"You know what it is I want of you, don't you?" Vidal asked.

A shiver ran down her spine. Whatever it was, she would give it freely. "I want to film you," he went on. "To see if the luminous quality you possess transfers to the screen.

The moon slid out from behind a bank of clouds. He had expected lavish thanks; vows of eternal gratitude; a silly stream of nonsense about how she had always wanted to be a movie star. Instead she remained silent, her face strangely serene.

His brows were pulled together, his silhouetted face that of a Roman emperor accustomed to wielding total power. "I expect complete obedience. Absolute discipline. Do you understand?"

Her head barely reached his shoulder. She turned her face up to his, the sea breeze fanning her hair softly against her cheeks. The moonlight accentuated the breathtaking purity of her cheekbone and jawline and he wondered how he could re-create the effect on film.

"Yes," she said, and at her composure his eyes gleamed with amusement.

"Where the devil did you spring from?" he asked, a smile touching his mouth.

Her eyes sparkled in the darkness as she said with steely determination, "Wherever it was, I'm not going back. . . ."

GODDESS

Margaret Pemberton

BANTAM BOOKS
TORONTO • NEW YORK • LONDON • SYDNEY • AUCKLAND

GODDESS
*Published in Great Britain
as
Silver Shadows Golden Dreams
A Bantam Book / December 1985*

ISBN 0-553-25561-4

PRINTED IN THE UNITED STATES OF AMERICA

H   0 9 8 7 6 5 4 3 2 1

For Mike, as always.

GODDESS

Chapter One

"I don't want her and I'm damned if I'll keep her," the girl said viciously, thrusting the squalling bundle into the startled arms of the young nun.

Sister Francesca stared at her thunderstruck. "But you can't leave her here," she protested, horrified. "This is an orphanage. We only take children who have no parents. There are rules. . . . Regulations . . ."

"Damn the rules," the girl said crudely, with no respect for Sister Francesca's calling. "I don't want her. I'm not keeping her and that's final."

"Do come on, Lou," called the young man in the battered Model T Ford parked some yards away. He revved the engine impatiently.

Sister Francesca stared around wildly for help. She had been on her way to collect the convent's daily supply of eggs when the automobile had bucketed down the dusty road and halted, blocking her path. The convent stood some hundred yards away overlooking the Pacific, its high white walls blind to her plight. The children were at class. Her fellow sisters, about their tasks. Beneath its tightly wrapped shawl, the baby struggled, fighting to be free.

"I'll be going, then," the girl said, smoothing an imaginary crease from the cheap, shiny material of her skirt, turning on a suicidally high heel.

"No!" Sister Francesca's voice was anguished. The girl was no older than herself. Eighteen or nineteen at the most. Her hair had been inexpertly bleached and frizzed. Sister Francesca was irrationally aware that beneath the dark lipstick and masklike makeup was a face of uncommon prettiness.

The girl was opening the door of the Ford, slamming it behind her. Sister Francesca ran after her, the baby and the long skirts of her habit hampering her speed. "No! Wait! You

1

can't leave your child like this! I don't know your name . . .
your address . . ."

The girl turned her head and held Sister Francesca's
gaze reflectively as the wheels of the Model T spun and
gained a hold on the rough road.

"My name doesn't matter. Hers"—she nodded indiffer-
ently in the direction of the baby—"is Daisy."

She leaned back against the cracked leather upholstery
and closed her eyes as if overcome with boredom as the Ford
pulled away, quickly gathering speed.

Desperately, Sister Francesca began to run in its wake.
"Stop! Oh, please, stop!"

Her pleas went unheeded. She ran until she was breathless, until the Model T was nothing but a black speck heading
toward the Santa Ana highway. Then she stumbled to a halt,
standing on the dust-blown road, the baby clasped tightly in
her arms.

The Ford had disappeared. A bird swooped low overhead. In the distance a farmer was tending the trees in his
orange grove.

She looked down at the child. It continued to squall, fists
clenched tight, eyes bright with rage. It was no more than a
week old.

Sister Francesca lifted it to her breast, holding it close,
soothing it with gentle words as she began to walk back
toward the convent.

The pearl gray of early dawn filtered through the wooden
slats of the room. Daisy woke with a sense of elation. Today
was Saint Joseph's Day. Today was special. There would be
extra prayers before breakfast, dedicated to the saint the tiny
Californian town of San Juan Capistrano had made its own.
But it was not the prospect of venerating Saint Joseph that
filled eight-year-old Daisy's heart with excited anticipation. It
was because Saint Joseph's Day had become her very own,
treasured anniversary. Saint Joseph's Day was the day the
swallows returned to Capistrano.

She couldn't remember how old she had been when she
had first seen the thousands of birds winging their way inland
from the Pacific, darkening the sky with the rhythmic beat of
their wings. All she could remember was the awe she had
felt. The delight and the wonderment.

They were so beautiful, so graceful, so free. She had known that miracles occurred. Sister Dominica, who was old and strict, and into whose care Daisy was placed daily with her twenty companions, had told her so. There was the miracle of the Virgin Mary appearing to Saint Bernadette. The miracle of the Lord turning the water into wine. But this was the first miracle Daisy had ever witnessed: the sweeping flight of birds returning on the same day every year, their return hardly varying by so much as an hour.

It was still only five-thirty. Small, curled bodies lay asleep in the narrow beds that ranged the length of the sparsely furnished dormitory. It would be another half hour before Sister Dominica's handbell roused them into unwelcome wakefulness.

Daisy swung bare feet onto the polished wood floor. Sister Dominica would scold her for rising before the correct and appointed time, but Daisy didn't care. There would be a penance to do. Maybe a half hour of reciting her rosary or an extra confession. It was small punishment for seeing the glory of the first of the swallows on the distant skyline.

She slipped her uniform dress of coarse blue linen over her head and tiptoed quietly into the washroom. The cold water stung her cheeks. She rubbed her face dry and then brushed and braided her hair as she had been taught. By the time she had finished, her arms ached and she knew with despair that the result would not please Sister Dominica's critical eye.

She paused and stared into the cracked mirror above the sinks. Huge eyes in a small pointed face stared back at her. Jessie Sullivan's hair sprang into curls no matter how tightly it was braided and Sister Dominica never chided her. Sister Dominica liked Jessie, but then, Jessie was pretty. She had pink cheeks and eyes as blue as those in a painting of the Virgin in the convent's chapel. Daisy wondered if Sister Dominica knew that Jessie lied and had twice not owned up to hiding the chalk, so that lessons had been delayed while more was obtained from the storeroom.

The whole class had suffered for Jessie's silence when Sister Dominica had sternly asked that the culprit stand and step forward. There had been no supper that night, but Jessie had disappeared for fifteen minutes between evening prayers and bed, and Daisy had uncharitably wondered if those fif-

teen minutes had been spent with Sister Dominica and if
Jessie had been less hungry on her return than her roommates.

She shrugged her shoulders and dismissed all thoughts
of Jessie Sullivan and Sister Dominica from her mind. There
were more important things to think about: Where the swallows had come from. Where they were going. Hurriedly, she
ran along the deserted corridor and down the shallow flight of
steps that led to the classrooms and refectory. Bypassing
them, she opened the heavy oak door with difficulty and
stepped out into the early morning air.

The convent had originally been a Spanish mission and
had changed little in style since the Franciscans had founded
it in the late eighteenth century. A covered walkway inter-
spersed with delicate arches surrounded a central square.
Thick adobe walls supported a roof of rose-red tiles and
protected the inmates from the intrusion of the outside world.
In all her eight years, Daisy had never stepped outside the
giant wrought-iron gates. Only girls who had been selected
for adoption did so.

Daisy had watched these departures with envy. Adoption meant a real home. It meant not having to wear the same
blue dress day in, day out. It meant freedom from Sister
Dominica. One day she, too, would be adopted. She would
miss Sister Francesca, who was Reverend Mother's secretary,
and who was kind to her, but maybe Sister Francesca would
write to her, or maybe even visit her.

Shivering a little in the early morning chill, she crossed
the square and stood before the high, forbidding gates. Somewhere out there people lived different lives. Exciting lives.
She wound her fingers round the cold wrought-iron scrolls.
In the distance a truck could be heard thundering north on
the Santa Ana highway. Her fingers tightened on the curling
loops of iron. Sister Francesca had journeyed north on the
highway; she had gone to a city called Los Angeles and had
stayed there, on convent business, a whole week. When she
returned, Daisy had asked her longingly what Los Angeles
was like and a slight flush had heightened Sister Francesca's
pretty face. She had told Daisy that it was a Babylon, too
sinful to be mentioned. Daisy had been only the more intrigued and had asked coaxingly why, if the city was such a
Babylon, Reverend Mother had sent her there.

"Our church offices are in Los Angeles, Daisy," Sister

Francesca had said patiently. "Sometimes problems arise that cannot be dealt with satisfactorily by correspondence. When they do, I act as Reverend Mother's spokeswoman, and travel to Los Angeles to settle them."

Daisy had been silent for a while. If Los Angeles was like the Babylon of the Old Testament, she could understand why the Reverend Mother did not wish to travel there, but it seemed unfair that Sister Francesca, who was so kind and good, should be obliged to do so.

"Why does the church have offices in such a wicked city?"

"It wasn't always a wicked city, Daisy. Not before they began to make moving pictures there."

They had been walking the length of the cloisters. Daisy stopped and stared at her. "*Moving* pictures?" she asked, her eyes widening.

Sister Francesca had smiled down at her, reminded of her younger sisters. "Yes, Daisy. They flash them on a big white screen and you can see people moving around and waving their arms and even making faces."

Daisy had regarded her in disbelief. "Have *you* seen a moving picture, Sister Francesca?" she asked.

"No," Sister Francesca had said, and there was a touch of regret in her voice. "It wouldn't be seemly, Daisy."

Afterward, whenever Sister Francesca went to Los Angeles on business, Daisy would ask her for the latest news of moving pictures. Sister Francesca told her of a moving picture called *Quo Vadis* in which there were not only people but lions, and Daisy had known that Sister Francesca wanted to see *Quo Vadis* almost as badly as she did.

"How do you know so much about moving pictures if you haven't seen any?" she asked naïvely.

Two bright spots of color had appeared on Sister Francesca's cheeks. "There are magazines with stories in them about the pictures that appear and the people who star in them," she had said sheepishly.

Daisy's mouth had rounded on a gasp of incredulity. "Oh! Can I see them, Sister Francesca? *Please*."

Sister Francesca had looked down into her eager eyes and her heart had to overcome her common sense.

"Of course," she had said, and had been rewarded by a

small pair of arms hugging her tight. "But it must be our secret, Daisy. You do understand, don't you?"

"Oh, yes," Daisy had said fervently. "I shall never tell, Sister Francesca, I promise."

The magazines had captured her imagination, feeding her mind just as surely as the food in the refectory fed her body. In the world of moving pictures anything was possible. A beggar maid could quite easily become a princess.

She had never given away the secret. Jessie had traded ruthlessly with the other girls when an aunt had sent her pinup photographs of Lillian Gish, and Barbara La Marr, but Daisy had not even been tempted to follow suit. The movie magazines from Los Angeles were her and Sister Francesca's secret, and she would have died rather than betray it.

She scuffed the toe of her shoe in the dust, waiting with increasing anxiety for the first faint speck to appear on the skyline. The swallows had to come. They were her talisman of hope for the future. In some primitive way that she could not understand, it was as if her very existence were bound up with theirs.

"Please," she whispered, her eyes hurting with the effort of staring at the empty skyline. "Oh, *please come!*"

As if in answer to her prayer, first one dark speck appeared, and then another. She clasped her hands together, her eyes shining. They were coming. At first only a few, but soon they would be flying overhead in their thousands, the sun glinting on their blue-black wings.

"I wish I were a swallow," Daisy whispered to herself ardently in the silence of the courtyard. "I'd fly higher and farther than all the other birds. I'd fly so high I'd touch the sun!"

There were more birds now, speckling the gold-streaked sky like a vast army. Wave upon wave of them, heading with blind, primitive instinct toward Capistrano and the sun-parched hills beyond. Daisy felt her heart soar. One day she would be as free as the birds that flew with such single-minded determination to their breeding grounds in the north. One day the giant wrought-iron gates would open and she would step outside just as Sister Francesca did. Only, unlike Sister Francesca, she would never return.

The blissful stillness was broken by the harsh ringing of Sister Dominica's handbell. Daisy felt a surge of despair. Her absence would be noticed. She would have to return indoors: attend prayers, breakfast, classes. And all the time the swallows would stream overhead and she would catch only glimpses of them from the high, narrow windows. Why, oh, why could she not be left in solitude for just one hour, one day?

Sister Dominica's voice rose stridently. Daisy sighed, knowing to the second the length of time it would take Sister Dominica to storm down the stairs and shatter the almost unearthly beauty of the morning.

In all her years in the convent Daisy had never cried, but her throat tightened now as the door slammed back on its hinges and Sister Dominica strode angrily toward her.

"Daisy Ford, return to the dormitory instantly! I shall report your behavior to Reverend Mother. Never in my life have I met such a disobedient, intractable child!"

A gaunt hand seized Daisy's shoulder and began to propel her forcibly toward the still open door. Daisy raised her head for a last precious glimpse of the swallows as the door closed, banishing them from view. They were free and she was a prisoner. Overcome with desolation she followed Sister Dominica down the endless whitewashed corridors to the chapel and early morning prayers.

"Jessie Sullivan is going to be adopted!" The words ran excitedly from mouth to mouth around the room as the girls made their beds with military precision.

Daisy stared at them. It had been a long time since anyone from their dormitory had left, small cardboard valise holding the obligatory set of new underclothes that the sisters regarded as a necessary start in life. They were eleven years old now. Adoptive parents liked younger children. Over the years the girls who had shared her dormitory had all been called to the Reverend Mother's office and returned exultant, leaving the convent shortly afterward. Only she and Jessie had remained. All the other girls were relatively new. Girls who had been orphaned at nine or ten. Girls who cried bitterly when the dormitory lights were turned off and only loneliness and darkness remained.

"Of course, I would have been adopted *ages* ago," Jessie was saying grandly to those gathering around her bed, "only my uncle was alive and he wouldn't give permission. He's dead now," she added with undisguised satisfaction.

Daisy folded her top sheet the regulation ten inches below the edge of her blanket, a slight frown furrowing her brow.

"You'll all be gone soon," Jessie was saying brightly. "Everyone gets adopted eventually."

"I haven't," Daisy said, tucking the bottom of her blanket in as neatly as if she were a nurse on a ward.

Jessie sat on her bed and swung her legs, her eyes gleaming maliciously. "Well, of course not. Only *orphans* get adopted."

Daisy halted in her task and stared at her. "We're all orphans. Otherwise we wouldn't be here."

Jessie smiled. It wasn't a pleasant smile and Daisy felt a curious sense of unease.

"Not all of us," Jessie continued, putting a sweet into her mouth and sucking it slowly.

The room fell silent and those around Jessie's bed stared at Daisy with open curiosity. Daisy looked beyond them into Jessie Sullivan's knowing eyes and felt suddenly cold.

"The Convent of the Sacred Heart is an orphanage," she said tightly, her hands clenching involuntarily, the knuckles showing white.

Jessie nodded. "In which case you should think yourself very lucky to be here."

Their eyes held. Daisy had never liked Jessie and was well aware that the feeling was mutual. Jessie was a trouble-maker and a liar. The most sensible thing for her to do would be to ignore Jessie's foolish remarks and leave the room. Yet there was something in the tone of Jessie's voice that held her fast. Slowly she began to cross the polished wood floor to Jessie's bed. Instinctively, the girls who had gathered around it retreated.

"What exactly do you mean by that remark, Jessie Sullivan?"

Jessie laughed. Her teeth were very white, very small.

"Only that as you're not an orphan you shouldn't be here. You should be in a home for children whose mothers don't want them."

Daisy moved so swiftly that Jessie did not even have the chance to spring from bed. Her hands closed around Jessie's wrists, her eyes blazing in her pale face.

"My mother *did* want me, only she's dead!"

"No, she isn't!" Jessie spat out triumphantly. "She brought you here. Sister Dominica told me so. She brought you here and she left you. Sister Dominica said you should have gone to a home for the abandoned but that Reverend Mother decided to make an exception in your case. I suppose she thought that if you stayed here, your mother would eventually return for you."

Taking advantage of Daisy's stunned incredulity, she snatched her wrists from Daisy's grasp.

Daisy's heart felt as if it were about to burst. She couldn't get her breath. "You're lying!"

"No, I'm not!" Jessie scrambled to comparative safety on the far side of the bed. "You ask Reverend Mother! Ask Sister Dominica! Ask anyone!"

Jessie's face swam distortedly before Daisy. She wanted to reach out and grasp something to prevent herself from falling, but there was only Jessie's bed and the ring of watching girls.

"I'm going to Reverend Mother now." The blood pounded in her ears. "I'm going to prove to everyone what a liar you are, Jessie Sullivan!"

Jessie leaned back against her pillows, her blue eyes gloating. "You'll only prove to everyone that you're a bastard and shouldn't be here. Sister Dominica says—"

She never finished the sentence. Daisy leapt onto the bed, seized Jessie's braids and wrenched them hard. Jessie screamed and kept on screaming, lashing out vainly at Daisy with her feet, clawing at her face with her nails.

Daisy's knee drove hard into Jessie's stomach, and as Jessie choked for breath she knelt astride her, releasing her braids and pinning her wrists high above her head.

"Apologize for what you said, Jessie Sullivan! Apologize or I'll scratch your eyes out!"

Jessie sobbed and gasped for air. "No . . . it's true! Your mother left you here because you were born in sin. Sister Dominica says so. Sister Dominica said—"

Daisy's nails dug so deep into Jessie's wrist that blood seeped beneath them. "You're lying! Tell me you're lying!"

"No . . . never . . . You're a bastard. A bas—"

Daisy sobbed and slapped Jessie across the mouth. *"Liar!"*

"Bastard!"

As Jessie writhed to be free they tumbled to the floor, feet kicking, nails clawing.

As the horrified spectators gathered their scattered wits, some of them ran for help. None of them ventured to intervene. Blood was pouring from Jessie's mouth. Daisy's face was scored with scratch marks. To intervene could result in being scarred for life.

Help was not far away. Sister Dominica, mottle-faced, was already marching toward the dormitory, where the screams and sobs were reaching crescendo pitch.

"It's Daisy Ford, Sister! She's trying to murder Jessie!"

"No she isn't. Jessie said that . . ."

"There's blood everywhere, Sister Dominica . . ."

Sister Dominica strode through the clamoring girls, her crucifix swinging against the heavy black folds of her habit. At the open door of the dormitory she halted, momentarily transfixed. Lockers had been overturned, their contents spilled onto the floor as Daisy and Jessie rolled and fought and kicked and screamed.

"Stop it! Stop it this instant!"

Neither girl obeyed, or even seemed to hear her. Glass from a shattered photograph frame crunched ominously beneath the flailing bodies. Jessie's face was smeared with blood. Daisy's was contorted with rage and hate.

Sister Dominica stepped forward, grasping Daisy's shoulders, hauling her with surprising strength away from her struggling victim. With authority in evidence, the other girls moved forward, helping a hysterical Jessie to her feet.

"How dare you . . . desecrate . . . this convent in this way?" Sister Dominica panted at Daisy. "You are a wicked, degenerate, ungodly, ungrateful—"

"Let go of me!" Daisy swung around with such force that she nearly knocked Sister Dominica off-balance. Her chest hurt as she gasped for air. "It is you who are wicked, Sister Dominica! Lying about me to Jessie Sullivan! Telling her that I was born in sin! That my mother didn't want me!"

The blood drained from Sister Dominica's face. Jessie lay in a crumpled heap on her bed, crying piteously, surrounded by sympathizers.

"You will go immediately to the chapel," Sister Dominica said, clasping her hands together as they began to tremble. "You will say the rosary twelve times. You will—"

"I will do no such thing." Daisy's eyes flashed. "I am going to Reverend Mother. I'm going to tell her of your lies . . . your wickedness."

"You will do as you are told, Daisy Ford, or your punishment will be one you will never forget as long as you live."

Daisy's breathing had steadied. She held Sister Dominica's gaze implacably. "I am going to Reverend Mother," she repeated, and turned on her heel, watched by a dozen horrified, and admiring, pairs of eyes.

Sister Dominica felt sweat break out on the palms of her hands. The Reverend Mother's wrath was rarely vented, but when it was, it was awesome. And on this occasion it would be vented on her. Swiftly, she began to march after Daisy.

"You are only going to make things worse for yourself," she said, trying to make her voice conciliatory. "There was damage done to personal property. Jessie is obviously in need of medical attention. To bring the incident to the attention of Reverend Mother is both foolish and unwise."

Daisy continued to walk along the white-plastered corridor, Sister Dominica half running in her attempt to keep pace with her.

"Jessie was a naughty girl to fill your head with such stories and I will see to it that it never happens again."

Daisy continued undeterred. The Reverend Mother's door was only yards away.

"Daisy Ford, I *forbid* you to disturb Reverend Mother over such a triviality!"

Daisy paused and turned. "My parentage is no trivial matter, Sister Dominica," she said tightly, and for the first time in her life Sister Dominica was aware that she was facing a child she could not intimidate.

She sucked in her breath, restraining the urge to slap Daisy's face, knowing it was too late to exert force as Daisy knocked on the pinewood door and the Reverend Mother's voice bade her enter.

The Reverend Mother had been in consultation with Sister Francesca. From behind her large oak desk she stared in surprise as Daisy walked purposefully into the center of the room. Girls entered her office only when specifically requested to do so. Her eyes widened even farther at the sight of the vicious scratch marks on Daisy's face, and the bruises fast coloring on her forehead and cheeks.

"Yes, Daisy?" The Reverend Mother lay down the sheaf of papers in her hand. "Can I help you?"

Daisy took in a deep, steadying breath. "Jessie Sullivan has told me that I am not an orphan. That my mother brought me to the convent and that I am illegitimate. She told me in front of the whole dormitory and now everyone believes her, and I would like you to tell them that she is lying."

Sister Francesca gave a little gasp, and the letter she had been holding fluttered from her grasp, falling gently onto a brilliantly colored hooked rug.

The Reverend Mother's eyes moved from Daisy's white, drawn face to Sister Dominica standing apprehensively in the doorway. Fear flickered in Sister Dominica's eyes and was quickly suppressed. Very carefully the Reverend Mother lay down the papers in her hands.

"You may leave us, Sister Dominica," she said authoritatively.

"I . . . But . . ."

The Reverend Mother's glance froze her. Unhappily, Sister Dominica obeyed. The door closed behind her. The room remained silent.

There was no need for the Reverend Mother to ask where Jessie Sullivan had received her information. There was only one possible source and she would deal with Sister Dominica later. She smiled gently at Daisy.

"Please sit down, Daisy."

"No, thank you, Reverend Mother." Daisy's lips felt dry. "I only need you to tell the girls that Jessie lied."

The Reverend Mother picked up a paperweight and replaced it. Daisy could feel a pulse begin to beat wildly in her throat. Why wasn't the Reverend Mother angry? Why wasn't she escorting her back to the dormitory to refute Jessie's allegations? Her eyes flew to Sister Francesca, and at the expression of pity in Sister Francesca's eyes fear seized her, crippling in its intensity. There was such pain in her throat that she could hardly speak.

"Jessie did lie, didn't she, Reverend Mother?"

The Reverend Mother stood up and slowly moved around the enormous desk, resting her hands lightly on Daisy's shoulders.

"No, Daisy," she said quietly. "Jessie did not lie. You

did not come to the orphanage as other children come. It is something that I would have told you myself at the right and proper time."

"But I *am* an orphan! My mother wouldn't have left me! It isn't possible. . . ." The huge eyes in the small face burned with anguish, desperate for affirmation.

"Your mother was very young, little more than a child herself. No doubt she thought that placing you in our care was the best thing she could do for you."

Daisy felt as if she were falling into a vortex of brilliant colors and black rushing winds. She stared desperately from the Reverend Mother to Sister Francesca.

"Then I shouldn't be here! Not if my mother's alive! There's been a dreadful, terrible mistake!"

"Your mother left you and did not return for you," the Reverend Mother was saying firmly. "Therefore you are as much an orphan as the other children in our care."

"No!" Daisy backed away from her like an animal at bay, her hand splayed behind her, seeking the door, the wall. "No!" She gave a small, inarticulate cry that sounded as if it had been torn from her heart. "She thinks you've had me adopted! She's looking for me. I know she is. I want to find her. I'm not an orphan. I'm *not!*"

Daisy was vaguely aware of Sister Francesca's moving toward her, and then the spiraling colors sucked her down and down until only blackness remained and she pitched headlong onto the rug, lying in a small, insensible heap at Sister Francesca's feet.

Her eyes were bleak as she watched the swallows return. She had been removed from Sister Dominica's care and was no longer obliged to obey the sound of the imperiously ringing handbell. Sister Francesca knew that Saint Joseph's Day was special to her and Sister Francesca was tolerant and understanding.

She leaned her back against an archway, her knees drawn up to her chin, her arms circling them, her head resting against the warmth of the golden stone. It was nearing midday and for hours she had watched the birds on their annual migration. This time no joy filled her heart. Only bitterness and envy.

Jessie Sullivan had long since departed. The other girls

in her dormitory never referred to Jessie's allegations, but from that day on she had become an outsider. Her own temperament had made her so.

The other girls were orphans. She was not. Somewhere, beyond the high white walls, her mother lived and worked and waited for her. She picked up a pebble and skimmed it across the sun-filled courtyard. But her mother did not come for her.

Her companions relied on the Sisters for all the indiscriminate affection they received, but they had known love in the lives they had lived before entering the convent. She had known only routine and regimentation and Sister Dominica's harsh discipline.

A swallow swooped low and circled her head as if enticing her to follow it. Before Jessie's outburst she had believed herself to be happy. Now, knowing that she was different from all those around her, she knew only a long, never-ending misery.

Sister Francesca stepped quietly from the shadows and stood at her side.

"We should have been studying Latin an hour ago, Daisy."

"I know." Daisy was truly repentant. Sister Francesca was kind and good and beautiful. She did not deserve disappointment, especially from a child it was not truly her duty to instruct.

Sister Francesca gazed upward. "They are very beautiful, aren't they?"

Daisy nodded, unshed tears glistening in her eyes. Sister Francesca slid down into a sitting position beside Daisy in a manner that would have startled the Reverend Mother, and appalled Sister Dominica.

"Does it hurt so much, Daisy? It's been nearly a year now."

Daisy did not dare to meet Sister Francesca's compassionate gaze. If she did, the tears so bravely held in check would fall unrestrainedly. "Yes," she answered, her voice muffled as she pressed her face against her drawn-up knees.

Sister Francesca remained silent. Ever since that dreadful day in the Reverend Mother's study, Daisy had withdrawn into a world that even she could not enter. There had been no more questions. No hysterics. From the moment she had recovered consciousness, she had been a changed girl.

Silent and intense, spurning all friendship, remaining constantly alone, her only solace the movie magazines that came with such pitiful irregularity from Los Angeles.

Wave after wave of swallows flew in from the sea and they watched them together in silence. At last the moment Sister Francesca had both prayed for and feared arrived.

Daisy traced a pattern in the dust on the ground and asked hesitantly, "Did you ever meet my mother, Sister Francesca?"

A swallow broke free of its companions and darted low over the convent walls, landing on the moss-covered lip of the fountain.

"It was to me that your mother gave you."

Daisy gasped, the blood draining from her face. Aware of her distress, Sister Francesca took her hand.

"I was going for eggs when a couple in a Model T Ford halted some yards ahead of me."

Sister Francesca was aware of the sudden jerk of Daisy's head. She continued undeterred. "A young . . . lady . . . stepped from the Ford. She was carrying you in her arms." Sister Francesca hesitated, remembering the hard, pretty, overpainted face, the harsh words as she thrust Daisy from her. "She gave you to me and asked that you be cared for in the convent."

"What was she like?" Daisy asked urgently. "Was her hair dark, like mine?"

Reluctantly, Sister Francesca shook her head. "No, Daisy. Her hair was blond."

Daisy stared at her incredulously. Over the years she had conjured up many images of her mother, but they had always been blurred. Now, incredibly, the image became more defined. Her mother had been blond. And had left her. The breath was so tight in her chest that she could hardly breathe as she asked, "Was she crying?"

"No, Daisy, she wasn't crying." She tightened her hold on Daisy's hand as the blood pounded in Daisy's ears and the child fought to come to terms with the fact that her mother had said good-bye to her without shedding a tear.

"Was she pretty?" Her voice was low, her mouth buried once more against her knees.

"Yes." She did not add that the prettiness had had to be

sought beneath masklike makeup, and that the sulky, petulant mouth had made it nearly indiscernible.

Sister Francesca could sense that Daisy was steeling
herself for an even more important question. She waited
patiently. It was too late for Latin now, but Latin was not as
important as the peace of mind of a twelve-year-old child.

"You said there was someone else with my mother in the
Ford. . . ."

Sister Francesca hesitated fractionally and then said, "A
young man was driving."

"My father?" The words were little more than a whisper.

"I don't know," Sister Francesca replied truthfully.

"It must have been!" Daisy's eyes were fevered. "They
were poor and they wanted the best for me. They brought
me here and then when they came back for me they were
told I had been adopted!" She sprang to her feet. "Don't you
see, Sister Francesca? All I have to do is find them and we'll
be a family again!"

"Daisy . . ." Sister Francesca rose and caught hold of her
hand once again, remorse engulfing her. She had told Daisy
as much of the truth as was palatable because she believed it
was in Daisy's best interests that she did so. Now she was not
so sure.

"What was my father's name?"

"I don't know. Daisy—"

"My mother's? What was my mother's Christian name?"

"The young man called her Lou, but, Daisy—"

Daisy broke free of her hold, her face radiant. "Lou!
That must be short for Louise or Louella. Oh, Sister Francesca, surely we can find her now? Louise or Louella Ford.
My birth must have been registered. There must be some
place that keeps everyone's birth certificate. If you could go
there for me . . . find it. Perhaps even find my parents'
marriage certificate! There'll be addresses on it. They must
have lived near here. Perhaps even in Capistrano!"

She whirled around ecstatically on the tip of one toe and
Sister Francesca watched her in despair, knowing she had
made a terrible error in believing she could tell part and not
the whole of the truth.

The whirling figure steadied, stretched out her arms,
and ran lovingly toward her. Sister Francesca held her close,

doubting if ever again there would be such a joyful expression of affection between them.

"Daisy . . ." Gently she held Daisy away from her. "Daisy, you will never be able to find your mother."

Bewilderment flooded her eyes. "Why not?"

"I do not believe your mother was married, Daisy," she said as gently as possible. "She wore no wedding ring."

Daisy stood so still, it seemed to Sister Francesca that she had ceased to breathe. Then she rallied with a courage that tore at Sister Francesca's heart.

"That doesn't mean I can't find her. Not now that I know her name."

Sister Francesca was suddenly aware that the last swallow had flown over Capistrano. The air was silent. The heat hung in the high-walled courtyard. Sister Francesca felt beads of sweat roll down her body. She could not allow Daisy to cling to a hope that was futile. To waste her life looking for a woman she would never find.

"We never knew your mother's last name, Daisy," she said softly. "She refused to give it. We know only that her companion referred to her as Lou. And that your name was Daisy."

Daisy stared up at her, puzzled. "But my name is Daisy Ford. It's always been Daisy Ford. My mother's name must have been Ford, too."

Sister Francesca strove to keep her voice calm. "Sometimes, when children enter a home without a name, someone on the staff gives them one. A little girl was left on the steps of the Los Angeles mission on Christmas Day and the nuns decided to call her Holly."

Slowly, Daisy began to back away from her, the blood draining from her face.

"Is that what happened to me? Did *you* call me Daisy? Did Reverend Mother?" Her voice began to rise hysterically. "Did, Sister Dominica?"

"No, Daisy. Your mother gave you your name."

Momentarily, Daisy halted, her breath coming in short, harsh gasps. "And Ford? Who gave me the name of Ford?"

"The choice of your surname was a . . . unanimous . . . decision," Sister Francesca said with difficulty.

"But why . . .?" She choked, suddenly understanding,

her eyes black with horror. "You named me Ford because of the motorcar they brought me in!"

Sister Francesca reached out for her hand to hold and comfort her, but Daisy brushed her away sightlessly, stumbling backward, a fist pressed to her mouth to stifle a rising scream. "*You named me after a motorcar!*" She began to shake, her eyes huge in her white face. "*I hate you! I hate you all! I won't be named after a motorcar! I won't! I won't be known as Daisy Ford ever again!*"

She hurled herself against the giant gates, her fingers curling around the cold iron, and her cry of pain was such that a hunter high in the hills thought he heard the death throes of a small wild animal.

It was four hours before a weeping Sister Francesca, helped by the Reverend Mother, managed to prise Daisy's numbed fingers from their grip on the flamboyant, baroque swirls of the gates and carry her indoors; and it was six years before Daisy was able to fulfill her vow.

She did so on the day she left the Convent of the Sacred Heart, never to return. Her belongings were in her cardboard valise. The name and address of the lady the Reverend Mother had arranged to employ her as a maid was in her hand. Mrs. Helen Morley of Chalcedony Street, San Diego. On the Santa Ana highway, waiting for the southbound bus, she tore up her letter of introduction and the card with Mrs. Morley's address on it. Daisy Ford would not be going to San Diego. Daisy Ford no longer existed. She would not be known by the name given her by a woman who had abandoned her. She would not be known by the name the nuns had so unimaginatively allotted to her. And she would never, *never* be a maid to anyone.

She crossed the highway and began to walk north, a delicate, fragile figure, graceful despite the clumsy convent shoes and elegant despite the shabby valise.

Bob Kelly was not in the habit of giving lifts, but there was something vulnerable about the slender figure ahead of him and he took his foot off the gas and slowed down, halting in a cloud of gasoline fumes, at her side.

"Want a lift?" he asked compassionately. Wherever she was going, she had a long walk ahead of her and close up she looked as if the merest breath of wind would blow her away.

Daisy gazed up into a pleasing face with blue eyes that crinkled at the corners and a mouth etched with deep laughter lines.

"Yes, please," she said gratefully.

"Where are you heading?"

She hesitated, uncertain. "Where are you going?"

"Los Angeles." He nodded to the sign on the side of the truck. "Worldwide Pictures, Los Angeles."

It was as if a fist had been slammed into her breastbone. As if all her life she had been walking toward this one moment. "Are you a movie star?" she asked, hardly able to breathe as he hauled her into the seat beside him. He laughed, letting out the clutch, picking up speed. His hair was thick and fair, bleached blond by the sun. His hands on the wheel were strong and capable, and any nervousness she had felt at first fast disappeared. She knew instinctively that with the man at her side she was safe.

"No, I'm not a movie star," he said with amusement. "I ferry things around—scenery, lights. Yesterday we shot a scene down at Del Coronado. Today I have to tote it all back again."

Elation surged through her. She knew all about scenery and lights. All about the world of which he was a part. She smiled at him and he caught his breath. He had thought that he'd picked up a kid with braids. Now he saw that he'd picked up much more.

"What's your name?" he asked, trying to regain his composure.

Autographed photographs were taped all around the cabin of the truck. Marlene Dietrich, Greta Garbo, Gloria Swanson, Rudolph Valentino. The smoldering eyes of the tragically dead embodiment of Hollywood seemed to burn into hers and she knew what her name would be. What it would always be.

"Valentina," she said, smiling, as the past was left behind and they approached the outskirts of Los Angeles.

Chapter Two

"Where's it to be?" he asked as the truck hurtled through the downtown part of the city.

She stared at the bewildering array of buildings, momentarily nonplussed. "I . . . Anywhere," she said, a slight frown puckering her brow.

Where would she go? What would she do? Reverend Mother had given her the name and address of that lady in San Diego who needed a maid, but she had torn the card into pieces, determined never to be a maid to anyone. Now, for the first time, she began to feel doubt and she turned her head abruptly, avoiding Bob's all too perceptive gaze. She should never have thrown that address away. What had been the name on the card? Morgan? Manley?

It was no good. She had paid it scant attention and now the memory of it was beyond recall.

Bob navigated around a motorcycle with only one hand on the steering wheel, reaching for a fresh piece of gum with the other.

"Los Angeles is a big place," he said laconically, dropping a silver wrapper to the already littered floor. "You tell me whereabouts your folks live and I'll drop you nearby. I've got the time."

He began to chew, his eyes no longer on her but on the road ahead.

Daisy cleared her throat. No matter how hard she tried, she couldn't tell him a lie. That here was near enough. That her folks lived only minutes away from the large building now looming up on her right-hand side. Nor could she tell him a place farther away where her nonexistent family might live. The only place name she knew of in Los Angeles was Hollywood, and as Hollywood was Bob's destination he would probably insist on dropping her at the door of a house she would be embarrassingly unable to enter.

"I . . . Here will do fine," she said bravely, looking suddenly very vulnerable.

Bob Kelly looked away from the traffic and regarded her thoughtfully. There was an almost elusive quality about her. Her beauty was bone-deep, far beyond mere prettiness.

He said, keeping his voice casual, "Of course, you never *did* say you had folks in Los Angeles. It could be that I was mistaken. I just figured that with you leaving your convent, home would be the first place you would head."

A truck passed, horn blaring. A movie house had a giant billboard of Marlene Dietrich and Clive Brook. The film was *Shanghai Express* and she wondered if Bob had toted the props for it.

Bob continued through downtown Los Angeles at a speed much slower than normal. He needed to give her time to think and he needed time to think himself.

Daisy's throat was uncomfortably tight. Nothing she had ever experienced had prepared her for the seething hubbub beyond the safety of the truck.

"I don't have any family," she said at last, keeping her eyes fixed firmly on Bob's photograph of a languorously smiling Gloria Swanson.

Bob rolled the gum around his mouth and tried to remain nonchalant, terrified that at any moment she would open the cab door and run.

A Plymouth roadster cut in on him and he braked sharply. One thing was for sure. If he deposited her on the sidewalk, she wouldn't last a minute, convent clothes or no convent clothes. Los Angeles was a city of wolves and sharks, and her haunting seductiveness was apparent, despite her coarse cotton dress and thick stockings. Beads of sweat broke out on his forehead. He was twenty-eight and he had certainly never met anyone like her before. Whether she knew it or not, she needed protection, and it was beginning to be obvious that there was no one to offer her that protection unless he himself took on the task.

He shook his head as if to clear it, and swore again. He'd given a kid a lift. She'd said she wanted to go to Los Angeles. He'd taken her to Los Angeles. Now was good-bye time. He liked his life exactly the way it was. No responsibilities. No troubles. Don't ask, he said to himself. For Christ's sake, don't ask.

"So who are you staying with?" he said aloud grimly.

She tried to inject a note of nonchalance into her voice. "No one."

He swung his head sharply and she continued hurriedly, "But that's no problem, I'll get a job . . . living in. A maid. I'd make a very good maid."

Bob ground his teeth and Daisy reflected bitterly on how quickly she was prepared to renege on her vow never to be a maid to anyone.

"You'd make a godawful maid," Bob said. Then, as the silence grew uncomfortable, "Know any agencies?"

"Agencies?" Daisy was bewildered.

Bob's temper flared at her naïveté. "Yes, agencies! What do you think this place is? Fairyland? What the hell were those people doing in Capistrano? Do they usually turn kids out onto the streets with no job, no place to stay?" He ran his hand through his thick shock of hair. "Know what I should do?" he continued angrily as she shrank into the corner of her seat, "I should turn this goddamn truck round and take you right back there!"

Her heart began to beat so hard, she thought she would faint. "No. You can't do that. I won't go, and besides, they wouldn't take me back."

"They'd *have* to take you," Bob said as he narrowly missed a Gray Line bus. "They should have made arrangements for you. Given you an address; gotten you a job. Not to do so is downright negligent. It's crass stupidity. It's practically criminal!"

"They did give me an address," she said in a small voice. "It was to live in with a lady in San Diego. As a maid."

Bob sighed and spat the gum out of the open window. There was no way he could turn around and make the 120-mile trip to San Diego. His load was needed at the studios. He was already taking too much time in delivering it. Tomorrow he finished early. He could take her there then. She'd have to sleep on his sofa for the night, but in another twenty-four hours his unsought role of father figure and protector would be over.

"Tomorrow," he said grimly. "I'll take you there tomorrow."

She eyed him nervously. "You can't," she said, her gaze

fixed on his profile, on the bunched muscles of his jaw. "I threw away the paper with the address on it, and I can't remember the lady's name."

"Christ Almighty! Do you mean to tell me you've nowhere to go? Nowhere to stay?"

"I can manage," she said, her trembling voice holding a hint of defiance. "Just stop the truck and let me out."

"Over my dead body!" Bob's mouth was set in a harsh line, the blue of his eyes glacial. "You're about as equipped to deal with this town as I am to star as Cinderella."

Despite her distress a smile tinged the corners of her mouth. "What are you going to do with me, then?"

"Look after you until you've the sense to look after yourself. First of all we dump this load up on the lot. Next, we get rid of that damned cardboard valise."

"You can't," she protested mildly, aware of a sudden feeling of safety and refuge. "All my clothes are in it."

"And I can guess what they look like," Bob said darkly. "Tomorrow we'll buy you a couple of dresses and some shoes."

"I haven't any money."

Bob's lips twitched in a suspicion of a smile. "I never for one moment reckoned you had."

Downtown Los Angeles was behind them now. They were climbing a steep, winding road that led high into the San Gabriel Mountains, and Daisy looked around her with interest. Fuchsias grew wild and instead of gasoline fumes, the air was heavy with the scent of mimosa and honeysuckle.

"I like it up here," she said disarmingly.

Bob looked across at her, marveling at the calm way she had accepted his protection; at her innocence and trust. "Don't you want to know if my intentions are honorable?" he asked curiously.

A faint frown furrowed her brow. "Are they?" she asked, and for a fleeting moment he saw the frightened-little-girl look dart into her eyes again and instantly regretted his question.

His expression softened. "Hell, yes. You take the bed, I'll take the sofa."

"Shouldn't it be the other way around?" she asked as they approached a vast array of sprawling, hangarlike buildings behind iron gates.

"It should be," Bob agreed dryly, "but I'm just an old-fashioned boy at heart. Always the gentleman."

They were laughing again as the truck drew up to the gates and a small, heavily built man dragged the gate open wide so that they could drive through.

Bob was aware of a glare of disapproval. It was strictly against company policy to give lifts, much less admit anyone unauthorized to the lot. He didn't give a damn. He did his work well and was a good timekeeper, and this was the first time he had so much as infringed on a company rule.

Daisy's heart began to slam hard and fast. "Is this the film studio?"

Bob nodded, driving steadily past the enormous hangars with their infuriatingly closed doors. Beyond them she glimpsed a whole street that looked as if it had been transported in its entirety from the Wild West. Then a castle, turreted and crenellated; and then a bizarre semicircle of fake Amazonian trees and trailing creepers. She wanted to ask Bob to slow down, to stop, so that she could see better, but sensed that to do so would be futile.

There were people everywhere. Ethereally slim, pencil-skirted girls hurrying purposefully in and out of glass-fronted offices; muscular men hauling heavy cables. Young girls in tutus and ballet shoes. Young men with sheafs of paper under their arms. All carried with them an air of importance and barely suppressed excitement. It was as if they were all privy to a glorious secret, and Daisy passionately wanted to be one of them. To have a destination to hurry to. A task to undertake.

Suddenly there was a distant shout of command and she gasped as scores of soldiers armored in brass began to surge toward the battlements of the castle. Before she could catch her breath, Bob had driven into a building so large, Daisy could see no end to it. He halted the truck, opened the door, and sprang to the ground. "Stay there, I'll be twenty minutes, maybe thirty."

Daisy's eyes adjusted to the dimness. Stacked high on either side of the truck, stretching into seeming infinity, were piles of what she could only imagine were the props Bob had spoken of. Another male voice joined Bob's. The rear doors of the truck were opened and the contents were lifted out, checked off, and added to the overwhelming array surrounding them.

It was only twenty yards from the hangar entrance to the point where she had seen the intriguing mock battle. She peeped out of the truck. Bob was lifting the heavy props, the strong muscles of his arms gleaming with sweat. She paused for a second and then opened the cab door and jumped lightly to the ground. Neither man heard her or looked up as she ran, fleet-footedly, out of the shadowed hangar and into the brilliant sunlight.

The battle was still raging.

"To the death, men!" shouted a brave figure with a huge black cross emblazoned on his silver mail, as he led yet another charge against the brass-armored enemies scaling the castle walls.

"Cut! For Christ's sake, cut!" The deep voice cracked like a whip across the set, silencing the uproar instantly. "The invaders are to be *repelled*, Tennant. There's so many of them over the battlements there's not a knight to be seen."

The men groaned, retreating down the ladders and slumping defeatedly against the walls. Fascinated, Daisy edged nearer. The harsh voice that had brought a halt to the proceedings belonged to a powerfully built man sitting in a canvas chair with his back to her. Hair as black as her own curled low over the collar of his shirt. The clenched knuckles that drummed impatiently on the wooden arm of the chair were olive-toned. Everything about him indicated command. The tense set of his shoulders, the undisputed authority in his voice.

A minion approached and was waved impatiently away. Electricians and cameramen surrounded the foot of the castle. Close up Daisy saw that it was nothing more than a facade of gray-painted plywood with platforms behind it on which the knights could stand.

"Okay, let's take it again and this time put some guts into it." There was an intriguing quality to his voice. An accent that was not quite American.

"Quiet on the set!" called one of the men near the cameras. "Tennant. *The Black Knights*. Scene sixteen. Roll 'em."

Again the air was filled with the sound of battle. Again the walls were scaled, but this time the knights succeeded in repelling the onslaught.

The formidable figure in the canvas chair rose to his feet and Daisy held her breath, willing him to turn in her direction so that she could catch a glimpse of his face.

Suddenly a door only yards away from her opened and a figure she recognized from Sister Francesca's movie magazines stepped out into the sunlight, saying petulantly to the retinue in her wake, "If my call doesn't come soon, I'll need to be completely made-up again."

Daisy gazed at her in disbelief. Her hair was a golden halo, her eyes, large and blue, her glossy lips forming an almost perfect Cupid's bow. A wimple of floating chiffon crowned her head and a belt of braided silver hung seductively low on her hips, falling in two glorious streams to the hem of a clinging white gown.

"Just another few minutes, Miss de Santa," one of the girls hurrying after her said.

"A glass of water, Miss de Santa?" suggested another deferentially.

A glass of water with ice appeared as if by magic. Miss de Santa sipped it daintily and then, surrounded by her acolytes, drifted goddess-like toward the dominant figure surveying the scene before him with rapt concentration.

"Darling, can't we get my take over and done with? I can't possibly wait any longer. I shall wilt."

With an impatient expletive the broad-shouldered figure swung around and Daisy felt as if all the breath had been sucked from her body.

Black eyes slanted under winged brows. There was something harsh, almost Arabic, about the sun-dark planes of his face, the high, lean cheekbones, the strong nose and jutting jaw. It was the face of a man used to being obeyed. Hard and uncompromising. A face that once seen would never be forgotten. In the heat of the sun his hair had a blue sheen as it tumbled low over his forehead. His shirt was gashed open at the throat and Daisy was aware of whipcord muscles and the sense of power barely under restraint. There was something feral and primitive about him that sent a shiver down her spine. He frowned fiercely as Miss de Santa laid a hand upon his arm and said, "It's so insufferably hot, darling, and . . ."

Behind her Daisy heard the throb of the truck's engine. Reluctantly she moved in its direction and as she did so his eyes flashed across at her.

"Who the hell are you?" His voice halted her instantly. She turned to face him and tried to speak, but the words choked in her throat. Her legs had suddenly lost their strength and she leaned weakly against the hangar wall, her fingers splayed behind her.

His eyes narrowed and he gasped for breath. God in heaven, where had she come from? At first he had seen only the cheap dress, the ugly stockings and clumsy shoes, and then her head had jerked upward, startled and afraid, and he had seen her face.

He had been in Hollywood for two years. Five years before that he had made films in his native Hungary, and in all that time he had never seen a face so exquisitely photogenic. It was angular and delicate, full of shadows and light, the hollows beneath her cheekbones balanced perfectly by a mouth full and sensually curved. But it was her eyes that held him, almond-shaped and thick-lashed, the color of smoked crystal. Luminous, haunting eyes that screamed out to be filmed. Eyes that belonged to a woman, not a child. A woman who had suffered pain and loneliness and defied them with courage, as she was defying him now. He began to stride toward her, oblivious of the waiting set, the curious crew. The long, lovely line of her neck was flawless. The shapeless dress she wore was no concealment for a body supple and slender and unbelievably graceful. There was an incandescent quality about her that took his breath away. It was as though she were lit by an inner flame. She was fire and air and he wanted to film her more than he had wanted to film any other woman in his life. He halted, a scant foot away from her.

"Who are you? What are you doing here?" His voice had lost its snarl. He was gazing at her with such a curious expression on his face that she wondered if he were mad.

"I'm a visitor," she said, drawing a deep, ragged breath into her lungs, and struggling for composure.

Vidal Rakoczi stared down at the cloud of dark hair and bravely tilted chin.

"I'll be damned," he said softly, and gazing up into his dark, devil's face, Daisy felt that he very well might be.

For a long moment their eyes held. Time wavered in the sun-scorched heat and seemed to halt. The cast and crew fell silent, watching them. She could no longer hear the throb of the truck's engine. She was aware of nothing but the overpowering presence and masculinity of the man standing so close to her now that she could feel the warmth of his breath on her cheek.

"What is your name?" he asked, his voice scorching her nerve ends.

"Valentina." Her lips trembled slightly, her sexual vulnerability so palpable it inflamed even his hardened senses. He stemmed his surge of desire and stared at her hideous shoes, the ugliness of her stockings.

"How old are you?"

He was so close to her that her hair blew against his skin.

"Seventeen."

His eyes narrowed speculatively and tiny white lines appeared at the corners of his mouth. She looked nearer fifteen, and if she was, Worldwide would never agree to her appearing in his films. Not in the parts her eyes destined her for. "Did your mother bring you?" They usually did. Laying siege to the casting director's office for hour after hour.

"No . . . I . . ." His eyes were consuming her. She felt as if she were about to faint. His hand reached out to steady her and she swayed against him like a petal in the breeze.

"*Valentina!*" Bob's voice was raw with urgency.

She stared dazedly in his direction. He was halfway out of the truck and there was murder in his eyes.

She had to move, had to prevent a confrontation between him and the powerful figure at her side.

"I'm coming, Bob," she gasped, tearing herself free, running, stumbling toward the truck. "I'm coming, I'm sorry!"

Her hand closed on the handle of the passenger-seat door and Bob hauled her up savagely beside him, slamming the truck into gear and speeding away without a backward glance in Rakoczi's direction.

His face was set in a terrifying mask as he slewed the truck around the last of the hangars and made for the studio's parking lot. He didn't know what he wanted to do most—throttle Valentina for her stupidity in leaving the anonymity of the truck, or punch the hell out of Rakoczi for reducing her to a quivering wreck. The tires screeched as he brought the truck to a halt.

"Out," he ordered tersely, his jaw clenched, a nerve throbbing angrily.

Daisy obeyed, silent sobs rising in her throat as she remembered the dark voice that had called after her as she had broken free of him. He had called after her and against every instinct in her body she had continued to run.

Bob stormed across to a Buick and unlocked the door. "Get in and let's get the hell out of here."

She half fell into the seat beside him.

"I . . . Who was he?" she asked at last as they sped between the studio gates and spun around the first of the bends in the long, descending road.

"Vidal Rakoczi." Bob spat the name venomously. "Of all the people to tangle with you have to choose the most powerful man on the lot. Christ. *No one* goes on a Rakoczi set unless they're part of the team. It's a wonder he didn't hurl you physically over the studio gates."

The blood surged through his veins in a raging tide. "Was he foulmouthed to you?" he asked tensely. If Rakoczi had been, Bob knew he would hit him square on the jaw, job or no job.

Daisy looked at him in astonishment. "No. . . . He was . . . kind."

"*Kind?*" Daisy thought Bob was going to explode. "Rakoczi hasn't been kind to anyone in his life! He's reduced the biggest stars of the studio to tears, and he's the only director I've ever known who defies the studio chiefs and gets away with it. He's known as the Hungàrian devil and it's a reputation he lives up to."

Daisy looked down at her arm where Rakozci had so fleetingly held it. It felt as if it had been branded.

"He only asked my name," she said, her voice a barely discernible whisper.

Bob looked at her in astonishment. "He didn't tell you to get off the set, or ask how you got onto it?"

"No." She shook her head and the light caught in her hair. "He asked me how old I was. That's all."

Bob's blue eyes narrowed. "Son of a bitch," he said as he turned into Van Ness with scant regard for traffic. There was only one reason Rakozci would ask such a question. The only surprise he felt was that Rakozci should care whether she was underage or not.

"That lady . . . it was Romana de Santa, wasn't it?"

Bob's anger was already ebbing away. He suppressed a

grin, doubting that anyone had ever before described Romana as a lady.

"Yep, she's Worldwide's latest acquisition. The bosses are all set to make her into a rival to Gloria Swanson."

"She's very beautiful. Just like a princess in a fairy tale." Daisy remembered the proprietorial way Miss de Santa had called Rakozci "darling" and an icy chill entered her soul.

Bob grinned. Romana de Santa was more like a bitch in heat than a fairy-tale princess. She had fought, slept, and bribed her way to the position she now held.

"Is Romana a Spanish name?" she asked reflectively. "She didn't look Spanish."

Bob turned right on Santa Monica. "She isn't, and she was born Dolly Munff in Calico Springs, Idaho. Does that dispel your fairy-tale illusions?"

Daisy stared at him. "Do many people change their names in Hollywood?"

"Ninety-nine percent. The studios like a fancy name on the billboards. The public will flock to see Romana de Santa in her latest epic. They wouldn't be quite so keen to see Dolly Munff."

Daisy was aware of a sudden stillness in the very center of her being. The movie magazines had never hinted that the stars adorning their pages had been born with names far different from those they were known by. Dolly Munff had changed her name to Romana de Santa just as she had changed *her* name to Valentina, and Romana de Santa was famous, feted wherever she went. More important still, Romana de Santa was a woman who could call Vidal Rakoczi "darling."

"Valentina isn't my real name either," she said tentatively.

Bob resisted the urge to laugh. "I never thought it was, sweetheart."

"Aren't you going to ask me what it is?"

"No. In this town you can be anyone or anything you want to be. If you want to be Valentina, that's fine by me."

"And if I want to be an actress like Romana de Santa?"

"Then it isn't," Bob said, his mood changing abruptly. "For every Romana there are thousands who don't make it, and break their hearts in the process."

She didn't care about the thousands who didn't make it. She was not one of them. All her life she had had to rely on her inner resources. On the world of her imagination. That world had sustained her through all the bleak days of her childhood. The movie magazines had shown her how easy it was to slip inside the skin of another character. When Sister Francesca had lent her a copy of Emily Brontë's *Wuthering Heights*, she had *been* Cathy. Though she had never walked on moorland, she had felt the northern winds tugging at her hair and staining her cheeks with color. Her throat had ached as she cried silently after Heathcliff. She had loved and she had suffered, and she had relished every single moment of it. In religious education she had been Rachel, weeping for her children; Rebecca, determining her destiny by lowering her pitcher into the well and giving water to the servant of Abraham; Pharaoh's daughter, lifting the infant Moses out of the ark of bulrushes.

She had defeated loneliness by bringing to life the characters of books and the characters that peopled her imagination and making friends of them. Now, with devastating clarity, she saw that her ability was not only a panacea for unhappiness. It was her lifeblood. Part of the very fiber of her being. And here, in Hollywood, it could be fulfilled.

She could be anything she wanted to be. A maiden in distress being saved by a black knight; a cowgirl on the wooden street that brought the Wild West to the studio lot; an adventuress lost in the jungle of artificial creepers. She didn't want to be an actress. She was one. All she had to do to be a star was to be true to herself.

Seeing the expression on her face, Bob ran a hand through his hair and wondered if he were mad. In the space of a few hours he had become a surrogate father to a girl so hauntingly beautiful that even Rakoczi had noticed her. He was taking her home to share his roof, but not his bed. No one would believe the truth of the situation. He doubted if he believed it himself. With a screech of tires, he drove down Heliotrope and halted outside a wooden frame house, its shabby paint job barely discernible beneath a riotous mass of jasmine and honeysuckle.

"We're home," he said, unhappily aware that his feelings toward Valentina were not paternal, and never would be.

Chapter Three

Bob's words roused Valentina from her stupor. "Home." It was a word she had never heard before. Slow pleasure seeped through her as she stood at his side and stared at the simple, wooden-framed house almost drowning beneath its load of ivy and flowering creepers.

"It's beautiful," she said softly.

Bob looked down at her compassionately. If this was beautiful, the convent had indeed been a bleak place to live.

"Let's go in," he said gently, picking up her valise and leading the way up a narrow walk edged in by boxwood hedges.

The door creaked on unoiled hinges and Bob winced at the sight of unwashed dishes and the film of dust on the coffee table and woodwork.

Daisy was blissfully unaware of any such flaws. She saw only the cozy intimacy of a small room with books and pictures and gaily scattered rugs. All her life she had existed with a minimum of personal possessions. To her, Bob's room seemed to be overflowing with riches. In wonder she walked slowly across to the open door leading to a cubbyhole of a kitchen. A few bottles of beer sat on top of the refrigerator, waiting to be stowed away. A spray of eucalyptus bobbed in at the open window.

Bob stood in the center of the main room as she retraced her steps and paused tentatively before a closed door. She looked across at him and he nodded permission. Tenderness flooded through him. At least the bed had been made, he recalled with relief.

She opened the door and stood on the threshold. The bed was old-fashioned with a brass head and a hand-crocheted coverlet. There was a small dresser, a mirror, a host of glossy autographed photographs and a pile of discarded clothing, topped by a battered tennis racket.

"It's all yours," Bob said as he entered the room and scooped up the dirty linen.

"Do you mean it?" She had never slept in a room of her own before.

"Of course I mean it." He swung the valise onto the bed. "Now, let's eat. I've got some steak and tomatoes and mushrooms. If you want to shower, the bathroom's through there." He nodded in the direction of a glass-fronted door adjoining the kitchen.

She looked up at him, at the crinkled corners of his eyes and the laughter-lined mouth, and was overwhelmed at his kindness.

"Thank you," she said simply.

He smiled. "There's no need for thanks," he said, making his way to the kitchen. "Just run a duster over the place now and again. That'll be thanks enough."

Later, as music from Bob's record player filled the room and she sat on the floor with her back against the sofa and Bob sipped at the beer, she said dreamily, "I don't think I've ever been so happy."

Bob put down his beer carefully. Her head was a mere few inches from his knees, and he resisted the urge to move closer; to reach out and touch the silky softness of her hair.

"That convent of yours must have been a pretty grim place."

Her eyes clouded. "No, not really. Just . . . lonely."

"But there must have been lots of other kids."

She drew her knees up to her chin and folded her arms around them. "Sometimes there were twenty, sometimes thirty."

"Then how come it was lonely?" Bob's brow furrowed in a faint frown.

"They weren't like me. They were orphans."

"And you weren't?"

"No . . ." A lamp cast a soft light in the room. Through an open window came the sound of a distant coyote. "My mother left me at the convent when I was a baby. They couldn't allow me to be adopted in case she came back for me."

"Only she didn't?"

"No."

"Holy shit." This time he did reach out and touch her, his hand resting comfortingly on her shoulder. He glanced at his watch and saw it was nearly midnight. It had been a cataclysmic day: for himself as well as for her. "Bedtime, sweetheart," he said, rising to his feet. "I have an early start tomorrow."

His pillow and blanket, folded neatly, lay in readiness at the end of the sofa.

She stood up, suddenly uncertain. "What will I do? About a job, I mean?"

"Don't worry. I'll soon fix you up with something," he said, but as the bedroom door closed behind her, he knew he would not do so in a hurry. She was too special to wait tables at Franco's or Garnett's. He stretched his long frame out on the sofa and passed his hand across his eyes. She trusted him and it was a trust he could not abuse—or let others abuse. His mouth hardened as he remembered Vidal Rakoczi and the way he had caught hold of her. It would not happen again. No matter what pressure the Hungarian brought to bear on him.

Vidal was waiting for him the next morning as Bob parked the Buick.

"Who is she?" he asked with narrowed eyes before Bob could even get out of the car.

Bob didn't answer until he was standing upright. "I don't know who you mean," he said tightly, moving toward the truck.

Rakoczi barred the way. "You know damned well who I mean, Kelly," he said softly.

Bob felt the anger he had been determined to control lick along his veins. Rakoczi had wasted no time in finding out his identity. No doubt he would waste equally little time in reporting him for bringing Valentina onto the lot.

"I've told you, I don't know who you mean," he repeated through clenched teeth.

Rakoczi had been riding in the hills since dawn. The whip he still carried cracked menacingly against the leather of his knee-high boots. His black eyes glittered. "You know damned well who I mean. The girl you brought onto the lot yesterday. I want to know who she is. Where she lives."

Bob felt his hands slowly clenching. "She's my sister and she went back home to Oregon last night. She has no interest in films or filmmaking."

He was speaking to a director. He should have addressed him as "Mr. Rakoczi." Have ended his sentences with a deferential "sir." He did neither. He knew instinctively that the man before him was his enemy, that given the chance, he would take Valentina away from him.

Rakoczi moved toward him threateningly. "You're lying."

Bob shook his head and stood his ground, his eyes brilliant with a rage that matched that of the man before him. "No, I'm not. You frightened her half to death yesterday. She's not a city girl. She's gone back home where she belongs."

"She belongs on film!" Rakoczi snarled, his eyes blazing.

"No, she doesn't. She belongs with the man she's going to marry. Now, if you'll excuse me, I have work to do."

Vidal's breath hissed between his teeth as he stepped out of the way and Bob swung himself up into the truck's cab. There had been the certainty of truth in Bob Kelly's words and Vidal wasn't a man accustomed to wasting time and energy. He would find out where Kelly came from; which part of Oregon. If he had to search the whole damned state, he'd find her. And film her.

Bob allowed himself a triumphant smile as the engine throbbed into life and the truck rolled away from the thwarted Hungarian. He didn't envy the staff or crew of *The Black Knights*. Rakoczi's temper, legendary at the best of times, would be doubly explosive today.

When he got back to the house that evening, every surface sparkled and shone and a vase overspilling with poppies and yellow daisies graced the center of the dining table. An inviting aroma drifted from the kitchen as Valentina took his jacket and led him to his chair.

Bob grinned at her. "Have you been enjoying yourself, sweetheart?"

She nodded, her eyes anxious, eager to please. "You like chili, don't you? And tacos?"

"I love them," Bob said, sitting down, aware that his days of hamburgers and hot dogs were temporarily at an end.

"I . . . I wondered if you'd seen Mr. Rakoczi today," she said hesitantly.

"No." Bob's voice was steady as he shoveled chili into a

taco shell. "He's a director. I'm a truck driver. Our paths don't cross."

In some subtle way he had withdrawn from her, and she knew that to continue would be to make things worse, but she had to ask.

"Could I come with you tomorrow? To the studio . . . ? Maybe I could get a job there."

"No!" This time there was no mistaking the steeliness of his voice. "I've told you before, Worldwide is no place for you. It's corrupt and degenerate, and you should stay well clear of it."

She swallowed a mouthful of chili with difficulty, her appetite gone. "I wouldn't get in anyone's way, Bob. Not like yesterday. I thought I could work in the offices. Sister Francesca taught me to type and to keep books and—"

"No!" Their gazes met and held and he knew that he was right in refusing her request. There was something about her. Some indefinable quality that he didn't understand but that he knew would not go unnoticed if she were seen by the boys in the casting office.

She lowered her eyes and blinked back hot tears. There was no compromise in Bob's voice. He had said no and he had meant it. But if she didn't return to the studio, how could she ever see Vidal Rakoczi again? Her shoulders drooped with disappointment, and Bob pushed his plate away.

"Would you like to see a movie this evening?" he asked, wanting to make amends.

She gasped, the color draining from her face. A movie! Incredibly, she had never seen one. Nearly all of the other girls in the convent had. Aunts and uncles came for them sporadically, taking them out at Christmas or at Easter. No one had ever come for her. She had become resigned to it, withdrawing so far inside herself that the hurt of such total rejection had numbed. Now at last, after all these years, she was about to see her first movie. She could hardly believe it.

"Oh, I'd love to, Bob," she said, her eyes shining.

Feeling like a king at being able to dispense such happiness so easily, Bob hurried her out to the car. The movie everyone was raving about was Josef von Sternberg's *Shanghai Express*.

"Do you like Marlene Dietrich?" he asked as they drove downtown.

"Oh, yes!" She had seen stills of Marlene in *The Blue Angel* and had followed the story line of her next movie, *Morocco*, avidly. When Sister Dominica's upper Latin class had become too tedious to tolerate, she had rested her chin on her hand and mentally eased herself far away. Following Gary Cooper into the desert in high-heeled shoes as Marlene had done. Now at last she would see her on the screen.

When they stepped from the Buick and walked into the theater, she was seized by momentary panic. What if the movie was nothing like in her dreams? What if the magic world that had sustained her for so long was finally to disillusion her? She took a deep, steadying breath and, with her heart palpitating wildly, stepped with Bob into the darkness.

It was magnificent. An experience so wonderful that she knew she would remember it for the rest of her life. Marlene played Shanghai Lily, a fallen woman with a heart of gold. Dressed in black feathers, like an exotic bird, she graced scenes so beautifully lit they reminded Daisy of Renaissance etchings. Clive Brook was her chilly ex-lover who doubted her faithfulness, a stuffy English bore whom Daisy knew *she* would never have loved. To save his life, Marlene offered herself to a rebel leader and Daisy shivered as her own emotions were scorched raw. At long last, after years of apprenticeship, she had entered the glittering, fanciful, magical world of the movies.

She went at every opportunity. Bob did not want her to work, but she insisted. She told him that if he did not allow her to work, she would have to leave the house and find a room in a boardinghouse. Seeing the defiant tilt of her chin, he had conceded defeat. She could work. But not at the studio. On that he was so adamant that she curbed her bitter disappointment and ceased to ask to be taken with him. Instead, she waited on tables in Garnett's.

The hours were long and the work was hard, but she enjoyed it. She enjoyed meeting people; enjoyed the chatter of the girls that she worked with, the good-natured bantering of the customers. She was a world away from the convent. She was free and she exulted in it.

The novelty of the little house on Heliotrope never wore thin. As their first days together merged into a week and then a month, she dusted and polished with pride. In the evenings they would go to the movies, to the beach, to the local tennis

club, where her standard of play was soon equal to Bob's.
Her coarse linen dress and thick, dark stockings were burned
and she went bare-legged in sandals and gay summer dresses.

Her days off from Garnett's usually fell through the week
when Bob was working. On those days she would go for long,
pleasurable walks in the hills, or maybe down to the beach.
In March, when her day off coincided with Saint Joseph's
Day, she knew that neither alternative would suffice. Saint
Joseph's Day was her own private anniversary and it could
not be spent in Los Angeles.

She left a note for Bob telling him where she had gone in
case he should be worried if she were late getting back,
packed a picnic lunch, and caught the early morning bus
south.

It was a strange sensation to be returning. The bus was
full of trippers heading for the same destination, cameras and
binoculars slung over their shoulders and around their necks.
A small smile tugged at the corners of her mouth. For none
of them could the return of the swallows mean as much as it
did to her.

When they reached Capistrano, she disentangled herself
from the gathering sightseers, walking swiftly and strongly
away from the town and toward the convent. Nothing had
changed. It was as if it were caught in a time warp. The high
wrought-iron gates and blazing white walls still enclosed it.
She could glimpse the courtyard and the cloisters, the vivid
mass of bougainvillea and the searing pink of geraniums, and
the fountain with its perpetual small trickle of water. No
small child stood beside it, her face upturned to the sky,
waiting with anxious heart for the first dark speck to appear
on the skyline. Abruptly she turned as remembered pain
sliced through her, striding through wild grass until she
reached the crown of the hill.

Only a few birds were winging their way inland. Square-
tailed, with glossy dark throat patches, they swooped in a
long elipse and then soared high again, their cries a soft churr
in the warm March air. A couple of them landed on the eaves
of the convent far below her and she sat down on the grass,
hugging her knees to her chest.

So much had happened since she had last waited for
their return. Her life with Bob had taken on a routine that
she had accepted unquestioningly. She knew now that it was

innocence that had enabled her to do so. In the beginning Bob had succeeded in shielding her from the wisecracking remarks of his friends, but had been unable to do so for long. To her surprise she had discovered that everyone, neighbors and friends, assumed they were lovers. Bob had said, his cheeks flushed with color, that she was not to pay any attention to their gossip, and she hadn't.

A swallow flew low, skimming her head, and she watched it, her eyes troubled. She was no longer as unsophisticated as she had been. She knew now that Bob was in love with her. That they could not continue for much longer as they were. Their relationship would have to change and deepen, or come to a painful end. The swallow darted away and she sighed, aware of a disturbing feeling of restlessness. If only she could work at the studio, she was sure that it would fade, but Bob, so indulgent in many ways, stood firm. She was not to go to the studio. She was not even to aspire to being a tea girl at the studio. She had tried not to mind, but it was as if she was denying her very birthright.

The swallows soared in, wave after wave of them, the air thick with the sound of their beating wings. She tilted her chin defiantly. She would ask him again. She would try and explain to him how very much it meant to her. She cared for him very deeply, and she did not want to hurt him, but she had to be herself. She had to be Valentina.

She returned home before he did, tore the note that she had left for him in half and threw it away, busying herself with the dinner, trying to think of the best way to broach once more the subject of Worldwide.

When he walked into the house that evening, she turned with the words ready on her lips, but he forestalled her. "We're invited to a party," he announced, striding into the kitchen and giving her a hug.

"Whose party?" she asked, momentarily disconcerted.

"Lilli Rainer's. She was a big name in the old days. Her son, Jeff Claybourne, is an electrician at Worldwide."

In all the time they had been together they had never attended any parties given by his fellow Worldwide employees.

"That will be lovely," she said, setting a casserole dish down on the center of the table. "Bob, can we talk about Worldwide? I feel so restless and I'm sure that if only—"

"No," he said swiftly, his grin fading, a tight look about his mouth. "I absolutely refuse to discuss it, Valentina."

"But it means so much to me, Bob. Please listen to me and try and understand."

"No," he said again, avoiding looking at her. "You'll need a dress for Lilli's party. Do you want me to shop with you?"

She shook her head, her heart heavy. "No," she said, lifting a jug of ice water out of the refrigerator and carrying it to the table. "I'd like to make my own dress, Bob."

"But how will you know what it will look like, sweetheart?"

"Because I can imagine it," she said, and knew that he would not understand.

She bought a length of amethyst satin and cut out and sewed a dress of devastating simplicity. When Bob saw it, he whistled in amazement. "That sure is some dress, sweetheart."

She smiled up at him, her sadness at the growing gulf between them forgotten in the excitement of the evening.

"Do you like it, Bob? Truly?"

His eyes told her that he did. The dress clung seductively to her breasts and hips, swirling out around her knees. Her hair was a smoke-dark cloud dipping provocatively forward at the cheekbones, emphasizing the beauty of her eyes and the fragility of her face.

"You look like a million dollars, sweetheart," he said, his voice gruff with emotion.

She felt a surge of pleasure. She wanted to please him, to make him proud of her. With her arm tucked through his, she stepped outside into the warm night air.

They drove high up into an area she had never visited before. The houses were large and low, set well back from the road amid carefully tended lawns and trees. At last Bob swung the Buick off the road and drove with headlights blazing up a long, curving drive. The Buick halted and Bob opened the door for her. There was the sound of laughter, of glasses clinking. A sense of excitement seized her, so deep it nearly took her breath away. With glowing eyes she followed Bob and stepped into the noise and heat of the party.

"Do have a drink," urged a blue-eyed girl with a friendly smile. "Lilli has concocted the most fabulous cocktails with rose petals floating on the surface."

"Lilli wants to meet her," another girl said, grabbing

hold of Daisy's hand and tugging her free of the throng. "Hi. I'm Patsy Smythe. This sure is some party. Have you met Lilli before?"

"No," Daisy said, avoiding the appreciative touch of a strange male hand.

Patsy grinned. "Just treat her as if she's the Queen of Sheba and you won't go far wrong. Hell. Someone has spilled rum on my skirt. How do you get rum stains out of chiffon?"

Daisy didn't know. Her eyes met those of Lilli Rainer. Lilli's eyes were small and piercing, raisin-black in a powdered white face. She had been talking volubly, a long jade cigarette holder stabbing the air to emphasize her remarks. Now she halted, her anecdote forgotten. She had lived and breathed for the camera. Only talkies had defeated her. Her voice held the guttural tones of her native Germany and no amount of elocution lessons had been able to eradicate them. She had retired gracefully, allowing nobody to know of her bitter frustration. On seeing Daisy, she rose imperiously to her feet. No star or starlet from Worldwide had been invited to the party. She did not like to be outshone and the girl before her, with her effortless grace and dark, fathom-deep eyes, was doing just that. Everyone had turned in her direction as Patsy Smythe led her across the room.

Lilli's carmine-painted lips tightened. "This is not a studio party," she said icily. "Admittance is by invitation only."

Valentina smiled. "I've been invited," she said pleasantly. "I came with Bob Kelly."

Lilli sat down slowly and gestured away those surrounding them. The amethyst satin dress was pathetically cheap and yet it looked marvelous on the girl. A spasm of jealousy caught at her aged throat and was gone. It was only the second-rate that she could not tolerate. And the girl in front of her was far from second-rate. "Do you work at Worldwide?" she asked sharply.

"No."

"Then you ought to," Lilli said tersely, "It's a first-rate studio and it has one of the best directors in town." She drew on her cigarette, inhaling deeply. "Where is Bob going to take you? Warner Brothers? Universal?"

"Not to any one of them," Daisy said composedly, not allowing her emotions to show. "Bob doesn't want me to work at the studios."

Lilli blew a wreath of smoke into the air and stared at her. "Then he's a fool," she said tartly. "You belong in front of the cameras. Anyone with half an eye can see that."

Noise rose and ebbed about them. Neither of them heard it.

"I know," Daisy said simply and with breathtaking candor. "But Bob doesn't. Not yet."

Lilli crushed her cigarette out viciously. "And how long are you going to wait until he wakes up to reality? Whose life are you leading? Yours or his?" She leaned forward, grasping hold of Daisy's wrist, her eyes brilliant.

"There are very few, my child, a very tiny few, who can be instantly beloved by the cameras. It's nothing that can be learned. It's something you are born with. It's in here"—she stabbed at her head with a lacquered fingernail—"and in here . . ." She slapped her hand across her corseted stomach. "It's *inside* you. It's not actions and gestures, it's something that is innate." She released Daisy's wrist and leaned back in her chair. "And you have it."

Daisy could feel her heart beating in short, sharp strokes. Lilli was telling her what she already knew, and it was almost more than she could bear.

"I wondered where you'd gone to." It was Bob with Jeff Claybourne at his side.

"I see I'm a bit late to perform the introductions," Jeff said, bending and giving his mother a kiss on her white-powdered cheek.

Bob was talking, but Daisy did not hear him. A cocktail glass was pressed into her hand and she took it numbly. Bob was talking to Jeff; Patsy Smythe was admiring her dress, and Lilli Rainer was looking at her, as if seeing into her very soul.

She had to get away. She needed peace and quiet in order to be able to think clearly. To still the unsettling emotions Lilli's words had aroused.

She fought her way from the crowded room into the ornate entrance hall. A chandelier hung brilliantly above her head; the carpet was wine-red, the walls covered in silk. There was a marble telephone stand and a dark, carved wooden chair beside it. She sat down, her legs trembling as if she were on the edge of an abyss. Someone had left cigarettes and a lighter on the telephone table. Clumsily she spilled them from their pack, picking one up, struggling with the lighter.

"Allow me," a deep-timbered voice said from the shadow of the stairs. The lighter clattered to the table, the cigarette dropped from her fingers as she whirled her head around.

He had been sitting on the stairs, just out of range of the chandelier's brilliance. Now he moved, rising to his feet, walking toward her with the athletic ease and sexual negligence of a born predator.

She couldn't speak, couldn't move. He withdrew a black Sobranie from a gold cigarette case, lit it, inhaling deeply, and then removed the cigarette from his mouth and set it gently between her lips.

She was shaking. Over an abyss and falling. Falling as Vidal Rakoczi said softly, "I don't believe you've ever been to Oregon in your life."

Chapter Four

There was still noise. Laughter and music were still loud in the nearby rooms, but Valentina was oblivious to it. She was aware of nothing but the dark, magnetic face staring down at her, the eyes pinning her in place, consuming her the way a forest fire consumes dry tinder. She tried to stand, to gather some semblance of dignity, but could do neither. The wine-red of the walls and carpet, the brilliance of the chandelier, all spun around her in a dizzy vortex of light and color and in the center, drawing her like a moth to a flame, were the burning eyes of Vidal Rakoczi. She was suffocating, unable to breathe, to draw air into her lungs. The cigarette fell from her lips, scorching the amethyst satin. Swiftly he swept it from her knees, crushing it beneath his foot.

"Are you hurt?" The depth of feeling in his voice shocked her into mobility.

"I . . . No. . . ." Unsteadily she rose to her feet. He made no movement to stand aside, to allow her to pass.

He was so close that she could feel the warmth of his breath on her cheek, smell the indefinable aroma of his maleness.

"Will you excuse me?" she asked, a pulse beating wildly in her throat.

"No." The gravity in his voice held her transfixed. His eyes had narrowed. They were bold and black and blatantly determined. "Now that I have found you again, I shall never excuse you to leave me. Not ever."

She felt herself sway and his hand grasped her arm, steadying her.

"Let's go where we can talk."

"No," she whispered, suddenly terrified as her dreams took on reality. She tried to pull away from him, but he held her easily.

"Why not?" A black brow rose questioningly.

The touch of his hand seared her flesh. She could not go with him. To go with him would be to abandon Bob, and that was unthinkable. He had done nothing to deserve such disloyalty. He had been kind to her. Kinder than anyone else had ever been. Sobs choked her throat. She loved Bob, but not in the way that he needed her to love him. The day would have come when she would have had to tell him so . . . but it hadn't come, and she couldn't just leave with Rakoczi. Not like this.

"No," she said again, her lips dry, her mouth parched. "Please let me go."

The strong, olive-toned hand tightened on her arm and the earth seemed to tremble beneath her feet. It was as if the very foundations upon which she had built her life since leaving the convent were cracking and crumbling around her. Lilli's words echoed in her brain. Bob's life or her own? To go or to stay? Pain sliced through her and she knew with despair that Bob's life could never be hers. He loved her, but he had no understanding of her. And instinct, ages old, told her that the man at her side understood her utterly. She made one last, valiant attempt to cling to the world that had been her haven.

"I came with Bob Kelly," she said, knowing even as she spoke that her battle was lost. "He will be looking for me."

A slight smile curved the corners of his mouth. "But he won't find you," he said, and with devastating assurance he took her hand and the course of her life changed.

She wasn't aware of leaving the house. She wasn't aware of anything but Vidal Rakoczi's hand tightly imprisoning hers as she ran to keep up with his swift stride. They crossed the night-wet lawn to the dryness of the gravel drive and he opened the doors of a pale blue Duesenberg. She didn't ask where they were going. She didn't care. She was with him and it was sufficient.

He didn't drive the way Bob did; he drove with breathtaking recklessness, taking the swooping downward curves of the canyon at suicidal speeds, his hands strong and firm on the wheel. Distant houses, trees, lights, flashed by and were gone, swallowed up in the darkness.

She sat in silence at his side, peace and contentment lost to her forever. Something long dormant had at last been released. A zest, a recklessness for life that caused the blood to pound along her veins, and her nerve ends to throb. Like had met like. She had known it instinctively the day he had stalked across to her on the studio lot. Now there was no going back. No acceptance of anything less than life with the man who was at her side.

He bypassed La Cienega Boulevard, heading out toward the coast.

"A cigarette?" he asked, breaking the silence for the first time.

She nodded, and he removed one hand from the wheel and gold gleamed dully as he flicked open his cigarette case. As he closed it and returned it to his inside breast pocket, she saw that instead of initials, a coat of arms was engraved on one corner, embellished with a diamond.

The spurt of flame as he lit her cigarette threw his face into sharp relief and she understood all too well why his handsome, almost satanic features had earned him the nickname of a devil. His black bow tie had been discarded long since and his austere white evening shirt was open at the throat. At her swift intake of breath his eyes flicked from the highway ahead and held hers. Heat flooded through her as she returned his gaze in the darkness and then his white teeth flashed in a devastating smile and she asked, "Why did you think I came from Oregon?"

He laughed, and as he did so her shyness and awe of him evaporated like dew on a sun-hot morning. He was her kindred spirit. The other being she had waited for all her life.

"Your brother said you had left California and returned there."

"I don't have a brother."

He swung the Duesenberg off the highway, roaring down a dirt track to where giant waves rolled onto a deserted beach.

"I know that. It was a remarkable performance from a man who isn't an actor."

She didn't ask who he meant. She already knew.

The car crowned a dune and he braked and halted. In the moonlight the heaving Pacific was silk-black, the swelling waves breaking into surging foam on a crescent of firm white sand. The night breeze from the sea was salt-laden and chilly. He took off his dinner jacket and draped it around her shoulders as they slipped and slid down the dunes to the beach. She stepped out of her high-heeled sandals, raising her face to the breeze.

"It's very beautiful here. And very lonely."

"That's why I come."

The breeze molded her gown to her body, outlining her breasts and hips, the hem trailing and fluttering in the sand behind her. Vidal's eyes narrowed appraisingly. She was both innocent and pagan. She would be even more devastating on the screen than Garbo.

They walked along in silence for a while, the Pacific breakers creaming and running up the shoreline only inches from their feet.

"You know what it is I want of you, don't you?" he asked at last, and a shiver ran down her spine. Whatever it was, she would give it freely. "I want to film you. To see if the luminous quality you possess transfers to the screen."

The moon slid out from behind a bank of clouds. He had expected lavish thanks; vows of eternal gratitude; a silly stream of nonsense about how she had always wanted to be a movie star. Instead she remained silent, her face strangely serene. There was an inner stillness to her that he found profoundly refreshing. He picked up a pebble and skimmed it far out into the night-black sea.

"I am a man of instincts," he said, stating a fact that no

one who had come into contact with him would deny. "I believe that you have a rare gift, Valentina." Their hands touched fleetingly and she trembled. "I expect complete obedience. Absolute discipline."

His brows were pulled close together, his silhouetted face that of a Roman emperor accustomed to wielding total power. He halted, staring down at her. "Do you understand?"

Her head barely reached his shoulder. She turned her face up to his, the sea breeze fanning her hair softly against her cheeks. The moonlight accentuated the breathtaking purity of her cheekbone and jawline and he wondered how he could re-create the effect with his chief lighting engineer, Don Symons.

"Yes," she said, and at her composure his eyes gleamed with amusement.

"Where the devil did you spring from?" he asked, a smile touching his mouth.

Her eyes sparkled in the darkness as she said with steely determination, "Wherever it was, I'm not going back."

He began to laugh and as he did so she stumbled, falling against him. His arms closed around her, steadying her. For a second they remained motionless and then the laughter faded from his eyes and he lowered his head, his mouth claiming hers in swift, sure contact.

Nothing had prepared her for Vidal's kiss. Her lips trembled and then parted willingly beneath his. There was sudden shock and an onrush of pleasure as his tongue sought and demanded hers, setting her on fire.

She was crushed against the hard length of his body. Heat flooded through her. She was his without reservation . . . and then, as suddenly as he had seized her, he released her.

"Let's go," he said curtly, his face savage as he pivoted on his heel, striding back along the sand so quickly that she had difficulty in keeping pace with him. "You have a long day ahead of you. I'll send a studio limousine to pick you up."

She stopped abruptly and he turned and looked down at her, lines of impatience around his mouth.

"Pick me up from where?" she asked, her heart beginning to slam in thick, heavy strokes.

He gave a slight shrug. "From wherever you live."

"I lived with Bob," she said, and the shaft of pain she felt was naked in her voice. "I can't go back. Not ever."

It was true. She had known it as she had stood in Lilli Rainer's chandelier-lit hall and she knew it now. Her life had changed irreversibly and for Bob's sake the break with the past had to be swift and clean. Like the cut of a surgeon's knife.

She shivered. Was that how her mother had felt the morning she had driven in the battered Model T Ford to the convent at Capistrano? Had she loved her but known that a future for them together was impossible? The breakers roared in from the sea, crashing and surging into foam only yards from her feet, stinging her cheeks with spray.

Bob would feel as abandoned as she had felt. Like her, he would not understand. Tears glittered on her long, dark lashes. She felt suddenly ages old. To stay with Bob would be to cheat him. He deserved far, far more from the woman in his life than she could give him. Gratitude was no substitute for love. And eventually, as she now understood and forgave her mother, he would understand and forgive her. Her eyes met Vidal's and her chin tilted a fraction higher. "Pick me up from where?" she asked again.

His facial muscles hardened. Already, like every woman, she was proving to be a damned nuisance. He swore inwardly. No one returned to Villada with him. It was a self-imposed rule that he had never broken. He sucked his breath between his teeth angrily. Tonight would have to be the exception. Tomorrow he would book her into the Beverly Hills or the Beverly Wilshire.

"Then you'd better come with me," he said tersely, opening the Duesenberg's door, hardly waiting for her to get into the car and be seated before he gunned the engine into life and swerved backward, circling in a cloud of dust and sand and speeding once more toward the highway.

She sat at his side, her moment of calm reasoning deserting her. He had said he would never let her escape him again. He had kissed her with passionate ferocity. Why, then, was he sitting at her side like a stranger, consumed by an inner rage she had no way of understanding?

Only when the highway was left behind and they began to climb a steep and pitch-dark canyon did she summon the courage to say tentatively, "Did you mean it? About wanting me at the studio tomorrow?"

"Yes." His voice was brusque. "I want a damned good screen test to persuade Worldwide to put you under contract and let me use you in the movie I have in mind."

"What movie is that?" she asked, seized by curiosity.

His eyes gleamed as they swerved round a hairpin turn. "A movie the Worldwide executives have no intention of making . . . yet."

"Will you be able to make them change their minds?"

"If they don't, I'll threaten to take the idea to Cecil De Mille over at the Lasky studios."

"Can you do that?"

"I do what I want," he said, the abrasive, masculine lines of his face hardening.

She felt the breath catch in her throat. She wanted to be like him. To have the same fearlessness, the same daring, the same insolence toward life. To face the world with fiery eyes and careless defiance. To do what *she* wanted to do. Not what Sister Dominica told her to do. Or Reverend Mother. Or Bob. To be Valentina. The person she herself had created.

In the darkness of the Duesenberg she closed her eyes and vowed that never again would she think of herself as Daisy. Daisy Ford was dead. Only Valentina remained.

The hills loomed menacingly above them, black silhouettes in the darkness. At last, when they had reached the barren heights, Vidal swung the Duesenberg off the narrow road toward a large, isolated villa.

A Filipino houseboy hurried to greet them as they entered, his eyes widening in astonishment as he saw Valentina in his employer's wake.

"Would you like a drink?" Vidal asked her as he took his customary tumbler of brandy and soda from the silver tray Chai proffered.

"No, thank you."

She was gazing around her in amazement. She had never been in a room like this one. One whole wall was glass, and far down the darkened hillside a solitary light signified a late-night party still in progress. The carpet was white and ankle-deep, the walls covered in sensuous black leather. There were paintings on the walls and shelf upon shelf of books. She was acutely aware of her windblown hair and her bare feet, and her cheeks warmed with mortification. What would the young man in Vidal's employ think of her? His eyes were inscrutable. He nodded impassively as Vidal said briefly, "Please show my guest into the Hispano-Mauresque room. We shall both need studio calls in the morning."

"Yes, sir."

Vidal moved to the foot of the stairs and then paused, his eyes holding hers, their dark depths revealing nothing.

"Good night," he said, and then, without a backward glance, he strode up the stairs to his room. A few seconds later there came the sound of a door slamming hard on its hinges.

Chai was at her side. "This way, please. The Hispano-Mauresque room is on the ground floor. It is a very pretty room."

She had thought she had left loneliness behind her when she had left the convent. Now she was consumed by it. Desolately she followed Chai into Vidal Rakoczi's guest room and then, bidding the houseboy an awkward good night, slipped out of her dress, letting the amethyst satin fall into a shining heap on the floor.

She was in Vidal Rakoczi's home. He was sleeping only rooms away from her. Wasn't that what she had dreamed about? Longed for? She slid between the sheets knowing that she should be content and knowing that she would never be so until she shared not only his roof, but his heart and his mind, his body and his bed.

She closed her eyes, but sleep would not come. Tomorrow she had to see Bob. Had to explain to Bob. But even that thought could not erase the burning memory of Vidal Rakoczi's lips on hers.

Determination seized her, as it had the day she resolved to leave the convent behind her. She would *make* Vidal Rakoczi fall in love with her. She brushed her lips with the tips of her fingers, and with a faint smile at last fell asleep.

Chai woke her in the morning with fresh coffee, warm rolls, and chilled orange juice. She dressed hurriedly, aware of how bizarre her dress looked in the light of early dawn.

As she closed the door of the room behind her, she was aware of Vidal waiting in the hallway. He had been riding. His boots were covered with a fine film of dust and his shirt was open at the throat.

"Have you had breakfast?" he asked, his tone implying that it would be a great inconvenience if she had not already done so.

"Yes." She moved toward him uncertainly. "What about my dress? How can I appear at Worldwide in the early morning in an evening dress?"

He suppressed a smile. "Don't worry. You won't be the first to do so. Your clothes are immaterial today. Wardrobe will take care of all your needs."

He turned on his heel and she followed him out and into the pale light of dawn. A chauffeur-driven Rolls, not the Duesenberg, was waiting to take them to the studio.

"Casting doesn't know a damned thing about you," he said as the Rolls took the first curve and the Cahuenga Valley lay spread before them. "If all hell breaks loose, smile sweetly and stay quiet. I'll handle it."

In the rear of the Rolls, the distance between them seemed vast. It was as if he had never touched her. Never kissed her. She clasped her hands tightly on her lap.

"How do you know that I can act?" she asked curiously.

"Because I am Rakoczi," he replied, and the timbre of his voice sent her heart pounding.

Her fingers began to twist and seeing her nervousness, he said a little less brusquely, "Do not worry about your ability to act. That will come naturally. It is not acting alone that makes great movie stars. Looks, movement, voice, talent . . . All are important, but they are not enough. If they were, thousands of people could be stars."

"Then, what is it?" she asked as the Santa Monica Mountains took on a rose-red hue and lemon and orange groves became discernible in the distance.

"Personality. The quality that flows out of you. That draws attention, commanding and holding it."

"And do I have that?"

"Yes," he said abruptly, leaning forward and releasing a catch allowing a small mahogany cupboard to fall open. Inside were glasses and silver flasks. It was not yet six in the morning.

She tried to tear her eyes away from him and could not. His hands were so strong. She wanted to reach out and touch them. To bury her fingers in his hair.

"What will happen when we reach the studio?" she asked.

"First you'll go into makeup, then hairdressing, and then wardrobe."

"And will I play a scene?"

"Yes." He hesitated and then said, "For years I have wanted to make a picture about the struggle between the House of York and the House of Lancaster for the throne of England in the fifteenth century."

"You mean a picture like *The Black Knights?*"

His mouth twisted in a brief smile. "Not remotely like *The Black Knights*. That movie could have been made by a blind, deaf, and dumb man. I want to make a picture that people will still want to see in fifty years from now. A classic. There was a time when I thought Garbo could play the lead. I still thought so until you wandered on to the set of *The Black Knights*." He paused and his voice took on a different quality. "Then I knew differently."

Her eyes were troubled. "I don't know anything about English history except that William the Conqueror invaded in 1066 and that the present king's son is very handsome."

Vidal's brows flew together. The blond, mild-mannered Prince of Wales was the very antithesis of himself.

"You'll have to learn," he said tightly. "I don't want you to play the part of Margaret of Anjou. I want you to *be* her."

They were nearly at the studio gates.

"Who *was* Margaret of Anjou?" she asked ingenuously.

A smile tugged at the corners of his mouth. Any other woman would have feigned knowledge rather than admit ignorance.

"Margaret of Anjou was a tigress. Quick-tempered, courageous, and passionate. She was French by birth, and the wife of Henry VI of England." There was a wicked glint in his eyes. "They were not a very compatible pair. Henry was a prude and conducted his kingship in sackcloth and ashes. When their son was born, Henry said he must have been conceived by the Holy Ghost."

For a moment it seemed as if the barrier that had risen up between them was on the verge of breaking down, and then they were approaching the studio gates and he fell silent. Itinerant workers clustered in small groups in the hope of being needed as extras. The elderly man who had glared so fiercely at Bob the previous time she had entered, now saluted smartly and wished Mr. Rakoczi a good day.

They drove past the casting office, entering the heart of the lot. The scene set for *The Black Knights* had long since been dismantled. In its place was a railroad station complete with rolling stock. She remembered the breathtaking beauty of Romana de Santa as the medieval princess, and sudden doubt assailed her. Surely it was Romana who should be playing the part of Margaret of Anjou. Romana, with her spun-gold hair and china-blue eyes.

The Rolls had halted, the chauffeur was opening the door.

"It doesn't matter what they do to me in makeup," she said, overcome by momentary panic, "I shall never be able to look like Romana de Santa."

"Heaven forbid!" Vidal said explosively, picking up the folder that lay on the seat beside him. "There must be a hundred Romanas in this studio alone and one is more than enough."

The chauffeur held open the door. She hesitated for only a fraction of a second and then stepped out onto the pavement of Worldwide. Heads turned immediately in her direction. Anyone seen in the company of Vidal Rakoczi excited attention, and several hurrying executives stopped and stared as she followed Vidal up a flight of wooden steps and into the makeup department.

"Good morning, Mr. Rakoczi," Wally Barren said, leaving his task of turning a bored-looking actor into a Spanish conquistador and hurrying to greet them. A visit from Worldwide's enfant terrible was a rare event.

"Good morning, Wally. Let me introduce you to Valentina."

Wally looked worriedly at his notes on his clipboard. "I don't have her name down here, Mr. Rakoczi. Is she testing for *Thunder Dawn?*"

"She's not testing for *Thunder Dawn*, nor for anything else you have down there, Wally."

"Casting always stipulates the parts actresses are testing for, Mr. Rakoczi."

"Casting didn't send her."

"Oh . . ." Wally swallowed hard. "I see. What is it you want me to do, Mr. Rakoczi?"

"What I *don't* want you to do is to make her into a replica of every glamour girl on Worldwide's assembly line."

"No, Mr. Rakoczi." Wally suppressed a grin. "Does Mr. Gambetta know of Miss . . . of Valentina's screen test?"

"It isn't any of Mr. Gambetta's affair—yet."

Wally smiled broadly and seated Valentina, placing a cape around her shoulders while his minions attended to the conquistador. Theodore Gambetta was the self-styled emperor of Worldwide. From a huddle of huts on a sun-scorched patch of no-man's-land he had built Worldwide into a major studio. Babylon had risen and fallen on a Worldwide lot. Moses had descended Mount Sinai; the Red Sea had parted; the Civil War had been fought. Until Vidal Rakoczi arrived, no one had claimed that Worldwide Pictures made great art, but no one disputed that they created great box-office attractions.

Valentina sat before a large, brilliantly lit mirror, and Vidal flicked open the folder in his hand.

"These are the costume sketches, Wally. The period is mid-fifteenth century, but the woman is no pining princess locked in an ivory tower. She is a fighter. A woman who led troops into battle because her husband was too weak to do so."

Wally tilted Valentina's chin, moving her head from one side to the other, staring thoughtfully at her.

"I think the focus should be on the eyes, Mr. Rakoczi. They're the most damned expressive eyes I've seen since Rudy's. And see the jawline? Perfect. Absolutely perfect."

Valentina remained motionless. They were discussing her as if she were an inanimate object.

"I'll be back to take her to hairdressing myself, Wally. If anyone asks any questions, just refer them to me."

"Sure thing, Mr. Rakoczi."

The volatile Hungarian had many enemies at Worldwide, but Wally was not one of them. All the man demanded was the same exacting efficiency he demanded of himself. If he didn't get it, then it was best to run for cover. Wally always gave it.

He turned his attention to Valentina. In the two years Mr. Rakoczi had been at Worldwide, he had never before personally escorted anybody—star or starlet—into makeup. And Mr. Gambetta didn't know of her existence. It was an interesting situation. He speculated about it briefly and then forgot it as he became immersed in his work. And it was sheer joy; the bone structure beneath his dexterous fingers was superb. There were no blemishes to conceal; no faults to hide from the all-seeing studio lights.

"Have you known Mr. Rakoczi long?" Valentina asked Wally, finding pleasure in just the utterance of his name.

"Two years," Wally said, discarding one brush and selecting another. "Ever since Mr. Gambetta brought him to Worldwide." He grinned. "That caused the biggest uproar this studio has ever known—and I've been here for twenty years."

He began to accentuate the hollows of her cheekbones. "No one here had heard of him. Mr. Gambetta had been to Europe and seen his movies and figured he was a genius. Said that he could bring a prestige to Worldwide that no one else could." He stood back to survey his handiwork. "He sure doesn't put up with some of the shit other directors have to put up with. Mr. Gambetta"—he lowered his voice confidentially— "is not the easiest of men to work for."

"I doubt that Mr. Rakoczi is either," Valentina said with a smile.

Wally chuckled. "You're right there. When Mr. Rakoczi and Mr. Gambetta meet head-on, the vibrations can be heard as far away as La Jolla." He began to apply color to her lids. "Funny thing is, Mr. Gambetta always gives Mr. Rakoczi his head, and Mr. Rakoczi is never wrong. Every studio in town is after him. Mayer and Thalberg at MGM have offered him so much money that when La Swanson heard of it, she fainted dead away."

"Gloria Swanson?"

"Yeah. She earned nine hundred thousand dollars a year when she was at Paramount. Her clothes bill alone was eighty thousand dollars a year."

Valentina blinked. She knew the stars earned colossal sums of money, but nine hundred thousand dollars a year was beyond her imagination.

"With Mr. Rakoczi directing you, you could find yourself in the same income bracket," Wally said encouragingly.

"I wouldn't know what to do with so much money."

"Spend it, kid, spend it," Wally said, highlighting here, powdering there. He liked Mr. Rakoczi's latest find. There was a simple directness about her that made a welcome change from the affected posturings of most of Worldwide's starlets.

"I'll let you in on a secret. You're the only girl I've ever had in here brought in by a director. The system is that potential contract players come through central casting. I guess Mr. Rakoczi has something special in mind for you." He began to outline her lips with a brush. "Everything Mr. Rakoczi touches turns to gold. If he's singled you out, then you can bet your last dollar that you're on your way to the top."

He began to mix two different colors together on his palette in order to obtain a lip color that was strong enough for the studio lights without being too harsh.

"Mind you, you'll have to work yourself to near collapse. He doesn't spare himself, and he doesn't spare his crew. If your screen test is a success, you can look forward to eighteen hours of work a day, every day, until the movie is finished. When the last reel of *The Black Knights* was safely in the can, Romana de Santa booked herself into a sanatorium, claiming that she was suffering from exhaustion and that Mr. Rakoczi had subjected her to mental cruelty that would have been grounds for divorce if they'd been married."

"Were Mr. Rakoczi and Miss de Santa very close?" Valentina asked hesitantly, remembering the proprietorial way Romana had laid her hand on his arm.

Wally laughed. "Hell no. Mr. Rakoczi's faithfulness to his wife is legendary."

She stared into the mirror as Wally busily finished painting her lips and returned his attention to her eyes. For a second she didn't feel anything. It was as if her heart had ceased to beat.

Wally erased one carefully penciled eyebrow with cold cream and began work on it again. Her hands closed tightly over the arms of the makeup chair.

"Did you say that Mr. Rakoczi was married?" Her voice sounded strange, even to her ears. It was as if someone else were speaking; as if she were watching the scene from a vast distance.

"Biggest wedding this town's ever seen," Wally affirmed. "Mrs. Rakoczi comes from an old New England family. If you believe all they say, her ancestors came over on the *Mayflower*."

Her mirrored face swam distortedly before her eyes. If she had not been sitting, she would have fallen. She had a strange sense of déjà vu. It was as if she were once again in the Reverend Mother's study, faced with a truth so appalling that it robbed her of coherent thought. She wondered if she would die. It seemed impossible to live and to hurt so much.

"She spends a lot of time in Europe. She's in Switzerland now," Wally was saying, and then there came the sound of Vidal's swift steps on the wooden stairs and she struggled to draw air into her lungs as the door burst open.

Chapter Five

He strode across the room and surveyed her appraisingly. "You've done a good job, Wally."

"My pleasure, Mr. Rakoczi."

He was only inches away from her. She could smell his cologne, the inherent maleness of him.

"Hairdressing is waiting," he said, and she nodded, incapable of speech.

Wally frowned as they left the makeup department. His sharp eyes had registered her reaction when he had mentioned Mr. Rakoczi's marriage. He felt a surge of pity for her. She was a nice girl, but she would have to develop a much tougher exterior if she was to survive in the Hollywood jungle. He shook his head despairingly and turned his attention to an actress waiting to be transformed into a Southern belle. It was none of his affair. He had long since ceased giving out unheeded advice to the stars and starlets who passed daily through his hands.

In hairdressing, she avoided Vidal's eyes and touch. It was as if a sliver of ice had entered her heart, chilling her blood so that no amount of summer sun could warm it. If he noticed her silence, he gave no sign of it. Not until they were crossing to wardrobe did he speak.

"I'm not going to do the usual screen test. I want to show Gambetta more." He handed her several pages of script. "The first scene is where the fifteen-year-old Margaret of Anjou is told by her uncle, Charles VII, that she is to marry Henry of England in order to effect a lasting peace with France."

Her throat was parched and her heart hammered as she said with difficulty, "Were England and France at war?"

He grinned and she turned her head away swiftly before he should see the pain in her eyes.

"Didn't they teach you anything at school? In the early fifteenth century, much of France was held by England. After Henry's disastrous reign, only Calais remained in their control."

"There is no reason why I should know English history," she retorted spiritedly.

"Maybe not, but you will before the next few weeks are over. The second scene is where Margaret, despairing over her vapid husband, decides to raise and lead an army herself in order to save the English crown for her husband and her son."

His nearness was almost more than she could bear. "Who will play the parts of Charles VII and Henry?" she asked, keeping her eyes firmly averted from his.

"Today, no one. Read through the script of that scene, and memorize what you can. It doesn't matter if you have to read from it. It's how you come across on camera that matters."

They entered wardrobe and she stood as far from him as possible, wondering how she would endure his physical presence in the close confines of the studio.

"Is everything ready?" he asked a tiny, spry lady with gray hair and a pince-nez.

"Just as you requested, Mr. Rakoczi. This is the costume here."

"Very well," he said, then turned on his heel and walked briskly out of the room.

The wardrobe mistress asked Valentina to undress in a small changing room. She lifted the sumptuous gown of velvet from a hanger and followed. Ermine edged the canopy of the skirt and the long, trailing hem. She slipped the gown over Valentina's head, and then led her out to the fitting area. As the costume was pinned, Valentina read the script carefully. Confidence seeped through her. She was going to do what she had always done. Bring words on paper alive with her voice. She had been eight when she first memorized Tennyson's *Lady of Shalott*, tears dampening her cheeks by the time she reached the last sad verse. Longfellow's *Song of Hiawatha* had been committed to memory with voracious ease, as had *Paul Revere's Ride*. As she had grown older she had tackled more difficult subjects. Her favorite passages of Scripture; whole pages from whichever book of American history was being studied in class. Her ability had enabled her to survive in the book-deprived dormitory. Now it was going to become her life.

When she finally put the script down and looked into the mirror, her eyes widened and she gasped with pleasure. The heavy, medieval robe had transformed her. She was Margaret of Anjou—fifteen, dutifully, but not submissively, facing her uncle, the most powerful king in Europe. Her hair streamed down her back and around her shoulders, crowned by a coronal of gold inlaid with imitation pearls and precious stones.

Vidal returned. "Ready?" he asked, and his voice caught and deepened. For years, Margaret of Anjou had lived only in his imagination. Now she stood before him, flesh and blood.

"Yes." Margaret of Anjou was not in love with Vidal Rakoczi, a married man. Margaret of Anjou was mistress of her own heart. She did not have to suffer. She did not have to tremble at a glance or a word from the man at her side. The knowledge gave her an inner freedom she had not thought possible. Holding her head high, she met his eyes fearlessly and walked from the room as if surrounded by a score of ladies in waiting.

Behind her, Vidal grinned. Theodore Gambetta did not know it yet, but he had found his biggest star and she had as yet to face the cameras.

He had given orders for a closed set. He didn't want a word of what was he was doing to leak to Gambetta before he was able to show him the rushes. There were more people about now. It was nearly nine o'clock and executives and their staffs flooded through the main gate, hurrying purposefully to their offices.

The commissary counter was surrounded by writers and technicians, all gulping down hot coffee, bracing themselves for the demands of the day. Extras hastened to the studios to be costumed and given their instructions. The paint and plaster shops were hives of activity. There was a line at the barber and a line at the shoeshine stand.

Vidal stalked through the human mass of Theodore Gambetta's employees, Valentina at his side. He could feel excitement building within him. He would know whether he had been right or wrong before he even saw the rushes. He would know the instant she set foot before the cameras.

A door closed behind them and they were in shadow. Valentina blinked, her eyes adjusting to the dimness of the interior of a small studio.

"Morning, Mr. Rakoczi."

"Good morning, Harris. Let me have a closer look at that set."

"We've been working on it flat out ever since you gave the orders, but three hours isn't any time at all. If we'd known last night . . ."

Vidal was no longer listening to him. He was striding across coils of cable toward the hastily constructed set. The backdrop was a painted canvas of medieval grandeur. The interior of a fifteenth-century palace. In front of it stood a dark oak table and a high-backed chair, intricately carved.

Valentina remained where he had left her. There were sixteen or more men in the room: cameramen, electricians, grips. None paid her any attention. Their eyes were focused on the tense, lithe figure of Vidal Rakoczi.

"I thought perhaps we should put straw down on the floor, Mr. Rakoczi," the man called Harris began.

"No." Vidal's voice was decisive. "I want her to walk forward toward camera. I want her robes to sweep the stone slabs of the floor, to rustle. I want no other sound at all. None. Just the girl walking forward until she faces her uncle and speaks directly to camera."

"Okay, Mr. Rakoczi."

Vidal gave the set a last, dismissive glance and turned to the crew. "Let's move. I want that klieg farther to the left."

Valentina stood silently behind the lights as they were maneuvered into place. It was the fifteen-year-old princess, summoned from comparative obscurity to her uncle's presence, that Vidal wanted her to portray in the first scene. How would she have felt, that young girl, on being told that she was to marry a man she had never met? A man who did not love her, but wanted her hand in marriage to strengthen his hold on the throne of England.

Vidal was at her side, his gaze disturbingly intense. "First, I want right and left profile shots. Then I want you to stand at the very rear of the set. When I tell you to move, I want you to walk forward—slowly. Remember, it's a king you're facing. The king of France. He may be your uncle, but he has the power of life or death over you. You have no idea why you have been summoned into his presence. I want to feel your uncertainty. England wants you as a queen in order to salvage something of the wreckage of her former power in France. When Charles VII tells you that you are to marry Henry, both you and he know the reasons. As far as Charles is concerned, you will exert your influence as queen of England to his advantage. You are, after all, only a girl and, in his eyes, malleable. He expects that, even married to Henry, your loyalty will be to France."

She could feel the warmth of his breath on her cheek and began to tremble. She clenched her hands tightly. She must not think of him. She must forget her own existence and that of Vidal Rakoczi, the man she loved. Only Margaret of Anjou and Rakoczi, the director, could be allowed to exist if she was to live and breathe on the screen.

"Everything's ready, Mr. Rakoczi," a voice called.

Vidal turned swiftly, the planes of his face harsh. "Thanks, Harris. Valentina, I want you to stand at the side of the chair. We'll do some straight shots first, and then we'll take it from the script."

They were waiting for her. She had to move. She had to forget her heartbreak and become Margaret of Anjou.

She walked forward uncertainly, standing with one hand resting lightly on the carved back of the chair. The grips, the electricians, the cameramen, momentarily disconcerted her. She had not known they would be so close. Then, as if they were Sister Dominica, she closed her mind to them and they no longer existed.

The obligatory casting shots were taken and she moved to the rear of the set to face the brilliant glare of the klieg lights. With a sharp intake of breath, Vidal saw that her script was nowhere in sight, and then she moved forward and he knew that it did not matter. The first time he had seen her, he had seen magic in her face and as the cameras started to whirr, the magic shone through. It was as if an electric current existed between her and the lens.

"Jesus," Harris whispered in awe to Vidal, "this dame's coming across in another dimension."

Valentina halted on the chalk line before the camera and the nonexistent king of France.

"My liege," she said, curtsying deeply, the haunting smoky quality of her voice silencing the set, "you wished to speak with me?" Her smile was hesitant and flickering, the smile of a girl who does not know her fate. But when she raised her head, her eyes were surprisingly bold . . . the eyes of a woman no man had as yet taken into account.

When she had finished, Vidal contained his excitement and said smoothly, "And now for the Warrior Queen speech, Valentina. Remove the coronal and stand two paces to the left."

She did as he told her, pausing briefly with her back to him and the crew. She was no longer young and vulnerable. She was queen of a divided country, and she was fighting to secure the throne for her husband and her son.

"Right," said a distant voice. "One, two, three. Roll 'em."

She spun round on her heel, her skirts whipping about her ankles. She was fire and lightning and the very air sizzled as she rallied her troops against the oncoming army, intent on taking her prisoner.

At last it was all over. Valentina stood, momentarily disoriented, as once again she became aware of the camera and crew, and then to her utter amazement she heard first one man begin to applaud and then another.

Vidal strode forward and seized her so tightly that his hands seemed to crush the bones in her wrists. "You were sensational! Once Gambetta's seen these rushes, we'll be able to have *The Warrior Queen* in production within a few months!"

Harris was patting her on the back. "Boy, oh, boy, I just couldn't believe my eyes. You've sure got some future ahead of you, lady."

Don Symons, the lighting engineer, was staring at her,

mesmerized. Hollywood history had just been made and he had been part of it.

The rest of the crew gathered around, shouting out congratulations.

"Come on." Vidal was tugging her away. "I want you out of the studio before the word spreads."

"Where are we going?" His touch was scorching her skin and she knew that she should pull away from him.

"The Beverly Hills Hotel," he said, striding toward wardrobe, pulling her in his wake. "I want you out of that costume in two minutes flat. Is that understood?"

"Yes," she gasped, convinced that he would drag the costume from her back if she did not comply.

A seamstress with an armful of costumes skipped nimbly out of their way.

"Two minutes!" he thundered, thrusting her crumpled amethyst satin dress toward her.

Within seconds she was surrounded by helpful hands. Pins were expertly unpinned, hooks were unhooked, the heavy brocade was lifted over her head and carried reverently away. The amethyst satin seemed wan and pathetic in contrast. She stepped into it, her hands trembling slightly. It was an incongruous dress to be wearing around noon.

"I can't go to a hotel," she said as she emerged from wardrobe and he immediately seized hold of her wrist. "I have no money and no clothes."

The Rolls was waiting at the studio exit and he half threw her into its luxurious interior. "You're going to have so much money you'll never be able to count it," he said as the Rolls sped through the studio gates. "Theodore Gambetta isn't going to let you escape from Worldwide now. Not after he sees the rushes from this morning."

She tried to steady her breathing. "Was I really so good?"

"Yes." His smile was sudden and devastating. "You were really so good."

She turned her head away swiftly. His smile was not for her. It was for himself. Because his judgment had been proved correct. Because the movie that was his private passion could now be put into production. She hugged her arms as if holding herself together against an inner disintegration. As Margaret of Anjou she had been able to forget her anguish. Now there seemed no escape. He was married. He had never loved her, had never pretended that he loved her. Would never love her. The Rolls glided up the porte cochere of the Beverly Hills Hotel and her fingers tightened on her arms.

The chauffeur opened the door. She was obliged to follow Vidal past liveried bellboys and to the front desk.

"A bungalow for the lady," he requested curtly.

"Of course, Mr. Rakoczi."

"Madam's luggage will follow shortly."

"Of course, sir. This way, sir."

She was vaguely aware of a decor of pink and green banana leaves swirling over the walls, of a log fire burning in the lobby, despite the heat, and then they were outside in the gardens. Diminutive hummingbirds darted between the trees, their turquoise and gold plumage flashing in the sunlight. Tropical flowers grew lushly, encroaching on carefully tended lawns.

The bellboy inserted a key into a bungalow door. She saw Vidal crush dollar bills into his hand and then the door swung open and she stepped into an oasis of white lace drapery and spun-sugar-pink carpeting.

"This will be your home until I can find you somewhere more permanent." He held the key out to her and her fingers closed over the cold metal. "I don't want you to leave this room until I telephone after Gambetta has seen the rushes, understand?"

"Yes," she said, holding his eyes steadily, "but I must see Bob."

Vidal frowned. He had already forgotten Bob Kelly and was strangely annoyed that she had not done so too. He gazed down at her with narrowed eyes.

"He's a truck driver," he said coldly. "You don't have any reason to see or speak to him again."

Her eyes sparkled dangerously. "He was good to me," she said defiantly.

He shrugged. "Telephone him, if you must, but don't leave this suite." There was a distinct edge to his voice that he made no attempt to conceal. "When Gambetta wants to see anyone, he doesn't wait around." He paused at the door, his eyes unwillingly drawn to the seductive curve of her mouth. "And neither do I," he added brutally, hating his weakness, swinging on his heel and striding out into the sunlight and the gardens, leaving the door wide open behind him.

She stood without moving until he had disappeared from sight and the sound of his receding footsteps had faded into silence. Then, very slowly, she closed the door and leaned against it.

When the tears fell, they fell silently, blinding her until she slid down against the door, sinking onto the carpet in a crumpled heap, the key clutched so tightly that it pierced her flesh and a spot of bright red blood dripped onto the candy-floss pink.

It was the bellboy who roused her from her stupor of grief, knocking at the door, delivering flowers and a basket of fruit with the management's compliments. She took them dazedly and then, with trembling fingers, she picked up the telephone receiver and asked to be connected with Worldwide.

"Could I have the drivers' depot, please?" she asked when the telephone operator at the studio came onto the line.

"Sorry, no private calls are accepted," a metallic voice said uncaringly.

"It's very important . . . a family matter . . . there's been an accident," she lied.

There was a bored sigh from the other end of the line. "Okay, who is it you wish to speak to?"

"Bob Kelly."

"I'll try for you, but I doubt he'll be in at this time of day. Hope you realize what a favor I'm doing you, lady."

"Oh, yes. Yes, I do." Nervously she waited, cradling the mouthpiece until at last Bob's familiar voice said, "Okay, Gladys, I've got it," and then, in a different tone, "Who's speaking?"

"Valentina," she said quietly.

"Where the hell *are* you?" he yelled. "I thought you were dead or something!"

"I'm at the Beverly Hills Hotel."

"The *where*? Are you sick? Did someone give you a shot of dope? Just tell me where you are and I'll come and get you."

"I'm at the Beverly Hills Hotel," she repeated, looking down at the key in her hand. "Bungalow eight."

"I'm on my way!" The telephone sounded as if it had been thrown down. She replaced her own receiver with care and wondered what she would say to Bob when he arrived.

The afternoon sunlight streamed into the room and she rose, half closing the shutters. Whatever Bob said or did, there could be no going back. Standing beneath Lilli Rainer's glittering chandelier, her life had changed direction. It had not been predestined. She had had a choice. To go or to stay. To take one turning at the crossroads to the future or to take another. She had walked away from anonymity and Bob, lured by a world of make-believe. That make-believe world was the only one she could now inhabit. A sense deep within her had told her so the first morning she had come into contact with it and even now, knowing the loneliness that lay ahead of her, she could envisage no other way of life.

Whatever Bob had expected when he had arrived at the Beverly Hills, it was not to be conducted with perfect propriety through the gardens and to a bungalow that must be costing at least a couple of hundred dollars a day. As Valentina opened the door to him, his anxiety turned to perplexity.

"What are you *doing* here, for Christ's sake? The guy at the desk knows damn well you're in here. It'll have to be paid for. . . ."

She took his arm and led him into the room, closing the door behind them. "Please don't worry about that, Bob."

He looked at her suspiciously, his eyes narrowing. "You haven't done something real foolish, have you?"

"Yes," she said, "I think that I have, Bob."

He sat down slowly. "Tell me," he said, his face grim.

"Last night at the party, I met Vidal Rakoczi."

Bob sucked in his breath.

"He asked me if I would do a screen test." She knelt beside his chair. "I'm sorry, Bob. Truly. This is something that I have to do. Please try and understand."

There was utter certainty in her voice and he knew that nothing he could say or do would change her mind. He felt suddenly old. It was all over. For the first time he realized how very much he had loved her. Loved her and lost her. He sat quietly for minutes absorbing the knowledge, schooling himself to accept all of it. At last he smiled lopsidedly.

"If you're going to be a star, Valentina, be a big star. The biggest and the best."

Her eyes were overly bright. "I will, Bob. I promise."

He rose to his feet. "It was fun," he said, a catch in his voice as he took hold of her hands. "No one makes better chili and tacos."

Her hands tightened in his. "I can make them for you again, Bob."

"Yes," he said, releasing his hold of her and walking across to the door. "Sure you can, sweetheart." But as he stepped out into the sunlight, both of them knew that the days of chili and tacos were over.

The door closed behind him and she remained sitting where he had left her until the sun began to fade and the telephone rang. It was the desk clerk informing her that Mr. Rakoczi would be coming for her in half an hour.

Chapter Six

He was preceded by a covey of bellboys ferrying load after load of hide luggage with *Valentina* stamped in letters of gold across the corners. Hat boxes followed. Vanity cases. Dozens of sumptuous furs. She caught a glimpse of sable. Of mink. Of leopard. Bemusedly she watched as the cases and trunks were piled high in the center of the pink-carpeted room.

She thanked the bellboys and dismissed them. A small frown furrowing her brow. The trunks would contain dresses as splendid as the furs. She touched the cheap silk of the amethyst dress. It seemed a lifetime since she had stepped into it in the bedroom of the little house on Heliotrope. In discarding it, she would be irrevocably discarding the past. Nothing would ever be the same again.

The last vanity case was placed on top of a brass-cornered trunk, and the bellboys retreated. Slowly she ran her fingers over the gold letters of her name, remembering the moment on the beach before she had known that Vidal Rakoczi was married. When he had kissed her and she had believed that he loved her. That he was taking her home with him. That they would be together for ever and ever. For eternity.

The silence was broken by the swift sound of approaching footsteps. She whirled around as he threw open the door, striding into the room, filling it with his presence.

"What the devil are you doing?" he snapped, staring at her. "I told you to be ready the instant I came for you!"

Angrily he heaved the first available trunk into the center of the room and slammed open the lid. Tissue paper billowed out over chiffon and silk.

"Here." He scooped up a swirl of white satin. "Put this on and be quick about it."

He hurled the dress toward her and she caught hold of it, retreating hastily into the bathroom. As she turned the shower on she could hear his muffled curse of impatience. A smile tugged at the corners of her mouth. Mr. Vidal Rakoczi would just have to wait until she was ready.

When she had toweled herself dry and sprayed herself with cologne, she stepped into the sinuous sleekness of the dress he had chosen so peremptorily. It was long and clinging, encrusted with crystal beads. The halter strap was a mere ribbon of silver, exposing her naked shoulders and back.

"If you don't finish dressing this instant, I shall come in and finish dressing you myself!" Vidal thundered furiously from the other room.

Hastily she brushed her hair, coiling it low on the nape of her neck, securing it with an orchid from the shoulder of her amethyst gown. The reflection in the mirror looked like that of a stranger. It seemed impossible that she should look so beautiful and alluring. The material skimmed her breasts, plunging nearly as low in the front as it did at the back, leaving her with the sensation of nakedness.

"*Uristen!*" Vidal swore in Hungarian, yanking open the bathroom door in a fever of impatience. At what he saw he halted. She hadn't a trace of makeup on and she looked like a goddess. A strange sense of unease touched his spine and was immediately banished.

"Come on! Do you realize that you're the only woman

who has ever kept Gambetta waiting?" he shouted, seizing hold of her wrist.

Her dress was so tight that she had to run in tiny little steps to keep pace with him as he marched her out of the bungalow toward the waiting Rolls.

"You're hurting me," she said, gasping for breath as he dragged her mercilessly in his wake.

"If I lose Gambetta's enthusiasm for this project because of your lateness, I'll do more than hurt you. I'll beat you to death," he threatened, pushing her unceremoniously into the rear of the Rolls.

As they began to speed out of the hotel grounds she rubbed her wrists and said, "Was Mr. Gambetta pleased with the rushes?"

"Mr. Gambetta was ecstatic," Vidal said with grim pleasure. "He's given the go-ahead for immediate production on *The Warrior Queen*."

"With me as Margaret of Anjou?"

His teeth flashed in a sudden smile. "With you as Margaret of Anjou," he confirmed.

"I'm not sure that I believe it," she said dazedly.

"You'd better. You're going to have to work, work, work from now on."

"Who will play the part of Henry?"

"Desmond Brookes, Raymund Mullone. There's going to be a lot of time spent getting that particular piece of casting perfect. Gambetta naturally sees Henry as being the male lead, but he isn't. He's too insipid. He doesn't motivate events. Doesn't dominate in any way. The real male lead is the earl of Suffolk. He's the masculine presence in the movie. The noble who fights for Queen Margaret's cause. The man who leads her troops. Who rides into battle beside her. Who loves her and dies for her. For that part I want Rogan Tennant and I've told Gambetta so."

She looked across at him in surprise. "Wasn't Tennant the star of *The Black Knights*?"

He nodded. "Without Tennant in that movie I'd have folded it long before the finish. He carried it with sheer sexual exuberance. I want explosions on that screen and together the two of you will be dynamite."

She felt a spark of excitement leap along her veins. She had never appeared in the smallest part and Vidal Rakoczi,

Hollywood's greatest director, was telling her that she would be the lead in the biggest film of his career. That she would be playing opposite Rogan Tennant, the screen idol of millions.

She said suddenly. "What if Mr. Gambetta doesn't like me?"

"He likes what he sees on the screen. To Gambetta, that's all that matters."

They were sweeping up the driveway of a sprawling colonial mansion. "You'll have to sign a contract and it will have to be for seven years, I hate the damned things, but there's no way around them for the moment."

"What will the contract mean? That I can work only for Worldwide?"

"Unless it's to their financial advantage for you to do otherwise. There'll be renewal options on it, but don't take any notice of them for now. They're the least of your worries. And the contract guarantees you a salary."

"What sort of salary?"

He gave her a down-slanting smile that sent her blood churning. "The usual starting salary varies from two hundred and fifty dollars a week to five hundred, depending on the studio's views of how useful you are going to be."

Her eyes widened. "I've earned so little money in my life. Bob took care of me at first when I left the convent. I wanted to work and he got me a job, but it didn't pay much."

Vidal's eyes narrowed as he regarded her. A convent. So that was where she had come from. It explained a lot. Her vulnerability. Her naïveté.

"You're going to have quite a lot of adjusting to do," he said dryly. "No star in a Rakoczi movie picks up small-time checks. You'll be on a salary of two thousand dollars a week for the duration of *The Warrior Queen*, and we'll negotiate more when it's finished."

"Two *thousand!*" For a second she wondered if he was making fun of her and then knew instantly that he was not.

He laughed at her stunned expression and the chauffeur raised his eyebrows. Mr. Rakoczi was not in the habit of laughing. It was an event he could never remember happening before.

"We're here." The Rolls had glided up to a brilliantly lit porch. "Just be yourself. You're an original and there's nothing Gambetta likes better."

He was laughing at her and her eyes flashed. She wanted him to take her seriously. She wanted him to admire and respect her.

Gambetta opened the door to them himself, embracing Vidal in a bearlike hug and then standing back and surveying Valentina.

He was short and stocky with powerful shoulders and sharp, piercing blue eyes. As he looked down at Valentina he sucked in his breath. Her dress and body were those of a wanton. Her face, that of an angel. Her eyes met his directly, without coyness or flirtation. There was an honesty about her that was palpable. He took hold of her hands and kissed them reverently.

"Welcome to Worldwide, my dear. I am sure we are going to have a very profitable relationship."

He led them through into a vast drawing room with a full-sized movie screen at the far end.

"Vidal tells me that you haven't seen the rushes yet."

"No."

"They are remarkable. Truly remarkable. Jeffers!" He turned, calling to his manservant. "Drinks, please." He looked questioningly at Valentina. "What is it to be? A margarita? A dry martini? Scotch on the rocks?"

Vidal regarded her with amusement, wondering how she would handle the first of the new situations in which she found herself. He was certain she had never drunk a cocktail in her life and that martinis and Scotch had played no part in her homelife with Bob Kelly.

She hesitated and then said disarmingly, "I only drink wine, Mr. Gambetta."

"Then we'll have champagne to celebrate. Jeffers! Open a bottle of Grande Dame."

Jeffers complied and as Gambetta ushered her to a deeply upholstered armchair opposite an Adams fireplace, Vidal mentally gave her ten out of ten. If she had any sense, she would stick to wine and avoid the exotic-cocktail circuit altogether.

The champagne cork exploded skyward, and Jeffers poured the frothing champagne into crystal fluted glasses.

"To Worldwide's newest star!" Theodore Gambetta raised his glass high, beaming at the thought of all the dollars that would pour into Worldwide's coffers when Vidal's master-piece was released.

"To Valentina," Vidal said, and Valentina felt a faint flush heighten the color of her cheeks.

"Now for the rushes," Gambetta said, settling himself back in his chair with satisfaction. "Lights, Jeffers."

The lights dimmed and from behind them came the whirr of a projector. Valentina gasped, spilling champagne onto her gown as her image flickered onto the screen.

She was larger than life. Never had she seen herself as the camera saw her. As Vidal had seen her that first, fateful day. After the statuesque profile, sitting and standing shots, she appeared as Margaret of Anjou. Valentina slowly lowered her glass and gazed at the screen in wonder.

Now she knew why the crew had clapped. Why Vidal had been so pleased and why Gambetta had invited her to his home. It was as if something shone out of her. As if she were a diamond and a host of facets sparkled at once.

Pleasure seeped through her. Pleasure and a growing confidence. She had seen scores of movies with Bob, but never before had her eyes been so riveted to the screen. And it wasn't because it was herself she was watching. It was because the creature on the screen compelled attention. Radiated a glow that was tangible.

All too soon it was over. "To St. Albans and to victory!" Margaret of Anjou cried, and then her image faded from the screen and the opulent room was again bathed in light.

For a second no one spoke, and then Gambetta said with feeling, "When God created you, little girl, he did so for the camera."

"Flesh impact," Vidal said as Jeffers refilled his glass. "Her image on-screen doesn't look like a reflection of flesh, but real flesh. That's the secret. No matter who else is in a scene, Valentina will be the one the audiences will be looking at."

"She's as compelling as Garbo," Gambetta said, lighting a cigar, "and that can't be said for another actress in Hollywood at the moment." He exhaled a wreath of blue smoke. "She's got something more than Garbo as well. Something utterly feminine. I'd defy any man not to feel protective toward her."

Again, Vidal felt a primeval sense of unease. Gambetta was right and it wasn't only on-screen that she evoked such feelings. He cursed himself again for his momentary lapse of self-control on the beach.

It had been completely uncalculated. She had fallen against him and he had kissed her. His knuckles whitened and he rose, crossing to the drinks cart. Kariana was away for months on end and what he did in his private life was his own affair, but he had long ago forged a code of conduct that forbade any intimacies with the stars he directed because those kinds of affairs led to complications . . . and his life was complicated enough. He poured himself a large measure of vodka and topped it up with blue curaçao and soda.

Valentina watched him, feeling once more like a piece of merchandise as they spoke of her as if she weren't in the room.

"She has a mobility of expression I've never come across before," he said to Gambetta as he returned to his seat with his drink.

Gambetta rubbed his hands together joyously. "Mayer and Thalberg are going to eat their hearts out when they see her on screen. Jeffers! Bring me that contract, please."

"Yes, sir."

The ubiquitous Jeffers left the room for a minute and returned with a lengthy document that Theodore Gambetta placed before Valentina.

"Just sign your name here on the bottom, where there's a penciled cross, and at the bottom of all the subsequent pages."

"But shouldn't I read it first?"

Vidal's black eyes danced at the expression on Gambetta's face.

"Legal jargon isn't easy to understand," he said impatiently. "I know you haven't an agent, and believe me, you don't need one. Just accept my word that this document is going to give you everything you've ever dreamed of."

"Is my salary written in here?" she asked sensibly.

Gambetta stabbed at the print with his forefinger. His latest acquisition was showing signs of intelligence and he wasn't too used to that in the starlets he signed on. They usually were so grateful at being given a Worldwide contract that they'd have signed their lives away for a dollar if it meant appearing before millions on the silver screen.

Vidal's enjoyment deepened. There had been nothing

mercenary in Valentina's request. Only a genuine interest. It would be fascinating to see what sort of business acumen she developed in the months and years ahead. That she had a head for finance he didn't doubt.

Valentina signed the document that bound her to Worldwide for seven years and that officially gave her the profession of actress. Gambetta sighed with relief and quickly pocketed it before she started asking more questions.

"Now then," he said, leaning back in his deeply upholstered chair and lighting another Havana. "What name are we going to give you? Something rare and exotic, I think. Perhaps we could pass you off as princess of some exiled European royal house. I can get publicity to build up an entire background for you within a few days. What about a Spanish royal? Your hair and eyes are dark enough to make Spanish blood credible and there're hundreds of minor Spanish royals who've come to America now that the republicans are in power." He sighed with satisfaction and blew a wreath of blue smoke upwards. "We'll say you've fled Spain for America, land of freedom. The public will love that. It makes a great story. We'll say that in the interest of your adopted country you no longer wish to be addressed by your title, but we'll make damned sure they mention the word *princess* at every opportunity. And for the safety of your remaining family in Spain we'll decline to give them the kind of details some wise boy can disprove."

He beamed. "Now what name? Carlotta de Vallellano? Lucia de Pelayo? Isabella de Salamanca? Which takes your fancy, princess?"

"I am not a princess, Mr. Gambetta," Valentina said, her voice firm. "And I have no intention of misleading people into believing that I am one."

Gambetta stared at her. His question had been purely rhetorical. If he said a Worldwide star was an exiled princess, then she was an exiled princess. That the star in question should object never entered his head.

"I already have a name," she continued, undeterred. "It is Valentina. That is the name I have signed on my contract and that is the name that I wish to be known by."

Theodore Gambetta removed his cigar from his clamped teeth with difficulty and said, "All this is very new to you, little girl. Let me assure you that we know best." His waving arm indicated Vidal, who sat some distance away from them, nursing his drink. "So that's settled. You're Spanish. A princess. Now what name is it to be? Isabella or Lucia or Carlotta?"

"I think," Vidal said, a gleam in his black eyes, "that Valentina is correct. Her present name is more suitable than any that we can give her. As for the Spanish background, it's a good idea, but for someone else."

Gambetta frowned and summoned Jeffers to pour him a large Scotch on the rocks.

"Valentina," he said experimentally. "It sure is better than some of the damned names these girls arrive with. But what about her last name? Whatever it is, it's bound to need to be changed."

"I don't have a last name," Valentina said composedly.

Gambetta stared at her and then snatched the contract from his inside pocket and scanned the bottom of the first page.

"I asked for your signature," he said, an angry flush staining his face and neck. "That means first name and last name." He slammed the document back onto the small table that held her champagne glass. "Unless it's got both it isn't legal!"

Valentina remained unperturbed, a slight smile on her lips. "I'm sorry, Mr. Gambetta, but I don't have a surname."

"God damn it! Everyone has a surname!" Gambetta raged, swallowing his whiskey and holding his glass out to be refilled.

"I am an orphan, Mr. Gambetta," she said, holding his gaze unflinchingly. "Therefore I have only the name by which I am known. And that is Valentina."

Gambetta stared at her. She wasn't pulling his leg. She was telling the truth.

"But that's a great story!" His rage evaporated as quickly as it had surfaced. "A lonely, tortured childhood. A heartbreaking search for love and affection . . ." He jumped to his feet and began to pace excitedly around the room.

There was a flash of pain in Valentina's eyes and Vidal said quickly, "The best publicity you can give her, Theo, is that of absolute mystery. No past at all. Let everyone wonder. Let them talk. But tell them nothing."

Gambetta halted, swirling his Scotch and drinking deeply. He wasn't accustomed to being outmaneuvered. A deep frown creased his brow. It might work. It was a ploy Worldwide had never tried before and there *was* something essentially mysterious and elusive about the girl sitting opposite him.

At last he waved his cigar in acquiescence. "Okay, okay. I think you're right, Vidal. No childhood story. No artificial packaging. We'll let everyone in this whole damned town speculate to their hearts' content. That way there'll be even *more* talk about her." He regarded Valentina through half-closed eyes. "But we'll have to come up with a sellable surname. Valentina Veronese," he said experimentally to himself. "Valentina Vada. Valentina Vila." He savored each as he reeled them off.

Vidal noticed Valentina's chin set willfully and waited with enjoyment for the next confrontation.

"I will not be given a surname," Valentina said, and this time there was steel in the low tones. She had been given a surname once. She would not be given one again.

Gambetta's patience was fast running out. "Now look here . . ." he began threateningly.

Vidal deduced it was time to intervene. "She doesn't need one, Theodore," he said smoothly. "The greatest actresses have always been known by a single name. We speak of Duse or Bernhardt. Goddesses don't need two names to identify them. One is sufficient. And Valentina will be enough for Worldwide's greatest star."

"You really think she's going to be so big?" Gambetta growled, unwilling to concede yet again.

"You've seen how she comes across on film," Vidal said, rising and replenishing his drink. "None of the big five has anyone to touch her."

"Who are the big five?" Valentina asked, unaware that she had just gone three rounds with one of the toughest men in Hollywood and won every round.

"Metro-Goldwyn-Mayer, Warner Brothers, Paramount, and RKO," Vidal said, returning to his seat. "The smaller studios are Columbia, Universal, and United Artists."

"And Worldwide?"

Vidal grinned. "Worldwide refuses to be numbered with the big five, but it's as big and possibly bigger."

"Worldwide," Theodore Gambetta said, with a return of humor, "is the greatest studio in this town."

"I'll drink to that," Valentina said impishly, raising her glass.

Gambetta chuckled. Despite her obstinacy he liked his new acquisition. She had spirit and it was a quality that he admired. He strolled over to the drinks cart, dismissing Jeffers with a slight movement of his hand.

"When does Kariana return from Europe?" he asked, pouring a generous amount of Scotch into his glass and swirling it around thoughtfully.

"I'm not sure. Probably by the end of the month."

The room had gone suddenly quiet. The voices of both men had changed subtly. Valentina looked from one to the other and knew that they were talking about Vidal's wife. There was a long silence and then Gambetta said, avoiding Vidal's eyes, "We must have a party for her when she returns."

Vidal's fingers tightened on his glass. "I don't think so, Theo," he said, putting down his glass on a low, glass-topped table. "Kariana doesn't like parties."

There was another long, uncomfortable silence, and then Vidal said, "About *The Warrior Queen*, Theo, I don't want any interference from the front office."

Gambetta turned to Valentina. "How do you like this guy? I give him a cast of thousands and a budget of millions and he's still not happy." He chuckled, but Vidal did not share his joviality.

Thin white lines had appeared around his mouth. Incredibly he had not given Kariana a thought all evening. Now he was forced to do so and it was as if a palpable burden had settled on his shoulders.

Valentina remained immobile. Kariana. His wife's name was Kariana. It was a pretty name, and she would be returning soon. Taking her rightful place at Vidal's side, happily unaware of the girl who had slept in the guest room of her home and who had fallen irrevocably in love with her husband.

"Tennant was scheduled for *Pirate King*; he may not be too happy at being withdrawn on such short notice," Theodore Gambetta was saying.

Vidal forced his mind back to the conversation. "I'll talk to him," he said, well aware that his doing so would be mere formality. If Gambetta had agreed that Rogan Tennant could star in *The Warrior Queen*, any objections the actor might have to the contrary would be immaterial.

Valentina's thoughts were far from *The Warrior Queen*.

She looked up startled as Vidal said for the second time, "Are you ready, Valentina?"

He was standing, holding his hand out to her. Trembling, she laid her hand in his and rose to her feet.

"You need a wrap," Theodore Gambetta said, seeing the tremor that ran through her body and mistaking its cause. "Jeffers! Bring the lady a wrap."

"No, thank you. I'm quite warm enough."

Vidal had released her hand. The shivering was subsiding.

"Nonsense," Theodore said genially. "What's a mink here or there?"

A white mink stole was draped around her naked shoulders. Its warmth was strangely comforting.

"Thank you," she said, with an effort at a smile. "I'll see that it is returned to you tomorrow."

Theodore Gambetta roared with laughter. "I do believe you mean it," he said at last, wiping his eyes with his handkerchief. "It's yours, little girl. The first of many."

Jeffers showed them to the door, and as they stepped onto the porch they could still hear deep rumbles of laughter coming from the room they had just left.

"I told you he'd like you," Vidal said dryly as the chauffeur opened the rear door of the Rolls and she stepped inside.

It was several minutes before her voice was steady enough for her to speak. At last she asked, "How long will it be before *The Warrior Queen* is in production?"

"Under normal circumstances it could be six months to a year." He laughed at the expression of horror on her face. "Don't worry. There's nothing normal about *The Warrior Queen*. The script is written and the budget approved. We'll be in production within six weeks."

She was silent for a few moments. "What will I do until then?"

"Plenty. I'll have the script sent around to you tomorrow and from then on you learn it." His gaze was disconcerting. "If the way you memorized your lines for this morning's shooting are anything to go by, you shouldn't have any problems."

He felt something twist deep inside him as he gazed down into the shadowed oval of her upturned face. The most curious longing swept through him. His senses were filled with her presence. He wanted to kiss her again, and there wasn't a damned thing he could do about it.

His mouth tightened. The hell of his private life could be shared with no one. Least of all the innocent young girl at his side. Any consolation he sought would have to come from other quarters. Meaningless and ephemeral.

She sensed his withdrawal from her and the line of her jaw tensed as she struggled to remain calm. Why did he smile at her one moment and frown at her the next? Tears of anger and frustration stung her eyes, but she choked them back. It was better if he was cold and distant to her. His harshness was easier to bear than his kindness. When he was kind, he opened up visions of a relationship that could never be.

The Rolls swept up the porte cochere and when it halted she did not wait to see if he would escort her through the gardens to her bungalow.

"Good night, Mr. Rakoczi," she said, pulling the mink closer around her shoulders.

"Good night, Valentina."

For an instant their eyes met and held. His, dark with an expression she could not understand; hers, anguished. The chauffeur opened the door and without another word she slid from his side, running past the gold-epauletted doorman. Running until she reached the sanctuary of her bungalow and turned the key in the lock behind her.

Chapter Seven

When she woke next morning, she was naked and lying between satin sheets. Bewildered for a moment, she stared around her until memory came flooding back. Vidal. Vidal was married and she was about to become a star. Her limbs felt strangely heavy as she swung her legs to the thickly

carpeted floor. Her old life was over. She had to accustom
herself to a new way of life.

She surveyed the trunks that Vidal had sent and cautiously opened the lid of the first one. A sable opera cloak lay
cradled in a layer of tissue. The fur felt alien and strange
beneath her fingers as she lifted it out of the trunk. Beneath
it were two silver fox furs, a white satin evening gown with a
matching jacket edged with ermine, and a long, flowing gown
of emerald-green chiffon.

She leaned back on her heels, wondering if she was
destined to spend the rest of her life in plunging, exotic
evening wear. Apprehensively she turned to the next trunk
and breathed a sigh of relief. There were swimsuits and the
sort of women's trousers that Dietrich was making so popular. Day dresses with Lucien Lelong labels, crepe de chine
pajamas and sumptuous shantung day robes. She picked out a
loose-flowing caftan edged at the neck and hem with gold
braid and slipped it over her head before continuing with her
task.

In another trunk were shoes: backless shoes, high-heeled
shoes, peep-toe shoes. She slipped her feet into a pair of gold
slip-on sandals and stared down at them wonderingly. They
fitted perfectly. As did the dress. She laughed, her puzzlement vanishing. Wardrobe would have supplied him with her
dress and shoe sizes. She knew before she looked that even
the lingerie would fit as if it had been custom-made for her.

There were hatboxes containing picture hats, turbans,
tiny hats decorated with feathers and wisps of veiling. There
was more perfume. She sprayed it on her wrists, overawed
by Vidal's ability to command so much, so swiftly and so
easily. She was just about to lift a silver lamé evening gown
from its tissue when from outside the door there was a rattle
of a breakfast cart and a second later came a knock on the
door. A maid entered, carrying a tray.

"But I didn't order breakfast," Valentina said, disconcerted, thinking of the bill.

The maid smiled. Young ladies, conscious of their figures, often didn't. But the breakfast had been ordered and
she was well aware by whom.

When the maid had left, Valentina stared incredulously
at her tray. There was fresh orange juice, Kadota figs, an
omelet with creamed smoked salmon, tea, served with a

second silver pot filled with hot water, and a flute-thin vase holding a single perfect rose.

She abandoned her search through the trunks until she had eaten and then warily eyed several unopened jewel cases. If the contents were as lavish as those in the trunks, they would have to be returned. As, eventually, would the dresses. She was just about to satisfy her curiosity and open the smallest of the black leather cases when she was disturbed again, this time by a bellboy delivering the script of *The Warrior Queen*. The jewelry cases were forgotten. She settled herself comfortably against the pillows and began to read.

Within seconds she was utterly absorbed. Vidal had prefaced the script with two excerpts from Shakespeare and a historical resumé of the events leading up to the Wars of the Roses. She had never before read Shakespeare and she found the language difficult, yet intriguing.

The more she read, the more she understood why the character of Margaret so fascinated Vidal. She was a woman worthy of Greek mythology. A woman who evoked either passionate love or raging hate. A woman whose beauty was legendary. She was a femme fatale; a leader of armies; a chief of state; a heroine and an executioner. She was a seductress who enslaved poets and princes, and yet who never deserted the husband who was so unworthy of her. Her life affected the destinies of both England and France, and changed the history of the world. And she, Valentina, was to depict her. She put the pages down slowly, realizing for the first time the enormity of the task ahead of her.

There was a sharp knock on the door and it opened before she could even call out or move from the bed. As Vidal strode into the room she began to gather the scattered pages together in confusion.

"I hadn't expected to see you again so soon," she said, color mounting her cheeks as he stood in the center of the room, dominating it with his presence.

"You need to be seen in all the right places," he said curtly. "We're lunching at the Brown Derby. You'll need to wear something more suitable than that."

The shimmering caftan made her look like a royal queen.

"Yes, of course." She slipped from the bed and stood

barefoot, wondering why he was staring at her with such a strange expression in his eyes.

"There are drinks in the sitting room," she said awkwardly.

With faint surprise he realized that she was waiting for him to leave the bedroom. With a shrug of impatience he turned and walked into the adjoining room, where he poured himself a large vodka.

Valentina slid back the mirrored doors of the wall-length wardrobe and slipped a white silk dress from its hanger. There were high-heeled, sling-back calf shoes to complement it and she twisted her hair into the simple chignon that suited her so well. When she emerged, Vidal's eyes were appraising. She took seconds to change where other women took hours to achieve that stunning effect. The white she favored set off her dramatic looks to perfection.

"The gold bracelets will look best with that dress," he said, careful not to betray his admiration.

She looked at the array of unopened jewel cases.

"Yes. Which case?" Her hand hovered uncertainly.

This time it was his turn to stare. "Haven't you opened them yet?"

"No. I've been reading the script you sent."

"The gold bracelets are in the red velvet case," he said, wondering how many other women would have regarded a script as more important than the contents of unopened jewelry cases.

She lifted the lid and removed a broad bracelet of hammered gold and clasped it around her wrist.

"Do I need anything else?" she asked, forcing herself to meet his gaze.

"No." His voice was surprisingly gentle. "You look perfect." He led the way out of the bungalow. "Rogan Tennant will be lunching with us. He's anxious to meet you."

She smiled, her mouth unknowingly soft and sensuous.

"Rogan Tennant wants to meet *me*?"

He grinned. "He's curious as to why Gambetta has cast an unknown for the lead."

"Perhaps he thinks I'll let him down."

"Or steal the picture," Vidal said, laughing.

She looked across at him curiously. He laughed rarely, but when he did he became a different person. It was at moments like this that she knew that his company, and his company alone, would suffice her for the rest of her days.

There was chatter and laughter from the hotel's pool. A mockingbird and a blue jay swooped low overhead, disappearing with a rustle of leaves into the thick foliage. She was having lunch with Vidal Rakoczi. She was about to meet Rogan Tennant, the screen idol of millions. She had just signed a seven-year contract with Worldwide Pictures. A slow happiness seeped through her, replacing the misery of the previous evening. She would not let thoughts of Kariana Rakoczi spoil the magic of the present. There was time enough for her happiness to be darkened by Kariana. No doubt the rest of her life. For the moment she would pretend as she pretended when she was in front of the cameras. She would pretend that Kariana Rakoczi did not exist and that Vidal was a free man.

She smiled at the chauffeur as he opened the rear door of the Rolls for her, amazed at how quickly and how easily she had become accustomed to such attentiveness and luxury.

"What did you think of the script?" Vidal asked as the Rolls headed the short distance to the restaurant.

"I haven't read all of it yet. I've been reading the extracts from Shakespeare and the historical notes."

"What did you think of the Shakespeare?" he asked, suddenly aware that her reply would mean a good deal to him.

"I knew *why* you had prefaced the script with Shakespeare's description of her. Shakespeare lived much nearer to Margaret's day. Her memory would be comparatively fresh to him."

Vidal nodded. He had not been wrong about her intelligence.

"I had to read the pages a few times to really understand them, but after a while it all made sense. Especially when I read it out loud."

"That, I would have liked to have heard."

She looked across at him doubtfully, wondering if he was mocking her, but the sun-bronzed face showed no sign of it and she continued to discuss the Shakespeare and the historical notes with growing confidence.

Interested bystanders watched them as they entered the Brown Derby on Vine Street. Inside, Valentina found it pleasantly informal. It was designed so that everyone could see everyone else with the tables set at a series of semicircular brown leather banquettes. A waiter addressed Vidal deferentially by name and led them to where a blond-haired Greek god sat swirling bourbon and ice around in his glass.

He looked up as they approached, immediately rising to his feet and stretching out his hand.

"Valentina, Rogan Tennant, who I know you have seen many times on the screen. Rogan, Valentina. Your new co-star."

Vidal saw with satisfaction that Rogan Tennant was looking slightly dazed as he sat down, still staring at Valentina. Vidal knew what Rogan had expected—a flashy, affected replica of Romana de Santa. Style and class had been the last things he had expected to be confronted by.

Vidal's customary vodka and blue curaçao and soda was brought across to him and he ordered a bottle of Piper-Heidsieck.

"Valentina," he said, turning to Rogan, "drinks only wine." He grinned suddenly and Rogan Tennant stared. He had worked with Rakoczi on three movies. He admired and respected him but did not like him. It was impossible to get close enough to Rakoczi to like him. In all the time he had known him, this was the first time he had ever seen him relaxed and in a good mood.

"Valentina has a copy of the script and knows what is wanted of her," Vidal continued, ignoring the menu as he surveyed Rogan Tennant. "I understand from Gambetta that you're not happy at being removed from *Pirate King*."

Rogan Tennant's perfect features were marred by a frown.

"It isn't being removed from *Pirate King* that I object to. It's being given a supporting role. If I'm going to be in this movie at all, then I want star billing."

"You've got star billing," Vidal said reasonably.

"I haven't got the leading part!" Rogan Tennant looked like a petulant child. "If I don't have the leading part, everyone will think I'm on my way out. I'm Worldwide's hottest property. I *have* to have the starring role."

"You have," Valentina said, drawing the eyes of both men to her immediately.

"No, I haven't!" Rogan's mouth was set in a sulky line. "The king is the leading part. I'm not playing in this movie unless I play the king."

"It would ruin your reputation."

Rogan stared at her. She had the most incredible eyes he had ever seen. They were like smoked quartz. He struggled to concentrate on the conversation. Rakoczi and Gambetta were easing him down and out and he had no intention of allowing them to have their way. He was a star. A big star. And he had every intention of staying one.

"In this movie there's a king and queen. You're playing the part of the queen. How could playing the king ruin my reputation? It will be ruined if I don't!"

"You don't understand," Valentina said, leaning forward slightly, the cowl neck of her silk dress dipping low and revealing creamy white breasts. "The king isn't important. He's a weakling. That's why the title is *The Warrior Queen*. It is his wife who leads the armies into battle." She tilted her head slightly to one side and looked intently at the criminally handsome Rogan Tennant, swashbuckler and virile screen lover. "When a young lady tried to seduce him, he was so horrified that he had removed her from court."

Rogan stared at her in horror. "You mean the guy was a homo?"

Valentina had only a vague idea what Rogan might mean. She shook her head. "I don't think so. He was holy. He liked books and learning. He couldn't fight. He couldn't do anything that was manly. It was really all most unfair. He shouldn't have been a king. He should have been a monk."

"Do you want to play the part of a sexless monk?" Vidal asked, his eyes gleaming with amusement. "It can be arranged if that's what you want, Tennant."

"No! No!" The smoothly sophisticated Rogan Tennant was growing increasingly agitated. "What kind of guy is this Suffolk, the guy you want me to play?"

"He," Vidal said with a touch of impatience, "is the male lead. I told you that before. He's a warrior. A lover."

"Whose lover?"

"Mine," Valentina said, and smiled.

Rogan felt his manhood harden and swell. A bead of sweat broke out on his forehead.

"You're not trying to put something over on me, are you, Rakoczi?"

Vidal's eyes narrowed dangerously. "No, I am not. I am offering you the greatest part of your career. I am giving you the chance to show that you can act. If you don't want to seize the chance, then don't. There'll be other actors who will be only too willing."

Rogan Tennant stared from Vidal to Valentina and back to Vidal. "Is this movie really going to be so big?"

"This movie," Vidal said, summoning the waiter to their table, "is going to be the biggest movie this town has ever seen."

Rogan swallowed. In his books, the kings were the heroes. It was hard to accept that being a mere earl could be the main part. Yet if he played the part of the king and was made to look a fool . . .

"This king. Was he really so all wet?"

"Saturated," Valentina said.

Vidal's grin widened and Rogan gave a lopsided smile and said, "Okay, count me in."

Steak and mushrooms and broccoli appeared accompanied by the champagne.

"So what's the theme?" Rogan asked, spearing a mushroom.

"England in the fourteen hundreds," Vidal said briefly. "The Wars of the Roses."

"Sounds kinda pretty," Rogan said, wondering why Rakoczi was so enthused by wars of flowers and hoping to God he wasn't going to have his reputation ruined by starring in this picture.

Valentina waited for Vidal to explain and when he didn't, put her fork down and said passionately, "It wasn't pretty at all! It was called the Wars of the Roses because King Henry's symbol was a red rose and the nobles who were trying to take the crown from him had white roses as their symbols."

"I see," Rogan said, wondering if he would be requested to ride into battle carrying a flower and determining that no force on earth would persuade him to do so. Not even Vidal Rakoczi.

"Margaret was young and beautiful, and yet, because she married Henry, she became known as the Bloody Rose. She was . . ." Valentina struggled for the right words to convey to Rogan the magnitude of the events they were going to depict on screen. Her religious upbringing came to her aid. "She was like a figure of the Apocalypse!"

Both men stared at her. Rogan because he had never met anyone so beautiful, so extraordinarily passionate. Vidal because she never ceased to amaze him. Twenty-four hours ago she had never heard of Margaret of Anjou. Now she was conjuring her up in words that fired even his imagination.

She faltered, aware of the way both men were looking at her.

"Go on," Vidal said encouragingly.

"I don't know much else about it. Not yet. But I do know that it wasn't pretty. For thirty years the English spilled each other's blood in a hideous struggle for the throne. Hundreds and hundreds of people were destroyed and the whole of European history was changed."

Rogan blinked. He had had some funny conversations in the Derby, but nothing to equal this one.

"That, I think, just about sums it all up," Vidal said, regarding the bewildered Rogan with a wide grin.

"I guess so," Rogan said, rallying manfully. "You a teacher before you came out here?"

Valentina giggled. "No. I wasn't anything before I came out here."

"Oh, God, here comes Lucrezia Borgia," Rogan said suddenly, smiling falsely at someone behind Valentina.

Valentina gazed around to see a small, energetic-looking woman bearing down on them, her pin-bright eyes alive with curiosity.

"Darling, there are rumors of great things afoot at Worldwide," she said as Vidal took her hand. "I think perhaps it would be mutually beneficial if I drove up to Villada and we discussed them."

"Meaning that if I tell you what you want to hear, you won't print any more blatant lies about my private life," Vidal said dryly.

The little birdlike woman at his side was unperturbed.

"Something like that, darling." Her eyes swiveled to Valentina.

"Louella, let me introduce you to Valentina," Vidal said, wondering how Valentina would handle the most formidable gossip columnist in Hollywood. "Valentina. Miss Louella Parsons, columnist for the Hearst press."

"And is this your new star?" Louella asked, surveying Valentina as if she were an interesting and possibly valuable piece of merchandise.

Vidal nodded.

Valentina met Miss Parsons's gaze without any of the simpering nervousness the gossip columnist was accustomed to. Louella's eyes gleamed. This was no run-of-the-mill glamour girl being given a chance to show her mettle or fall flat on her face. This girl was special. It showed in the very fact that Vidal Rakoczi was out to lunch with her. For over a year she had ferreted in his private life for a story and failed to find one. Now, for the first time, he had appeared in public with a woman other than Kariana Rakoczi. It was all very interesting.

"Where are you from?" she asked Valentina with her usual directness.

"From here," Valentina replied, unruffled.

"If you'd come from here, you'd have been spotted long before now," Louella said bluntly. "I want to know all about your past. Who you are . . . where you come from . . . how Mr. Rakoczi found you."

Valentina smiled gently and did the near impossible. She charmed Louella Parsons within three minutes of meeting her. "I don't have a past," she replied in low, measured tones. "I only have a future."

Louella cackled appreciatively. "If there were bets running, I think I'd make a high wager on that one. I'll be seeing you again, Miss . . ."

"Valentina."

"No surname?"

Valentina's eyes sparkled wickedly. "Screen goddesses don't need last names, Miss Parsons."

"Indeed they don't," Louella Parsons said, lights dancing in her eyes. She would forgo her lunch interview and get the present conversation, suitably embellished, down on paper as fast as possible. "Good-bye, Valentina. I'm sure we'll be seeing a lot of you in the future."

She blew Rogan a kiss, aware that Worldwide's leading male star was seething at being ignored, and hurried off to find paper and typewriter.

"Bitch," Rogan Tennant hissed when she was safely out of earshot.

"I should have thought after the last little piece she did on you, you would be grateful that her interest was centered elsewhere," Vidal said wryly.

Rogan shrugged and, conscious of Valentina's presence, forced a laugh. "She's the least of my worries," he lied, aware, as every other movie star was aware, of the importance of appearing regularly in Louella's column.

"I thought she was nice," Valentina said, wondering who the people were in the other booths and why they were so interested in the table at which she sat.

"You'll learn," Rogan said darkly, replenishing his champagne glass.

When the meal was finished, they left Rogan nursing a large brandy and exited amid curious stares.

"I thought the dame was with Tennant," she heard a masculine voice say as they passed, and then, more faintly, "Hell, no. She came in with Rakoczi."

"Rakoczi? Now that's interesting . . . ."

"Would you like to read the complete plays I took the extracts from?" Vidal asked as they seated themselves in the rear of the Rolls and the brown-painted cement bowler with the reddish trim was left behind.

Her eyes shone. "Oh, yes!"

"I'll drop them off to you. And some other books as well. Have you read Dickens? Jane Austen? Tolstoy?"

She shook her head and lights danced in her hair.

"Then you should. Margaret was a great lover as well as a great fighter. You should read about the great lovers of history. Abelard and Heloise; Rochester and Jane Eyre; Emma and Mr. Knightley; Anna and Count Vronsky. And you should extend your reading: give Proust a try. Flaubert. Henry James . . ."

They were at the Beverly Hills Hotel.

"I'd love to. Thank you, for the lunch and for the offer of the books." She resisted the urge to reach out and touch him. "Good-bye, Mr. Rakoczi."

Something hot flickered at the back of his eyes. "Off the set the name is Vidal."

She clenched her hands imperceptibly and said, "Yes, Mr. Rakoczi . . . Vidal."

The chauffeur was standing at attention, the door open wide. "Good-bye," she said again, and then walked swiftly away and into the hotel.

His sense of loss was acute. The day had lost its sparkle. He swore viciously to himself in Hungarian as the Rolls moved away from the hotel's entrance. For two years he had not let anyone come close to him. Not a man. Not a woman.

He had lived joylessly and despairingly, putting all his passion into his work. Now the thing that he had always feared was beginning to take on reality. He was beginning to feel again, to respond to another human being. To feel with them, laugh with them. His eyes darkened. Not them. Her. Valentina. And in less than a month Kariana would be home.

Chapter Eight

He worked twenty hours out of twenty-four for the next two weeks and then could stand it no longer. Grim-visaged, he dispensed with his Rolls-Royce Phantom II and drove his Duesenberg at breakneck speed over to the Beverly Hills Hotel.

She was there as he had known she would be. He had told her not to leave the bungalow. To stay there and to study her script until she became word-perfect and she had done so. He had rung reception every day. The lady occupying bungalow eight was eating well, working hard, playing the occasional game of tennis, and making casual acquaintances among the other guests.

Vidal's voice had sharpened over the telephone. What other residents? What kind of casual acquaintances? The desk clerk, well used to the tempers of jealous lovers, had assured the volatile director that Miss Valentina's acquaintances were merely that: certain residents that she saw on her way to and from the tennis courts and to whom she passed a word of greeting.

"Who," Vidal had stormed, "did she play tennis with?"

"With the resident tennis coach," the desk clerk had replied calmly.

"And the pool?" Vidal's doubts had been raised.

He was assured that Valentina did not join the laughing groups around the poolside, though it had been observed that she was in the habit of taking a late-night swim if the pool was deserted.

Jealousy tormented him. Even when he was working, he found his thoughts kept straying back to her. Wondering what she was doing. If she was smiling her soft, sensuous smile, and if so, at whom?

When he entered the bungalow with the passkey the desk clerk had circumspectly given him, she did not at first hear him.

Words and memory came easily to her. She had already mastered the bulk of the script, though many of the technical directions still remained a mystery. As relaxation she had turned once again to the Shakespearean extracts Vidal had prefaced the script with. The old English words were no longer difficult for her. She loved their ancient sound, their poetry.

She was reading a long scene between Margaret and the earl of Suffolk aloud. In answer to the earl's imperious query as to her identity, she lifted her head and said proudly, "Margaret my name, and daughter to a king. The King of Naples—whosoe'er thou art."

"An earl I am," the rich timbre of Vidal's voice declared as he stepped into the room, "and Suffolk am I call'd. Be not offended, nature's miracle, Thou art allotted to be ta'en by me . . ."

She could scarcely breathe. It seemed as if there were only the two of them in the whole world. This was the point where Margaret turned swiftly from Suffolk, intrigued, yet feigning contempt for him. She spun on her heel and he noted the swell of her breasts beneath the loose-fitting robe and the curve of her hips as the material swirled around her legs.

"Fain would I woo her, yet I dare not speak," he continued, his voice throbbing. The words were not those of the earl's for Margaret, but those of himself for Valentina.

She faced him again and this time there were only inches between them.

"Say, Earl of Suffolk," she said, her lips parched, "if thy name be so—What ransom must I pay before I pass?" Her voice faltered. "For I perceive, I am thy prisoner."

She could smell his skin. If she stretched out her fingers, she would be able to feel his heart beating.

He gazed down at her and then slowly unloosened the ribbon holding her hair, spilling it free in a dark cloud around her shoulders. She was a virgin. He had known it instinctively the night they had walked on the beach and been vaguely surprised by it. She had been living with Kelly, and Kelly's reputation was that of a healthy heartbreaker. Until he had met Valentina.

Where and when had that been? He suddenly wanted to know with desperate urgency. He wanted to know everything about her. He wanted to know what gave her smiles their intriguing quality of underlying sadness. He wanted to know what had forged the steel beneath her fragility. He wanted her. Not for the *The Warrior Queen*. Not for any other movie he might make. But for himself. He knew only too well why Bob Kelly had kept her hidden in his little house on Heliotrope. Why he had not casually seduced her. Why she had meant so much to him.

He was on the brink of an abyss and he knew it. The tiny pulsebeats of time stretched out between them, and then he turned away from her so suddenly that she nearly fell.

"You read Shakespeare well," he said, his lips stiff, his brows pulled together, furrowing the lines of his forehead as he strode toward the books he had brought with him. "Here is the complete play that you were reading from." He tossed a slim leather-bound volume onto the nearest table. "And here are the works of Jane Austen." He carried an armful of books through into the bedroom and scattered them in a heap on the white lace bedspread. "There's Tolstoy, as I promised. And Flaubert. And that frightening English troika of talent, Anne, Emily, and Charlotte Brontë. Not forgetting your own Henry James by way of patriotism." He talked rapidly, avoiding her eyes. "There's Proust as well, and Turgenev."

"I shall never be able to read all these books," she said, moving and talking with difficulty.

"Then read what interests you." To his fevered gaze the virginal white-draped bed seemed to dominate the room.

"Which would you suggest?"

His hair curled low in the nape of his neck, coal-black, springy and unruly. His shoulders were tense, the muscles taut beneath the exquisite cut of his lightweight jacket.

His inner battle was fought and won. He said with a cool edge to his voice, "You could start with Heloise and Abelard."

It seemed apt. He was beginning to feel more like the castrated Abelard with every passing day. "I'll help you. You can't enter Hollywood society without a rudimentary education."

It was a lie and he knew it. If a knowledge of the classics were essential equipment for Hollywood society, then Hollywood society would expire overnight.

"Thank you."

The hard line of his mouth softened slightly. He selected a book and sat down cross-legged on the floor, Indian fashion. "Abelard and Heloise," he said dryly. "Lovers worthy of a Hollywood epic." His shirt was silk and open at the throat. His eyes were narrow, slanting above high, Slavic cheekbones. It was a face to be photographed. Painted. Loved.

She sat down some distance from him as he began to read, her back resting against the wall as the beauty of the words and his voice flowed over her. She was his protégée and she had to be whatever he wanted her to be. And what he wanted her to be was a star.

"Rumor has it that you're thrashing the hell out of the Beverly Hills' tennis coach. Mind if I come over and give you a game and see if the rumors are true?" It was Rogan Tennant.

He had waited impatiently to see Valentina at the incestuous round of Hollywood parties and had waited in vain. Half a dozen times he had picked up the telephone and put it down again. No one knew a thing about her, except that she was Vidal Rakoczi's discovery. And like Rakoczi, she wasn't partying. That could mean one of two things: That she was shy and reserved, or that her time was being spent with Rakoczi.

"The rumors are wrong," she said, amused.

"Then can I come around and find out for myself?"

She hesitated, but only fractionally. Rogan Tennant was to be her co-star. Vidal would want her to be on good terms with him and it would be interesting to see what he thought of the way Vidal had envisaged Margaret and Suffolk.

"Yes, please do. The desk clerk will tell you where to find me."

If Rogan had hoped it was in her bungalow he was disappointed. She was on the courts, playing an energetic game against the hotel coach, her dark hair tied back from her face with a scarlet headband, her provocatively short white tennis dress revealing perfectly shaped legs. She broke off when she saw him and waved in greeting.

"Hi. Do you want to play right away or have a drink first?"

"I'll have a drink," Rogan said, aware that for the first time in his life he had been taken at his word. He had suggested a game of tennis and a game of tennis was what was expected of him.

"A margarita," he said to the waiter who approached them as they sat down at a table beneath a gaily striped awning.

He looked questioningly across at Valentina.

"A lemonade, please," she said disarmingly. "It's really hot out there, Rogan. I'm glad you didn't want to play now."

"That's all right," Rogan said magnanimously. "Do you know that these are the finest courts in Hollywood?"

"They're certainly a lot different from where I used to play," Valentina said, and there was a faint trace of wistfulness in her voice.

"And where was that?" Like everyone else in town, Rogan was intrigued by her, anxious to learn something, anything, about the mysterious beauty Rakoczi had demanded play the lead in a movie it was already being whispered was going to be the greatest of his formidable career.

"Oh, nowhere." She dismissed the past and said with genuine interest, "How are you getting along with your script?"

"With tedium," Rogan said with a laugh. He had a facile memory and learning lines presented no problems to him. But he never found them interesting. The only printed words that ever held him in thrall were those written in his contract.

Valentina stared at him, slightly shocked. She lived and breathed *The Warrior Queen* and it had not occurred to her that her co-star would feel any differently.

Rogan's sleek blond hair gleamed in the sun as he said casually, "Have you seen much of Rakoczi lately? Word has it that he's been working twenty hours a day getting this damned movie set up."

"No, not much." If Vidal was working so hard, he would not want it known that he had to spend two hours a day educating his future star.

Those hours were the highlight of her day. He came every evening between seven and nine. His greeting was always cursory. Sometimes he hardly glanced at her. They sat as they had sat the first time: Vidal cross-legged in the center of the floor; she, at the far side of the room, curled up on the candy-pink carpet, her back resting against the wall.

On the completion of *Heloise and Abelard* he had told her that the book was hers to keep, and she treasured it more than all the jewels, dresses, and furs that hung in her wardrobe. From Heloise and Peter Abelard, they had moved on to Flaubert's *Madame Bovary* and were now deep into the tortured world of *Anna Karenina*.

Rogan's words made her realize how hard Vidal drove himself. *The Warrior Queen* was everything to him. He had spent years planning it and was feverishly impatient to start filming. Yet he spared time for her.

A shadow fell across her eyes and Rogan noted it perceptively. There had been no hidden smile in her eyes when he had mentioned Rakoczi's name. No heightening of color in her cheeks.

"That man can be the very devil to work for, though it helps if you're on close terms with him. You probably don't see the fiendish side of him quite as often as we do."

"Me? Why not?" Her puzzlement was genuine. He noticed with a sudden surge of heat to his loins that her amazingly colored eyes were double-lashed. She was the most beautiful woman he had ever seen, and he understood full well why Theodore Gambetta had been prepared to take such a risk on her. She was no carbon copy of any other star. She wasn't another Swanson or another Crawford. She wasn't another anybody. She was uniquely and originally herself. She would make Worldwide a fortune.

He shrugged and smiled. "You two *are* a going concern, aren't you?"

She stared at him, a frown marring her forehead, and Rogan knew that not only did she not understand what he meant, but that the answer was no.

He signaled for the waiter, feeling buoyant. "Another margarita, and another lemonade with ice, please," he said, and then turned once more to Valentina.

"Sorry. A Hollywood expression. I just thought that if you were friends from way back, Torquemada might be easier with you than he is with his other leading ladies."

"Torquemada? Is that your nickname for Mr. Rakoczi?"

"Mine, and everyone else who works for him." Rogan flashed her a smile that made feminine hearts quiver from Arizona to Maine.

"Why?" she asked curiously. "Is it Hungarian? What does it mean?"

Rogan laughed. "Tomás de Torquemada was a Spanish Dominican monk: very active in the Spanish Inquisition, which was hard to beat for torture and cruelty."

She raised an eyebrow. It was her first intimation that Rogan did not like Vidal. "Have you known Mr. Rakoczi a long time?" she asked, swirling the ice cubes around in her drink.

"I've done more movies for him than anyone else," he replied, with studied carelessness.

She hesitated a moment and then asked, "Do you know Mrs. Rakoczi as well?"

"Kariana Rakoczi is one of the loveliest ladies in Hollywood," Rogan said easily, as if he were on intimate terms with her. For a second he pondered on the enigma that was Kariana Rakoczi. Her public appearances were rare and when she did attend a Hollywood function, there was a tenseness about Vidal that was almost akin to fear. Rogan grinned to himself. It was impossible to imagine Vidal Rakoczi afraid. He was jealous. He had married a woman in a class way beyond him and he was determined not to lose her.

There were fingers of ice around Valentina's heart.

"Would you like to play now?" she asked, indicating a vacant court, her smile masking the desolation that held her in its grip.

"No," he said disarmingly. "I want to sit here and look at you. How does Rakoczi keep Lucrezia Borgia at bay? It can't be easy."

A smile tugged at the corners of her mouth. "Who is Lucrezia Borgia?"

"Why Louella Parsons, of course. You can bet your sweet life she's been hounding the hotel desk night and day. You're news, Valentina. You appear from nowhere, and suddenly you're the hottest property in town. Rakoczi wants you for a movie it's rumored is going to be the biggest thing he's ever done. Gambetta signs you on at a fabulous sum, and no one has seen you on the screen yet."

"Mr. Gambetta has."

"He must have, and you must have been pretty impressive. Gambetta doesn't throw his money around and he only bets on certainties. We should be celebrating. Let's call a halt to those lemonades and have a real drink. Champagne, isn't it?" He ordered a bottle of Piper-Heidsieck. "We're the envy of the whole town, Valentina. Every Rakoczi movie is news but this one more so than all the others put together. And we're the stars. Hell! We didn't even have to fight for the parts!"

"Mr. Rakoczi wanted you right from the beginning," Valentina said as the champagne cork exploded skyward.

"That'll be because of *The Black Knights*," Rogan said confidently. "That film has grossed more at the box office this year than any other Worldwide production."

Valentina did not tell Rogan what Vidal's private opinion of *The Black Knights* was. Instead she said, her eyes sparkling mischievously, "Mr. Rakoczi said you carried the movie on sheer sexual exuberance."

"Rakoczi said that?" Rogan visibly preened. It made a nice change from the things he had called him during the shooting of it.

"Say, do you spend all your time here? You should get out and about more. What about dining with me at Ciro's this evening? It's the kind of place you should be seen at, and it's fun."

She shook her head. "Mr. Rakoczi doesn't like me leaving the hotel."

Rogan's savoir faire momentarily deserted him. "You mean he's keeping you a prisoner here?"

Her smile widened. "No. It's just that he wants me word-perfect by the time shooting starts and so I spend most of my time going over my lines."

"Hell. He's beginning to bully you already!" Rogan said indignantly. "The man's a sadist and it's about time someone told him so to his face!"

"Then why don't you, Tennant?" Vidal's voice sliced like a whip through the still afternoon air.

Rogan spun round in his chair, blood draining from his face.

Vidal was a mere three feet away from them.

"I'm waiting, Tennant."

Rogan felt sick. "I was just warning Valentina, in the

friendliest way, that your attitude could often be mistaken for bullying and that someone should tell you so."

Vidal's face was taut with anger. "You don't tell me anything, Tennant. Is that understood? And I don't want to see you here again. Now leave."

Rogan rose to his feet, impotent with fury. To object could well mean losing the most important part of his career. Almost incoherently he said good-bye to Valentina and stormed past Vidal.

"Bastard," he muttered viciously beneath his breath when he was safely out of earshot. "Son-of-a-bitching *bastard!*"

As Vidal watched Rogan's undignified departure, Valentina rose from her wicker chair. Immediately, Vidal swung around. "I told you not to see anybody. *Anybody!*" he rasped.

Heads were beginning to turn in their direction, but Vidal was uncaring. He slammed a book down on the table. "From now on, I'll be too busy to discuss literature with an empty-headed trollop who can't wait to get her hands on her leading man!"

Valentina gasped and then her hand shot out, slapping him full across the face. "How *dare* you speak to me like that!" she hissed, her face white with fury.

He seized her wrist in a steellike grip, his eyes glittering. "I dare do anything," he rasped through clenched teeth. "Never forget it! From now on, no Rogan. Understand?"

"No," she flared, wrenching her wrist from his grasp. "I'm not your property! I'll go where I want and see who I choose!"

He shook his head, and at the expression in his eyes she flinched. "*You will not! You will do exactly as I say!*" and spinning on his heel, he strode away from her, leaving her alone among the flowers.

Her chest hurt so much that she could hardly breathe. It was as if there were an iron band around it, squeezing it tight. Their altercation had aroused fervent interest and she knew that scores of eyes were on her as she tilted her chin a fraction higher and walked toward her bungalow. In a few savage seconds her world had been once more ripped apart. Her head ached and as she pressed a hand to her temple she saw the ugly bruises darkening her wrist. Only days ago he had sat with her on the pink-carpeted floor, reading from *Heloise and Abelard*, his rich, deep voice smoking across her senses. She knew with despair that he meant what he said. He would not come and read to her again. She had unwittingly aroused his anger and there would be no forgiveness.

Tears glittered on her lashes as she stepped into the merciful coolness of her bungalow. She had merely sat with her co-star thinking that they would be able to discuss their respective parts, and he had called her a trollop for doing so. The pain behind her eyes intensified. She didn't understand him. She didn't understand what devil drove him and she didn't understand why she couldn't free herself of him.

With a heavy heart she closed the blinds in both rooms, plunging the bungalow into shade. All she wanted to do was to please him, but it seemed an impossible task. She eased off her tennis shoes and lay on the bed. The last few weeks had been a whirlwind of new experiences, new situations. She had barely been able to adjust to one before another had come hard on its heels.

The sun filtered through the slatted blinds and dust motes danced in the air. She knew that she could do whatever he asked of her in the studio. The transition from being herself to becoming Margaret of Anjou was one that came naturally to her. The ability to perform was in her blood and her bones. It was not anticipation of the stresses of the studio that disturbed her and filled her with nameless fear; it was Vidal. It was his mercurial temper, the devastating way in which his mood could suddenly change. She found it almost impossible to believe that a voice that could be so tender, could also be so harsh.

She gazed bleakly at the ceiling. And what of Kariana? The woman Rogan had described as "one of the loveliest in Hollywood." How was she ever to come to terms with the fact that Kariana was the woman who dominated his life? Perhaps if she saw Vidal's wife, just once, she would become more real. Perhaps then her heart would obey her head and she would cease to love him. Her nails dug deeply into her palms. It would be easier to stop breathing. There was no escape from Vidal, and in her heart she knew that she didn't want there to be one.

He did not come again to visit her. There were no telephone calls; no messages. She continued her reading alone. She studied her script. She played an occasional game of tennis with the hotel coach, and she swam when she thought she was unobserved.

She did not read the *Los Angeles Times* or the *Examiner* and so she did not know that a readership of millions now knew her name; that she was gaining publicity by shunning it. That Hollywood and its adoring fans were being told that Vidal Rakoczi, the controversial Hungarian director, had searched for years to find an actress to play the lead in a mammoth movie he had written and would direct. That he had found the girl he had predicted would be the star of the decade and brought her out of obscurity. That Valentina was going to be a name to rank alongside Valentino's in Hollywood history.

Vidal dismissed the euphoric prose impatiently. He had no time for the publicity office, nor for the gossip columnists who fed the hungry appetites of their adoring readership. He installed a brawny young man in the bungalow adjoining Valentina's, giving him strict instructions to see that no one from the press approached or spoke to her. He also took the precaution of renting the bungalow on the other side of her in a further attempt to secure privacy.

All the members of the hotel staff were under strict instructions to deny that she was staying at the Beverly Hills, and his own personal telephone calls to the desk clerk increased. Totally unaware of it, Valentina was under twenty-four-hours surveillance. With relief, Vidal learned that Rogan Tennant had not been foolish enough to try and contact Valentina again. When his rage had burned itself out, he tortured himself for the isolation he had imposed on her. She knew no one in Hollywood apart from himself, Tennant, and Bob Kelly. And he knew that she had made no effort to contact Kelly. She was living alone, eating alone, and sleeping alone.

He tried to expiate his guilt through his work, and failed. She was in his thoughts continuously. The longer he went without seeing her, the more desperately he longed to feast his eyes on her, and to renew the magical hours when he had been able to share his love of literature with her. Because he could not trust himself to see her, he turned with increasing regularity to his one method of escape: racing his Duesenberg at suicidal speeds when the long, punishing days he set himself were over. Striding the beach, consumed by the darkness of his thoughts. Fighting a desire that could lead only to misery and unhappiness.

On the first of July, a bellboy delivered a message to Valentina. The letter was typed. It asked that she be ready for work at five the next morning and informed her that a studio car would pick her up, and take her to Worldwide.

She slept badly, more from fearful excitement at the prospect of seeing Vidal again than at nervousness about what might be required of her on the set.

She dressed the next morning with care and the Worldwide chauffeur looked at her with admiration as she walked down the shallow flight of steps toward the car. The rumors flying about Worldwide had not been wrong. She was certainly different from any other star he had been ordered to pick up, and he determined there and then to request that he become her permanent driver.

As they entered the canyon that led to Worldwide, her heart began to beat in slow, thick strokes. This time, it was she who received a deferential salute from the man at the gates. She regarded him coolly, remembering the way he had spoken to Bob. She wondered where Bob was now; if she would get the opportunity to speak to him.

As the car slid to a halt, Vidal strode across to greet her. He had still not changed from his riding breeches and boots, and there were damp patches of sweat on his silk shirt. He had been up even earlier than Valentina to ride through the hills like a whirlwind, as if by doing so he could lessen the physical tension he felt. His efforts had been in vain.

"Wally is waiting for you in makeup," he said, frowning down at her, and then he turned on his heel, rasping a volley of orders to the minions who hurried in his wake.

Wally was genuinely pleased to see her. His friendliness did much to calm the tumult raging under her calm exterior.

A young boy whose eyes held both curiosity and awe led her from makeup to hairdressing and then to wardrobe. Wherever she went, she was watched, treated with respect. The whole of Worldwide knew who she was. For the first time she realized the enormity of the risk Vidal and Theodore Gambetta had taken, and she determined that no matter what the situation was between her and Vidal, she would not let them down.

The set fell silent when she entered the studio. She saw

Rogan and he immediately came up to her, putting her at ease, quietly explaining just what it was that the electricians and lighting men were doing. She felt a flood of warmth toward him. He was being kind to her and she badly needed some human kindness. Vidal continued to ignore her except to give her curt orders. The day passed in a haze that she afterward found difficult to remember.

There were their lines to go through. Endless rehearsals. Changes. She had to become accustomed to the marks on the floor, and understand what Vidal meant when he told her to hit them.

The first time she had looked at him in bewilderment and Rogan had quietly crossed to her and said, "See those chalk marks on the floor? The assistant cameraman puts them there and that's exactly where he wants us to stand for the various takes. If an actor fails to stand at, or hit, the marks accurately, the cameraman in charge of focus may run into difficulties."

"I see. Thank you."

"Have you quite finished playing nursemaid, Tennant?" Vidal snapped harshly. "Now, let's try again. One, two, three. Hit those marks! Watch those lights, Tennant! Jesus God! You're supposed to be an *earl*! Let's have a bit of dignity for crissakes!"

Crew members looked at each other silently with raised eyebrows. If this was a foretaste of how the shooting was to continue, the movie was going to be a rough ride.

As Vidal strode across to a seething Rogan, Valentina quietly studied the marks on the floor. There were three or four sets of marks and once she had looked at them she knew that she would never again have to look down for them.

"Right, let's try it once more. And *act*, for God's sake, Tennant! Head up, Valentina! You look more like a scullery maid than a princess! Quiet, please! Hold it down! Roll 'em! Take six! Speed! Go!"

And again and again and again: "Smile, Valentina, but don't move your chin! Hold it! She's sweating again. Makeup!"

She stood under the unbearably hot lights as her face was powdered.

"Right. Let's make this the last take. Quiet on the set, please. Hold it down! Roll 'em. Take seven."

Again, Valentina greeted Suffolk, who was to play such

an important part in her life—arrange her marriage, become her champion, her lover. With overwhelming relief she heard Vidal rasp, "That's it. Print it."

The cameraman gave an audible sigh of relief. As the long, arduous day drew to a close, Valentina asked Rogan, "How long will what we have done today be on-screen?"

"Three minutes, if we're lucky," Rogan said dryly. Rakoczi was being as much of a bastard to Valentina as he was to everyone else. He was certainly not romantically interested in her.

"Let's have dinner tonight and talk about it."

"I'm very tired, Rogan."

"So am I, but the more you know about how this place works, the easier it will be for you. I'll pick you up an hour after we break from here."

"You're being paid to act, Tennant," Vidal said coldly. "Could we please have your attention back where it belongs."

His eyes did not even flicker in her direction. The long, taut, tense day finally drew to a close. Throughout it all, Vidal had not given her one word of praise or encouragement.

When she left the set, walking tall and proud and showing none of the rejection she felt, Don Symons, Vidal's chief lighting man, said, "When that camera starts whirring, she turns it on, the magic, and you can't believe your eyes."

"No," said Vidal, his eyes bleak. "You can't."

Valentina entered her bungalow slowly and sat down on the edge of her bed. So this was what it was going to be like. Day in and day out. No wonder Rogan had nicknamed him Torquemada. He had been nice to her until he had got what he wanted. Her signature on Theodore Gambetta's contract; Gambetta's agreement that she should play the lead in *The Warrior Queen*.

There was no more reason to stay endlessly in the pink-carpeted suite. Vidal would not be calling with another armful of books, or to discuss the movie. She knew her lines. There was nothing to stop her from going out with Rogan.

She showered and changed into a backless evening dress decorated with seed pearls. Rogan, at least, was kind to her.

He arrived on time, eying her appreciatively. They went to Ciro's and Valentina ate enchiladas and cobb salad and watched in fascination as Rogan waved endlessly to his acquaintances. After they had eaten, they danced and then Rogan led her from table to table, introducing her to movie stars she had never dreamed she would see in the flesh and who now, incredibly, seemed passionately eager to meet her.

They returned to their table and Rogan had a Scotch. "Let's make a night of it," he suggested, taking her hand in his. "Have you ever gambled?"

A smile lurked at the corners of her mouth. "No, but I've an awful feeling I'd like to."

He grinned. "We'll go on to the Clover Club. It's the smartest gambling house in town. Roulette, chemin de fer, blackjack. You name it and they've got it."

His arm slid around her shoulder in the intimacy of the car on the way to the Clover Club, and for a brief moment she stiffened as if to pull away from him. Rogan was aware of the movement, and his desire for her increased. She wasn't going to be an easy lay, but that was precisely why he was putting himself to so much trouble. It had been a long time since he had had to make an effort where a woman was concerned.

At the club he sat her down at a roulette wheel with a stack of chips and proceeded to teach her the rules of the game.

"I don't believe it," she said to him, "it can't be that easy."

Rogan laughed. "It is, Valentina, it is."

The spinning wheel and the rattle of the ball fascinated her. When she won, she was as delighted as a child. When she lost, her disappointment was endearing.

"Having fun?" he asked, his knee brushing hers.

She laughed and raised her head. "Yes," she said, and then the smile froze on her face.

Vidal was leaning against a far wall, every line of his body lithe and tense like that of a panther about to spring. Her hand faltered over the chips that were being pushed in her direction. She could not tear her eyes from his. They were blazingly angry; demonic in their fury.

"Come on, Valentina. Stake again on the red," Rogan said encouragingly.

Mechanically she did as she was told, but her eyes were not on the table. They were on Vidal. She could not tear them away. She felt as if a band of steel were tightening around her chest, squeezing the breath from her body. What had she done to arouse such fury? Surely he could not expect her to remain a prisoner of the hotel forever? She had done all that he had asked of her. She had studied her part, learned her lines. What more did he want of her?

The answer came unerringly. He wanted to control her the way Svengali had Trilby in one of the books they had read. He saw her not as a person but as an object. Like one of his precious cameras or an expensive piece of lighting equipment. And like them, he wanted her to remain under lock and key until such time as he required her.

Anger licked through her and her eyes flashed dangerously. He was not her husband. Not her lover. Not even her friend. He had no right to decree where she would go; who she would see; what she would do. She saw shock register in the black glitter of his eyes. Whatever reaction he had expected when their gazes met and held, it had not been one of defiant rage. For a second she thought she saw pain and then he had wheeled away, striding from the room, ignoring every greeting and leaving a trail of raised eyebrows behind him.

For an insane moment she wanted to leave Rogan and the table, and run after him. She wanted to ask what it was she had done that had so aroused his wrath. She wanted to see him smile again; become the person it seemed she saw only in privacy. See his black, glossy hair tumble thickly over his forehead. See his eyes fill with laughter. Hear his voice lose its harsh rasp and become deep and rich and gentle.

Reason asserted itself and with a dull ache she returned her attention to the roulette wheel and forced herself to smile as Rogan continued to chat and joke with her, telling her outrageous anecdotes about the various stars playing at the other tables.

Vidal strode across to his Duesenberg and slammed the door behind him. Savagely, he revved the engine and slewed the car out and onto the road. The buildup of pain behind his eyes was crucifying. A pulse began to beat at his temple as he headed out toward the coast. For the first time in his life, he was racked by indecision. He passed a hand across his eyes despairingly. Other Hollywood marriages ended in divorce every day. But other Hollywood marriages were not like his. No amount of alimony could compensate Kariana if he abandoned her.

He pressed his foot down harder on the accelerator and

the needle flicked from eighty to eighty-five miles an hour. The highway stretched out in front of him, empty and stark, the waves creaming ghostly white on the beach to his left, the mountains, barely discernible in the darkness, on his right. Kariana's personal nightmare had engulfed him as surely as it had engulfed her. There could be no escape. Not now. Not ever.

"God in heaven!" he cried aloud, beating the wheel with his fists. "What am I to *do*?" In a cloud of dust and the scorching fumes of burning tires, he screeched to a halt and buried his head in his hands and wept.

Chapter Nine

Valentina tried to concentrate on the game and failed. "I'm sorry," she said as she made a foolish mistake for the third time. "I have a headache, Rogan. Would you take me back to the hotel, please?"

"Sure, honey." Taking her arm, he excused himself from the table, calling out many good-byes as he left the room. It would be all over Hollywood next morning that Rogan Tennant was living up to his reputation as Worldwide's greatest stud, off-screen as well as on.

As they drove back to the Beverly Hills Hotel and he told her what a hit she had made at Ciro's and the Clover Club, she was subdued. It had been kind of Rogan to take her out, but Vidal's appearance at the Clover Club had spoiled the evening. She could almost feel his presence teasing and tormenting her.

Unlike Vidal, Rogan started to leave the car and escort her to her bungalow. She put a hand lightly on his arm.

"It's only a little walk, Rogan. Thank you for the evening." She remembered that he had promised to tell her more about the way the set worked and that the conversation had never once veered around to the topic of *The Warrior*

Queen and Worldwide. She felt guilty. She had been a poor companion, barely answering him as he had spoken to her on the way back to the hotel, her thoughts elsewhere and far away from him.

Rogan leaned back in his seat and slid his arm around her shoulders.

"You're a tease, Valentina," he said softly. "Shall we drive farther on and find a little privacy?"

She shook her head, her hair brushing his hand. He laughed, hooking a finger under her chin and tilting her face to his. "We can hardly say good night in the full glare of the porch lights, can we?"

"I'm afraid that we'll have to," she said gently, aware that she had led him on unfairly.

His cologne was heavier and sweeter than the one Vidal used. His hand caressed the nakedness of her shoulder. "I want to make love to you, Valentina." He leaned forward, taking the lobe of her ear gently between his teeth. "I've wanted to make love to you ever since we met," he said huskily. His hand slipped down, cupping her breast, and she pulled away.

"Good night, Rogan," she said firmly, and then was silenced as his mouth came down on hers. She tried to free herself and failed. Her hands pushed in vain against his chest. For a moment she wondered if she was mad. She was in the arms of a man who looked like a hero from the Greek myths. A man millions of women swooned over. And she was trying to free herself from his embrace.

"You're a witch, Valentina. A beautiful, tormenting, glorious witch and I want you so much I'm burning up." His voice was thick with desire, his mouth skimming her neck, her shoulders, the soft warm flesh of her breasts.

She drew in a ragged breath and pushed herself away from him. "Stop it, Rogan! I don't want to be kissed. To be touched!"

At the vehemence in her voice he pulled away from her, stunned. It was the first time in his life that he had been rejected. "Do you go the other way?" he asked incredulously.

"Do I what?"

"Do you prefer girls?" It was the only conceivable explanation for her behavior that he could think of.

She put a hand to her throbbing head. "I'm sorry, Rogan.

I don't understand you. I have a terrible headache and I really am very tired. Today has been a long one for me." She managed a smile. "I'm sorry if I overreacted. I'm just not used to . . . to being touched like that."

She slid across the seat and opened the car door.

"Good night, Rogan. It was a nice evening. I'm sorry if I spoiled it."

The door closed behind her. There was the rapid tip-tap of her high-heeled sandals as she crossed the lobby, and then silence.

Rogan shook his head as if to clear it, and then reached for his cigarettes. His hand was unsteady. He gazed down at it in disbelief. If he wasn't careful, he was going to find himself in deep water. Hooked and landed like a kid just out of high school. Unassuaged desire washed over him in waves. It wasn't a feeling he was accustomed to. Crushing out the cigarette he'd only just lit, he revved the engine and set off at high speed for a house where he knew he would be made more welcome.

Valentina hung up her evening dress and bleakly slipped on a lace-edged nightdress. She was in Hollywood, not the Convent of the Sacred Heart. She should have been prepared for Rogan's kiss, and she should have handled the situation with more sophistication.

She took two aspirins and lay down in the darkness. She could only hope that Rogan's masculinity had not been so offended that it would alter his attitude to her on the set. If it did, then she would be totally friendless. The electricians and lighting men were helpful and kind, but she knew that they dare not take the time to talk to her without incurring Vidal's wrath.

Vidal. Why was it impossible to think of anyone or anything but Vidal? His face burned against her mind. Sensually aware; mocking, confident. And tonight, furiously angry. But why?

She tossed and turned restlessly, finding no answer. At last she rose and crossed to the window, staring out into the darkness. *Had* it been pain she had seen so fleetingly in the black glitter of his eyes? And if so, why? She rested her cheek against the coolness of the windowpane. Was it because the woman he loved spent so much time away from him? Valentina wondered. If she were married to him, she would not leave his side for a second. Not for a moment. She blinked away weary tears. But she was not married to him. She could not ease his pain, nor comfort him. She could only act for him. Be Margaret of Anjou.

Heavyhearted, she returned to her bed and wondered how long it would be before the love she felt for him would wither and die from lack of nourishment. From the moment she had known that he was married, she had not wanted to love him. But the knowledge had come too late. From the first moment she had seen him, it was as if he had entered her blood and her bones. And now, try as she might, she could not free herself of the need to see him, to be near him. She closed her eyes. She must sleep. She had to be at the studio by six and the day ahead would be long and arduous— and joyless.

Vidal's mood the next day was even more explosive than it had been the previous day. He watched with legs astride and his hands on his hips as final touches were made by carpenters to Rogan's huge dressing room. Then he brusquely ordered everyone who had anything to do with the production to be in his office before shooting started.

There were murmurs of discontent at his attitude from both cast and crew as they walked en masse across to Vidal's white stucco bungalow.

"The man's an egomaniac," said Sutton Hyde, the actor who was cast as Henry.

"He's certainly the most uncompromising director in town," Leila Crane, the girl who played Valentina's handmaid, said a little more charitably.

"He's a shit," Rogan Tennant said, scowling fiercely and looking as if he had had very little sleep.

Don Symons, Vidal's chief lighting man, chewed gum laconically and said, "He's a man of genius and vision and you're all damned lucky to be working for him and not producing a fifth-rate B movie on lot nine."

There were groans and blasphemies from those around him, but they were quickly silenced as they entered the bungalow.

Valentina looked around with interest. It was a big room taken up almost completely by a massive desk. There was a vast clutter of costume sketches on it and several pages of the screenplay that Vidal had obviously been in the process of changing. On the walls were shooting schedules and sketches of the sets already built and being built on the back lot.

Vidal glared at them as they entered. "Yesterday's rushes were garbage!" he said grimly. "I want you all here to tell you for one last time that this isn't just any Hollywood epic we're producing. This is a film that is going to be a classic."

He stalked round to the front of his desk and there was a shuffling retreat.

"None of you is giving enough. Not the so-called male lead . . ." He cast a withering look in Rogan's direction. ". . . or the crew. I want everything you've got. I want sixteen hours a day solid work and I want you to live in purdah till the last reel is in the can. No nightlife, no parties, no drink and no drugs. *Nothing* but this movie, is that understood?"

Valentina waited for the sound of protest. There was none. Nobody liked it, but no one wanted to be off the movie.

"That's okay with me, Mr. Rakoczi," a voice said from the back of the room.

There were other mumbled assents.

Vidal's eyes narrowed to mere slits. "That means everyone from the lighting man to the script girl. Got it?"

"Yes, sir, Mr. Rakoczi," they said in unison.

There was a cruel edge to his voice as his eyes rested finally on Valentina. "There's no one on this set who can't be replaced. I hope that's understood."

She held his gaze steadfastly, refusing to be intimidated. "Yes, Mr. Rakoczi," she said with a composure she was far from feeling. "I think you've made everything perfectly clear."

A pulse began to throb at his jawline. He had been right about the steel beneath the fragility of her beauty. He clenched his fists.

"I want everyone on the set in fifteen minutes."

With relief, cast and crew dispersed and Rogan, already in costume, crossed over to her. "About last night, Valentina. No hard feelings?"

She smiled. "None at all, Rogan."

The doublet and breeches he wore suited him. His bucket-top boots were of soft yellow leather and trimmed with lace. There was more lace at his neck and cuffs. A short velvet cloak hung jauntily from one shoulder, exposing a fine sword and giving him an air of martial swagger. If in life the earl of Suffolk had been as handsome, then Valentina could well understand the attraction he had held for Margaret of Anjou. It if wasn't for Vidal, she would probably be falling in love with her handsome co-star.

"Then let me make amends," Rogan said, his eyes warm and concerned. "How about dinner tonight? Somewhere quiet where we can talk and really get to know each other."

She shook her head. "I'm not used to late nights and early mornings. I need sleep if I'm to survive this sort of routine."

He felt an emotion akin to panic. What had started off as an entertaining diversion had now become all-important. No woman had rejected him. Not ever. And there was something special about this one. Something that could not be easily forgotten.

"Sunday?" he asked desperately. "We could meet Sunday. Take a picnic. Go down to the beach."

At the mention of the beach her eyes darkened. "No, Rogan. It sounds to me as if Mr. Rakoczi may well want us on the set weekends as well as weekdays."

Vidal's assistant director was walking toward her and she turned her attention to him, leaving Rogan thwarted.

As the morning progressed Vidal's verbal lashings became more severe. They were redoing all the work they had done the day before, and for the cast, in their heavy medieval robes, the heat was crippling. Valentina nearly sank to the ground with relief when Vidal's voice shouted curtly, "Okay, wrap it up for an hour."

While the others staggered off gratefully to the commissary, Rogan escaped to his dressing room and Valentina set off in the direction of the drivers' depot. Though costumes attracted very little attention on the lot, she was aware of people stopping and staring at her. Everyone had heard of the girl Theodore Gambetta had declared was going to be Worldwide's biggest star, and this was the first chance many had had to see her at close quarters.

She didn't have to ask for Bob. He was standing near a truck, a cup of coffee in his hand.

She felt a pang in her heart. He looked so dearly familiar. So reliable and steady. She remembered the little flower-drowned house on Heliotrope. The simplicity of evenings spent at the tennis club or at the local movie theater. It was a whole wide world away. The only part of her life that had been normal and conventional.

Her shadow fell across him and he looked up. She had caught him unaware and for a moment the pain he still felt at losing her was naked in his eyes. He grinned, concealing it as best he could, saying with forced jauntiness, "Hi. What are you doing around here? Are you lost?"

Her throat felt uncomfortably tight. "No," she replied, wishing that he would call her sweetheart again and knowing that the gulf between them was too deep for the old, safe familiarity. "I just wanted to see how you are."

Something dark flashed through his eyes and he averted his head swiftly for a moment, and then said, "I'm fine." The old grin was back on his face. "I hear you're knocking them off their feet down there on the set."

"I'm doing my best," she said, aware that beneath the banter was a feeling of constraint on Bob's part that she had been unable to overcome. "But it's harder than waiting tables."

He laughed, and then the laughter died in his eyes and he said awkwardly, "It's prettier."

They were hiding behind words. None of the real things they wanted to say to each other were being said, and she knew in despair that they never would be.

"I'm playing the part of a princess," she said, blinking back tears for the loss of their old ease with each other.

He flashed her another overly bright grin. "That explains it," he said. Silence hung between them, saying far more than their falsely casual words. Tenderly he reached out and took her hand. "Are you happy, Valentina?" he asked, his grin fading. "Is everything working out okay?"

She wanted to throw her arms around him and hug him tight. "Yes," she lied, thinking of the tense, nerve-racking atmosphere on the set. "Everything's fine, Bob."

"Good." His voice was thick with emotion. "If ever things change, you know where to find me."

Their hands tightened and then he cleared his throat. "I have to go now. They're waiting for this load down at La Jolla." He let go of her hand, swinging himself up into his cab, looking down at her with a lopsided smile. "Bye, Valentina."

Her eyes held his and she knew it was their last good-
bye. "Good-bye, Bob," she said, blowing a kiss. "And thanks.
I shall never forget."

"Where the hell have you been? You're late!" From
beneath black brows, equally black eyes blazed in Vidal's
lean, dark face.

She tilted her chin defiantly. "I'm not late. There're still
five minutes to go before the hour is up."

"You weren't at the commissary!" His voice was accusing.

"I went to see a friend."

"You went to see Bob Kelly!" he said, jealousy flaring
through him. "From now on, you have no contact with him
whatsoever! You're a star and he's a truck driver. Is that
understood?"

Her eyes held his unflinchingly. "I told you before, Mr.
Rakoczi, Bob Kelly is a friend. If I want to see him, I shall
see him."

He covered the distance between them in one stride.
"Not on my time, you won't!" he said, his rage overwhelming
as he seized her shoulders with strong, large hands.

At the physical contact a vibration of shock ran through
both of them. She gasped and he let go of her as if he had
touched a volt of electricity. *"Damn it to hell!"* he rasped out,
striding away from her toward the set.

She stood for a little while, struggling to regulate her
breathing, and then followed. If anyone had seen the scene
between them, they did not mention it. The harsher Vidal's
demands, the kinder the crew became to her. And despite
the rigorous pressure of transforming herself again and again
into Margaret of Anjou, Valentina found that she was enjoying herself.

She was beginning to be able to tell when a take was
successful, and it sent an enormous surge of adrenaline through
her veins. Exhilaration banished tiredness and she felt only
disappointment when Vidal said finally, "That's it for today. I
hope for all your sakes the rushes are better than yesterday's."

"Autocrat," said a perspiring Sutton Hyde under his
breath.

Leila grinned. "They say his name is written in letters of
fire on his contract."

"It wouldn't surprise me," Sutton said darkly. "He directs as if he's been chosen by God."

"I have, Sutton, I have," Vidal said tightly, striding past them without glancing in Valentina's direction.

He was once more in control of himself and he felt an inner sense of elation. His bullying of Rogan Tennant had paid off. For once in his life, Worldwide's heartthrob was acting superbly. And Valentina had been magnificent. Valentina. He felt a familiar buildup of pain behind his eyes. He should never have touched her again. Even touching her in anger inflamed his senses.

He entered his bungalow and poured himself a large vodka and blue curaçao. Then he telephoned the Beverly Hills and asked the desk clerk to inform him if she left the hotel. He swallowed his vodka and frowned, drumming his fingers on the leather surface of his desk. There was no need for Valentina to leave the hotel via the lobby. The bungalows had been built specifically for privacy, and the narrow, winding pathways through the gardens made it easy to enter and leave without being seen.

He placed another call; this time to the employee he had posted in the bungalow nearest Valentina.

"If she goes out, Bains, I want to know. And I want to know who with."

"Yes, sir." Bains was intrigued. Rokoczi was behaving like a jealous lover. He settled himself where he could clearly see the door of Valentina's bungalow, and poured himself a bourbon.

When Vidal saw the rushes that night, he knew his elation at the end of the day's shooting had been justified. And with grim satisfaction, he learned that Valentina had not left her bungalow all evening.

The next morning he invited Rogan and Valentina, Sutton and Leila, to see the rushes of their previous day's work.

"No, thank you, Mr. Rakoczi," Leila said nervously. "I just hate to see rushes. It makes me terribly self-conscious and then my work suffers."

Vidal nodded. He had met many other actors and actresses who felt the same way.

"Were they good?" Rogan asked.

"Adequate," Vidal said curtly, disturbingly aware of Valentina as they walked into the projection room.

"I *always* see the previous day's rushes," Rogan was saying to Sutton. "I like to have *some* say in what takes are chosen."

Sutton smiled as the projection room lights dimmed. He doubted if Rogan would have any say at all with Vidal Rakoczi.

Within minutes, Rogan was groaning. "*Why* do they keep taking my left side, for God's sake?" and then in another take, "Oh, shit. I look *awful* in that one. Now that one's better!" He enthusiastically leaned forward in his seat. "I look really good in that one."

Sutton's remarks, too, were restricted to how he came across personally on the screen. Vidal had never known an actor who thought in any other way. Their appearance, their image, was all-important to them. He wondered how Valentina would react and was not disappointed.

"She looks too confident in that one," she said of the scene where she was summoned to the presence of the king of France. "She would be wary, wouldn't she? That one is better. Her uncertainty is showing through."

Vidal's eyes were appraising. She was seeing not herself on the screen, but Margaret of Anjou. It was how the character came across that mattered to her. Not how she herself looked.

The next scene was between Sutton and Rogan. In the flickering light of the small projection room, she became uncomfortably aware of Vidal's nearness. Slowly she slid her eyes across to him and her heart seemed to freeze in her throat.

For an insane second she thought that he was looking at her with desire in his eyes, and then she blinked and saw that she had been mistaken. His eyes were as cold and as dark as obsidian and she turned her head away, striving to concentrate once more on the screen before her.

Rogan and Sutton effusively complimented each other's performance, and then the rushes came to an end and the room was flooded with light.

"Which take have you decided on in the scene between Sutton and me?" Rogan asked.

"The eighteenth."

"I can't argue with that," Sutton said affably. "They were all so damned good, I don't know why there had to be so many."

"Because Mr. Rakoczi is a perfectionist," Don Symons said as they filed from the room and out into the sunlight.

Rogan was at Valentina's side, supremely pleased with himself. Rakoczi might be a bastard to work for, but as a director he was a genius.

"You were sensational, Valentina. Absolutely stunning."

"Thank you, Rogan."

Rogan eyed her with a certain amount of reservation. She *had* been sensational. She glowed on-screen, commanding all attention. Which meant that there would be less attention directed to him.

"I hope you've changed your mind about Sunday."

"No. If we're not working on the set, then I'll be going over my lines, Rogan."

"I'm not just trying to be friendly," Rogan said, a hint of desperation in his voice. "You're driving me crazy, Valentina. I can't sleep for thinking of you. I can't eat . . ."

"Places, everyone," Vidal said, his voice raw with naked anger. He had seen Tennant's blond head indecently close to Valentina's and knew that Tennant was not discussing the scene they were about to play.

Harris, the assistant director, looked across at him in surprise. The rushes had been good. The cast was working together without any problems. Yet there was a throb of uncontrolled fury in Vidal's voice. For the life of him, he couldn't understand why.

"Lights," he called. "All right, everyone. Cameras. Action!"

The day set the pattern for all those that followed. The work was hard, demanding, and utterly absorbing, and it was soon common knowledge that something extraordinary was going on down on lot fourteen.

Vidal continued to subject Rogan to verbal abuse in order to gain from him the kind of performance he would be too lazy to give otherwise.

He spoke to Valentina only when absolutely necessary, and the occasions became fewer and fewer. She seemed to know what he wanted from her, even before he asked for it. As the weeks passed, rapport, total and absolute, grew between them. She responded utterly to his trust in her, his total conviction that she could play the part of Margaret as no one else could. Her performance was alive with a magic that neither the other members of the cast nor the crew had ever seen before.

Rogan continued to ply her for dates, and as she steadfastly refused, realized that for the first time in his life he was feeling genuine emotion for someone other than himself. He sought consolation elsewhere. But it was Valentina he wanted. Valentina whom he craved.

At the end of each day's shooting, she returned to the Beverly Hills Hotel, circumnavigating the lobby and wandering wearily down the pathways between palms and eucalyptus to spend her evenings alone, counting the hours until she would be in Vidal's presence again.

"The schedule should be letting up soon," Rogan said to her one morning as their stand-ins stood patiently in the center of a mock battlefield and the cameras were adjusted to Vidal's satisfaction.

"What do you mean? We haven't shot a quarter of the movie yet."

"Kariana Rakoczi is on her way home. She's terminated her European tour and is staying with her family in New England. In a few days' time she'll be crossing America by rail on the *Chief*."

Valentina swayed slightly and Rogan grasped her arm. "Be grateful we don't have to stand out there for hour after hour while Rakoczi checks that every single camera is exactly as he wants it. Did you hear him earlier, ranting about historical detail? Apparently one of Henry's soldiers arrived on the lot wearing a wristwatch! Rakoczi vowed he'd never again work on one of his productions and he gave the continuity girl such hell she's been in floods of tears ever since."

Rogan chuckled and did not notice that all the color had left Valentina's face.

Vidal's wife, Valentina thought. The woman had been absent for so long that she had nearly managed to convince herself that Kariana didn't exist.

Vidal was striding toward the center of the ravaged battlefield. The battle had been fought and was over. All that was left was the churned-up earth, the bodies, and Queen Margaret and the earl of Suffolk in battle-weary triumph. She could hear Vidal's volley of orders to the hundreds of extras as he arranged and rearranged them in grotesque attitudes of death; she could see the lean, tanned contours of his body beneath the light silk shirt he wore.

A black stallion and a white stallion pawed impatiently at the ground. Soon, when everything was as Vidal wanted it, she and Rogan would have to walk across to the horses and replace the stand-ins who had been mounted on their backs for over an hour.

Vidal turned, speaking to Don Symons. His profile was grim. He didn't look like a man about to welcome home his wife. Perhaps he didn't yet know that she was on her way west. Studio gossip was so refined an art that often the source of the gossip was the last person to know that his marriage was on the rocks, that he was being dropped from a major production, or that, in Vidal's case, his wife was coming home.

He was striding back toward them. The cameras, the bodies, were in position. Rogan sighed. "Come on. Once more into the breach. How I hate that damned horse."

Vidal halted a mere foot away from them. She could smell his sweat, almost feel the heat of the flesh she was unable to touch.

"I want it just like the reruns yesterday. The horses are slightly abreast and you sit facing each other." His white shirt was open to the waist. She averted her gaze from a crisp pelt of darkly curling hair. "You're exhausted, mud-splattered, and triumphant. It is the first major battle against the Yorkists and it is a battle that you have won. So I want weariness, elation, and I want to be aware of the unspoken passion between the two of you." There was a cool edge to his voice. "Any problems, Valentina?"

She avoided his eyes. He had been almost courteous of late and surprisingly gentle when she had first had to mount the white stallion for close-up shots.

"No," she lied. "Everything is fine."

"Good. Replace the stand-ins and let's do it in as few takes as possible."

She began to walk with Rogan across the field that had been so carefully churned the previous day.

"I swear to God he can't wait for that horse to bolt with me," Rogan said savagely. "Have you ever seen such a temperamental beast? It's a wonder I haven't been thrown and had my back broken."

Valentina didn't answer. She wondered if Kariana shared her husband's love of riding. She knew that Vidal rode every morning. When Kariana was home, did she join him on those early morning canters into the hills? Did they laugh and talk and did they perhaps lie down on the grass and make love?

She pressed her hands to her eyes in an effort to erase the tormenting images.

Rogan took hold of her. "Are you okay? If you're sick, there's no need to go through with this shot today. They can take the distance shots with the stand-ins."

"No." She lowered her hands from her face and managed a shaky smile. "I'm fine, Rogan. Really I am."

She patted the stallion's velvet-soft muzzle. The nostrils dilated and liquid-brown eyes surveyed her compassionately. It was as if, instinctively, the animal knew of her inner suffering and was trying to give her sympathy. His name was Sapphire and she wondered if she dare ask Vidal where he had come from. Who owned him? And if they would be prepared to sell him.

She swung herself up onto his back and her robes were meticulously arranged, her makeup checked.

"Okay. Camera one, ready? Camera two? . . ." The familiar directions were given. With a determined effort, she banished Kariana Rakoczi from her mind. She was Margaret, queen of England, a tigress who never accepted defeat.

Chapter Ten

"Thank goodness that's over," Rogan said with fervent gratitude when he was at last able to dismount from his horse and the day's shooting was finished. "If I don't have a drink, I'll die. How about seeing me in the bar in an hour?"

She managed a smile and shook her head. Rogan groaned in despair. "You're turning into a recluse, Valentina. It isn't healthy. Hell. It isn't even normal!"

"I'm tired. We're shooting in the studio tomorrow and I want to make sure I'm word-perfect."

"You use that excuse all the time and it isn't valid. You're *always* word-perfect."

"That's because I don't go out at night," she said, but her smile did not reach her eyes. For the first time Rogan noticed that beneath the heavy makeup, she was paler than normal. Perhaps she did need rest. Rakoczi had been working them all to the point of exhaustion.

"Okay," he said, capitulating gracefully. "But I'm not going to continue to take no for an answer. In the scene between King Henry and the earl of Warwick we won't be needed for days. There'll be no excuse for tiredness then."

She shivered. Not to be needed on the set seemed inconceivable. Pushing the thought away, she walked wearily toward the luxurious bungalow that Theodore Gambetta had assigned to her as a dressing room. Ellie, the maid from the Beverly Hills Hotel, was now her own personal maid and was waiting to remove her makeup and help her out of her heavy costume of mud-splashed velvet.

As her royal robes were replaced by a beige silk shirt and neatly fitting slacks, Valentina said, "There's no need to wait for me tonight, Ellie. I'm staying at the studio for a little while. Have the chauffeur drop you off and then return for me."

"All right," Ellie said doubtfully. "If you're sure. . . ."

Such a thing had never happened before. When the day's work was over, Valentina always returned immediately to the hotel.

When Ellie had left, Valentina wandered restlessly around the bungalow, loathing the idea of leaving the familiarity of the studio. Picking up a sweater, she closed the door behind her and walked down the shrub-shrouded pathway that gave her dressing room its illusion of privacy.

There was the sound of hammering as a distant set was constructed ready for the morning. She continued without direction or purpose, past the sound stages, the photographic studios, the cutting rooms. She paused at the door of the projection room and wondered what time it would be when Vidal looked at the day's rushes. Then she continued on past the story department and the publicity offices.

This was Theodore Gambetta's dream factory and this was where she belonged. She was as avidly interested in the set designer's job as she was in her own. Everything fascinated her and aroused her curiosity. She wanted to learn about lighting, about camera work. About anything and everything.

The scene scheduled for tomorrow was a particularly tense one between herself and Rogan. No doubt some of the crew would still be working on the set. They wouldn't mind if she wandered in for a few moments to familiarize herself with it.

For a few seconds the darkness was all-engulfing. The only lights were at the far side of the set, where the carpenters were still at work. She stepped over a cable and sat down. The chalk marks had not as yet been put in place. She thought she knew where Vidal would require them. She murmured her opening lines and then fell silent. There was something awesome about a soundstage when it was deserted. She rose to leave and was halted by the sound of Vidal's voice.

"They'll be working all night on this set. Our schedule is pretty tight."

"Is it a palace? It looks very beautiful."

The voice was soft and melodious. With racing heart, Valentina tried to move and failed.

"The ceilings are to be vaulted." Once again she heard the timbre of his voice and then they strolled into view.

Rogan's studio gossips had been wrong. Kariana Rakoczi was not about to leave New England for Hollywood. She had already arrived. Everything about her was ethereal and insubstantial. Her gown was of floating chiffon, gossamer sheer. Her hair was pale gold, falling forward in stunning simplicity on either side of her face. As Valentina watched she saw Vidal slip his arm protectively around his wife's shoulders and glance down at her with an expression she had not thought him capable of. An expression of exquisite tenderness.

This time, when she tried to move, she succeeded, stumbling out into the blessed coolness of the evening, the nebulous dreams she had cherished, withering and dying.

The Rakoczi marriage was not on the brink of divorce. There was no hope of a future in which Vidal would love her as she loved him. She half ran to her waiting Cadillac, hurling herself on to the rear seat, trembling convulsively, wondering how she would live through the next minute. The next day. Her chauffeur eyed her through the mirror with a troubled gaze and then drove smoothly out of the studio and toward Sunset Boulevard. As he drew to a halt beneath the porte cochere of the hotel, Rogan was just about to step into his limousine. He had been drinking in the hotel bar and was now en route for Ciro's and his date for the evening. On seeing Valentina, he halted.

"Hi," he said as her chauffeur opened her door for her. "How about a drink?"

She looked up at him, her face bleak. "Thank you," she said, a curious inflection in her voice. "I'd like a drink very much."

The dark and cozy bar was already full. At first very little notice was taken of them. Everyone knew Rogan and had already exchanged friendly words with him earlier on in the evening. Then the whispers began to fly from banquette to banquette. The casually dressed girl at Rogan's side was the elusive co-star of his new movie. The girl Theodore Gambetta was betting millions on.

Within minutes some of the most illustrious names in town were strolling casually past their table, exchanging words with Rogan and being introduced to Valentina. A photographer snapped Rogan and a Paramount male star, drinks held high, grins wide on their faces, a smiling Valentina between them. The next day the *Examiner* printed it beneath the headline MYSTERY STAR EMERGES AT LAST!

When Vidal strode on the set the next morning, there were white lines etched round his mouth and his eyes glinted dangerously. For six months Valentina had shunned the glittering social world she was eligible to enter, and now it seemed she was shunning it no longer. And the man she had chosen as her escort was Tennant. Vidal could hardly control himself as he surveyed the finished set and went over the lighting with Don Symons. There wasn't a damned thing he could do. Tennant was between marriages and Valentina was single. The publicity department would be ecstatic.

He paced the set, ordering first one camera to be moved and then another. When shooting finally commenced, both cast and crew knew that they were in for a rough day.

"Tilt your chin to the *left*, Tennant! *Uristen!* You are an English earl. Be arrogant! Proud!" He stormed back to his director's chair. "Camera one?" he rasped out, "Two? Three? Sound? Okay. Turn them over."

Valentina kept her eyes steadfastly averted from him. It was the first rule she had made for herself through the long, sleepless night. She had fallen in love with him in an instant. Falling out of love with him would be a hard, painful process, but she would do it. She would shut him out of her mind and her heart. She would love someone else. Rogan, perhaps. Anybody. But she would not love Vidal Rakoczi.

She obeyed his directions as impeccably as always, but something had changed between them and it was apparent to everyone on the set. When he spoke to her, she no longer held his gaze with fevered intensity, and there was a cruel edge to his voice that made even Harris and Don Symons wince.

"What devil is riding Rakoczi today?" Sutton asked Leila Crane in a whisper.

Leila shrugged. "Perhaps he doesn't like his two stars becoming so friendly off the set."

Sutton raised his eyebrows. "When did that interesting event take place?"

"I don't know, but I don't think there's any doubt that it has." She nodded in the direction of Rogan and Valentina, who were waiting together at the far side of the set for the lighting to be perfected for their next scene. They were drinking Cokes and there was something about the easy intimacy in the way they were standing. Their unnecessary closeness. And then, as Rogan put down his Coke, his hand slid down Valentina's arm and he lightly clasped her hand.

"So the young lady is not quite so remarkable as I first thought her," Sutton said with regret. "A pity, but no reason for Rakoczi to behave like a fiend. It isn't as if he's an interested party. If he had been, we would have known about it by now."

"Yes . . ." Leila's voice held doubt. "Yet when they're together, when he is directing her, there is such a feeling." She shivered expressively. "It's like electricity."

"He is a great director," Sutton said simply. "And he has at last found a star worthy of his talents."

"Is she really so remarkable?"

"Incredible," Sutton said. He had been in the business more than a decade and was one of the few who had successfully made the transition from silent movies to talkies. Leila listened and believed.

"Yet off-screen she's so quiet. So self-contained."

"Look into those eyes and you'll see nothing quiet or self-contained," Sutton said dryly. "You'll see a passion that is quite frightening in its intensity. For Rogan's sake I hope she doesn't make him the object of it. He isn't equal to such fire. There are no soul-dark depths to Worldwide's leading lover boy."

Harris's voice silenced them. "All right, now. Places, everybody. This is a take."

Queen Margaret was leaving her lover to return to her monastic husband. It was one of the most important scenes in the movie and had been rehearsed by Rogan and Valentina countless times. Even with Rakoczi in a good mood, it would be a hard scene to shoot. In his present mood both cast and crew mentally prepared themselves for a harrowing afternoon.

"Are you ready?" Valentina could sense Vidal's eyes burning into her as he snapped the question.

She merely nodded, continuing to keep her eyes averted.

"Okay," he said tightly. "I want everything you've got." There was complete silence on the set. "Right. Camera. Action!"

Leila and Sutton and the watching extras held their breath. Don Symons crossed his fingers. They could be days on this one scene. Possibly weeks.

Valentina lifted her head and her hauntingly beautiful eyes were misted with unshed tears.

"My duty is with my husband," she began heartbrokenly, and Vidal felt his blood begin to churn. She was flawless and she continued flawlessly, lifting Rogan along with her, releasing in him a power of emotion that no one at Worldwide had ever suspected he possessed.

"You are my life. You have my heart, my body, my soul." The earl of Suffolk's hand was held against her cheek. She was playing the scene with a nervous vulnerability and sensitivity that rendered Vidal breathless. There was a sense of open, daringly expressed pain and despair about her that he had never seen equaled.

When it was over, no one moved or spoke. At last Vidal said brusquely, "That's it. Print it." One of the most difficult scenes in the whole movie had been shot in one take.

Valentina felt a wave of relief. She had been terrified that her own tormented emotions would have crippled her ability to act. Instead, they had intensified it. She said shakily, to a perspiring Rogan, "I think I'd like a coffee, please."

"You deserve champagne," he said, aware that thanks to her he had just played the most stunning scene of his career.

She laughed, aware of a surge of adrenaline. An I-can-do-anything feeling. In some mysterious way she had just proved something to herself and she knew that she would never be quite the same again. The uncertainty had gone. She knew who she was and what she could achieve. As a child she had developed an inner life in order to survive, and that inner life was now sustaining her.

Vidal's shadow fell across her. "You were good," he said tersely.

All day long she had avoided his glance. Now she raised her eyes to his.

"Yes," she said, and there was defiance in her voice. "I was, wasn't I?"

All his life he had been in control. He had never broken any vow he had taken or made. And he had vowed never to succumb to the affinity of spirit he felt for the smoky-eyed waif who had wandered into his life wearing a coarse linen dress and thick, unbecoming stockings.

"I would like to see you tonight," he said, and the dark, smoke-rich quality of his voice held her rigid. "Perhaps we could have dinner together?"

Her heart began to beat more slowly. There were flecks of gold near the pupils of his eyes and she could smell the faint tang of his cologne. Desire shot through her, and she suppressed it ruthlessly.

"I'm dining with Mr. Tennant tonight," she said coolly.

His jaw tightened. "Then tell him you now have other arrangements."

Pride gave her strength. If he wanted to discuss *The Warrior Queen* with her, then he could do it when it was convenient for her. Through the day, on the set.

"But I haven't," she said, and a demon of jealousy drove her to add recklessly, "though if I ask him, I'm sure he won't mind if you and Mrs. Rakoczi join us for dinner."

The blood drained from his face, leaving the strongly defined cheekbones and jutting nose and chin menacing and hawklike. For a second an expression of such raw pain flared in his eyes that she physically flinched, then it was gone and she was staring up into a face shadowed and shuttered and devoid of all emotion.

"Thank you," he said, and the coldness of his voice chilled her. "But that will not be possible."

She tried to smile politely, to think of some brittle, bright remark, and failed. Her hands groped behind her in search of something to hold on to. He looked down at her for another long moment and then shrugged, his shoulders lifting dismissively beneath his immaculately tailored jacket as he turned on his heel and strode away.

She fought an onrush of tears, aware that friendship, as well as love, was now beyond her grasp.

"What did our lord and master want?" Rogan asked, handing her a cup of coffee, his blue eyes glinting with pleasure at the knowledge that his changed status with Valéntina was arousing the Hungarian's wrath.

"I . . . nothing."

Vidal was deep in conversation with Harris. With difficulty she tore her gaze from the lean, tanned contours of his body and gave her attention to Rogan.

"He must have wanted something." Rogan raised a fair, sleek brow and the corner of his mouth quirked in an amused smile.

She sipped at her coffee and then said, her voice steadier, "He wanted to talk to me about *The Warrior Queen.*"

"He didn't look as if your comments had pleased him very much. He was scowling like the devil when he walked away from you."

"Was he?" She tried to smile. "You mustn't take too much notice of Mr. Rakoczi's scowls, Rogan. He has a volatile mid-European temperament."

"Is that what it is?" He grinned. "I thought it was just sheer damned rudeness."

"That's it for today," Harris said, strolling toward them. "I'd take advantage of it and get down to the beach if I were you. It looks like we'll be here till midnight doing the Henry and Warwick scenes."

Rogan put down his empty cup. "Come on, Queen Margaret, let's escape before Torquemada changes his mind."

She looked around her helplessly as Rogan seized hold of her hand and began to pull her in his wake off the set. She didn't want to leave. Other people's scenes were as important to her as her own. Away from the set she felt edgy and ill at ease, as if she were not in her rightful place.

"Come *on*," Rogan repeated impatiently. "We have time to enjoy ourselves for once. Let's leave while the going's good."

Reluctantly she followed him. Vidal would not want her on the set when her presence was not required. No doubt he had instructed Harris specifically to make sure both she and Rogan left Worldwide the instant they were no longer needed.

The thought filled her with desolation. She remembered how, in the early days, he had talked to her long and enthusiastically about his plans for *The Warrior Queen*. How she had felt part of those plans. As if the movie were a shared venture. Now she was no more than a puppet to be moved around at will.

Rogan kissed her enthusiastically and hurried off to his trailer to shower and change.

Despondently she wandered down the pathway to her dressing room. No doubt Kariana now listened to all of Vidal's plans. She probably saw the day's rushes with him and helped him select takes. Whenever they saw the rushes on a morning, Vidal had already made his selection. It was only courtesy on his part that gave Rogan and Sutton the illusion that they had any say in the matter.

Her fingers clenched. Only hours ago she had determined to shut him out of her thoughts completely and here she was, imagining him with his wife, torturing herself unnecessarily.

"Could I have a drink, Ellie?" she asked as she entered the privacy of her bungalow.

Ellie put down the heavy satin court dress she had been stitching.

"Of course. Would you like a Coke or a bottle of mineral water?"

"Neither," Valentina said wearily, unhooking her bodice with its heavy weight of fake jewels. "White wine. There's a bottle of Moselle at the back of the refrigerator."

She shed the burden of her medieval robes and slipped a terry-cloth robe on. "The scene went well, Ellie, we did it in one take."

"That's tremendous!" Ellie's eyes glowed. Any triumph

of Valentina's was a triumph of hers also. "Mr. Rakoczi must have been very pleased."

Valentina gave a wry smile. "If he was, he didn't go overboard in showing it."

Ellie handed her a glass of chilled wine, disturbed anew by the sadness that lurked at the back of Valentina's smoke-gray eyes. It was never completely absent. Even when she was laughing, the sorrow remained. Somehow, somewhere, she had been hurt deeply, and not even her present heady status as Worldwide's number one potential star had succeeded in eradicating her pain.

As Valentina was finishing her glass of wine there came a loud rap on the door.

"That will be Mr. Tennant," she said, rising to her feet. "Tell him I'm in the shower, Ellie. I'll be ready in ten minutes."

She disappeared into her bedroom with its adjoining bathroom and Rogan was obliged to wait impatiently, helping himself to the Moselle and wondering which would be the best location for her seduction.

They could go down to the beach and he could borrow Sutton's beach house. They could stay the night there. Or he could dine with her at Ciro's and take her back for drinks to his own sprawling mansion.

Excitement built up in him till he could hardly bear it. Damn it all. He didn't want to bother with the beach or with Ciro's. He wanted to take her straight back to her Beverly Hills bungalow and fuck until he was exhausted. He grinned to himself complacently. Which wouldn't be for hours. He wasn't known as Worldwide's sexual athlete for nothing. They could have food and champagne sent in and stay in bed for days.

His sex throbbed and he poured himself another glass of wine. Never in his life had he wanted a woman so intensely. He felt light-headed with anticipation. No wonder even Rakoczi was jealous of him.

Valentina emerged in a simple white silk dress and low-heeled shoes.

He eyed her appraisingly. "You look a million dollars."

Ellie continued with her sewing. So that was how it was. She had never noticed that her young employer was as devastated by Mr. Tennant as the rest of the female population.

Still, it wasn't surprising. She snapped off her thread and began to sew on a button. When Miss Parsons caught a whiff of the new romance, there would be reams more about Valentina in the fan magazines and gossip columns. She sighed with satisfaction. Her cuttings box was nearly full already. Soon she would have to start another one.

Rogan rolled away from her and stared at her in astonishment. Initially he had been pleased that she had been reluctant to follow Harris's suggestion and go down to the beach. Instead, they had driven straight to Mulholland Drive and he had been euphoric.

She had adamantly refused any of his exotic cocktails but had drunk a healthy amount of champagne. In showing her his opulently furnished house, he had left the bedroom till last of all. It was a room he had no intention of leaving in a hurry.

"I'm not sure I like the African masks," she said, a smile of amusement playing about her lips as she observed that the ceiling was mirrored, as was the wall behind the bed. Rogan obviously took his label of great screen lover seriously.

"They came from *African Enchantment*," he said, steering her toward the center of the room and the vast, silk-sheeted bed. "They're extremely rare." His arm slid around her and his lips kissed the nape of her neck softly. "Like you, Valentina."

She waited for desire to shoot through her as it did when Vidal touched her. As it did when Vidal merely looked at her. She felt only an agreeable warmth. The comfort of touching and being touched; the comfort that she had been denied throughout her childhood.

"You nearly drove me mad in the love scenes today," Rogan said, his voice thickening as he turned her around, his hands sliding slowly up and down her back, caressing her hips as he pressed her hard against the length of his body. "You're a tease, Valentina. I can't eat or sleep for thinking of you." His mouth claimed hers, hot and demanding, and then he pressed her backward and fell with her onto the bed.

It was a full thirty seconds before he realized that his action had been unwelcome.

"What's the matter?" he panted, his leg straddling her,

pinioning her beneath him. "There's no one here. We won't be disturbed."

His hand had slipped into her dress and cupped her breast. She arched her back, trying to free herself of his weight.

"I don't care if we *are* disturbed! I didn't come here to go to bed with you!"

It was then that he had rolled away from her and stared down at her in incredulity.

"But of course you did. Hell. Why else do you think we came here?"

His fingertip brushed her nipple and he smiled, his confidence returning. "We have all evening. All night. And if Rakoczi is shooting the Henry and Warwick scenes, probably all next week as well."

His mouth silenced her protests, his leg pressing hard between hers.

With all the strength she had, she pushed at his shoulders, twisting her head to free her mouth from his.

"Stop it, Rogan! If it's my fault you misunderstood, I'm sorry! Now please let me go!"

"Is that how you like it?" His hand was sliding up the nakedness of her leg, pushing the white silk upward. "Do you like to struggle? To fight?"

She grasped hold of his sleek fair hair with her hands and tugged hard, ignoring his yell of pain.

"No!" she gasped, wriggling free of him. "I don't like it at all! I don't even know what you mean by 'it'! I've never been to bed with anybody in my life!"

"Jesus God!" Rogan held his head in his hands. "You nearly scalped me!"

She sat up and pushed her skirt down over her exposed thighs. "You deserved it," she said grimly, swinging her legs off the bed.

He raised his throbbing head. "Are you trying to tell me that you're a virgin?" he asked incredulously.

"Yes." Her anger was disappearing. Rogan's perplexity was comic.

"But this is Hollywood. There *aren't* any virgins in Hollywood."

"There are now."

Rogan staggered from the bed, still holding his head, and made his way to the nearest bottle of bourbon.

"Hell," he said again. "I thought the only virgins were the ones Cecil B. De Mille offered up as sacrifices in his biblical epics!"

"I'm sorry." She joined him at the lavishly stocked bar in the corner of the bedroom. "Do you mind if I join you? I'm not used to fighting for my virtue."

He swallowed three fingers of bourbon and poured some more. "No hard feelings?" he asked.

She smiled. "No."

He was silent for a little while, and then he said, in dazed disbelief, "Valentina, will you marry me?"

Chapter Eleven

Vidal was not concentrating and he knew it. The scenes between Henry and Warwick were going badly. Exasperated, he ran his fingers through his hair and strode across to the two actors.

"There must not be even the slightest show of arrogance from Henry. He *knows* Warwick is his enemy. But he is a man who forgives his enemies. A man totally out of touch with the age in which he lives. He is gentle and meek and the swaggering Warwick sees nothing admirable in these qualities. We must. Right. Let's try it again."

He returned to his director's chair and watched with growing despair as Sutton failed yet again to depict the innate saintliness that was Henry's downfall.

Reluctantly he called an end to work for the day. Both cast and crew breathed sighs of relief and scurried away as soon as they could. Don Symons lingered behind.

"I hear Mrs. Rakoczi is back home."

Vidal tensed imperceptibly.

"Yes, Don. She arrived home yesterday."

"Did she enjoy her trip, Mr. Rakoczi?"

Don's question was well-meaning. Vidal managed a brief smile.

"Yes, thank you, Don. She did."

Don turned and looked at the set. "I guess we try again tomorrow."

"Hopefully with a little more success," Vidal said dryly.

Don grinned. "It can't always be magic like it was this morning."

Vidal's eyes were bleak. "No," he said. "It can't. Good night, Don."

Vidal stepped into his waiting Rolls. Don, he knew, had a pretty, vivacious wife and three small daughters. No doubt there would be shrieks of welcome when he returned home. Wearily, Vidal poured himself a drink. Envy was an unpleasant emotion and not one that he often yielded to.

The Rolls swept around the first curve of a steeply climbing canyon and he sank back against the leather upholstery, gazing unseeingly at the scrub-covered hills. There would be no children waiting to greet him when he arrived home. The relationship he and Kariana had so fleetingly enjoyed in the early days of their marriage could no longer be recaptured. His love for her had become that of a protective guardian. It could never be sexual again. And he could not leave her. To leave her would be to destroy her. Without him as a shield the press would soon discover the reason for her rare public appearances. The word *strange* would deteriorate into the word *neurotic* and then the hideous word *insanity* would begin to be whispered at dinner parties and cocktail parties. Kariana's sweetness and gentleness would be no protection against the gossipmongers. They would ignore the shy, soft-spoken Kariana Rakoczi and concentrate only on the stranger that she became whenever she was sick.

The Rolls took a hairpin bend at high speed and Vidal's mouth tightened. The Dansarts wouldn't wait until the snide remarks reached the point of publication. Long before then they would recall Kariana to the bosom of her family—and quietly and expensively institutionalize her. She had begged him never to leave her, and knowing the consequences if he did so, he had promised that he never would.

Until now the promise had not caused him agony. His work had consumed him. He had closed the door on human contact and passion and believed that it was closed for good. And then a convent-dressed waif had wandered onto his set and the door had been wrenched from its hinges. Desire and longing had surged through him and in one devastating moment he had known that he would never have peace of mind again.

He tried to remember what he had felt when he had first met Kariana. It had been at a party given by friends to welcome him to America. He had thought her exquisite. Everything about her was delicate. The pure line of her jaw; the graceful movements of her hands when she spoke; the dove-gray and the lavender chiffon dresses that she favored. His friends had told him that he was a fool. The Dansarts were American aristocracy. They were as obsessed with the pedigree of their name as any family in the *Almanach de Gotha*. If he wanted to marry Kariana, then he would have to elope with her. There was no way the Dansarts would welcome into the family a Hungarian, with only his talent to recommend him. Yet the Dansarts had.

The reason had come soon enough. Kariana's behavior had already caused deep concern. There had been scenes in the privacy of the Dansart home. A minor breakdown that the family doctor had diagnosed as hysteria. Unexplained bouts of temper that left her strangely withdrawn, as if her mind and spirit had become disembodied.

At eighteen she had become engaged to the son of family friend but the engagement had been embarrassingly short-lived. Then she had met him and Vidal could well imagine the relief that the Dansarts must have felt. From that time on, if Kariana showed signs of instability, it could be safely assumed to be caused by her unsuitable marriage and bizarre life-style in the film world.

They had honeymooned in Europe. Hand in hand they had visited the cathedral at Rheims; the Roman arena at Arles; the Sistine Chapel in Rome. He had been, briefly and sublimely, a happy man.

It was on the evening before they left Paris for Boulogne and the boat home that disaster had struck. He had no idea what started it off nor was he ever to have such an understanding in all the subsequent nightmares they endured. One minute she was herself, beautiful and soft-spoken; the next, a

barely recognizable stranger shouting foulmouthed obscenities at him.

He had stumbled from the room, unable to believe what
he was seeing and hearing. When he returned, she had gone
and had not reappeared for three days. When she did, she
was disheveled and vacant-eyed and her body and clothes
had reeked of stale sex. He never knew where she had been
or with whom, and fear had been his constant companion
ever since.

It could happen anywhere and at any time, and the
ultimate horror was that Kariana had no recall of what had
occurred. In London he had left her at Harrods to shop while
he had luncheon with Alex Korda, a fellow Hungarian. They
had eaten with zest, drunk with relish, and argued exuberantly. He had returned to their hotel in high spirits and
found Kariana in bed with a cabdriver. Her bewilderment at
his rage had been pathetic. She had come home early from
her shopping trip because she had a headache. She had gone
to bed to sleep it off. His accusations were horrible and
untrue. She had wept copiously and taken to going to bed
early and sleeping late.

On the journey home he had spent hour after hour
staring sightlessly into the surging trough of bilious green
waves, wishing heartily that he were dead. He could have
coped with her promiscuity if it had been open and defiant.
He would have beaten her, satiated her with his own lovemaking, locked her in the bedroom if necessary. What he
couldn't cope with was the fearsome knowledge that there
were hours and days in her life that were lost to her. Days
that she steadfastly refused to discuss or to contemplate.

Her fastidiousness in the periods he had begun to think
of as ones of normality, increased. Her sumptuous lingerie
was worn only once and destroyed. She wore a fresh pair of
gloves daily and dropped them in the trash can when she
removed them. There were times when he felt that he was
drowning beneath hundreds of pairs of cellophane-wrapped
gloves and delivery after delivery of bras and slips and panties.

In New York she had tried hard to please him. Detesting
cold, she had accompanied him willingly on his long walks
through the snow-filled streets. His tension and fear had
begun to ebb. They had thrown snowballs at each other in
Central Park; visited art galleries; sat through every movie in

town. They had laughed together; talked together; made love together. And then the whole precarious sense of normality and well-being was shattered at a stroke. This time it wasn't a cabdriver who willingly took thirty minutes out of his working day. It was one of the waiters at the hotel.

His fury had been white-hot. He had known that if he touched her, he would kill her. He had hurled himself out of the room, out of the hotel, and walked through the night. At dawn he had found himself freezing and exhausted on an empty pier on the Hudson River. Oil slicks had coagulated on the inky-black surface, and as he watched the debris bobbing against the side of the wharf he was filled with a savage desire to throw himself into the icy depths and end it all. He had not done so. Instead he had visited Kariana's family.

The Dansarts had received him with frigid civility. When he had tried to talk to them about Kariana's lapses of memory, the atmosphere had turned hostile. They refused adamantly to allow him to speak to their family doctor and they left him in no doubt as to what their solution to the problem would be if Kariana returned home. It would be to ensure that Kariana did not bring disgrace on the family name. And the only way they could make sure of that would be by institutionalizing her.

Sick and angry at their attitude, Vidal had returned home and had continued to shield and protect his wife unaided.

It was not a thankless task. For the most part Kariana was sweet-tempered and charmingly shy. He grew to be grateful for her shyness. It meant that she had no desire for a hectic social life and potential disasters could be avoided. Her cataclysmic mood swings took place at home and he was the only witness.

He began to feel more like a doctor than a director. He watched her constantly, desperately trying to discover what it was that triggered each attack. For a few hopeful weeks he believed that it was alcohol. Kariana drank very little. She didn't share his partiality for vodka and her drinking was limited to wine with her meals. To please him, she drank mineral water instead for a month.

Just as he was beginning to think that he had at last found a way of staving off future attacks, Kariana slid into a week-long fit of depression. It ended in a wild flood of tears and screaming, foulmouthed abuse.

Despairingly he had sought professional help. At a New York dinner party he had met Dr. Albert Grossman, an eminent psychiatrist with a clinic in Bern. He asked to speak to him privately and the next day, at the St. Regis, he spoke frankly about Kariana's behavior when she was ill. The relief had been enormous. Not until then had he realized what a burden he had been carrying.

Dr. Grossman had listened to him with interest and had accepted his invitation to meet Kariana socially. He did so many times and told Vidal that he thought Kariana was a nascent schizophrenic.

Vidal stared unseeingly out of the Rolls at the darkening silhouette of the hills. At that time, when Dr. Grossman had given Kariana's mental condition a name, he had been filled with hope. She needed treatment. And with treatment would come a cure.

His hopes had been in vain. Kariana would not admit that she was ill and refused to be treated by Dr. Grossman. The following year her mental lapses became more frequent and she grew less sure of herself and more aware of the nameless darkness with which she lived. At last she had reluctantly agreed to visit Dr. Grossman at his clinic in Switzerland.

She had remained a month and then, on one of the inevitable buoyant periods that followed her emergence from depression and hysteria, had discharged herself. She had stayed in London on her way to Southampton and the *Mauretania*. While there she had disappeared from her hotel suite for five days. She had taken no clothes and no money. The concerned hotel manager had informed the police and had cabled Vidal in Hollywood. He had gone immediately to London and been greeted by the news that his wife had been found walking along the banks of the Thames, barefoot and wearing only the evening gown she had been wearing on the night of her disappearance. The temperature had been below freezing.

The British had behaved admirably. The press reported only that Mrs. Rakozci had been taken ill during her visit to London and had suffered from temporary amnesia as a result. A photograph had showed them waving and smiling as they boarded the ship at the pier. Disaster had been averted, but only narrowly so. Switzerland was too far for Kariana to travel unescorted. In the future she would have to be treated by doctors in America.

Vidal tried reputed psychiatrists on both the East Coast and the West. None were satisfactory. A bond of trust had grown up between Kariana and Dr. Grossman and she would allow no one else to help her. At last, in despair, Vidal had informed Theodore Gambetta that he had to leave the studio for six months. Gambetta had raged, but Vidal had been adamant. The movie he was working on was handed to another director to complete. The movie he was to start was shelved. Hollywood gossiped and the rumor was that Rakoczi was returning to Hungary. It was a rumor Vidal did nothing to discourage. He wanted no one to know that he was accompanying his wife to Dr. Grossman's clinic in Bern.

It seemed as if the stay in Switzerland had been a success. On their return Kariana appeared rested and her behavior was less edgy and moody. When she had asked to be taken to the premiere of a Worldwide movie at Kahn's Persian Picture Palace, he had agreed cautiously.

The instant he had emerged from the Rolls, he knew he had made a mistake. The Los Angeles police were physically holding back thousands of shouting and screaming fans. A man with a portable microphone pushed it in his face, demanding his comments on the movie being screened.

The hysteria around her had at first bewildered Kariana and then filled her with childlike excitement. By the time they had made their way into the red-carpeted foyer, her eyes were shining and her cheeks were flushed. Theodore, gratified that Vidal had at last escorted his wife to a Worldwide premiere, had been lavishly attentive to her.

Louella Parsons had seen them, and not wanting to subject Kariana to Louella's scrutiny, Vidal had left her with Theodore and had elbowed through the tuxedo-jacketed throng to speak to the columnist by himself. When he returned, Kariana and Theodore had vanished.

Dread had curled and knotted deep within him. No one knew where the head of Worldwide Pictures was. All through the screening of the movie the place of honor remained empty.

Sick with anxiety, Vidal had pushed his way out of the Picture Palace and driven to Gambetta's home. Mr. Gambetta had not returned. He had driven wildly around Beverly Hills searching for Theodore Gambetta's distinctive Pierce-Arrow. It was nowhere to be seen. At last he had driven to Villada and paced the floor, drinking straight vodka, waiting in terror for the telephone to ring.

It had not done so. At three in the morning Gambetta's Pierce-Arrow had screamed to a halt outside. Vidal had run to the door, wrenching it open as Gambetta stumbled toward him.

There were vicious scratch marks down his face. Blood dripped onto the pristine whiteness of his evening shirt. His bow tie had been pulled adrift and his collar was askew, the first few studs of his shirt missing.

"I'm sorry!" he gasped almost incoherently as he half fell into Vidal's grasp. "I didn't know . . . didn't imagine . . ."

"What happened? Where is Kariana?" Vidal's voice was harsh with fear.

"I don't know! I'm sorry, Rakoczi! I—"

"*Where is she?*" Vidal had thundered, lifting Gambetta off the ground by the lapels of his tuxedo and shaking him till his teeth rattled.

"I don't know!" Gambetta had repeated helplessly. "I've been looking for her for ages! She felt faint. I took her outside at the rear of Kahn's, away from the crush. She said that the crowd frightened her. That she wanted to go for a drive."

"*And?*" Vidal demanded, his eyes blazing.

"And I thought it was a harmless idea. I know how it must look, Rakoczi, but I didn't intend—"

"*To hell with what you intended!*" Vidal had flung Gambetta away from him. "*What the fuck happened?*"

"I . . . we drove into the hills." He wiped a trickle of blood away from the corner of his mouth. "We kissed a few times. It was harmless, perfectly harmless, and then I suggested that we get back to the theater and she . . ." He shook his head as if trying to clear it. "She went mad. She began shouting at me. Using words . . . words I couldn't believe. I was out of my depth. I didn't know what the hell was happening. I figured the best thing I could do was to bring her back here."

"And?" Vidal asked again, his face ashen.

Theodore seemed to shrink inside his tuxedo. "She was screaming at me. Saying she didn't want to go back. She . . . she began tearing at her clothes. She just tugged and tore at them until she was naked. I was driving at about forty and she tried to jump from the car. I caught hold of her and the car was going haywire. She didn't seem to mind if we were killed or not. I slammed my foot on the brake and tried to get a firmer hold on her, but it was impossible. She was wriggling like an eel."

"Where were you when she jumped?"

"Just below Bellow's place. By the time I'd got the car under control and run back up the road, she had a head start on me. She ran into the trees and down the hill. There was no way I could catch her. I drove to the foot of the hill and cruised up and down, but there wasn't a sign of her." Something like a sob escaped from him. "Hell, Rakoczi! I didn't know what the shit to do! How could I come and tell you your wife was running around naked?"

"Did you go for help? Did you tell anybody?"

Gambetta shook his head and Vidal began to run toward his Duesenberg.

"Where are you going, Rakoczi? For the police?"

"No," Vidal shouted as he slammed the Duesenberg's door behind him. "I'm going to find my wife, for Christ's sake!"

Gambetta ran toward the car. "Take me with you. Let me help!"

Vidal had turned the Duesenberg around and, while the engine roared, flung open the passenger seat door.

Gambetta collapsed beside him. "I'm sorry, Rakoczi. So goddamn sorry."

Vidal did not reply. His concentration was on the dark unlit road ahead of him and on the hillside where Gambetta had last seen Kariana. If she were picked up naked by a passing motorist, then nothing would prevent a scandal. Sweat trickled down his spine. Always, before, the worst times had been when she had been far from Hollywood. In London or Paris. The men had not known who she was. Scandal had been averted. Previously when she had fled Villada in one of her manic states, she had always headed for the anonymity of downtown Los Angeles. It was as if, bereft of sanity, a spark of self-preservation still flamed.

If she were found in Beverly Hills, there would be little chance of concealing her identity. When normality returned, she would have to face newspaper reports and lascivious stares and snickers. He had to find her and protect her. The very thought of what the press would do with the story if they got hold of it made his blood run cold.

It had taken them all night. She was near the foot of the hill, sitting like a wood nymph at the base of a giant spruce tree. She had twisted her ankle and, unable to run any farther, had simply sat staring up at the stars, waiting for deliverance like a small child.

She had turned her head at their approach, her eyes dazed and uncomprehending. Gently, Vidal had placed his jacket over her naked shoulders and lifted her up in his arms. His rage and fear had evaporated. He was aware only of a bone-deep tiredness. She would sleep and afterward, like an epileptic recovering from a seizure, would have no recall of what had happened. She was, he had thought wearily, more fortunate than he. He would have total recall. He would have to face Gambetta's pity. And he would have to write to Dr. Grossman and tell him that her condition was deteriorating.

When they returned to Villada and he had put her to bed, Gambetta had asked awkwardly, "How often does it happen, Vidal?"

Vidal's face was haggard. "There's no telling. Sometimes once a month. Sometimes not for six months."

"Can't something be done for her? Has she seen a doctor? A headshrinker?"

"She's seen every psychiatrist of repute on both coasts. The only one who seems to do any good is a Swiss with a clinic in Bern."

Gambetta poured a bourbon for himself and a vodka for Vidal. "I see. Now I understand why you sacrificed two movies to go to Europe."

Vidal took the proffered glass and leaned back against the cushions of the sofa, his shoulders slumped in defeat.

"I thought it had done some good. I thought there might be an end to it."

"There is always an end to everything," Gambetta said, his expression somber. "But it is not always the end we envisage, my friend." He had touched Vidal lightly on the shoulder. "As for me, tonight I left the premiere because I was unwell. I went home to bed. That is all I will ever tell and all I will remember."

The door had closed quietly behind him and Vidal had

remained downstairs, sitting on the sofa, staring unseeingly out of the vast windows as a blood-red sun rose over the Hollywood hills, staining the sky to gold.

After the incident with Gambetta something had changed in Kariana. It was as if a miasma of remembrance clung to her. Her dependence on him became suffocating and total. Day after day urgent telephone calls summoned him from the set to Villada. In despair he had suggested that she have a companion to live in. Hazel Renko was a twenty-six-year-old psychiatric nurse, and to Vidal's intense relief a genuine friendship quickly sprang up between her and Kariana.

The disruptions on the set ceased. They began to go out in the evenings and to entertain a little. They spent a week-end in the mountains at Arrowhead and another at the Santa Anita racetrack. Once again he began to feel faint stirrings of hope.

The call was put through to him when he was on location in Nevada. The temperature was a hundred degrees and he had been sweating and irritable when he was summoned to the telephone. It was Hazel Renko. In his absence Kariana had spiraled into a snakepit of amnesia and mania and neither Hazel nor Chai could control her.

He had returned at once to Villada. For a week he barely ate or slept. Together he and Hazel managed to prevent Kariana from leaving the house. Her violence and abuse had shaken even him. There wasn't a mirror that wasn't smashed, a room that wasn't damaged. And then it was over. Spent and exhausted, she had emerged from her sickness, blinking dazedly like a person stepping from darkness into sunlight. He had put her to bed. And he had telephoned Dr. Grossman.

Dr. Grossman had suggested that Kariana return to the clinic, this time for a longer stay. He had been optimistic, seeing no reason why her condition should not stabilize, especially now that she was experiencing a growing awareness of her illness.

It was arranged that the three of them would leave Los Angeles for Switzerland at the soonest possible opportunity. Vidal had told Gambetta that he would not be making any more movies that year, and Gambetta had received the news in silence and without protest.

It was then that Vidal experienced something very nearly

like hatred for Kariana. He didn't want to leave Hollywood. He didn't want to abandon his profession for six months, maybe a year. He didn't want to accompany her to Switzerland. Two days before they were due to leave, Hazel Renko had suggested that she and Kariana travel alone, and he had been ashamed at the relief he had felt.

The moon slid out from behind a bank of clouds as the Rolls cruised silently to a halt outside Villada. Kariana had gone to Switzerland with Hazel Renko and had stayed at the clinic for over six months. On the way home she had visited her family in Boston and Hazel had telephoned him and said there was no need for him to worry. Kariana was calm and showing no signs of stress. They were departing on the Twentieth Century for Los Angeles in three days.

He had felt as if high walls were closing in on him. In utter despair he knew that he did not want Kariana to return. He did not want to live with fear again, with every nerve end taut and tense as he returned home from the studio, not knowing what he would find. Yet there was no other way of life open to him. He could not divorce and abandon her. Without his support, she would be a lost soul.

Bleakly he had waited on the platform as the Twentieth Century pulled in from its long overland journey. Kariana had looked exquisite as she stepped down from the train, a silver mink jacket draped over her shoulders, her blond hair shining like gold in the morning sunlight. His arms had slid around her and the old protectiveness had revived. But it wasn't love. Love was an emotion he no longer felt for her and that he could not allow himself to feel for anyone else.

For an instant an image of Valentina suppressed all other thoughts. With her he had temporarily forgotten the hopelessness that he lived with. He remembered the hours of peace and calm in her pink-carpeted suite as he had read Shakespeare, and then he thought of her with Rogan Tennant and his hands clenched in a spasm of jealousy.

"Have a nice evening, Mr. Rakoczi," the chauffeur said as he opened the rear door for him.

"Thank you." If there was irony in his voice, the chauffeur was unaware of it.

He stepped out onto the loose gravel and then—instead of entering the house, handing his jacket to Chai, mixing himself a vodka and blue curaçao, and greeting his wife—he walked slowly over to the lip of the hill.

The ground fell away steeply. What had once been scrub had been carefully nurtured and the fragrance of bougainvillea and hibiscus lingered in the night air. He stood, a tall, lean, restless figure, staring out over the darkness of the Cahuenga Valley. Not until long after the chauffeur had let himself into his apartment above the garage and gone to bed did Vidal turn, his eyes bleak, the skin taut across his cheekbones as he began to walk slowly back toward the house.

Chapter Twelve

The next day the atmosphere on the set was claustrophobic. Valentina was unusually preoccupied and it was not with her lines. Twice she didn't hit her marks correctly, and Harris had to repeat his directions to her constantly.

Vidal had slumped in his director's chair, a deep scowl furrowing his brow, his silence unnerving the crew far more than the rages they were accustomed to.

Only Rogan seemed unaware of the strained mood around him. He quipped frequently to Sutton and Leila Crane. He breezed through his lines, blatantly uncaring of the repeated takes his shallow performance necessitated. Don Symons and Harris gave Vidal covert glances, aware that his concentration was not on the scene Rogan and Valentina were playing.

"What's the matter with him? Has someone died?" Harris whispered to Don as Rogan fluffed a line and Vidal did not notice.

"Search me," Don replied, mystified. "I've known him a long time but I've never known him to be like this before. We're shooting a load of crap this morning and he doesn't seem to care."

"He'll care when he sees the rushes," Harris said darkly. "I wish to God I knew why Rogan was looking so pleased with himself. If I was putting in his performance I'd be weeping, not smirking all over my goddamn face."

Vidal's secretary approached him nervously. "There's a telephone call for you, Mr. Rakoczi."

Vidal was staring at Valentina, his eyes dark, his mouth a tight, compressed line.

The secretary cleared her throat and repeated her message. Vidal dragged his gaze from Valentina and glared at his secretary.

"Yes? What is it?"

"Your wife is on the telephone for you, Mr. Rakoczi."

Vidal rose to his feet. "Take five," he said curtly to the crew. "And when I get back I want some acting on this set. Your performances so far wouldn't do credit to burlesque artists."

Rogan flushed an ugly red and turned his back on Vidal, drinking deeply from a silver hip flask. Vidal's eyes narrowed. When Tennant stepped from beneath the kliegs after his next take, he would find his pick-me-up flushed down the toilet, Vidal decided.

As Vidal strode toward the telephone, Rogan said savagely to Valentina, "The man's a barbarian. Thirty years ago he'd never have gotten any farther than Ellis Island."

Valentina didn't reply. Her head ached. All morning she had been torn by indecision. To marry Rogan or to continue through life alone.

"I'm wanted at home," Vidal said brusquely to Harris. "Keep Tennant here, going over his scene, but don't shoot a foot until I get back."

"Okay, Mr. Rokoczi," Harris said unhappily. "Anything you say."

Vidal snatched up his jacket and without a word or a glance at anyone strode from the set.

"What the hell was that all about?" Don asked, leaving his battery of lights and crossing the studio floor to Harris.

"Damned if I know. We're due to start shooting outdoors next week and we're still miles behind with these palace scenes. At this rate we're going to fall way behind schedule and Gambetta will be breathing fire and brimstone down all our necks."

"Relax, gentlemen," said Sutton soothingly, lighting a cigar and seating himself comfortably. "Whenever the divine

Kariana is in residence our dear director is easily distracted. It happened constantly on *Wild Summer*. No matter how vital the scene, one itsy-bitsy telephone call from his dearly beloved, and wham! Shooting came to an abrupt finale until the call of love had been answered."

Rogan stared at him. "Do you mean he's left us all high and dry while he goes home to fuck?"

Sutton shook his head in mock disapproval. "Your coarseness astounds me, Tennant. Let us just say that though we find our director less than amiable, his spouse does not share our feelings. Have you ever known her to attend any function without him?"

"No. But that doesn't mean she wouldn't like to, given the chance," Rogan said maliciously. "If she's so damned devoted to him, why does she spend so much time in Europe?"

"Culture, my dear boy. Culture," Sutton said, beaming genially. "Kariana Rakoczi is an easterner and a well-bred easterner. Amazing though it may seem to you, Hollywood is not the intellectual capital of the world. I shouldn't be at all surprised if a lady of Kariana Rakoczi's temperament finds it downright vulgar."

"Fucking at eleven o'clock in the morning ain't exactly refined," Rogan said caustically, "especially when it means seventy or eighty people have to stand around twiddling their thumbs while she exercises her conjugal rights."

There were sniggers from the listening cameramen and Valentina felt her cheeks burn.

"Right now is where you stop twiddling your thumbs and get down to some work," Harris said cuttingly. "I want this morning's scene gone over until it's perfect. When Mr. Rakoczi returns he'll expect us to be able to shoot it in one take."

"For Christ's sake, I know the damned thing backwards. If Rakoczi can take off in the middle of the day, why can't we?"

"Because you're an actor, not a director, and actors can be replaced, Tennant."

"Bullshit," Rogan said without sounding too convincing. "This movie would fall flat on its face without me."

"The way you've been acting this morning, it's going to fall flat on its face *with* you," Harris said darkly. "Right, places, everybody. Let's try it again."

"Gee, that Kariana sure is a lucky lady," Leila Crane said

to Valentina as they walked back onto the set. "Imagine having the hots and being able to summon a guy like Rakoczi just by picking up the phone."

"He's crazy about her," Don Symons said. "When they're together his eyes never leave her for a moment."

"I wish I could find a husband like that," Leila said feelingly. "I've had three so far and the bastards never kept their eyes off anything wearing a skirt."

"I heard the last one was partial to trousers as well," Rogan said with a grin.

Leila punched him on the shoulder and laughed. "You bet he was. From the tree of life I keep picking lemons. Maybe I'll be luckier next time."

"*Quiet!*" Harris yelled. "I want this scene a hundred percent perfect before Mr. Rakoczi returns. Take it from your entrance before Margaret and Henry, Tennant, and this time stop playing for the benefit of the extras and put some guts into it."

Valentina sat stiffly on the throne alongside Sutton's. Her robes were carefully adjusted and Don ordered a last-minute lighting change. Vidal had worked eighteen hours a day on *The Warrior Queen* and nothing had distracted him. Yet today he had done the inconceivable. He had walked off the set in the middle of shooting and for no more important reason than that his wife was feeling lonely and wanted to see him. Woodenly her mouth framed the words of her lines. She felt empty inside. Dead and cold and utterly alone.

"The great lords are raising private armies, my liege," Rogan said, falling on one knee before Sutton. "The Nevilles, the Beauchamps, the Cliffords, all are preparing to rise against the throne." A short cloak was thrown rakishly over one shoulder. His blond hair hung glossy and long over the high, stand-up collar of his doublet. He was an exceedingly handsome man, Valentina thought, and he loved her and wanted to marry her.

"Then we must soothe them, my good Suffolk," Sutton said with saintly tolerance. "We must love them and forgive them their hotheadedness."

At this point Rogan and Valentina were to look directly at each other, their shared despair and vexation at Henry's lack of fighting spirit blatantly apparent. As their gazes met,

Valentina was overcome with a surge of recklessness. Vidal did not love her and never would love her.

"Yes," she said as Harris yelled at them to do the scene again from the top. "I will marry you, Rogan."

For a second, Rogan stared at her disbelievingly and then let out a wild, triumphant whoop. He seized her around the waist, whirling her in his arms.

"What the hell?" Harris shouted in exasperation. "I'm trying to achieve something here, Tennant, and you're doing nothing but being damned disruptive."

"And I'm going to continue to be disruptive," Rogan said, walking across to him, his arm firmly around Valentina's waist. "I'm not going to go through that damned scene one more time. Instead, I'm going to send for some champagne and I'm going to celebrate my forthcoming nuptials."

"Your forthcoming *what?*" Harris asked, wiping the back of his neck with a silk handkerchief.

"Nuptials. That is, I believe, the correct lingo," Rogan said with a grin. "I'm getting hitched, wed, married."

Harris stared at him. "Are you serious?"

"I've never been more serious in my life. Allow me to introduce you to my future bride."

With a flourish in keeping with his role as the earl of Suffolk, he bowed low before Valentina.

There was a concert of gasps from both cast and crew. Harris felt himself pale. The last thing Gambetta would want was his future star turned into a hausfrau by Rogan Tennant.

"Well, Harris, I'm waiting to be congratulated." There was a touch of steel in Rogan's voice. He knew Harris didn't like him, but the least he could do was damned well be civil.

"Does Mr. Rakoczi know of your plans?"

Valentina stiffened imperceptibly and Rogan's anger flared into the open.

"No, he doesn't! It's none of his goddamn business! Christ, you'd think that man was the Lord Almighty the way you all defer to him! I'm surprised you go to the bathroom without asking his permission."

The muscles in Harris's neck and shoulders tightened and his fists clenched.

"I've just about had it with you, Tennant. Mr. Rakoczi's giving you the break of a lifetime and you do nothing but sneer at him whenever his back is turned."

Rogan let go of Valentina and stepped toward Harris threateningly. "I don't need *anyone* to give me a break! Not Rakoczi, not De Mille, not *anyone*! I'm a star, Harris. The biggest star this studio has!"

"Not in my eyes!" Harris said savagely. "You're a conceited, overbearing, arrogant piece of trash that this movie could well do without."

Rogan's fist shot straight and clean, hitting Harris full on the jaw. He stumbled backward, steadied himself, and with a roar of rage lunged toward Rogan. Cameramen, grips, and electricians rushed forward, grabbing hold of him, restraining him as Rogan backed away, white-faced. Harris was built like a bull and his punch had only succeeded because Harris was not expecting it. If Harris were let loose, he would probably kill him. He would certainly mess up his face and Rogan was well aware that his face was his fortune.

"Cool it," Don Symons said to Harris. "He isn't worth it. We've months of work to do on this movie and we aren't going to get it done if Tennant is in the Polyclinic with a broken jaw."

Harris shrugged off the hands grasping his arms and shoulders. "Then for all our sakes he'd better keep his smart remarks to himself in the future."

Before Rogan could antagonize Harris any further, Sutton stepped forward and said jovially, "Let me be the first to congratulate you, Tennant. You're a man to be envied." He took Valentina's hand and kissed it. "And you, my dear, will make the most stunning bride that this town has ever seen."

"Congratulations," Leila Crane said, kissing Valentina warmly on both cheeks. "I hope you'll be very happy."

Don Symons grasped both her hands in his. "You're certainly a dark horse," he said affectionately. "I hadn't even heard a rumor of this."

They were surrounded by well-wishers and even Harris pushed his way forward, pointedly ignoring Rogan but holding Valentina's hand as he said, "I'm sorry about the scene with Rogan. I hope it didn't spoil your big moment."

Valentina managed a shaky smile. The violence that had so suddenly erupted had shaken her profoundly. "No, Harris. It wasn't your fault. I guess Rogan is a little wound up. It isn't every day that he gets engaged."

Harris was tempted to point out that Tennant had had

some previous experience, having been married three times, but quelled the urge. He liked Valentina. She was beautiful, talented, and intelligent. Why she was marrying a schmuck like Tennant he couldn't imagine.

"Here comes the champagne!" the continuity girl cried as a stagehand hoisted a crate of Piper-Heidsieck onto the set.

"Where the hell did you get that?" Don asked, taking out a bottle and marveling at the vintage.

"A good stagehand knows where to get anything at a moment's notice."

"Can you get me an accommodating little redhead with rather spectacular feminine equipment for four-thirty this afternoon?" Sutton asked wistfully.

"Nothing easier," the stagehand said with a grin, and uncorked a bottle, spraying champagne over a laughing Rogan and Valentina as Sutton sighed in delicious anticipation.

"Come on, Harris, loosen up and enjoy the party. There's no way any more work is going to get done until Mr. Rakoczi returns," Leila said, offering Harris a glass of champagne.

He took it with a grimace. "Has it occurred to you that Mr. Rakoczi might be less than pleased with the news that Tennant and Valentina are getting hitched?"

"You're wrong. There's nothing going on there. I thought so too for a time, but their relationship is strictly for the cameras."

"I never thought otherwise," Harris said dryly. "But if she marries Tennant he'll start influencing her. Telling her what parts she should be angling for and which she should be turning down. And she's Mr. Rakoczi's protégée." He sipped his champagne thoughtfully. "I've got a gut feeling about this one, Leila. Mr. Rakoczi isn't going to like it. He isn't going to like it one little bit."

Vidal strode into his home, the familiar feeling of dread balled up inside his stomach. Kariana had been crying on the telephone, her words barely intelligible. Hazel had gone downtown to visit her dentist. The faucets in her bathroom had begun to leak, and Chai had driven to Beverly Hills to buy new washers for them. She was alone and she was afraid.

"Vidal! Is that you? Oh, thank goodness you're here!" Kariana, distraught, ran toward him. "Why has everyone left

me? They know I hate being on my own. It's not fair . . ."
She burst into tears as he put his arm around her and led her
gently into the lounge.

"Hazel had a raging toothache, Kariana. She *had* to go to
the dentist. She won't be long. Only an hour or so."

Kariana sat tensely on the sofa and began fraying her
lace-edged handkerchief with sharp, convulsive movements.
He knew the signs and he steeled himself for the coming
onslaught. She was entering one of the cataclysmic moods
that turned her within minutes into a total stranger.

"She planned to go out. I know she did. She doesn't like
me anymore, Vidal. She loosened the faucets on purpose so
that I would get upset."

"Hazel adores you," he said, striving to keep his voice
patient. "Let me fix you a coffee. By the time you've drunk
it, Hazel will be back."

If they were lucky, Kariana's distress would terminate in
a storm of tears. If they were unlucky, she would spiral into a
snakepit of darkness that only violence would end.

"And then *you'll* leave me." Her voice rose hysterically.
"You don't care about me either!"

"That's not true, Kariana," he said truthfully. "I care
about you very much and I hate to see you distressing yourself this way. Why don't you lie down for a while? Have a
sleep."

He put his arm around her shoulders and she sprang to
her feet, knocking him away, her pretty face feral.

"You make me sick! Always crawling around me because
of my money! Stealing thousands of dollars from me! Stealing
my ideas to make your movies!"

Vidal felt despair rise like a tide within him. It was a
well-worn theme. Kariana did not inherit her vast share of
her grandfather's millions until she was thirty. He had never
borrowed against her expectations and was uncaring of them.
Her accusation that he stole her ideas baffled him. She had
never shown the least desire for creativity and studio talk
bored her. She would listen passively for a while and then
change the subject. He had shown her the sets for *The
Warrior Queen* and she had delighted in the interior of the
palace that had been erected on lot fourteen, but had shown
no further interest. If he talked about his work, she drifted

away, turning on the record player, filling the house with the strains of Mozart and Chopin.

He wondered if music would soothe her now and slipped a recording of Rossini's *La Scala di Seta* from its sleeve and put it on the turntable.

"Turn that damned music off," she shouted. "I can't bear it! All I can hear is noise. Noise! Noise!" She pressed her hands to her ears, twisting her head convulsively from side to side as if the music were inescapable and in her brain.

The music ceased and Vidal walked into the kitchen and began to make coffee. There had been a time when he had believed such scenes could be halted simply by treating her as a disturbed child and taking her in his arms and soothing her. His attempts had ended in failure. Her distress could not be alleviated so easily.

He took down a bottle from a high shelf and shook three sleeping pills out onto the palm of his hand. Then he crushed them to a powder with the back of a spoon. When the coffee was ready, he poured a cup for himself, leaving it black, and then poured a cup for Kariana, adding cream and sugar and the crushed pills.

At first, when Hazel had suggested to him this way of ensuring Kariana took medication when she needed it, he had rebelled, finding the idea repellent. Time had taught him that it was in Kariana's best interests.

There were occasions when she would take sleeping pills when under stress, but they were few and far between. Bottles had been hurled at his head and through windows. There had been one terrifying occasion when she had said hysterically that if he thought she needed pills, she would take them all. Before he could stop her, she had raced upstairs and locked herself in the bathroom, a full bottle clutched in her hand.

He had hurled himself at the door till it gave on its hinges and found her curled up on the floor in a fetal position, pills clenched in her hands and scattered around her. The quantity she had swallowed had been minimal, but it was an experience he had no wish to repeat.

He walked back into the room and set the coffee cups down on the table.

"Sit down, Kariana, and try to relax," he said gently.

She swung on her heel and her eyes flashed. "Sit down,

Kariana; be good, Kariana," she mimicked, pacing to and fro on the ankle-deep carpet. "Why can't you leave me alone? You're always watching me. Spying on me!"

Vidal sighed. It would be useless to point out that he was with her because she had pleaded with him to be with her. That he had done the unforgivable on her account, as he had so many times in the past. He had left the set in the middle of shooting a scene. In his absence cast and crew would grow edgy and nervous. Tempers were likely to flare. Rumors would abound and incalculable damage would be done. He glanced at his watch. It was nearly midday. There was no sign of the tears that would lead Kariana to exhaustion and sleep. It was going to be a long, drawn-out harangue. Soon the obscenities would start. Then the violence. Neither he nor Hazel would be able to leave the house in case she foiled one of them and reached the Rolls or the Duesenberg.

"I'm here because I care about you, Kariana," he said wearily. "If you'd only go to bed and lie down, you would feel so much—"

"I'm not ill! Why should I go to bed?" The handkerchief disintegrated and she began to claw feverishly at her arms, making long, scarlet weals. "Why should I do anything that you say? You're a Polack, a wop, a Jew and I hate you! You're unclean!"

She began to laugh hysterically and Vidal looked away from her. It was impossible to believe that the gentle person he had said good-bye to only hours ago had turned into the ugly, vicious woman now facing him.

It was as if there were two Karianas. One, quiet-spoken and refined; the other, a coarse-mouthed banshee. Reason was lost on her. There was nothing he could now do or say that would halt the tirade. It would have to run its course and he would have to endure it.

Kariana raised her hand to the edge of the marble mantelpiece and with a triumphant sweep sent his rare collection of ivory and jade figurines crashing to the floor.

With supreme self-control he turned his back on her and poured himself a large, straight vodka. Dr. Grossman had told him that the worst thing he could do would be to seize her, to shake her, or to slap her. Steeling every nerve and muscle in his body, he swallowed the vodka and ignored the wreckage scattered on the carpet.

"Bastard!" Kariana screamed, hurling herself at him, her nails gouging at his face. "Bastard! *Bastard!* BASTARD!"

"There was no way I could keep the cast working," Harris said apologetically as Vidal walked onto the set at dusk, his face haggard. "I did my best. We went through the scene once and I think Don has perfected the lighting."

Vidal looked around the set briefly. Kariana was in bed asleep, spent and exhausted, Hazel by her side. Tomorrow she would have no memory of her vicious words or the wanton damage she had caused. Chai had swept up the smashed ivory and she would be pathetically curious when she noticed that the mantelpiece was denuded of its figurines.

He turned on his heel, saying to Harris, "I want to go over the schedules. It looks as if we have problems with the St. Albans battlefield set."

Harris nodded, hurrying to keep pace with him. As they stepped out of the studio he noticed the scratch marks on Vidal's face. He opened his mouth to remark on them and then thought better of it. Mr. Rakoczi's personal life was his own affair.

"The surrounding countryside just isn't green enough," Vidal was saying as he laid out the plans for the St. Albans set on his desk. "It's England. I want woods in the background. Meadows."

"There's a few thousand bucks' worth of turf been laid. . ."

"And that's exactly what it looks like," Vidal said sharply. "The usual effects aren't going to turn a tract of the San Fernando Valley into the green tranquillity of England. I want poetic countryside raped by the hooves of a thousand horses."

"It's been done before," Harris pointed out doubtfully. "We have the best set dresser in town."

"Call him. I want him in here tonight. Unless he can give me what I want, I'm going to shift the whole unit to New England."

At the thought of organizing and preparing for a movie location on the East Coast, Harris paled. It wasn't possible. There would be hundreds of people to be fed and housed. Everything would have to be transported east. Costumes, props, horses, dressing rooms. The very idea made him feel sick.

"I'll call him now," he said weakly to Vidal. "And I'll call my wife and tell her I'll be home late."

"Tell her you'll be here all night," Vidal said brusquely. "The budget's off and I want estimates of how much more we're going to have to spend. I want to be prepared if Gambetta panics and tries to call the whole thing off."

Harris swallowed. If they were over budget now, they'd be criminally so if the unit went east to a new location. He dialed a number and after a brief pause said tightly, "You'd better get down here immediately. It looks like we have problems."

They worked through the night and at dawn, when Vidal pushed his chair away from his desk, the whole San Fernando location had been redesigned. As Harris and the special effects man stumbled home to grab a couple of hours sleep, Vidal remained in his office. He couldn't face the thought of returning to Villada. Instead, he stretched out on his long leather sofa and stared into the darkness. Louella Parsons had recently headlined him as the man who had everything. His mouth twisted in a bitter smile. Louella was devastatingly wrong. He was a man who had nothing of true value.

Next morning on the set Harris approached him nervously, his face tired and drawn from lack of sleep.

"Rogan Tennant and Valentina haven't turned up for costumes or makeup."

Vidal glanced at his watch, his mouth tightening. "Are they in hairdressing or the commissary?"

"No, Mr. Rakoczi. They're nowhere in the studio."

"Have their studio cars returned?"

Harris shifted uncomfortably on his feet. "Tennant's has, there's no sign of Valentina's."

"Let me speak to Tennant's driver. I don't care how sick he is, he's going to have to come in today."

Don Symons, who had been listening to the conversation, said uneasily, "I don't think he's sick, Mr. Rakoczi. There was a little trouble on the set yesterday, and Tennant turned nasty and threw a punch at Harris."

Vidal cursed volubly in Hungarian. It had been bound to happen sooner or later. A movie company's cast and crew were a spawning ground of intense personal relationships. People who would never normally talk to each other were thrust for long periods into daily physical and mental contact.

The results were often explosive, and it could well explain Valentina's absence.

"Did she seem distressed at the time?" he asked sharply.

Harris blinked uncomprehendingly and Vidal resisted the urge to imitate Tennant's behavior. "Valentina," he said through clenched teeth. "Did she seem distressed at the time by the scene between you and Tennant?"

"She looked a bit shaken," Don said.

"She must have been more than shaken to stay home rather than face the two of you this morning," Vidal said savagely, turning on his heel. "I'll put a call through to the Beverly Hills now. You get Tennant on the phone and tell him if he doesn't get his ass over here in thirty minutes, he's off the movie."

Don and Harris exchanged glances, well aware that wherever Valentina and Tennant were, they were together.

"Use a passkey!" Vidal thundered into the telephone receiver. "If she's not answering, it means she's sick!" The flesh tightened over his cheekbones. He couldn't imagine a small thing like a disagreement between Harris and Tennant disturbing her so deeply that she would ruin a day's shooting by willfully absenting herself from the studio. Perhaps she'd been unable to sleep and had taken sleeping pills. She would be unused to them. Perhaps she had accidentally overdosed. His knuckles showed white as he clenched the receiver, and there were beads of perspiration on his forehead.

"The lady in bungalow eight has requested specifically not to be disturbed, sir," the distant voice said respectfully.

"This is Rakoczi!" Vidal thundered. "I want you to get in that bungalow, do you understand me?"

There was an awkward pause at the other end of the line, and then an apologetic voice said, "I believe the lady is entertaining, sir."

Vidal froze, well aware of what the polite euphemism meant. For a second he thought he was going to black out. Very slowly he replaced the receiver on its cradle.

Don cleared his throat uncomfortably. The voice from the Beverly Hills Hotel had been clear enough for them all to hear.

"I guess they were celebrating late and slept in. I'll get someone over there right away."

"Just who do you mean by 'they,' and exactly what were they celebrating?" Vidal asked, turning toward Don, his voice so full of menace that Don automatically took a step backward.

"Rogan Tennant and Valentina. That's what caused the disruption on the set yesterday. Tennant insisted on throwing an impromptu party to celebrate their engagement."

"Jesus God," Vidal said softly, his face draining of blood. Don and Harris looked away in embarrassment. They had been wrong in their conjectures. There *was* something going on between Mr. Rakoczi and Valentina, only they had been too blind to see it.

No one spoke. The moment seemed to stretch out endlessly. At last Vidal forced himself to move. His feral, primitive quality, barely veneered by the politeness that civilization demanded, was now naked. He looked like a man about to commit murder. His eyes blazed in a fury that was white-hot as he rounded his desk, hurtling out of the room and toward his Rolls.

"Mr. Rakoczi . . ." Harris called after him in vain.

The rear door of the Rolls slammed and the startled chauffeur hurriedly put the car into gear, speeding toward the studio gates with scant regard for the strictly enforced five-miles-an-hour limit.

As the cloud of dust in the Rolls's wake dispersed, Harris walked weakly back into Vidal's office and sat down. "For once in my life I feel sincerely sorry for that bastard Tennant," he said, fumbling for his cigarettes. "Rakoczi's going to make mincemeat out of him."

Don remained silent. Unless Rakoczi's temper cooled on the short drive from the studio to the Beverly Hills Hotel, Rogan Tennant could be facing far more than a severe beating. He could be facing extinction and Rakoczi could be facing a murder rap. He walked somberly out of the room, filled with a sense of foreboding, crushing in its intensity.

Chapter Thirteen

For once in his life Vidal had no coherent thought or plan. He only knew that to see Valentina married to Rogan Tennant would be an agony beyond endurance. The blood pounded behind his eyes as the Rolls flashed down the winding road of the dusty canyon and out onto a wide, eucalyptus-lined boulevard.

The pink stuccoed fairy-tale cupolas of the Beverly Hills Hotel came into view and before the Rolls could slide to a halt Vidal had opened the rear door and leapt from the still moving car. His chauffeur stared after him, shrugged his shoulders, and then eased the car away from the front entrance until it should again be requested.

Vidal raced through the immaculately kept gardens to the ocher-tiled bungalow. He didn't have his passkey with him and he had no intention of wasting time by presenting himself at the front lobby and requesting one. Tennant would open the door to him or never set foot before a camera again. Bile rose in his throat. If Tennant *was* in the bungalow, then it meant that he and Valentina were already lovers.

The drapes were drawn and he hurled himself at the door, beating on it with his fists.

"What the hell . . . " he heard Rogan exclaim before he threw his shoulder against the door, yelling, "Open this goddamn door, Tennant!"

A passing waiter, wheeling a breakfast cart away from one of the other bungalows, left his silverware unattended and rushed to inform security that a disturbance was taking place outside bungalow eight.

Rogan stumbled, half naked and bleary-eyed, from the bed. He had drunk far too much the previous evening. He had a vague recollection of leaping joyously into a fountain in front of a hotel and of being helped through the grounds by a

157

bevy of companions, all wishing him well and shouting drunken congratulations. He stared around dazedly for Valentina and saw a pillow and blanket in rumpled disarray on the sofa.

"What the hell . . ." he repeated as the pounding on the door continued and a string of Hungarian oaths and profanities filled the air.

"It's Vidal," Valentina said, ashen-faced, emerging from the living room, bare feet peeping from beneath a tightly wrapped rose-silk negligee. "I told reception I didn't wish to be disturbed. They must have thought I meant this morning, not last night. There's been no studio call. Nothing."

"What the fuck *happened* last night?" Rogan asked, beads of perspiration breaking out on his forehead as the door began to give on its hinges.

Valentina stared from him to the door and back again, her voice unsteady.

"We had a celebration dinner and then we went for drinks in the bar and Sutton was there. He toasted us with champagne and then the word spread and the whole thing got out of hand. Sutton said the trade papers would hear of the story within hours and that I should tell reception I didn't want to be disturbed."

"Christ!" Rogan said despairingly as the door splintered on its hinges. "We're sure as hell being disturbed now!"

Vidal burst into the room like a tornado. In one glance he took in the disheveled bed, the empty champagne bottle and glasses, Rogan scrambling frantically for his shirt and jacket; and Valentina, perfectly still, perfectly composed. And unutterably beautiful.

All the passion, all the jealousy, all the possessiveness he had kept damned within him for so long, burst free. He had wanted her since he had first set eyes on her and he had fooled himself into believing that he wanted her only to film. For weeks now, he had known the truth and he had fought against it. He was incapable of fighting any longer.

With the agility and speed of a rampaging Magyar, he seized hold of the still half-naked Rogan and pitched him headfirst through the open door and onto the rose-bordered gravel outside. Then he kicked the damaged door shut with his heel and faced Valentina, his breath coming in harsh gasps, his eyes blacker than the coals of hell.

"It was my fault . . ." she began with difficulty, the

words strangling in her throat as his blazing eyes riveted her so that she could not move, could hardly breathe. "I told reception yesterday that I was not to be disturbed. They misunderstood. There was no studio call this morning. Nothing."

"You were in bed with Tennant!" he said ferociously, seizing her wrist, encircling it with a lean, strong hand.

She stared up at him dazedly. Surely his fury was because she hadn't turned up on the set on time? Not because of Rogan.

"We got engaged yesterday," she said, feeling herself begin to tremble.

"The devil you did!"

The heat of his touch burned her. He was holding her so savagely that she felt faint with pain. His mouth was etched with white lines and even his nostrils seemed pinched with fury.

"You're hurting me!"

Vidal was uncaring. "Of all the men in the world, you have to lose your virginity to a mindless, conceited cretin like Tennant!"

"What is it to you if I did?" she flared, shock giving way to answering fury. "I'm not your property! I have a life of my own to lead and I'll lead it in any way I choose!"

"No, you damn well won't!" Vidal roared. Grasping hold of her shoulders, he dragged her against him, kissing her with the pent-up urgency and hunger of months.

For a brief second she remained rigid as his arms imprisoned her, and then with a sob that relinquished reason, her arms circled his neck and her mouth parted willingly beneath his.

Vidal was ablaze with sensations he had never given rein to before. As her lips opened like a flower beneath his, he knew that he was experiencing not mere passion but a love that was all-consuming.

With a groan he swept her up in his arms and carried her toward the bed. Her hair brushed his flesh, fine and soft and silky. He lowered her beneath him, her robe falling apart at her breasts. His mouth was on her lips, her throat, her shoulders, and then his hand slid down, touching and possessing. She heard herself gasp, and then her breath was lost in the passion of his mouth and her body was no longer her own.

"I love you," he said urgently as her pulse thundered in her temples and her heart thudded against her breastbone. "I shall find no peace without you!"

If there was pain as he entered her, she was unaware of it. She felt only his swift intake of breath and then was lost in the near mindless pleasure of loving and being loved. Her body felt as if it were parched earth, saturated by soft, sweet rain after years of drought.

"I love you," she gasped, her body arching to meet his, her fingers burrowing deep in the thick mass of his hair. "I love you! I love you! I love you!"

Afterward there was utter stillness. His body still imprisoned her, her arms wrapped tight against him as if she would never let him go. Outside, birds twittered and the morning sunlight fell through the shutters, bathing them in golden light. Very slowly, he raised himself on one arm and looked down at her, tenderly smoothing a tendril of hair away from her damp forehead.

"You never slept with Tennant, did you?"

She smiled the gentle, intoxicated smile of a woman fulfilled. "No," she said, brushing his shoulder with her lips. "I never did."

He kissed her lingeringly and she sighed, her whole being suffused with a joy that was bone-deep.

"I should have made love to you that night on the beach," he said, his eyes glittering wickedly.

"Yes," she said, her fingers touching his body in the familiar, intimate way they had longed to do for so long. "You should."

When he made love to her again, it was with the gentleness of absolute love. Their bodies moved together in a harmony that was beyond the expectations or experience of either of them.

The sun was high in the sky when she reached across for the telephone and asked room service for breakfast for two.

"And a bottle of Bollinger," Vidal prompted, tracing the delicious curve of her breasts with his forefinger.

"And a bottle of Bollinger," she repeated, her eyes dancing. "And Beluga caviar and lots of black coffee and scrambled eggs."

"*Uristen*," Vidal groaned, "what a mixture!"

She slid down beside him, her lips burned and bruised by his kisses. "After we eat, shall we return to the studio?"

Vidal winced. For two days not a foot of film had been shot. Even now Gambetta might be rampaging over the set like a maddened bull.

"I doubt if Tennant will show his face today, but we'd better. Both the cast and the crew are going to wonder what the hell is going on."

Valentina gurgled with laughter as she pressed her naked body closer to his.

"And will you tell them?"

His eyes gleamed. "You're a wanton hussy," he said, pulling her down on top of him, his hands caressing her thighs and buttocks.

"Not so wanton that I will forgo my breakfast," Valentina said, laughing as she bit his earlobe, then slipping off the bed and into her discarded negligee as the waiter knocked on the door, a midday breakfast cart complete with champagne and caviar at his side.

Vidal sat Indian-fashion on the bed and she knelt beside him, the champagne cork flying upward. They toasted each other joyously and the champagne was ice-cold and delicious, not jaded as the many bottles of the previous evening had seemed.

"I suppose," she said, nibbling at toast and caviar, "that I shall have to unengage myself."

"At the very soonest opportunity," he said, kissing away champagne droplets that had fallen on her breast.

"And you?" she asked, resting her head against his shoulder. "How long will it take for you to unmarry yourself?"

His glass remained motionless in midair for a second or so, and then he said, with a peculiar edge to his voice, "I won't be unmarrying myself, Valentina."

She stared up at him, the joy fading from her eyes. "But you love me! I *know* that you love me! Surely you'll be getting a divorce."

"No." His sun-bronzed face was suddenly hard and uncompromising. "I do love you, but I shall never get a divorce." His voice was raw with pain as he set his champagne glass down and took her hand in his. "I shall never be able to marry you, Valentina."

For a long minute she simply did not believe him, and then, when the enormity of what he had said sank in, she backed away from him, shivering convulsively.

"I don't understand. . . . We love each other. We belong together. . . ."

He made no move toward her. "I'm married, Valentina. I have a responsibility toward my wife. She needs me."

Disappointment and hurt flooded through her. "*I* need you!" she cried, her eyes anguished. "I love you! I've always loved you! I always will love you! But I can't continue to be your lover if you stay with your wife."

Slowly he stood up and reached for his shirt. "My wife is ill," he said in low, measured tones. "I can't leave her, Valentina. Please don't ask it of me."

"But she'll get better." She threw herself on her knees before him, filled with wild hope. It wasn't that he didn't love her enough. It was that beneath his go-to-the-devil attitude he was a man of honor. "We can marry then! Oh, please, Vidal! I couldn't live if I thought we would never be married!"

The sunlight was behind her so that a nimbus of gold seemed to halo her dark hair. He cupped her chin in his hands and raised her face to his.

"No matter how bad things are, Valentina, we can always live through them."

She gazed up at him, the expression on his face awakening within her a nameless fear. For the first time she realized that the deep lines running from nose to mouth had been etched there by suffering.

"Is it so bad?" she whispered, her eyes pleading for him to deny it. To renew her hope. To make everything all right again. In that moment his eyes seemed ages old.

"Yes," he said quietly. "It's so bad."

Their eyes held and she knew that she had no decision to make. It had been made long ago when she had stood on the set of *The Black Knights* and had not even known his name.

"Then we won't speak of it again," she said with devastating simplicity. "We'll just love each other for as long as we live."

He drew her to her feet, kissing her long and deeply, knowing that she had an inner core of strength that he would always derive sustenance from. He felt no guilt toward Kariana for there was none to feel. Their life as husband and wife had ended long ago. She demanded only that he remain with her, protecting and shielding her, and he would do so.

As their lips parted they gazed at each other, aware that they were embarking on no transient affair, but a lifelong comitment.

In one brief, sunlit morning she had been transformed from a girl into a woman. She began to laugh. "The studio!" she said, her eyes dancing. "There's still time to save Rogan from drinking himself into oblivion. We could at least finish Henry's prevarication scene today."

Vidal glanced at his watch and began to dress swiftly. With luck, Harris would have held everything together. Valentina was right. They could still shoot considerable footage, if they moved fast.

As she slipped on lingerie, dress, and shoes, she watched Vidal. The strong muscles of his back rippled sensuously as he pulled on his shirt. His trousers hugged his hips, his fingers long and lean as he buckled his broad leather belt.

"Ready?" he asked as she hastily combed her disarrayed hair.

She nodded.

"Good. Let's see if we can get Tennant back on the set with the same speed."

He picked up the telephone receiver, asked for an outside line, and quickly dialed Rogan's Mulholland Drive number.

Valentina could not hear Rogan, but she could imagine his consternation as Vidal said curtly, "I'm leaving for the studio now and I expect you to be there when I arrive. If you're not, then you're off the film."

He didn't wait for Rogan to reply. The receiver crashed down on its cradle and he grabbed Valentina's hand. "I guess that gives him ten minutes at the most. Think he'll make it?"

"I hope so," she gasped as they raced through the gardens. "He's pretty resilient when he wants to be."

"He'll have to be to cope with a king-size hangover, the termination of his engagement, and the bruising he must have got when I kicked him out the door," Vidal said dryly as he bundled her into the back of the Rolls.

"Do you think he'll take it badly?" Valentina asked with concern as the car began to speed down the rhododendron-lined driveway and out onto Sunset Boulevard.

"The only thing Rogan takes badly is a bad press notice,"

Vidal said with a grin. "Don't worry about our handsome heartthrob. He'll survive."

Once at the studio, Valentina was hurried through makeup, hairdressing, and wardrobe at breakneck speed. When she walked onto the set, she was subjected to several curious glances and there were low murmurs of speculation. She smiled to herself. Let them speculate all they liked. Everything she had ever hoped for and dreamed of had come true. Vidal loved her. They would never again be apart, mentally or spiritually.

Makeup had done a skillful job of disguising the ugly bruise on Rogan's forehead.

"We'll have to shoot the whole scene from his left side," Don said, "It won't make any difference today, but we could run into difficulties tomorrow in the court scene."

"We'll shoot him in profile till it's healed," Vidal said, ignoring Rogan's malevolent glance.

"Barbarian," Rogan hissed beneath his breath to Leila. "He knows I photograph best on my right."

"What happened to you?" Leila asked curiously.

Rogan grimaced. His head hurt excruciatingly and his body felt as if it had been run over by a truck. "Hell knows," he said bitterly, "I don't."

"Places, everybody," Vidal called curtly. "I want one run-through and I want it faultless."

Rogan's eyes sought Valentina's, his eyebrows rising questioningly. They hadn't had a moment alone to talk and he wanted to know what had gone on between her and Rakoczi. After his humiliating exit he had driven home and swallowed a large brandy, terrified that Rakoczi was going to demand replacements for both of them. Then had come his telephone call and he had breathed a sigh of relief. Rakoczi had obviously realized that he wouldn't be easy to get rid of. His name carried weight at Worldwide. Gambetta wouldn't have invested so heavily in this movie if he hadn't had a star like himself to carry it. But Valentina did not have the same prestige. If she was replaced, it would mean weeks of re-shooting. The thought made him feel ill. One day longer than necessary with Rakoczi would be a day he could well do without.

Valentina, aware of his anxiety, gave him an encouraging smile as she sat on the throne next to Sutton. She would have to talk to Rogan, but the studio, with its scores of listening ears, was definitely not the right place to do so.

The anxiety in Rogan's eyes cleared. Rakoczi had obviously failed in reducing Valentina to a tearful wreck. And tonight would be a damned sight different from last night. There would be no heavy quantities of booze. He'd stay well clear of it. Tonight was a night he wanted to remember in glorious detail. He gave her the kind of smoldering glance that ladies from Cincinnati to Chattanooga lined up to see on screen, and fell on one knee before her and Sutton.

The makeup girl hurried forward and powdered the shine from Sutton's nose and forehead.

The set became suddenly quiet and there was an air of tenseness as the makeup girl retreated.

"Places, everyone," Vidal said, his eyes flicking over everything from the jaunty swing of Rogan's cloak to the carefully arranged folds of Valentina's gown. "This is a take."

"Tennant," one of the men near the cameras called, "*The Warrior Queen*, scene seven, roll 'em."

The scene was shot in two takes and there was an exhalation of relief from the cast. At last they were under way again. Rumors that Rakoczi had physically beaten Worldwide's highest-salaried male star could be indulged in later over drinks at Romanoff's or the Derby.

"Okay," Vidal said at last, well pleased with the work that had been accomplished. "That wraps it for today."

"Thank God," Rogan said to Valentina, careful that Vidal should not overhear him. "I'll pick you up from your dressing room after I've showered and changed."

She nodded. Her dressing room would be as private a place as any to break the news to Rogan that they were no longer engaged.

Vidal looked across at her, concern in his eyes. Without being told, he knew that she was about to sever her relationship with Rogan. She smiled and his concern faded. By the time she had finished with Rogan, he would think the termination of the engagement had been all his own idea.

His eyes traveled meaningfully from her eyes to her lips and she felt the color rise in her cheeks. He was making love to her without touching her, without speaking to her. Desire leapt along her veins, hot and insistent. He would be waiting for her when she had finished talking to Rogan. They would talk together, laugh together, make love together. Perhaps they would even view the day's rushes together.

"Well, well," Sutton said curiously as she hurried away to her dressing room, her eyes glowing, her face radiant. "I wouldn't have thought our dear Rogan capable of stirring such deep emotions. It seems that I've sadly underrated him."

"I'd give a lot to know how he came by those bruises," Don Symons said, picking up his jacket.

"Rakoczi, without a doubt," Sutton said, unperturbed at the thought of their director laying violent hands on his male lead.

Don shook his head. "That isn't Mr. Rakoczi's style. He can decimate Tennant verbally without resorting to physical violence."

"It does seem a little extreme," Sutton agreed. "I shall certainly ensure I don't commit the same misdemeanor. Physical abuse for the mere crime of not appearing on the set would mean my having to look for my livelihood elsewhere."

"If that was all the misdemeanor was," Don said dryly.

Sutton raised his eyebrows. "But, my dear boy, what else could it be?"

Don shrugged. "I don't know, but no doubt we'll soon find out. Tennant isn't exactly the soul of discretion."

"Mr. Tennant will be coming around in a few minutes," Valentina said as Ellie unhooked the constraining hooks and eyes on her heavy medieval robes and she stepped free of them. "Would you mind leaving when he arrives? I need to talk to him in private."

"Will you need me later?" Ellie asked, handing Valentina cleansing cream and tissues.

"No, take the evening off, Ellie."

Ellie went into the bathroom and turned on the shower, testing the water temperature carefully and putting body lotion and delicately perfumed talcum powder on the side so that they would be within Valentina's reach.

Valentina and Rogan Tennant had announced their intention of marrying only the day before. It would be natural enough if they wanted to be alone at every opportunity, but somehow she had the feeling that Valentina's request for privacy was not so that she could enjoy a lover's tryst. There was a faint frown marring her brow as she removed her makeup. Ellie felt a twinge of unease. She hoped that things had not started to go wrong already.

"What dress will you be wearing?" she asked as Valentina stepped into the shower.

"The white silk with the gold belt," Valentina called from beneath the noise of rushing water.

The Lucien Lelong white silk dress was withdrawn from the wardrobe and a pair of white kid sling-back shoes from the shoe rack. She was just about to open Valentina's jewel case for the gold earrings Valentina liked to wear with the dress, when there came a loud rap on the door.

"That will be Mr. Tennant," Valentina said, stepping from the shower and donning the terry-cloth bathrobe with satin lapels. "Let him in, please."

Ellie opened the door and Rogan stepped inside, his sleek blond hair still glistening with water from his shower, an aura of expensive cologne clinging to him.

"Good night, madam," Ellie said as Valentina moved to the drinks cart and began to pour Rogan a stiff Scotch.

The door closed behind her and Rogan put his arms around Valentina and kissed her on the nape of her neck.

"Jesus, baby, what a day. I've just had Rakoczi in my dressing room, apologizing for his behavior of this morning and begging me not to tell Gambetta."

Valentina turned and handed him his drink, knowing that he was lying. "I won't, but I didn't tell the bastard that. I'll let him suffer for a bit. If it hadn't been for you, I'd have made him suffer this morning. The hardest thing I ever did was control my temper and walk away."

Valentina felt a smile tug at her lips. Rogan hadn't walked. He had stumbled, and he hadn't been able to get away from Vidal's wrath quickly enough.

Rogan sat down and drew her on to his knee. "Did he give you a real hard time after I left?"

Valentina removed Rogan's hand from her waist and stood up, crossing the room and sitting on her dressing table stool.

"No," she said gently, "he didn't, Rogan."

Rogan looked mystified. "He was sure in one hell of a temper when I left. I was out of my mind with worry about you all morning."

Valentina dropped her eyes from his. If he had been at

all worried, he would have stayed. It made what she was about to say all the easier.

"Rogan, I want to talk to you. Not about this morning. About yesterday."

Remembering the debacle of the previous evening, Rogan felt an uncomfortable flush stain his cheeks. He forced a laugh and swallowed his drink.

"Sorry if I disappointed you, angel. Too many belts of celebration whiskey and too much champagne." He moved across to her meaningfully. "It won't happen tonight, I promise you."

"Nothing will happen tonight, Rogan," Valentina said firmly, catching his hand as he reached out to slip it beneath her robe. "I made a mistake yesterday in saying that I would marry you. It wouldn't work. I would make you terribly unhappy."

Rogan paused, wondering if he was hearing right.

"I'm sorry, and it was sweet of you to ask me," she continued, wishing that he would say something instead of looking so perplexed.

"Who told you that you'd be messing up my life if you married me?" Rogan asked at length, "Was it Romana? Honey, that woman is pure poison. There's no need to listen to a word she says."

Valentina hadn't known that Rogan had been romantically involved with Romana de Santa. The knowledge interested her, but did not disturb her.

"It wasn't Romana, Rogan. Yesterday was a mistake and I'm sorry."

"Then who the hell was it?" Rogan demanded irritably, pulling himself free of her restraining hold.

"It wasn't anyone, Rogan."

"It must have been *someone*," he said explosively, striding across to the bar and pouring himself another Scotch. "Hell, you wouldn't be playing the martyr unless someone had told you that if you loved me you'd set me free!"

Valentina regarded him with a mixture of affection and exasperation.

"No one has told me that I'd be ruining your life if I married you, Rogan," she said firmly. "That's a conclusion I came to all by myself."

Rogan drained his glass and put it down. It had been an

unpleasant day and he could have done without Valentina's sudden feelings of inferiority.

"Look, honey," he said patiently, "I know that I'm a big star and you're just starting out in this town. Sure, some people will talk and say that any future parts you get will be because you're my wife. It isn't going to bother me, so why let it bother you?"

Valentina sighed. "I'm not going to marry you, Rogan, because I don't want to."

Rogan stared at her as if she were out of her mind. She rose to her feet, wishing that he hadn't made it necessary for her to be so blunt. "I don't love you, Rogan. I never have. I've been very, very fond of you, and I thought that I could learn to love you, but now I know that I was wrong."

"You're crazy!" His voice had lost its conviction and his handsome face had paled. "Has Rakoczi been on to you? Has he told you it's against your contract to marry?"

"The decision is mine," she repeated, wondering what it would take to make Rogan believe her.

He stared at her. No one jilted Rogan Tennant. It was unheard of. "We told the whole goddamn unit," he said, his voice rising. "It'll be in the trades today! Louella will have got hold of it! The whole town will have heard of it!"

"Then you must tell Louella that it was a stunt dreamed up by the publicity department and that you felt you couldn't go along with it any longer."

"Damned right I'll tell her it was a stunt," Rogan said, white-faced. "But what about the cast and the crew? They know it was no fucking stunt!"

"I'll tell Sutton and Leila that you changed your mind," Valentina said, feeling sorry for him. "I'll tell them that you no longer wish to marry me. They'll soon spread the word."

"You'd better tell them goddamn quick!" Rogan said, his voice tight with rage and humiliation. "I'm not stepping out of here till you put the record straight and tell people the truth!"

"The truth being that you no longer wish to marry me," Valentina said soothingly.

"Damned right I don't!"

Valentina suppressed a smile, picked up the telephone receiver, and dialed Sutton's home number.

"Sutton, is that you?" Her voice held an underlying

tremble, as if she were suppressing an onrush of tears. "Sutton, the most hideous thing has happened. Rogan has walked out on me. He doesn't want to marry me. Doesn't want to see me anymore."

Rogan was mercifully too far away to hear Sutton sympathetically tell her that she was well rid of him. Next she rang Leila and listened dutifully as Leila sympathized effusively.

At last she replaced the receiver on its cradle. "Everyone will know by tomorrow morning," she said, turning toward a glowering Rogan.

"They'd better!" He seized hold of the door handle and paused. "I'm sorry about this, Valentina," he said with stiff formality, "but it just wouldn't have worked."

Valentina's eyes widened and then, as the door closed behind him, a broad smile came to her face. Rogan was already beginning to believe that the version of events she had told Leila and Sutton was the truth. By tomorrow he would have forgotten entirely that she had jilted him.

She removed her bathrobe and began to dress. Vidal would be in his office waiting for her. They would talk about *The Warrior Queen*, they would talk about themselves, they would talk about anything and everything under the sun. She slipped her feet into her shoes, slammed the door behind her, and began to run toward the ocher-tiled bungalow and the man she loved with all her heart.

He was sitting behind his desk, a score of sketches for the St. Albans location spread in front of him. He raised his head as she entered, and at the expression in his eyes her breath caught in her throat.

"Come here," he said, his dark, rich voice sending shivers down her spine. "I've waited eight hours to make love to you, and I'm not going to wait a minute longer!"

He rose to his feet and moved from behind his desk, pulling her into his arms, seeking her mouth and lowering her gently to the thickly carpeted floor.

Chapter Fourteen

Valentina stretched luxuriously against her lace-edged satin pillows as Ellie entered with her breakfast tray.

"News of tonight's premiere is splashed across the front page of both the *Examiner* and the *Times*," Ellie said, handing her the tabloids before setting the breakfast tray down.

Valentina motioned it away. "I'm sorry, Ellie, I couldn't possibly eat this morning. I'm too excited. I'll just have coffee."

Ellie looked disapproving but knew better than to waste her time arguing. She poured Valentina a strong black coffee and crossed to the vast wall of mirror-faced wardrobes as Valentina began eagerly to scan the headlines.

GAMBETTA'S MILLION-DOLLAR EPIC TO BE PREMIERED TONIGHT AT GRAUMAN'S! Louella's headline ran. *Valentina, the star set to tumble Garbo and Swanson from their thrones, must be a very nervous lady today.*

"Damned right," Valentina said, shaking open the *Los Angeles Times* and reading. The Warrior Queen *to conquer Hollywood tonight . . .* She took a sip of her coffee. . . . *The elite of the movie world will tonight judge whether Theodore Gambetta's million-dollar bet has paid off. Those in the know are already claiming that the volatile Hungarian director, Vidal Rakoczi, has produced a masterpiece.*

An inside column was headed: *Valentina: The Face of the Century.*

Valentina surveyed the accompanying photograph and then pushed the papers away. It wasn't what they said today that mattered. It was what they would say tomorrow.

The telephone rang, and she leapt for it, knowing that it would be Vidal.

"Oh, darling, I'm so nervous I can hardly breathe."

171

"Relax," Vidal said, a smile in his voice. "Tonight is going to be the biggest night of your life."

"What if they don't like it? What if . . ."

"Go down to the beach. Swim. Play tennis. Get rid of some of your nervous energy or you'll be in a state of collapse by tonight. I'll see you later."

"But you are coming for me, aren't you?" she asked anxiously. "We are still going to the theater together?"

For a year they had managed the impossible. They had managed to keep their affair untalked about in the most gossip-hungry town in the world. To arrive publicly, arm in arm, before a battery of cameras and microphones would be to invite the sort of speculation they had so far avoided. Vidal could take her because Kariana—with dark, subconscious memories of the last premiere she had attended—had no desire to meet Theodore Gambetta in the same scarlet-carpeted foyer.

"Yes," he said gently, wondering how much longer they could maintain the delicate balancing act of the last few months. "We're going together, Valentina."

"I love you," she said fervently. "Oh, God, why can't we spend the day together? Tonight is a lifetime away."

"I'm lunching with Theo. He has some damn fool idea of loaning you out to MGM simply because Mayer has offered an obscene amount for you. If he once starts to play those games, you could find yourself in all sorts of second-rate movies."

"But why does he want to loan me out?" Valentina asked, her hand tightening on the receiver. "I thought he was wild about *The Gethsemane Gate;* and *A Woman in Scarlet* is going without a hitch."

"*The Gethsemane Gate* won't be released for another six months and I've vetoed all his proposals for films to follow *A Woman in Scarlet.* He's just trying to put the screws on. Don't panic. I have a screenplay here that's perfect for you. When Theo sees it, he'll realize you're more valuable working at Worldwide than being loaned across town."

Theo was immediately forgotten. "What is it? Is it a costume drama? Is it a strong part?"

"It's a comedy," Vidal said, grinning as he heard her gasp of dismay. "Don't worry. You can handle it. You have the lightest touch I've ever seen and it will do you good to spread your wings, try something different."

"Theo will never buy it," she said despairingly. "He sees me as a femme fatale, not as a comedienne."

"You're an actress," Vidal said bluntly. "You can be anything you want to be."

"I want to be with you."

"You will be, in a few hours."

"I want to be with you all the time." Her voice was low, filled with sudden sadness. What she was really saying was that she wanted to be his wife.

"I love you," he said, knowing that he couldn't ask her the question she was longing to hear. "Be prepared for a crowd tonight. The world and his brother are going to be there and it's you that they'll want to see."

She put down the receiver slowly. There had been a time when she had firmly believed that she would never ask any more of him than he was prepared to give. But now, as their love for each other had matured and deepened, it seemed increasingly incongruous that he still remained married to someone else. A woman he no longer loved; a woman who shared none of his passion for his work. A woman he never voluntarily mentioned.

She began to dress. She was having lunch with Leila at the Beverly Hills Hotel, which she had long since vacated. Her home was now a long, low ranch house some distance from the fashionable cluster of Hollywood mansions. She liked her privacy. She had no desire to be part of the clique that met ceaselessly at a never-ending round of parties and dinners. And the remoteness of her home enabled her to see Vidal with comparative ease.

The Beverly Hills was the wrong place for lunch on a day when everyone was talking about her public debut on the screen. They left early and Leila, nearly as nervous as Valentina about the forthcoming evening, was only too happy to drive with her out along the coast road and to sit on a deserted stretch of shoreline.

"Have you any idea of what is the matter with Mrs. Rakoczi, Leila?" she asked, hugging her knees and watching the huge breakers crash into surging foam.

Leila shrugged. "Nothing that I know of," she said, picking up a pebble and spinning it out over the waves.

Valentina frowned. "She's sick, Leila. She's been sick for a long time. That's why she spends so much time away from Hollywood."

"It could be tuberculosis," Leila said reflectively. "That's the only disease I know about that requires people to spend a lot of time in places like Switzerland. That's where Mrs. Rakoczi vacations, isn't it?"

"Yes, I think so. I'm not sure." Valentina scooped up a handful of sand and let it sift through her fingers, her eyes thoughtful. If Kariana suffered from tuberculosis, it could well explain Vidal's reluctance to speak about her illness. Yet tuberculosis could be cured. And when Kariana was cured, there could be a divorce and the secrecy and discretion that they had to live with would be over. The more she thought about it, the more she was convinced that Leila was right. Tuberculosis was still regarded by many people as a shameful disease, and if Kariana received treatment in the dry mountain air near home, then it would soon have become public knowledge. Switzerland would ensure her the best doctors in the world and complete privacy.

Leila regarded her with concern. Since shooting of *The Warrior Queen* had ended, she had remained good friends with Valentina and was the only person to know that Valentina and Vidal were lovers and not just director and protégée.

"Does Vidal intend filing for divorce?" she asked tentatively.

Valentina's arms tightened around her knees. "No."

Leila bit her bottom lip, aware of problems that Valentina so far seemed oblivious of.

"It can't go on," she said quietly. "Adultery may be rife in this town, but only so long as the public doesn't get to hear of it. If they do, it's finito to any career. Even a career as prestigious as Vidal's."

Valentina felt a prickle of alarm. If loving Vidal meant sacrificing her career, then she had no qualms. Vidal came first. It had not occurred to her that Vidal's career, too, might be destroyed if news of their love for each other became public.

"That's ridiculous," she said sharply. "People change partners in Hollywood constantly."

"Yes, darling, but they tend to do it legally. They divorce and remarry."

"And then divorce and remarry again. Vidal and I aren't

like that. We're not going to change our minds about each other in a year's time. We're going to be together for always."

"Not if you're not married, you aren't," Leila said dryly. "Not in Hollywood."

Leila's words troubled Valentina for the rest of the day. As she dressed for the premiere she knew that what she had said was true. It had not taken her long to discover the hypocrisy of the new world she had entered. Anything went. Drugs, alcoholism, adultery, promiscuity, homosexuality. Every vice under the sun was happily indulged in, and condoned, just as long as news of it didn't reach the vast Bible Belt women's clubs of America via the gossip writers and the press. A damning paragraph in print could ruin a star overnight. She surveyed herself in her dressing table mirror. Her hair curved onto her cheekbones, dark and sleek. Her silver lamé gown clung sensuously, very décolleté, the back plunging to her waist. Tonight was not the time for dark thoughts. Tonight was going to be the most important night of her life. . . .

Vidal's white tie and tails failed to turn him into an archetypal socialite. He stood in the doorway, a tall, dark man with powerful shoulders and the lean grace of a jungle cat.

Valentina broke away from Ellie, her zip only half done up, and ran toward him. "You look marvelous, Vidal! Just like an aristocrat in one of Cecil B. De Mille's movies!"

He caught hold of her and held her against him tightly. "I *am* an aristocrat," he said dryly. "If I wanted, I could put a string of legitimate titles before my name."

She remembered his cigarette case and the diamond and the engraved crest. "Then why don't you?" she asked curiously. "Americans love titles."

"Because I left that part of my life behind a long time ago and I have no desire to drag the remnants of it into the present."

She slid her arms around him. He constantly surprised her. There were times when she wondered if she would ever know everything about him.

"I don't care if you're a prince or a peasant. I love you just the same," she said, her face alight with the love she felt for him.

"Then, perhaps Ellie wouldn't mind leaving us in privacy for a few moments."

"But I'm not ready!" she protested, horrified. "My hair isn't done. I haven't even finished dressing."

"It's very important," he said gravely.

She was seized with panic. Did Theo still want her to go to MGM?

Vidal raised an eyebrow slightly in Ellie's direction and she hastily left the room, closing the door behind her.

"Doesn't Theo like the idea of me doing comedy? Is he unhappy with the work I'm doing on *A Woman in Scarlet*. . . ?"

"Yes to the first question, no to the second," Vidal said, his voice thickening as he slid her zip down to the base of her spine and kissed the curve of her jaw.

"Then what was so important that you asked Ellie to leave?" she asked in bewilderment.

His lips brushed her ear, moving purposefully to her mouth as he slid the straps of her gown off her shoulders, and the lamé slithered into a silver pool around her ankles.

"Vidal! No! We haven't time! I'm late already and we're due at the theater in twenty minutes. People are waiting for us!" she protested as his intentions became transparently clear.

"Let them wait," he said in hungry, hoarse tones that sent desire leaping through her veins, so that her need for him was as primitive as his for her. Theo, the star-studded audience arriving at Grauman's, the throng outside—were all forgotten.

Within minutes he was as naked as she was while the mob of fans around the theater shrieked and screamed, as Sutton and Leila arrived and Rogan Tennant descended from his leopard-skin-upholstered Lancia, the star of the movie and its director made ferocious, savage love, uncaring of time and oblivious of anything and everything but each other.

"My goodness!" Valentina said, her hand clasped tightly in Vidal's as their Rolls edged toward the theater. "Is it always like this for a premiere?"

Shouting, cheering fans jostled the car, cramming the street for blocks in every direction.

"No, thank God. We have Theo's publicity machine to thank for this bear garden."

A motorcycle cop drew up at the side of the Rolls and Vidal lowered the window. The sound from outside was deafening.

"I'm sorry, sir. There's no way we can clear the street for the car to continue. I'm afraid we'll have to escort you on foot."

"Through that crowd?" Valentina asked, her face paling.

Vidal's eyes were grim. "He's right, Valentina. If this car moves another inch, it's going to mow someone down. Stay close to me and don't let go of my hand. Not for a second."

The police surrounded them when they stepped out of the Rolls. A great cheer went up and as they inched tortuously toward the theater's entrance, there were chants of "Val-en-tina! Val-en-tina!"

"This," Vidal shouted to her over the din, "is stardom!"

Valentina gasped, stumbling against him as the crowd jostled the encircling policemen. "They haven't seen me on screen yet!"

"They don't need to with all the brouhaha there's been about you. Don't look so frightened. Smile, even if the effort nearly kills you."

The incessant clicking of flashbulbs, some only inches away from her face, were blinding. Barricades had been erected in front of the theater and hysterical fans surged against them, so that Valentina expected any moment they would give way and she would be crushed underfoot. Hands from every direction were reaching out to touch her.

The only way she could cope with her rising panic was to pretend none of it was real. That it was the scene from a film. She blew kisses, she smiled, and the crowd went wild. The chants of "Valentina" could still be heard as they entered the lobby.

Theo and a troop of ushers rushed toward them.

"Have you ever seen anything like it?" Theo demanded ecstatically. "We're in the process of making Hollywood history! Tonight's a night that won't be repeated for a hundred years!"

Vidal, accustomed to Theo's extravagant superlatives, merely nodded, eager to escort Valentina away from the still blinding flashlights and toward the main aisle door.

"Let's move, Theo. Valentina isn't accustomed to all this ballyhoo."

"This ballyhoo is making her the most-talked-about star of the decade," Theo said, circling Valentina's naked shoulders with his arm for the benefit of the cameras. "She's a natural. Just listen to them! They love her!"

"They don't know a thing about me," Valentina protested with a smile as Theo blew wreaths of blue cigar smoke upward.

"And that's the way to keep it," Theo said, turning away from the cameras and reporters at last and moving toward the dark inner lobby. "Once they know anything resembling truth, they lose interest. Fantasy is what they want. Fantasy on screen and fantasy in their stars' private lives. Feed them plenty of fantasy, my dear, and you'll never go far wrong."

With her arm lightly through the crook of Vidal's arm, she entered the auditorium. There were faces she had seen only in movie magazines. Joan Crawford looking devastating in a high-necked black sequined gown, the expression on her face cynical. Bette Davis in scarlet silk, a white rose at her throat, a smile on her lips as their gazes met fleetingly. Clark Gable and Carole Lombard. Marion Davies and William Randolph Hearst. Irving Thalberg, production chief of MGM, cheek by jowl with his boss, Louis B. Mayer.

Dazedly she accompanied Vidal to the place of honor and then the lights dimmed and her fingers closed tightly around Vidal's. This was it. Her whole professional future lay in the reception of her performance by the movie stars, critics, columnists, and moguls in the audience. She couldn't bear to look at the screen. She kept her eyes tightly shut and prayed.

It seemed to take forever. At last she heard her final lines. A swift sword slash had ended the life of her seventeen-year-old son at the bloody battle of Tewkesbury. Her husband had been murdered on the orders of the usurper of the throne, Edward. All she had fought for so valiantly and courageously was lost. And yet as she sat on the prow of the boat taking her back to France and to exile, there was still something indomitable about her. Her inner spirit was unquenched. The white cliffs of England faded into the distance and she whispered a last good-bye to the land she had loved; to her dead husband and child.

There was a long silence and then the lights went up and there were tears in the eyes of everyone in the audience.

"They don't like it," she whispered frantically to Vidal. "They don't like it!" And then the cheering began and she thought she would faint with relief.

People were standing, clapping thunderously. The aisles were jammed and there was no way they could leave their seats. Flowers began to fly through the air in her direction. Corsages of orchids, carnations from buttonholes, roses, sprays of gardenias.

Theo climbed up onto the stage and made a speech that could barely be heard above the din of applause. Then he was gesturing for Vidal and Valentina and Rogan. The whole theater was a blaze of light. Laughing and crying at the same time, she was deluged with more flowers.

"It's a triumph!" Theo kept saying, tears of emotion in his eyes. "A triumph!"

There was no way they could leave by the front entrance. The head usher led them through the orchestra pit and backstage, the roar of those who had come to criticize and deride loud in their ears.

She sank back into the rear of the Rolls, exhausted.

"Happy?" Vidal asked as they sped through the darkened streets to her home.

"I'm speechless. I never expected anything like that. It was amazing. Unbelievable."

"It was a tribute to your talent," Vidal said as she rested her head against his shoulder. "Every star in town was there tonight thanks to Theo's publicity machine. Every director, every president of every movie company of any account. And they came to see you fall flat on your face. That's the kind of town Hollywood is. It can also be breathtakingly generous with praise when it's deserved."

"Do you think *The Gethsemane Gate* will be just as popular? It's such a different movie. Perhaps people will expect *The Warrior Queen* to be followed by another costume drama, not a story set in World War I."

"Every movie is a risk. That's what makes the business so exciting. I've no desire to make safe, uncontroversial pictures that don't stretch me creatively."

"And I've no desire to star in them," she said, sliding her arms around his waist, holding him close. "Do you think Theo will still want to loan me out to MGM?"

Vidal grinned down at her. "Now, now, my love. Mayer couldn't afford Theo's price!"

A Woman in Scarlet was completed and Vidal's comedy, *The Heiress Helena*, was already well under way when Valentina began to feel sick.

The Warrior Queen and *The Gethsemane Gate* were playing in packed houses all over the country. She had become the star that Theo had promised she would be. She had a luxurious house, a fabulous wardrobe, the adulation of millions, and the love of Vidal. Her cup was full and overflowing and she lived each moment with a joy that was contagious.

When she first began to vomit in the morning, Ellie had eyed her anxiously.

"Are you sure you're not overworking? You haven't taken any time off between pictures. What you need is a holiday."

"I love working, Ellie. I'm fine. It's probably the quenelles of lobster I ate last night at La Golondrina. I'll be okay in an hour or two."

She was. But the next day the same thing happened again. And the next.

"I think I'd better go to the doctor," she said, emerging from the bathroom, white-faced. "I feel dreadful. I can't even keep toast down. I must have a bug of some sort."

"Are you sure that's all you've got?" Ellie asked, straightening the sheets on the bed with unnecessary vigor.

"What else could it be?" Valentina asked, pushing away a cup of coffee before the sight of it should induce another attack of nausea.

"When was the last time you menstruated?" Ellie asked bluntly, thumping the pillows.

Valentina stared at her. "I don't know. What's that got to do with it?"

"Everything," Ellie said succinctly. "For a very bright lady you can be very dense at times. No periods and plenty of sickness adds up to one thing in my book."

Valentina sank onto her dressing table stool, her face drained of blood.

"I couldn't be. . . . It isn't possible. . . ."

"Well," Ellie said, her eyes dark with concern, "only you

know that, but if I were you I'd get along to a doctor right away."

Valentina passed a hand across her stomach wonderingly. A child? Vidal's child. It was something she had never imagined. "Call Dr. Helmann for me, Ellie. Tell him I want to see him right away. This morning."

"And the studio?"

"Call Mr. Rakoczi and tell him I won't be in till later. I'm not needed this morning. It won't disrupt his schedule."

Ellie did as Valentina asked, reflecting that if Valentina *were* pregnant, it would disrupt far more than his schedule.

"No doubt about it," Dr. Helmann said as she stepped back into her skirt. "You're at least two months pregnant. Possibly going on three."

Dr. Helmann was well aware of his patient's identity. And well aware of her single status.

"I don't perform abortions myself, but I recommend Dr. Gramercy highly. He's efficient and he's discreet. You'll need a week of rest afterward, but within ten days you'll be back before the cameras as if nothing had happened."

Valentina stared at him. "I have no intention of having an abortion, Dr. Helmann."

This time it was the doctor's turn to stare. "But, my dear girl, you have no choice! Haven't you seen the small print on your contract? 'Moral turpitude.' No studio in town could touch you if you flaunted an irregular sex life so openly. It's either an abortion or marriage, my dear. Anything else would be professional suicide."

She drew on her gloves. "Better professional suicide than the murder of my unborn child," she said quietly.

Dr. Helmann shrugged. "I think you're making a great mistake, but it's your decision. Come back to me if you change your mind and I'll give you a letter of introduction to Dr. Gramercy."

"Thank you, Dr. Helmann," she said, walking toward the door. "I don't think we'll be seeing each other again. Good-bye."

Valentina sat behind the wheel of her yellow Pierce-Arrow uncaring that without headscarf and dark glasses she was likely to draw attention.

The years rolled away and she was vividly aware of a young woman with blond hair and a baby in her arms, driving in a Model T Ford across the sun-parched earth to the convent at San Juan Capistrano. A woman who had not wanted the baby she had held. Who had given her child away and driven off, never returning. Never writing.

Her hands tightened on the wheel. The baby she was carrying would not be left loveless and alone. It would be loved and cherished. She felt such a surge of deep pleasure that she could hardly breathe. *Her* baby. Vidal's baby. There was only another four weeks of shooting on *The Heiress Helena*. She could accomplish those easily without arousing anyone's suspicions. But after that there could be no more films. Not for at least a year.

She put the car into gear and drew away from the curb. She would need to find a really good obstetrician; she would need to turn one of the rooms at the ranch into a nursery. She would need a hundred and one things. Baby clothes, a crib, a rocker. She edged into the stream of traffic going down Rodeo Drive. She had to see Vidal. She had to tell him the news immediately. The breeze lifted her smoke-dark hair away from her cheeks and she threw back her head, suffused with a feeling of pure joy.

A baby was the last thing either of them had intended, but it had happened. They were about to become parents. Vidal had six or seven months in which to persuade Kariana to divorce him and enable their baby to be born legitimately.

She headed out toward the studio. Both she and Vidal had more money than they knew what to do with. Whatever treatment Kariana required, it would not suffer in quality if she divorced Vidal. She had sympathized with his sense of responsibility toward Kariana, but now his responsibility was toward her and their unborn child. A Mexican divorce would take only a few months. In less than a year they would be a family.

The studio gates opened with swift deference as her Pierce-Arrow approached. Vidal's joy at the prospect of a child would be as deep as her own. A production director walked by and she waved and smiled. They would tell no one. She would take a vacation until his divorce was final, and once they were married they would ride out the ensuing storm together.

With the thunderous success of *The Warrior Queen*, Theo had insisted on teaming her with Rogan in both *A Woman in Scarlet* and her present movie, *The Heiress Helena*. Rogan's hurt pride had long been forgotten. He had married Romana de Santa a year ago and their marriage had already earned them the nickname of the "tussling Tennants."

"Hi, Rogan," she called as she walked onto the set. "Where's Vidal?"

"Answering a telephone call in his office. I guess it was private. He refused to take it here."

Valentina nodded and began to walk across to Vidal's bungalow. There were no secrets between them. He wouldn't mind her walking in on a business call. She smiled to herself, amused at how unaware he was that their lives were about to be devastatingly transformed.

"She's gone!" Hazel Renko said, her voice high-pitched with anxiety. "I knew she was heading for another breakdown. She's been edgy and moody for days. This morning she just went off on a tangent at Chai. I went to get some sleeping pills to knock her out before it got out of hand, but when I got back to the living room, she'd disappeared."

"Did she take a car?" Vidal rasped out.

"Yes, the Duesenberg."

"I'll be right over."

There was a sob in Hazel's throat. "She was only wearing her nightdress, Mr. Rakoczi. I've checked and all her coats are still here, and her negligees and wraps."

"Dear Christ!" Vidal slammed the receiver down and rounded his desk as Valentina opened the door.

"I've something to tell you," she said, her eyes glowing.

"Not now," he said, continuing his swift stride to the door. "I have to go."

"No!" She seized his arm. "This is important, Vidal. Please sit down for a moment and listen to me."

"Kariana is ill. I must get back to Villada immediately. I'll see you later. We'll have dinner at Chasen's."

"I said it was important," she said, her voice rising.

"Later," he said with a peremptory wave as he slid into the rear of the Rolls.

"*Vidal! Wait!*" She began to run after him, but it was too late. The Rolls was already speeding toward the main gates.

She halted, staring after it, all her joy of the morning replaced by a slow, burning anger.

Kariana. It was always Kariana. Yet he didn't love her. Didn't make love to her. Of that she had no doubt. Her fingers clenched tightly over the white leather of her purse. No woman could be ill with any disease for as long as Kariana and still appear in public, brimming with apparent good health. Even Vidal did not seem to know exactly what it was that was wrong with her. After her talk with Leila, she had asked him if it was tuberculosis, but he had said no, and that it wasn't such an easily defined disease.

"I bet it isn't!" Valentina said to herself, her eyes bright with fury. "That bitch hasn't a damned thing wrong with her!"

She marched purposefully across to her Pierce-Arrow. She was now certain of what she had suspected for a long time. Kariana Rakoczi was a hypochondriac. She enjoyed playing the invalid whenever it suited her. No doubt it gave her a sense of perverted power to be able to summon Vidal away from his work whenever she desired. Well, Kariana had done it for the last time. She was going up to Villada herself. She was going to confront the malingering Kariana, reclining like a latter-day Elizabeth Barrett Browning on her sickbed, and she was going to open Vidal's eyes once and for all to the triviality of his wife's so-called illness.

She swerved out onto the road, her face grim. She didn't like what she was going to do, but she had no choice. Vidal was being tied to a long-dead marriage under false pretenses. The sooner he realized the truth, the sooner they could start to build a life together. A life that would include their child.

As she approached Villada she was surprised to see that the high wrough-iron gates were open. She drove through, parking behind Vidal's Rolls.

Taking a deep breath, she stepped out onto the smoothly raked gravel and walked toward the main door. That, too, was open. She paused, and then knocked with all the firmness that she could muster.

Instead of Chai answering her, a young woman dashed to the door, her hair looking as if she had just run her hands through it, her eyes wild.

"Oh, God! I thought it was . . ." She paused, leaning against the door, regaining her composure with difficulty.

"I'm sorry. Mr. and Mrs. Rakoczi aren't home at the moment." Without even asking if she could take a message, she began to close the door in Valentina's face.

Valentina slipped past her into the marble-floored hall. "I know that Mrs. Rakoczi is not feeling very well, and I know that Mr. Rakoczi is home. I would like to see him, please," she said firmly.

"*Hazel!*" Vidal shouted urgently from an inner room.

"Will you please leave, I . . ."

Valentina ignored the hand that was physically pushing her toward the door and marched toward the sound of Vidal's voice.

"Stop! You can't go in there!" the woman cried, running after her and seizing her arm.

Valentina shook herself free, convinced that whoever the woman was, she needed psychiatric treatment.

At the threshold of the living room she paused, her eyes widening in amazement. Instead of Kariana reclining limply on a sofa, Vidal at her side, the room was a hive of feverish activity.

Vidal's chauffeur was on one telephone, Vidal on another, and Chai was wringing his hands and moaning as if he had just had news of a terrible disaster.

"Try every hospital in town!" Vidal yelled across to his chauffeur, and then to the person on the phone, "Someone must report seeing her soon. It's noon and she's only wearing a nightdress!"

"Was that the police?" the woman who had followed Valentina into the room asked, crossing to Vidal's side.

"Yes," he said tersely. "They've had no reports in yet. Riley, go downtown. Hazel, take your Packard and comb Beverly Hills. Chai, I want you here to take any calls that come in."

"Where are you going to search?" Hazel asked, grabbing her car keys.

"The home of every male she's on nodding acquaintance with," Vidal said, his nostrils pinched and white, his skin taut across his cheekbones.

They all turned, heading for the door. At the sight of Valentina everyone, including Vidal, momentarily halted.

"Get going," he said sharply to Hazel and Riley, and then to Valentina, "What the hell are you doing here?"

His rage had never before been directed at her. "I came to see you . . . to see Kariana. . . ." She faltered, aware that something was terribly, terribly wrong.

"I'll see you tonight. If she's found by then," he said curtly, striding past her and toward the open front door. Hazel's Packard could be heard roaring down the drive, Riley hot on her heels in the Rolls.

"What do you mean, found?" Valentina asked, running at his side in an effort to keep up with him as he marched across to the garage and the custom-built Voisin he rarely used. "I thought she was ill, not lost."

Vidal wrenched open the garage door. "She is ill," he said savagely, slamming the door of the car behind him and revving the engine. "But her illness isn't of the body, but the mind. My wife's a schizophrenic. Now do you understand?"

The car reversed sharply out onto the drive. "For weeks, months sometimes, she's sweet, gentle, sane, and then this happens!"

Valentina stumbled after the car. "But she'll be all right, won't she?"

"No, she won't!" Vidal yelled, his face contorted with agony. "She'll be sleeping with men she hasn't even met before! She'll be walking Sunset Boulevard at midday in nothing but a goddamn nightdress or less! She'll be getting herself jailed, raped, or beaten. And afterward, whatever happens to her, she'll have no goddamn memory of it!"

The Voisin roared away from her, leaving her standing in a cloud of dust. Slowly the dust settled. A hummingbird darted from the trees, its wings flashing gold and vermilion in the sunlight. She couldn't move. She stood there long after the sound of the Voisin had faded into the still air.

She was pregnant by a man who could never marry her, in a town where such a sin would be seen as an act of flagrant carelessness and would never be condoned. She would be ostracized by those who had fawned on her. The press would pillory her. The wrath of the Legion of Decency would descend on her like the wrath of God and every women's club in America would be outraged.

If she had her baby, her career would be over. Like a stab to the heart, piercing through the numbness she felt, came another realization. Not only would her career be over, but Vidal's as well.

She opened the car door and half fell into the seat. She could have her baby and ruin Vidal. Or she could have her baby and never identify the father. It would mean losing him. Living without his love. She felt faint, as if everything in her were being wrenched apart. She clenched the steering wheel tightly.

If she told Vidal the truth, he would have to choose between her and Kariana. She knew instinctively that he would choose her, and she knew also that their future life together would be tainted by Kariana's shadow. Loving him, she had no choice. She had to protect him from the scandal of being publicly denounced as a married man who had fathered a child outside wedlock. If that news were made public, he would never work in Hollywood again.

"Damn them for their hypocrisy," she whispered to herself, the tears coursing down her cheeks. "Why should it matter to anyone who the father of my baby is? Why should it matter to them if I am married or single? Why should it matter to anyone but me?" But in Hollywood, for a star as famous as she, it did matter and she knew it.

She eased the car through the still open gates. She would have to be seen around town with other men. There would have to be public doubt as to the identity of the father of her child. And there would have to be more than doubt in Vidal's mind. He would have to be told quite categorically that the baby was not his. And he would have to believe it.

She began to cry softly as the car took the first of the canyon's curving bends. Vidal had said that she was a great actress. She would have to be to carry out the part she now intended to play.

Chapter Fifteen

He telephoned her late that evening. "I'll pick you up in fifteen minutes," he said, sounding unutterably weary. "We'll eat at Chasen's."

"Kariana? Is she all right?" she asked anxiously.

"Hazel found her just as she was about to enter a club downtown. Fortunately there weren't many people around and those who did see her didn't recognize her. She's asleep now. Tomorrow morning she won't even remember leaving the house."

Her heart broke at the pain in his voice and the knowledge of the further pain she was about to inflict on him.

"I'll see you in a few minutes," she said, her voice unsteady, her hand trembling violently as she replaced the receiver.

Would tonight be the last time they would meet each other as lovers? The thought was unendurable. She would ask him one last time if they had any future together. Surely Kariana had a family who could care for her. Wally Barren had said she came from one of the most prestigious families on the East Coast.

Hope grew and she clung to it tenaciously as she sprayed Arpège on her throat and shoulders, then emphasized the deep color of her eyes with soft eye shadow.

"Please God, let him say yes," she whispered as she fastened a rope of pearls around her neck. "Please let everything be all right. Please! *Please!*"

He took her in his arms the minute he entered the room, kissing her long and lingeringly, and with deep need.

"Today has been hell," he said when he at last released her. "Let's have a drink, and dinner, and talk."

"Yes," she said, picking up her purse, striving for composure. "We have a lot to talk about, Vidal."

At Chasen's the headwaiter approached with a deferential inclination of the head and Vidal asked for a table in the most secluded booth in the restaurant. Neither of them was interested in perusing the menu and Vidal left their order to the waiter's discretion.

When they were alone, he took her hand in his across the table. "I'm sorry you walked in on that scene this morning. You must have wondered what in hell was going on."

"I did. At first . . ." Her fingers tightened in his. "Why didn't you tell me before, Vidal? I had no idea that Kariana was . . . was sick in that way."

"Nor does anyone else. Only the household staff, and Theo."

"What about her family?"

His expression became grim. "They know that she is unbalanced, but they don't know how badly."

"But why not? Surely you should tell them? They could help."

Vidal's voice was bitter. "I've spoken to them and don't intend doing so ever again. Their solution to any problem that might embarrass them is to pretend it doesn't exist. Failing that, their solution is to hide it."

"I don't understand." She was trembling. Kariana's parents *had* to help. If they did not, how could Vidal come to her? Marry her?

"If Kariana returns home and behaves just once as she did today, then the ultrarespectable Dansarts will have her very swiftly, and very privately, institutionalized."

Valentina's lips were so dry that she could hardly force the words past them. "Is that perhaps what she needs?" she asked falteringly, unable to make her eyes meet his.

"*No!*" Vidal snatched his hand from hers and ran it through his thick hair. "For most of the time she's perfectly sane. I know that's hard for you to believe after the way we behaved today when she was missing, but it's true. She's very gentle. Very shy."

"Then what is it?" she asked bewilderedly. "What happens to her?"

"I don't know," he said despairingly. "For no reason she begins to change. She becomes moody and edgy and irrational. Sometimes it culminates in a storm of tears and verbal abuse. Sometimes it's like today. She goes off with men she doesn't know. Even worse, she's quite likely to go off with men that she *does* know. Her language becomes vile and she doesn't seem to know if she's dressed or naked."

They fell silent as the waiter poured their wine. When he had gone, Vidal said, "An institution is no answer. It would terrify her. For most of the time she wouldn't know why she was there."

"But she must *know* that she is ill!"

"She knows there are days that she cannot recall. And she knows that her behavior during those periods is . . . embarrassing." He paused, his eyes darkening. "She knows enough now to live in fear."

"Is that why she goes away?" she asked, the hope that she had cherished diminishing.

"Yes, there's a doctor in Switzerland that she trusts implicitly. I've tried other doctors in New York and Los Angeles, but none of them has been able to help her."

Valentina remembered her brief glimpse of Kariana when Vidal had brought her down to the studio to see one of the sets for *The Warrior Queen*. She had been ethereally beautiful. There had been fragility in the delicate movements of her hands, sweetness in the low tones of her voice. And some monstrous affliction transformed that delicacy into coarseness and promiscuity. She felt sick. It was a horror too great to imagine. It was an obscenity.

"I'm so sorry," she said, her voice thick with unshed tears. She was sorry for Kariana. Sorry for Vidal. And sorry for herself and the child that she carried.

The waiter set two plates of hors d'oeuvres before them. Neither of them reached for a fork.

"Is there no solution? None at all?"

He shook his head. "Only to carry on as I have done for the last few years. To have Hazel Renko in the house when I am absent. To take Kariana out on her good days and to protect her from herself on her bad days."

In a mirror at the far side of the room Valentina could see herself clearly. Her soft dark hair dipped forward in deep waves at her cheekbones; her eyes were luminous and thick-lashed; her mouth full and generously curved, painted a warm pink instead of the fashionable red. She was beautiful.

She was rich. She was famous. She was loved. She could remain all those things if she accepted Dr. Helmann's advice and had an abortion. It would be so simple. So easy. And for her, so wrong. She could not murder Vidal's child. She would rather murder herself.

Her gaze returned to his. She could no longer put off asking the question that her future life depended upon. "Is there no way that we can ever be married?"

The deep pain in his eyes was her answer. "No," he said gently. "I have promised Kariana that she will never have to face the dark alone. It is a promise that I cannot break."

The walls of the restaurant seemed to close in on her. This was worse than the moment when she had stood in the Reverend Mother's study. It was even worse than the moment when she had discovered that Vidal was married. It was worse than anything she had ever experienced.

At a nearby table Ronald Colman could be heard ordering steak tartare. Gloria Swanson had just entered with her husband. All around her, people were eating, talking, laughing, and she was dying piecemeal, her world in ruins; her dreams turned to ashes.

"Why did you come to Villada this morning?" Vidal was asking curiously.

She stared at him, not understanding at first what it was that he was saying. He repeated the question and she replied, "I . . . I . . . I came instead of one of the crew. It wasn't important. A key had been lost. Don thought you might have had a spare one."

"Which key?" Vidal asked, puzzled.

"I don't know, I've forgotten. It's all right. It was found."

Dr. Helmann had been unable to say whether she was two months pregnant or three. If she was three months pregnant, she had no time to spare. Unless she made the break now, Vidal would know the baby was his.

And if he did? She closed her eyes. He would leave Kariana and acknowledge the baby. Kariana would be left to face the world and her nightmares alone. Her tragedy would continue to be their tragedy. Vidal would never be able to free himself of the guilt he would feel at abandoning her. Their happiness would be built upon the destruction of the woman he had once loved.

She opened her eyes and gazed across at him. His hair

curled low at the nape of his neck, thick and springy as heather. There were gold flecks near the pupils of his eyes so that in the restaurant's soft lights they seemed to flame like amber. Fatigue had etched deep lines around his mouth, but nothing could detract from the handsomeness of his lean, dark face. There was harshness as well as tenderness there. Sensuality as well as sensitivity. It was a face that would burn within her mind forever.

"Would you mind if I went home, Vidal?" she asked unsteadily. "I don't feel very well."

His brows flew together in concern. In the soft light of the restaurant her eyes were blue-shadowed, her face pale.

"Of course not. You should have said so earlier. We'll leave immediately."

"No." She put a hand on his restrainingly. It would be the last time she would touch him. A hot onrush of tears stung her eyes. "I'd rather go alone," she said, rising to her feet. "The chauffeur is waiting." Her lips were stiff and cracked, her voice that of a stranger.

He stared at her incredulously. "Of course I'm not going to let you go home alone!"

He rose to his feet and hysteria welled up in her like a submerging tide. If he touched her, held her, she would never be able to finish what she had set out to do. She tried to speak, to say good-bye, but her voice broke in an anguished gasp. Spinning on her heel, she ran blindly from the room before he could seize her. Running past startled diners and waiters. Running until she was out in the street, tears raining down her cheeks.

"Anywhere!" she gasped to her chauffeur, pulling open the rear door and stumbling inside. "Please! Quickly! Anywhere!"

"*Valentina!*" He was only yards behind her. She could hear the beat of his running feet, and then the limousine swerved away from the curb and entered the mainstream of traffic.

For a fleeting second she caught a glimpse of Vidal's agonized face as he shouted her name again and again, and then he was left far behind and she fell like a broken doll across the seat, crying as if she would never stop.

She didn't go to the studio the next day and she moved from the home she had grown to love into a small bungalow at the Garden of Allah hotel. Her residence there would not remain a secret for long, but it would ensure that Vidal would not appear on her doorstep that evening.

There was a bar, a swimming pool, and several other bungalows occupied mainly by screenwriters. She had no intention of staying for long. Only until *The Heiress Helena* was completed.

The books Vidal had given her looked strange in their new home. She ran her finger across their spines, reluctant to make the telephone call that had to be made. She was the most sought-after woman in Hollywood, and yet she had no date for that evening. And she could not wait until the word spread that she was no longer living the life of a hermit. She had only weeks in which to convince Vidal that the child she carried was not his.

Reluctantly she moved across to the cream-colored telephone and dialed Sutton Hyde's number.

"Darling, what a delightful surprise," Sutton said, putting down the script he had been reading. "To what do I owe this pleasure?"

"I wondered if you could do me a favor, Sutton?"

"I would be only too pleased," the English actor said sincerely. "Your wish is my command, my dear."

"I've lived the quiet life for too long, Sutton. I want to go out and enjoy myself."

"A reasonable enough desire," Sutton said equably. "In what way can I be of help?"

She fumbled for a cigarette and lighter with her free hand. "I know it sounds ridiculous, Sutton, but I want to go out this evening and I haven't a date. I thought perhaps you might know someone who could be my escort and that we could go out in a foursome."

Sutton chortled. "My dear Valentina, every male in town, including those under the age of puberty and over the age of senility, are simply panting to be seen at your side. Just leave it all to me. We'll pick you up at eight."

"I'm not at the ranch any longer, Sutton."

"Curiouser and curiouser. Just whereabouts are you?"

She told him and Sutton rang off, reaching for his address book. A little intrigue would be very welcome. Life had become rather dull of late.

His finger leafed the pages idly. Barrymore? Cooper? Donat? Grant?

His wife came in and leaned over his shoulder. "What are you doing, darling? You look very engrossed."

"I've just had an interesting telephone call from Valentina. She's lonely and would like to go out with us this evening in a foursome."

"And who is her escort?" his wife asked, perching on the arm of his chair.

"That, my dear, is just what is so intriguing. She hasn't one. I am to play matchmaker."

"Then, for goodness' sake, ignore all those men you named. Why not ask Paulos if he is free this evening?"

"Paulos Khairetis, the Greek pianist?"

"Yes, he would be far more suitable. He's cultured, intelligent, breathtakingly handsome, and mercifully free from the egotism and vanity afflicting most of your friends."

Sutton looked pained. "I hope I don't fall into the same category as my friends, my dear."

She kissed him on the top of a hairline too rapidly receding. "You, Sutton, are the vainest man I know. Ring Paulos and tell him Valentina is an angel and not at all like the screen goddesses he has avoided so far."

"Doesn't the fact that he *has* avoided them rather make you think Paulos's sexual proclivities may lead in other directions?"

Claire Hyde rose to her feet. "You really are the most awful fool, darling. Paulos Khairetis is undoubtedly heterosexual. Just because he doesn't hunt, shoot, fish, and whore doesn't make him any less masculine."

"Then Paulos it is," Sutton said, trusting his wife's judgment in this matter as he did in all others.

He reached for the telephone and dialed the Beverly Wilshire, asking to be put through to Mr. Khairetis.

"No, thank you, Sutton," Paulos said when Sutton had announced his reason for calling. "Your narcissistic ladies of the screen leave me cold."

"This one, dear boy, is far, far different," Sutton said chidingly. "She is one of nature's miracles. A natural beauty with flair and charisma and the sensitivity of a nun."

Paulos laughed. "I may not know Hollywood very well,

my friend, but one thing I do know, and that is that no nun would flourish in its midst."

"Convent-reared, as I live and breathe," Sutton continued, undeterred. "I have promised that we will pick her up at eight."

"No!" Paulos protested, a note of alarm creeping into his voice. But it was too late. Sutton had rung off.

He replaced the receiver slowly. Valentina: Would she be as stunningly beautiful in the flesh as she was on screen? He doubted it. It would be a physical impossibility. She would be like all the other actresses he had been introduced to in the three months he had been in town. She would have no conversation except when the subject was herself. She would be totally self-absorbed, self-centered, and a hollow mockery of the deep and dazzling personality she appeared to be on the screen. He had seen all her movies. His expression was suddenly somber. Where Valentina was concerned, he had no desire to have his illusions shattered.

Valentina surveyed herself in the mirror. She had to look vibrantly beautiful, sparklingly happy, this evening. Her eyes were swollen from the tears she had shed, bruised with grief. She had made her decision. Now she had to act on it. There could be no turning back.

At seven o'clock she took a gown of brilliant green flowing chiffon from her closet and began to dress. She picked up her perfume spray and then put it down again. It was Arpège. The perfume she had worn whenever she was with Vidal. She would not wear it again.

Rogan had long ago given her a present of Je Reviens by Worth. She sprayed it on her throat and wrists, wondering which famous Hollywood womanizer was to be her date for the evening. The doorbell rang and she answered it herself. She had told Ellie to take a holiday and did not expect to see her until her new way of life was firmly established. Ellie would know immediately what it was that she was doing, and she wasn't strong enough yet to face Ellie's censure.

"Darling, you look like a gift from the gods," Sutton cooed, kissing her on the cheek and entering her room to survey it with raised brows. It was, to say the least, modestly furnished and there was no sign of a maid.

"Let me introduce you to Paulos. He came over to compose music for Louis B., but he insists he is disenchanted with Hollywood and is returning as speedily as possible to the cultural worlds of Paris and Rome."

For a second Paulos did not move. Her hair looked as if it had been strung with beads of light. Everything about her glittered and shimmered. Everything but her eyes. They were smoke-dark, filled with inestimable sadness. He stepped forward and took her hand, aware of a growing sense of wonder.

Valentina was aware first of surprise, and then of relief. The young man holding her hand in a cool, firm grasp was not a familiar figure from the Hollywood merry-go-round of premieres and parties. His eyes were gray and intelligent. His face, fine-boned.

"I'm delighted to meet you," he said sincerely, and the speculating, lecherous look that she had become accustomed to was refreshingly absent.

"Is Paulos a Russian name?" she asked, picking up her wrap.

"No, Greek."

There was a pleasant quality to his voice, and though he took her arm as they stepped out toward the car, he released it once they were seated in the dark interior. Her relief intensified. At least she was not going to be bedeviled by unwelcome intimacies.

"Where is it to be?" Sutton asked as he seated himself beside his chauffeur.

"You're impossible, Sutton," his wife said exasperatedly. "Haven't you booked a table anywhere?"

"My dear girl, I had no idea where our guests would like to go. For all I know, Valentina is cherishing a secret desire to slum and—"

"Don't be ridiculous, darling," Claire said crisply. "Valentina has no desire to slum and neither do I. We'll go to Romanoff's. Mike will ensure we get a good table even without a reservation."

"I thought," said Sutton with pained indignation, "that you had no desire to slum. Mike Romanoff is a poseur."

"Mike Romanoff is a gentleman," Claire Hyde said, a note of steel in her voice effectively silencing her husband. "He is an absolute darling and one of the kindest men that I know."

"Romanoff's," Sutton said wearily to the chauffeur, and Valentina was aware that Paulos was grinning.

"I like His Imperial Highness," he said as the limousine headed out onto Sunset Strip. "We met the first week I was here."

"The man is a sham," Sutton said, lighting a cigar.

"Well, of course Mike's a sham," his wife agreed, "but he's a delightful sham, which is more than can be said for the other shams in town."

"I haven't met him," Valentina said, aware that the evening was not going to be the ordeal she had envisaged. "Is he really Russian?"

"Can't speak a word of it, my dear," replied Sutton. "Shouldn't be surprised if the fellow has been no farther east than New York's Battery."

"I think you are wrong there," Paulos said, and there was a gentle quality in his voice that Valentina liked. "He may not have been to Russia, but he has certainly been to Europe."

"I despair," Sutton said. "If a man of your intelligence is taken in, what hope is there for the rest of the credulous world?"

"Not taken in, Sutton," Paulos replied equably. "Just fascinated by a man with an indisputable flair for living."

"Poppycock," Sutton said, and then, when they had stepped from the limousine and entered the restaurant, he embraced His Imperial Highness, Prince Michael Alexandrovich Dmitry Obolensky Romanoff, warmly.

"Afraid we haven't booked a table, old boy. There's four of us."

Mike Romanoff surveyed Sutton's party, his eyes alighting on Valentina, a delighted smile spreading across his face.

"The divine Valentina!" he exclaimed, taking her hand and kissing it reverently. "My imperial greetings. Of course we can find a table." He turned to his headwaiter. "Remove those peasants from table four at once."

"But they are very important people, Mr. Romanoff. They are—"

"Peasants," Mike Romanoff finished for him. "Remove them."

"Yes, sir."

The peasants were removed. Valentina and Paulos, Claire and Sutton, sat down.

Their fellow diners turned and smiled and acknowledged their presence. Valentina could hear her name being whispered and queries made as to the identity of her escort. By tomorrow, Louella would have got hold of the news and there would be a tidbit in her column announcing that Valentina, seldom seen in public without her mentor and Svengali, Vidal Rakoczi, was last night in the company of the young classical pianist and composer, Mr. Paulos Khairetis.

A photographer, seeing his chance, walked smartly by their table and Valentina blinked as a double flash momentarily blinded her.

"I suppose this happens to you all the time," Paulos said as the photographer was unceremoniously hustled away by two of Mike Romanoff's henchmen. Mike was a professional. He knew the clients who welcomed such attentions and he knew instinctively the ones who did not. The alluring and breathtakingly beautiful Valentina fell into the rare but latter category.

"No," she said, aware that the purpose of the evening had been fulfilled. "I don't dine out very often."

Paulos regarded her long and measuringly. She was not at all what he had expected. She had none of the pretensions and affectations of the newly famous. There was something rare and intriguing about her. Something hidden below the surface. A quality he could not define. She raised her eyes to his and his hand clenched on the starched white tablecloth. The sadness he had seen in her eyes was no fleeting emotion. It was an integral part of her, so deep that he doubted if it could ever be erased. There was suffering in her eyes. Pain, loneliness, and despair. Yet she was a woman who was envied and emulated by millions.

He sat very quietly as Sutton and Claire discussed the wisdom of Sutton's starring in yet another medieval costume drama. There was something about the woman at his side that touched his heart. And in twenty-five years, only music had had that power.

"Sutton warned me that you would not be what I expected," he said, wishing that he could take her hand in his, yet knowing that she would instinctively withdraw from him if he did so. ". . . And he has been proved right."

"Have I disappointed you?" There was no coquetry in her question. She was lauded in public as a screen goddess. A great star. It would be only natural if Paulos Khairetis was disappointed with her in the flesh, for she was only Valentina—a woman who loved Vidal Rakoczi.

He smiled gently. "No. I doubt if you would ever do that."

"Then what is it about me that you did not expect?" she asked curiously.

"I did not expect such sadness," he said simply.

He saw alarm flare in her eyes and then she looked quickly away from him. "Is it so obvious?" she asked, staring unseeingly at silver and cut glass and white napery.

"To me it is."

There was a long silence. He studied her ringless hand only a fraction of an inch away from his.

"I think," he said slowly, "that you need a friend, Valentina. May I be that friend?"

His hair was dark, his skin olive-toned, and yet he was not remotely like Vidal. He had none of Vidal's drive and energy. He would never be able to kindle the flame that had consumed her whenever Vidal looked at her or spoke to her. There could never be another Vidal in her life. He had her heart and her soul, and they could never be given elsewhere. And the loneliness was crucifying.

"Yes," she said quietly, "I would like you for my friend, Paulos."

The next morning she appeared on the set, costumed and made up and outwardly composed. Vidal strode across to her, oblivious of the curious crew. "Where the hell have you been? I've been out of my mind with worry!" His face was haggard. He looked like a man who had not slept. A man who had come face-to-face with suffering of the worst kind.

She drew in a deep, ragged breath. "I went out with Sutton and Claire Hyde—"

"You did *what?*" he shouted, and the entire crew flinched. "You told me you were ill! You weren't home yesterday! No one knew where you were!"

"I'm sorry, I . . ."

He didn't wait for her to finish. He grasped her wrist and marched off the set, dragging her in his wake. Out in the open air he slammed her back against the studio wall. "What's going on?" he rasped, his eyes blazing. "You weren't just out with the Hydes! You were with some goddamn Greek! There are photographs in all the early editions!"

It was what she wanted. What she had schemed for. She dug her nails deep into her palms, praying for strength. "Yes," she said, as if it were the most natural thing in the world, "he's rather nice. He—"

"*Vigygzzon!*" he hissed, his hands crushing her wrists. "You haven't been home! Have you been with him? Sleeping with him?" Despite his rage, his eyes were disbelieving. It needed only one word from her. One little word, and everything would be as it had been before. She thought of the baby, of Kariana, of the madness she would spiral into if Vidal left her, and knew that the future could not be built on such a betrayal.

"Yes," she said, and cried out in pain as his hand slapped her face, sending her stumbling against the wall.

"Nem! *Nem! NEM!*" he roared, his face white, and then, as she pulled away from him, running back to the set, "*Valentina!*" His voice was anguished. She didn't look back. Didn't pause. Ashen-faced, she steadied her breathing and, ignoring the curious glances of the crew, walked across to the canvas chair with her name painted on the back, and sat, not moving, her face rigid. It was twenty minutes before Vidal followed her. When he did so, his face was grim, every muscle of his body tense.

"Right," he said tersely, ignoring her as if she didn't exist. "Places, everybody. Don, move that klieg farther to the left."

It was a day that took all of her stamina to survive. He didn't speak to her unless it was to give her directions, and when he did his icy voice slid across the vast soundstage like a whip.

At the end of the day she said good-bye to no one, simply walking off the set and into her limousine without even removing her costume or makeup.

"The ranch or the Garden of Allah?" her chauffeur inquired, wishing he knew what it was that was troubling her and that he could help.

"The Garden of Allah. I shan't be returning to the ranch. Not ever."

It held too many memories. Memories of Vidal's ringing laughter; of his down-slanting smiles; of his kisses and embraces.

There was a note waiting for her when she returned to her cottage at the Garden of Allah, inviting her to join her new neighbors for a drink in the bar that evening. She put it to one side and wearily began to run a bath. It was nice of them to ask her, but she couldn't face socializing. Not unless it was the kind of socializing that would find its way into the gossip columns and link her name romantically with her escort. News of her appearance with the Hydes and Paulos Khairetis had already spread through the movie community. Her telephone rang five times before she was able to step into her bath. Four of the men were married and the fifth had a reputation as a womanizer that was exactly what she needed. She had an hour to bathe and change and assume the part that the evening required.

As she stepped from the bath the doorbell rang. She froze, terror and hope fighting for dominance. Quickly she slipped her arms into a terry-cloth bathrobe and with trembling fingers tied it tightly around her waist. When she opened the door, it was Paulos who stood on the step, not Vidal.

"May I come in? I wondered if you would have dinner with me this evening?" His smile was charmingly hesitant.

"I . . . I have a date," she said, recovering herself with difficulty.

His smile faded. For the first time he realized how naïve he had been. Of course she would be going out. He had been a fool to expect anything else. Stars of her caliber dated only immensely rich men, European aristocrats, or stars of equal status. As a virtually unknown classical pianist he fell into none of the acceptable brackets. Last night had been a fluke. And her acceptance of his offer of friendship had been taken lightly and had not meant to her what it had meant to him.

"I'm sorry," he said politely, trying not to let his disappointment show. "Perhaps another evening. Good night, Valentina."

The door closed behind him and she was left alone. A weariness that was bone-deep suffused her. The Lothario she was to spend the evening with would undoubtedly try and get her into bed and behave like a spoiled child when he did not succeed. It would have been far nicer to have spent the evening with Paulos. She doubted if he would ask her again.

And she doubted if any of her future escorts would be as pleasant and as undemanding as the quiet-spoken, gentle-mannered Greek. Joy, which had been hers in such rich abundance, had now completely fled. All that remained was desolation. With a heavy heart she began to apply her makeup.

Chapter Sixteen

Vidal marched from the set and did not even remain to view the day's rushes. He dismissed his chauffeur, driving the Rolls high into the Hollywood hills, half crazed with rage and bewilderment. The last forty-eight hours had been a rapidly spiraling nightmare. Valentina's behavior was incomprehensible. They loved each other. He would have staked his life on her faithfulness and yet, without warning or reason, she had openly flaunted another man in his face. Had been seen in public with him. Had spent the night with him. Bile rose up in his throat as he slammed on the brakes and brought the Rolls to a halt in a cloud of dust. He gazed out over the spread of Los Angeles. It didn't make sense. Overnight she had turned into a stranger. A stranger who no longer cared for him. No longer loved him. Far away in the distance, beyond scrub-covered hills, the Pacific shimmered, silver-gray as dusk approached. His hands clenched white on the wheel. If he lost her, he would be destroyed. Life would have no purpose, no meaning. He felt as if a knife were twisting deep in his gut. He had lost her already. Her eyes, when she had told him about the Greek, had been cool and dispassionate. The future stretched bleakly before him. A parched desert in which he could find no comfort.

Dusk fell and still he remained at the wheel, his jaw tense, his eyes those of a man coming to terms with an inner hell. Not until the light faded and the coyotes began to howl did he force himself into movement, jamming the car into gear and slewing it back onto the road, heading God alone knew where.

* * *

Valentina laughed and danced, flirted and posed for newsmen, and no one seeing her would have guessed that she was hating every minute of the evening. Lex Dale was no Paulos Khairetis. He touched her constantly and his conversation left her in no doubt that he expected the evening to culminate in her lying spread-eagled beneath him. They had dined at La Maze and had then gone on to the Trocadero to drink and to dance, and to enable Lex to be seen in Valentina's company by as many people as possible.

"We'd love a photograph," he said expansively to the photographers who followed them from the restaurant to the nightclub.

The arm around her shoulders was hot and sweaty, unduly proprietorial. "Let's say, 'We're just good friends,'" he said with a leer at the gossip columnist of *The Hollywood Reporter*.

"How about a more friendly shot, Lex?" the *Daily Variety's* photographer demanded.

"Why not?" Lex Dale grinned. There was nothing he liked better than publicity, and this was publicity of the best kind. Valentina was front-page news. She was the hottest star in town. Effortlessly she had created an aura of mystery about herself, seldom being seen in public and rarely appearing without Vidal Rakoczi by her side. He would be the first man her name had been linked with romantically and he was going to play it to the hilt.

Valentina smiled seductively, a white mink stole around her throat, waterfalls of diamonds hanging from her ears.

"C'mon, honey, let's give the people what they want," Lex said, pulling her toward him and kissing her full on the mouth.

His breath smelled of rum. His mouth was wet, his tongue probing. She endured it as long as she could and then pressed her hands against his shoulders, pushing him coquettishly away.

"So when's the happy day?" the gossip columnist from *The Hollywood Reporter* asked.

"We're just good friends," Lex repeated, with a wink to indicate they were far more.

Paulos Khairetis stood on the far side of the dance floor. He had seen her the instant he entered the club. His first reaction had been to walk quickly away, but then he had been held in repelled fascination as Lex Dale had kissed her for the benefit of the watching newsmen. He would have staked his life that such behavior would have been anathema to her. He was filled with a sense of disappointment so deep, it was almost one of betrayal. And then he saw the fleeting expression in her eyes as Lex Dale lifted his head from hers, his arm still around her shoulders as he continued his repartee with the press.

His disappointment fled and he began to move purposefully toward her. Despite all appearances to the contrary—her smiles, her gestures—her eyes were desperate, the eyes of a trapped animal as the hunters closed in.

"Excuse me," he said with quiet authority, pushing his way through the crowd around her table.

"Hey . . . What the hell . . .?" An outraged photographer began indignantly as Paulos politely moved his camera out of the way.

Lex Dale blinked, staring up at him. It wasn't a face he knew and the guy was obviously not from the press.

"Let's go," said Paulos, holding out his hand to Valentina.

Her hesitation was minimal. With overpowering relief she grasped his hand and rose regally to her feet.

"Now, just a minute, buddy . . ." Lex Dale protested, his fists clenching.

"My cousin has only a few hours before his train leaves," Valentina said soothingly. "Please excuse me for now, Lex. I'll see you later."

It was a blatant lie. She had no intention of ever seeing him again.

Lex glanced at the watching photographers. Flashbulbs were popping all over the place. He ground his teeth together and managed a smile.

"Sure, honey," he said, and then with a wave of his hand in Paulos's direction, "Have a nice trip."

Paulos grinned. The longer he spent in Hollywood, the more ridiculous the pretenses that everyone lived with seemed to him.

Once they were outside the nightclub, he led the way across to an elegant Hispano-Suiza.

She sank thankfully into the wood and leather interior. He didn't speak again. Didn't ask her any questions. There was something infinitely restful about Paulos Khairetis. She closed her eyes and when she opened them they were cruising leisurely along a wide, neon-lit boulevard.

"Thank you," she said simply.

His voice did not betray his curiosity. "You looked like a damsel in distress," he said wryly.

For the first time in days a smile hovered at the corners of her mouth. "I was."

He didn't ask why. He was a man who valued his own privacy and would never invade the privacy of others. If she wanted to tell him what she was doing in the company of a man she obviously disliked, she would do so in her own good time.

"Would you like a drink?" he asked. It was still only ten o'clock.

"I'd like a cup of cocoa," she said with beguiling honesty.

He grinned. "That's quite a tall order in this town. Where do you suggest we go?"

She had no desire for the harsh lights of a soda fountain. "Let's go to my place," she said, a feeling of ease seeping through her. The man at her side would not misunderstand her invitation. She would not have to fight for her virtue as she had had to do with Rogan, or as she would have had to do with Lex Dale.

They drove to the Garden of Allah in silence, Paulos aware that he was no longer looking forward to leaving Hollywood; Valentina, aware that her plan of being seen publicly with different escorts was going to be even more distasteful than she had at first imagined.

"I haven't had cocoa since I was a child," Paulos said as he parked the car and they stepped out into the balmy warmth of the evening air.

"When I was a child, cocoa was one of my greatest luxuries. Here, where everyone drinks champagne, it's become something of a secret vice," Valentina confided.

They laughed as Valentina turned her key in the lock and opened the door, flicking on the switch and leading the way into a welcoming pool of soft light.

Paulos watched her as she entered the kitchen, putting milk on to heat, measuring out cocoa into ridiculously thin china cups. All her sadness was in her eyes. All her loneliness.

"When are you leaving Hollywood?" she asked as she set his cup before him on the glass-topped coffee table, knowing that when he did leave, she would miss him.

"Soon," he said, aware that he no longer wished to leave at all.

The sadness in her eyes returned and he resisted the urge to reach out and touch her. There was something about her that deeply moved him; that aroused in him emotions he had previously reserved for his music.

"I shall be sorry when you're gone," she said sincerely. "Will you come back and compose more music for Mr. Mayer?"

"Dear God, no!" Paulos said with an explosion of feeling. "I realized the first twenty-four hours I was here that I had been mad to imagine I could ever work away from the concert platform. Louis B. Mayer is in the business of manufacturing commercial entertainment. The creation of art is of secondary importance to him."

"And so what will you do?"

"Compose music that pleases me and that does not have to please tone-deaf producers."

She smiled and he felt his breath catch in his throat. Everything about her was soft and warm and beautiful. With Valentina at his side, he could compose music that would shake the world. Music that would live forever. But there was no place for him in her world; he could not prolong his stay indefinitely, and for all he knew, they would never meet again after tonight.

"What is the matter?" she asked, her eyes darkening with concern. "You look sad."

"I no longer want to leave Hollywood. I'm going to miss you."

She turned away from him. "I shall not be in Hollywood for much longer, Paulos. I, too, am leaving."

He frowned. "I don't understand. Where else would you go to make movies?"

"I don't think I shall be making any more movies, Paulos," and then, to her own astonishment, she said simply, "I'm expecting a child."

There was a moment's stunned silence. She waited for him to ask who the father was; why she didn't have an abortion. He said none of those things. He said only, "What will you do?"

"First of all, I'll have to tell Theo. That's Theodore Gambetta, head of Worldwide. I'm under contract for seven years. There's a clause in my contract called 'moral turpitude.'" She smiled wryly. "It means I can do what I like as long as it isn't made public."

"And having a baby . . . ?"

". . . is completely against the rules. Even if you're married, it's difficult. The studios worry about your figure. Your femme fatale image; if you're unmarried, it's a death knell." Her voice became bitter. "Abortion is the name of the game."

He didn't ask her why she hadn't considered it. He felt he knew her well enough to know why. "Will you marry?"

Her eyes clouded and she wrapped her arms around her knees. "No, he's already married."

Her shoulders were square and firm, her eyes full of courage. He knew then that he would marry her. "Let me make you another cocoa," he said gently, taking her cup from her lifeless fingers.

He went into the kitchen and she stared into the unlit log fire wondering where Vidal was; what he was doing.

"You would like Europe," Paulos said when he returned, setting a steaming cup of cocoa down in front of her. "There is sham and hypocrisy there, as there is all over the world, but it is not so obvious as it is here. It is not overpowering. London theater is marvelous. Paris is a poem and Rome is beyond description."

Her mouth softened once more into a smile. "I don't think that I shall go so far, Paulos. Perhaps I shall go to the East Coast; to New York."

Paulos stared at her, horrified. "The press will murder you in New York! The women's clubs! The Legion of Decency! Once the news becomes public property, the whole wrath of outraged America will fall on your head!"

"But why should it matter to anyone, once I have left Hollywood?" she asked in bewilderment.

He took her hands, his sculptured features sharpened by the intensity of his emotions. "Don't you understand what you *are* to the people who watch your movies? Don't you understand what you have become? Leaving Hollywood, not making any more pictures, is not going to be enough to protect you. You've become public property, Valentina. An idealized vision of beauty and femininity. You are on a pedestal and there is no way that you can step off that pedestal; you can only fall."

Her face had paled. She had not thought beyond leaving Vidal. Beyond leaving Hollywood.

"If people are cruel to me, I shall just have to bear it," Valentina she said at last, her voice barely audible.

Her vulnerability was total. If he had any lingering doubts about his decision, they were all dispelled.

"Your baby will have to grow up with the stigma as well, Valentina," he said quietly.

She gave a low moan, memories of her own childhood engulfing her. "No!" she whispered, pressing her hand against her mouth. "No, I couldn't bear that!"

He took her hand once again. "You don't have to bear it, Valentina," he said gently. "There is a way. . . ."

"How?" Her voice was anguished. "Everything you have said is true. I hadn't thought beyond leaving Hollywood! I hadn't realized my life would still be public property!" She slipped off the sofa onto her knees, her hands clasped tightly in her lap. "I *want* this baby, Paulos. I want to love it. To cherish it. Above all, I want it to be happy!"

"And I want *you* to be happy," he said tenderly. "Let me help you love and cherish your baby, Valentina."

She gazed up at him, not understanding.

"Marry me," he said simply. "If you marry me, the baby will have a father, and the only outcry will be because you have left Hollywood. I cannot remain here. My life and my work is in Europe, but they make films in Europe too, and—"

"Marry you?"

He nodded. "I don't mind if we only remain friends in marriage," he said. "I don't mind if you can never love me. But I want to be with you. I want to take care of you." His finger gently traced the outline of her cheek. "I want you to be my wife," he said with unnerving simplicity.

Chapter Seventeen

It was the longest night of her life. Paulos was offering her affection and security. Stability for her unborn child. She tossed and turned, pummeling her pillow. She was not in love with him. She was in love with Vidal. She would always be in love with Vidal. Yet she felt safe with Paulos. There was honesty between them, and she felt certain that, with time, there would be more. Much, much more.

She flung the bed covers aside and walked across to the window. The moon rode high in the sky. Serene and untroubled—and remote. She pressed her cheek against the cool pane. She had been going to marry Rogan, and she had never been in love with Rogan. She sighed. Nor had she ever been in real danger of marrying him. Her acceptance of his proposal had been an aberration. Accepted in the same mood of reckless impulsiveness in which it had been proffered.

Paulos was not Rogan. She knew instinctively that it would never be his habit to embark on violent and short-lived love affairs. Beneath his gentle manner was a depth that was reassuring. She liked Paulos Khairetis immensely. His sincerity and integrity were a welcome change from the sycophants who haunted Hollywood.

What would happen to her unborn child if she didn't marry? In the stillness of the night the years went whistling down the wind and she could smell again the waxed floors of the convent, see the jeering triumph in Jessie Sullivan's eyes as she shouted, "Bastard! Bastard!"

She shivered. Hollywood society would be even more cruel. There could be no future for them on the West Coast. Or the East, or Europe. Her face was too well known. However hard she sought it, obscurity was now beyond her grasp. But she could marry a man she liked and respected. A man who knew that she didn't love him. Suddenly it all seemed so very simple and so right.

She was going to marry Paulos Khairetis and she was going to bear Vidal's child. There were no more decisions to make. No more doubts to dispel.

The next morning she smiled at her chauffeur as he opened the door of her limousine. She would see Theodore Gambetta today. She would not telephone him. She would simply arrive at his office and insist on seeing him.

"You don't look quite so pale this morning," Wally Barren said to her as he applied her makeup. "Guess the end is in sight now."

"The end?" Startled, she looked up at him.

Wally grinned. "The movie. The last few weeks are always the worst. I don't suppose you have more than a few retakes to do now."

Her pulsebeat returned to normal. "No. I have only one. It should be wrapped up in two weeks, Wally."

"When it is, you should take a rest," Wally said sagely. "I'm probably the only guy who ever sees you without makeup, and let me tell you that your workload for this past two years has left you physically depleted. Look at those shadows beneath your eyes. It takes me twice as long to make you up these days."

"I've had a lot of late nights, Wally."

"Late nights, rubbish," Wally said, wielding a brush on her closed eyelids. "Your health is about to go. Don't argue with me. I've seen it happen too often. Too many pictures, too much pressure, too little rest. You're overworked. You give everything you've got to the part you're playing and it's depleting you. Don't let Mr. Gambetta or Mr. Rakoczi bully you. Insist on a rest. You need it."

Valentina smiled wryly. "Don't worry, Wally. I'm going to have one. And I think it's going to be a long one. Longer than even you would advise."

The cast and crew were unusually silent as Valentina took her place opposite her co-star for her last take of the film. The tension in the air could have been cut with a knife. Vidal had been on the set since five. Rumor had it that he had slept the night in his office. He had reduced the continuity girl to tears; yelled at Don Symons that his lighting was a disaster; and had stalked the soundstage with a face like thunder, finding fault with everyone and everything.

"Right," he snapped at last. "Let's take it in one."

Valentina drew in a deep breath. This was where she had to stop thinking about herself. Had to stop being so acutely aware of Vidal's nearness. *The Heiress Helena* was a comedy, not a tragedy. The lightness of touch that the part needed had to come from her very soul. She remembered the revelation that had changed her life. In a movie you could be anyone. Anyone at all. The crew waited with bated breath. Her co-star's expression was agonized. Valentina smiled at him reassuringly and shed her own personality as easily as if it were a silk-lined coat.

"Darling, spring in Rome will be divine," she said, her eyes dancing, her whole being suddenly suffused with tantalizing vitality.

Harris breathed a sigh of relief. It was going to be all right. Whatever had happened between Rakoczi and Valentina wasn't affecting Valentina's performance.

Vidal scowled in silence. The scene came to an end. Valentina and her co-star waited with increasing nervousness. The crew shifted from one foot to another and looked at each other with growing anxiety. The take had been perfect. If Mr. Rakoczi demanded another, then nothing would please him and they would still be working on the damned scene twelve hours later.

Vidal's eyes were on Valentina. Black and hard as obsidian. A minute went by and then another. Sweat broke out on the forehead of Valentina's co-star. *The Heiress Helena* was the first movie he had ever made with Mr. Rakoczi and he had not found the experience a happy one.

The makeup girl stepped forward to powder away the beads of sweat and then hesitated. Mr. Rakoczi had not requested that she do so and she had no desire to draw attention to herself.

Valentina clasped her hands lightly in front of her and kept her eyes firmly lowered. She could not look at him. The agony would be too great.

"Okay," he said at last. "Can it."

Harris breathed a sigh of relief. He'd worked with Mr. Rakoczi on a lot of movies, but he'd never seen him like this before. There was something terrible being restrained be-

neath Mr. Rakoczi's glowering exterior and he didn't want to
be around if and when it was unleashed.

Valentina glanced up at the studio clock. It was nine
o'clock. The perfect time to catch Mr. Gambetta before he
became involved in his first business meeting of the day.

Vidal's hands tightened over the wooden arms of his
director's chair as she walked away from the set. He half rose
to follow her, his eyes devouring her, his longing for her
overwhelming.

"Mr. Cassandetti wants to know if we're shooting him in
right profile or left profile in the next scene," Harris said
tentatively.

Vidal's eyes were still on Valentina.

She wasn't staying to watch the rest of the shooting as
she normally did. She was leaving the soundstage. What
could he say if he strode after her? He had said everything
that he could. He turned to face Harris.

"Tell him we're doing it from the left," he said curtly,
and there was a flare of such pain across the strongly boned
face that Harris stepped back as if from a blow.

"Yes, Mr. Rakoczi."

The crew's commissary talk was wrong. Rakoczi was not
an unfeeling bastard. He was a man capable of feeling—and
suffering—very deeply.

Valentina walked with hip-swaying grace across to her
car. He hadn't spoken to her, not one word. Yet wasn't that
what she wanted? She tilted her head a fraction higher. Vidal
Rakoczi was no longer any part of her life. His son would be
her whole life. She passed a hand lightly across her stomach
and began to walk toward her car. Strange how sure she was
that the child she was carrying was a boy.

"Mr. Gambetta's office, please," she said to her chauffeur, and sank back against the plush upholstery. There were
still some scenes to retake on *The Heiress Helena*, but she
was not required for any of them. She could leave Hollywood
just as soon as she had spoken to Mr. Gambetta.

He would threaten to sue her. He *would* sue her. A
smile touched the corners of her mouth. She was uncaring.
The three movies she had made with Vidal had grossed more
for Worldwide than all the movies it had produced in the
same period put together.

If she offered to stay and continue making movies for

Worldwide after the birth of her illegitimate child, he would have a coronary. He would insist that she have an abortion. He would probably also insist on knowing the identity of the father and coming to one rapid and very correct conclusion.

I'm sorry, Mr. Gambetta is on no account to be disturbed," his secretary said apologetically as Valentina entered Theodore's outer sanctum.

Valentina smiled. "I'm sorry, too," she said, "because I'm going to have to disturb him."

Theodore was lacing his morning coffee with a healthy amount of Scotch. He halted, bottle in the air, stunned by the uninvited intrusion.

"I had to see you, Mr. Gambetta," she said composedly, "and I knew that you would have a busy day ahead of you. I thought now would be the best time."

Theodore regained his equanimity with speed. He smiled broadly, mentally making a note to fire his damn fool secretary.

"Valentina, my dear. You couldn't *possibly* call at an inopportune moment. What is it? Some studio politics that need smoothing out?"

"No." She sat down opposite him and crossed her legs at the ankle, and Theodore made another mental note. They must get her into a movie that showed off those legs. They were sensational. Eye-riveting.

"I shan't be able to make *The Gypsy and the Marquis* when *The Heiress Helena* is finished."

Theodore drew in a deep breath, folded his hands on top of his desk, leaned toward her, and tried to look benign. It happened all the time: a starlet was grateful for anything. A star of Valentina's caliber began to want some choice in her parts. They never would have, as long as he ruled Worldwide. He knew the parts that would bring in cash at the box office. He also knew how to be patient when the need arose.

"It's a superb part, Valentina. Romana de Santa would screw Quasimodo to get it."

Valentina suppressed a grin. "I know it's a good part, Mr. Gambetta. I've been through the script several times."

"Well, then . . ." Theodore beamed expansively and spread his hands wide.

"It's just that I'll be pregnant all the time it's being filmed."

"You'll *what*?" Theodore's eyes bulged.

"I'll be having a baby," Valentina said as Theodore rose threateningly to his feet, his Scotch-laced coffee spilling in a stream across a mass of typewritten notes.

"*Over my dead body!*"

Valentina moved her legs away from the scalding downpour. Theodore Gambetta's face was mottled. The tendons in his neck bulged, straining at his restricting collar.

"*Jesus H. Christ!* Of all the stupid, idiotic, *dumb* things to do!" He marched around to her, controlling himself with difficulty. "You'll have to have an abortion. It'll take no time at all. Leave it all to me."

He mopped his face with his handkerchief, his composure returning. "You were right to come and tell me without trying to sort it out on your own. Hell, some abortionists in this town are nothing short of get-rich-quick butchers." He patted her hand. "It'll be okay, honey. We won't even have to delay the schedule on *The Gypsy and the Marquis*."

"I think it could make shooting *The Gypsy and the Marquis* quite difficult," Valentina said, trying not to feel sorry for the all-powerful Mr. Gambetta. "You see, I'm not going to have an abortion."

Theodore Gambetta stared at her. "But of course you are. . ."

Valentina shook her head firmly. "No," she said, her voice steady. "I'm not going to have an abortion. I'm going to have a baby."

"Now, look here." Theodore Gambetta leaned toward her threateningly. "There's no way in *this* town you're going to have a baby! There's certainly no way in *my* studio that you're going to have a baby! So what are your options? Come out of dreamland, honey, and face the real world. You're under contract for seven years and there's still another five to go. You're the biggest star in the studio. And you're *not going to have a baby!*"

Valentina rose to her feet. "I'm sorry, Mr. Gambetta. I didn't mean to get pregnant. However, now that I am, I'm not taking any so-called easy way out."

"*You have no choice!*" Gambetta yelled, spittle forming at the sides of his mouth.

"I have every choice," Valentina said quietly. "I can

choose to have my baby or I can choose to kill it. I've told you what my choice is."

Valentina's eyes met his unflinchingly. Gambetta felt sweat break out on his forehead. "By getting pregnant you've broken your contract." He paused, breathing harshly as a new thought occurred to him. "Is it more money that you're after? They're lining up all the way from Frisco to Boston to see *The Warrior Queen*. Money is no problem."

Valentina shook her head, her dark hair swinging close against her cheeks. "I'm not trying to blackmail you, Mr. Gambetta. I know that I have a contract. I know that by having the baby I will have broken it. I know that you can sue me and probably will. I made my decision before I came in here and I'm not going to change it."

"Have this baby and you'll never work in this town again!" Theodore Gambetta said ferociously.

"I know," she said, and at the tone of her voice Theo rapidly changed tactics.

With great difficulty he softened his voice. "He won't marry you, Valentina. An abortion will be the best thing for him as well."

The blood began to beat more rapidly along her veins. He was speaking of Vidal. Now was the time for the first inevitable lie. "That's just where you're wrong, Mr. Gambetta. He *is* marrying me."

Theodore Gambetta looked as if he had been hit with a sledgehammer. "*Rakoczi* is? Are you sure? Has he said so?"

Valentina looked steadily into Theodore Gambetta's incredulous eyes. "I'm not marrying Mr. Rakoczi. I'm marrying the father of my child."

"But I thought . . ."

"Then you thought wrong. I am marrying Paulos Khairetis. He is a Greek pianist and composer who came to Hollywood to work for MGM."

Theodore Gambetta let out his breath slowly. It wasn't so bad after all. There would be a marriage. A premature baby. It was nothing that the studio couldn't handle. Not for a star who pulled in the public the way Valentina did.

"We'll make a big thing of it," he said. "The wedding-of-the-year number. We can put *The Gypsy and the Marquis* on ice for twelve months. We'll tell Louella that the engagement has been secret for months. That you were only waiting for

The Heiress Helena to be completed. Hell, we'll even lay on a honeymoon for you!"

There was no relief in her eyes at his magnaminity; only a sadness that he couldn't understand.

"I'm sorry, Mr. Gambetta. My fiancé doesn't intend to stay in Hollywood."

Theodore gazed at her uncomprehendingly.

"I think he's going to New York. Probably even to Europe. Wherever he goes, I shall go with him."

"You'll *what?*" Theodore clutched at his desk for support. "You'll give up all this"—he waved his hand at the publicity photographs of her that lined his office walls—"for a two-bit *piano* player?"

Her eyes flashed dangerously. "I shall give up all this to be with my husband. Good-bye, Mr. Gambetta." She held out her hand to him.

Theodore's breath was coming in harsh gasps. Never before had he been beaten in a verbal battle. The biggest money-spinner he had ever put before the cameras was calmly telling him that she was walking out on him. He wondered if he was having a stroke. It certainly felt like it.

Her hand remained outstretched. He didn't take it.

Valentina shrugged, turned on her heel, and walked swiftly from the room.

Theodore Gambetta watched her go, his eyes admiring. She had courage and determination. He wished some of his studio executives would show the same kind of guts.

The door closed behind her and he reached for his telephone and asked his secretary to get his lawyer on the line. He was going to drag her through every court in the goddamn land.

"The studio, please," she said to her chauffeur as she walked across to the limousine, the morning breeze lifting her hair gently and filling it with light.

She had promised to ring Paulos as soon as she was through at the studio. They would be able to have lunch together. She would be able to tell him that she was not needed on any of the remaining scenes that still had to be shot on *The Heiress Helena*, and she would be able to tell him of her interview with Theodore Gambetta. Then they would be able to make plans for the future. She needed to remove the heavy makeup that Wally had applied so painstakingly and change from the dated twenties dress that her part demanded.

Paulos. A warm glow spread through her. They would have a good life together. There was affection. There was mutual respect. It was far more than most people started off with.

High in the hills the gigantic letters that spelt out H-O-L-L-Y-W-O-O-D-L-A-N-D glared white in the sun. It was a sign that she had lived beneath and flourished beneath and that she was now leaving, perhaps forever. It was a sign that would always mean the heat of klieg lights, the endless wait between takes, the nervous excitement of seeing rushes for the first time. It was a sign that would always mean Vidal.

She turned her head away swiftly. She loved him more than she would ever love anyone else. And loving him, she had to leave him.

The limousine slid through the open gates of Worldwide and halted at the end of the oleander-lined pathway that led to her bungalow.

"I shan't be long," she said to the chauffeur. "Thirty minutes at the most."

In the distance was the usual hive of activity. People rushing from one soundstage to another. The sound of sets being dismantled and new ones erected. The feeling of excitement was palpable in the growing heat of the morning. She paused for a second to savor it. Soon it would be lost to her, no longer a part of her life. She gave herself a mental shake and began to walk firmly toward the door of her bungalow. As she did so a dark shadow fell across her and she spun around, the blood draining from her face.

"I need to speak to you about *The Gypsy and the Marquis*," Vidal said tightly. It was a lie. He needed to do nothing of the kind.

Her throat was so tight, her lips so parched, that she could hardly utter the words.

"I've just been to see Mr. Gambetta. I won't be doing the movie."

Shock robbed Vidal of his facade of composure. "Have you taken leave of your senses? The costumes have been fitted, the sets erected; half the San Fernando Valley has been transformed into a medieval Spanish landscape. . . ."

"The movie will be going ahead as planned," she said, wishing that she could drag her eyes away from his, that her heart would stop drumming against her chest. "But I won't be playing the part of the gypsy."

He felt his blood chill. She wasn't being temperamental. She was hiding something from him. His nerve ends crawled with sudden fear.

"Why?" he demanded, a pulse beginning to beat at his jawline.

The oleanders pressed in on them on either side. She knew that for as long as she lived, she would hate their fragrance, that the very sight of them would always remind her of this final, terrible moment.

"I'm leaving Hollywood," she said, and despite all her courage there was an underlying tremble in her voice. "I'm marrying Paulos Khairetis and going east with him."

The skin seemed to stretch like parchment over his cheekbones. His eyes were black pits in which she could read nothing. He was silent for so long that she wondered if he had heard what she had said.

A studio executive strolling past her parked limousine called out a word of greeting that went unanswered. A group of secretaries could be heard approaching, giggling and laughing. Happy and carefree.

"*Nem lehet,*" he said softly, and there was contempt in his eyes. "Does Paulos Khairetis know what a shallow heart you possess, *liba?*"

His body was so near that she could feel its heat, smell the indefinable mixture of cologne and maleness. She stood straight and tall, her head and her abundant aureole of smoke-dark hair held high. "My heart is not shallow, Vidal Rakoczi, and never will be!" Her eyes flashed and then she was walking away from him, the blood pounding in her ears, the tears spilling down her cheeks.

"You look pale," Paulos said as she sat down at his table in the Derby.

She managed a smile. "That's exactly what the makeup man said to me this morning. He said that I needed a rest and I told him that I intended to take one—a very long one."

Paulos laughed and took her hand. "I have a present for

you," he said, closing her fingers around a small velvet-covered box.

His gray eyes were anxious as she opened the lid. Inside lay a heart-shaped aquamarine ring. "Oh, Paulos, it's beautiful!"

Gently he took it from its bed of satin and slipped it on to the fourth finger of her left hand. "I bought it because it reminds me of you," he said. "It's unusual and unexpected and Van Cleef cut it so that a host of facets seem to sparkle at once." His fingers tightened on hers and his voice was thick with emotion. "There isn't another ring like it anywhere, Valentina. Just as there isn't another woman in the whole world like you." He lifted her hand to his mouth and kissed it. "Now we really are engaged," he said, his fine-boned face alight with happiness.

Her hands were enclosed in his. The feeling of peace and calm that she had known would come when she was in his presence, seeped through her. Paulos was her haven. If he wanted to marry her that day, she would do so.

"I told Mr. Gambetta that I was getting married and would not be able to fulfill my contract," she said as the waiter put a bottle of Mumm's Extra Dry in an ice bucket at their side.

"And what did the great Mr. Gambetta say when you broke the news?" Paulos asked, his voice light but his eyes concerned. Gambetta would not lose Valentina without a fight, and the fight could prove an ugly one.

"Let's just say he wasn't very pleased," Valentina said, a smile touching the corners of her mouth. She twisted her fingers through his. "How soon can we leave Hollywood, Paulos? I did my last scene on *The Heiress Helena* this morning. They can finish the rest of the retakes without me."

"We need to get a marriage license. If we do it in Los Angeles, there will be a furor. The city hall is haunted by newspaper spies. Louella Parsons will know about it before we've left the building. Let's be married quickly on the East Coast by a judge."

Valentina looked across at the sensitive, classically sculpted face of her fiancé and said gently, "Is that the kind of wedding that you want, Paulos? A short ceremony in front of an American judge?"

Paulos's smile deepened. "It will do for now. The sooner

we get married, the better, and this is the quickest way. Later . . ." He paused, suddenly unsure of himself.

"Yes?" Valentina urged.

"Later I would like a proper wedding. A Greek Orthodox wedding with all my family present."

She squeezed his hands tightly. "Then that is exactly what you will have, but we'll have to make *that* wedding rather quick as well, won't we? Otherwise I'll shock all your family by being a very obviously pregnant bride!"

He laughed and then said, "I want to go home and introduce you to my family as soon as possible."

"Tell me about them," she said, trying desperately not to think of Vidal. "Where do they live? Have you brothers and sisters?"

"My family home is in Athens, but since my father died, my mother and my two sisters live mainly in our summer home on Crete."

"What are your sisters' names? How old are they?" she asked with eager interest.

"Aristea is fifteen and Maria is nineteen."

Valentina leaned back in her chair, amazed at the prospect of two young sisters-in-law, then a slight frown furrowed her smooth brow. "Your mother. Will she be distressed that you have not married a Greek girl?"

Paulos grinned. "She will wail and cry and tear her clothes, and say that I will never be happy and that I have disgraced them all."

Valentina's eyes widened in horror.

Paulos laughed. "Then she will meet you and she will fall in love with you, and she will tell everyone how lucky the Khairetis family is to have such a beautiful American for a daughter."

Valentina gave a gasp of relief. "Will she really like me?"

"She will love you. You have a family now. When you marry a Greek you gain not only a husband but a mother, sisters, cousins, as well."

She leaned toward him across the table. "Let's go this afternoon and apply for a license to marry, Paulos," she said urgently. "It doesn't matter about the fuss and publicity. We'll simply ignore it."

His eyes gleamed and his hand tightened in hers. "We'll go now," he said, rising to his feet, the champagne untouched. "We'll be married just as soon as I can get a judge to perform the ceremony."

Chapter Eighteen

The wedding was small and quiet and took only minutes to solemnize. Leila acted as her bridesmaid and Sutton and Claire Hyde were the witnesses. She wore a simple cream lace dress that reached to mid-calf, and carried a posy of small pink rosebuds. From the moment Paulos slipped the wedding ring on her finger, she never had a doubt as to the wisdom of her action.

They honeymooned in New York, and then sailed on the *Queen Mary* to Southampton. In the space of a few weeks her whole life-style changed. Paulos was the one who lived in the spotlight, appearing in concerts in London, in Paris, in Rome. Though reporters and photographers lay in wait for days for a glimpse of her, Paulos was adept at fending them off and of making sure that she had a measure of privacy.

"How would you like to be married again?" he asked her one morning as they ate breakfast on the balcony of their hotel in Rome. "In white and in church?"

She giggled. "Don't you think I would look a little . . . ripe. . . ?" she asked, regarding her rounded stomach with pleasure.

Paulos grinned. "Fruitful, certainly." He handed a letter across to her. "My mother is expecting us in Crete on the twenty-seventh, and she is appalled at our negligible nuptials. She wants a church wedding with priest and incense and candles and a bridal cake."

"But she can't!" Valentina protested. "She knows the baby is due in five months."

Paulos's eyes sparkled. "She doesn't care about the baby,

darling. She's a Greek mother who has been cheated out of her only son's wedding ceremony. She would like that remedied. What do you say?"

She began to laugh helplessly. "What *can* I say? Yes, we'll get married again, but I shall need a *tent* to disguise the existence of this baby!"

He leaned across the table and kissed her. "Don't worry, darling. Greeks are very practical. They only see what they want to see, and what they see will be a very beautiful and radiant bride."

The entire Khairetis family turned out in force when they arrived in Heraklion.

Paulos's mother welcomed her with a flood of Greek, engulfing her in an ecstatic hug.

"She says you are her daughter," said Paulos, grinning broadly. "That she is overcome at welcoming you into the family."

Mrs. Khairetis beamed, kissing her effusively on both cheeks. Maria and Aristea stepped forward shyly, their reserve fast disappearing as Valentina greeted them warmly.

"Now we go to Agios Georgios," Mrs. Khairetis said proudly in stilted English. "I show you, my daughter, Crete. In America there is nowhere so beautiful as Crete."

"Crete is a land of goddesses and legends," Paulos whispered to her as they walked toward the cars. "You should feel at home here!"

She did. Immediately. The road ran along the coast, past tiny bays and rust-colored cliffs. The hinterland was rural. There were small villages with whitewashed houses and tiny gardens massed with flowers and groups of women clothed from head to foot in heavy black serge. There were windmills, their great white sails fluttering like snowy blossoms in the breeze. An occasional shepherd with his flock and a barking dog passed by.

"You like?" Maria asked anxiously, eager that Crete should please her new sister-in-law.

"Oh, yes," Valentina said, her eyes shining. "I like very much, Maria."

Agios Georgios was on the southwest side of the island, remote and little visited. The car bumped and swayed over the ruts in the road that had petered out into a rough track. The White Mountains of Crete soared on their left, the foothills running down to the shore. Here and there clusters of houses clung to a crescent of fine shingle, goats and sheep scratching a precarious living from the inhospitable hillside. Blue sage brushed the sides of the car; asphodel nodded its golden head, Judas trees filled the air with their clouds of scented flowers, and the smell of verbena and lavender filled the air.

The track turned inland, climbing steadily, winding its way through high banks of maquis. The White Mountains truly were white: great soaring escarpments of silver rock, gashed by ravines, and crowned by scudding drifts of cirrus.

"Only the eagle and the mountain goat live up there," Maria said shyly as she saw Valentina gazing up in awe at the cruelly high ridges. Bare, gray rock glinted in the sun. "It is up there, far away where no man can climb, that Zeus, the father of the gods, was born," Maria whispered reverently.

Valentina felt a surge of affection for her new sister-in-law. Maria's English was far better than Paulos had led her to believe, but despite the polish of an expensive education she still believed as the ancients had. To Maria, the gods of Greece were fact and not legend, and her simple belief clothed them in flesh and blood so that Valentina, too, could well believe that Zeus had been fathered among the shining peaks; that Theseus had slain the Minotaur in the Palace of Knossos, and that Pan still played his pipes by the banks of the rushing mountain streams.

Paulos's hand closed over hers and she clasped it tightly. For the first time in her life she was part of a family. It was a heady, intoxicating feeling.

The road began to curve downward, snaking backward and forward across the steep slopes of the mountainside and then suddenly there was a lemon grove and a shining white villa, and the sea creaming up a stretch of golden sand.

"The Villa Ariadne," Paulos said. "It is the house from which my mother was married, and from which she wants us to be married. After the wedding she will return to Athens with Maria and Aristea and we will stay on for as long as we choose. The village is over there, to the right."

Sparkling white walls glittered in the sun and she could see olive trees and fruit trees and a donkey quietly grazing.

"This was my father's house," Evangelina Khairetis said proudly. "He was a man of Crete. Very brave. Very handsome."

They spilled out of the car and Valentina walked across a

terrace massed with jasmine and into cool, mosaic-floored rooms. It was a house she knew she would never willingly leave. A house she wanted to stay in until her baby was born.

An elderly maid, even plumper than Evangelina Khairetis, and dressed in ankle-length black with a starched white apron around her waist, greeted them, bobbing a deferential curtsy, as if Valentina were royalty, as she presented them with little glasses of almond-tasting liqueur.

Paulos downed his in a gulp, but Valentina, seeing that Maria and Aristea merely moistened their lips with it, did the same. A little dish of candied fruit followed, and then wineglasses full of sparkling, clear water. The traditional greeting over, Evangelina Khairetis formally led Valentina from room to room, her massive bosom heaving in satisfaction at Valentina's undisguised delight.

The walls were plain; the only decoration that of the waving shadows of the pomegranate trees beyond the open windows. The beds were covered with exquisitely embroidered and lace-flounced bedspreads. The furniture was delicate and intricately carved.

As they lay in bed that night, the air heavy and fragrant, she pressed Paulos's hand against her cheek. "You've made me very happy, Paulos. Happier than I ever thought possible."

He looked down into the pale ivory of her face. "I love you," he said simply, and took her in his arms, pressing her gently beneath him. In all the world there was only the silent, secret language of their bodies making love, and the distant surge of the sea as it creamed on the shingled shore.

The entire village turned out for the wedding. Maria and Aristea fulfilled the roles of *koumbaros*, holding the little wedding wreath over their heads as a bearded priest married Valentina and Paulos. Valentina wore the white lace gown Paulos's mother had worn for *her* wedding, the waist discreetly altered. The Khairetis family wedding veil floated over her dark hair and she carried Aristea's prayer book in her hand and a spray of roses that Maria had picked from the wild.

The wedding feast was held beneath the plane trees in the village square. On white tablecloths were dishes of *styphádo* and *dolmádes*. *Bougatsa* and *paidákia*. There were honey cakes and fresh figs, mulberries and pomegranates.

Paulos changed into traditional dress, magnificent in black, knee-length boots and pantaloons, black shirt and cummerbund, and gaily embroidered waistcoat.

Maria and Aristea wore long skirts covered by beautiful hand-embroidered white aprons and thickly embroidered peasant blouses. Light veils covered their faces and gold necklaces and bracelets hugged their throats and wrists.

Everyone, from the very young to the very old, danced. Paulos quoted from Homer's *Iliad,* describing how "Daedalus in Knossos once contrived a dancing-floor for fair-haired Ariadne," telling her that every true Greek loved to dance.

Ouzo and wine flowed freely, and even the stove-hatted priest drummed his feet beneath his black robes in time to the music of the lyre.

There were breathless, swinging dances with arms interlocked. Sedate circle dances, and dances where only the men participated.

"*Stin iyassas,*" the villagers said, raising their glasses to Valentina. "Your health."

"*Pánta yiá,*" the priest said, beaming. "May you always be happy."

She whirled and danced, her wedding gown swirling around her ankles. There were no photographers. No reporters. To the people of Agios Georgios she was not Valentina, a Hollywood star. She was Kyrie Khairetis, Evangelina Khairetis's daughter-in-law, Paulos Khairetis's wife. It was a world she felt she would be content to remain in forever.

Chapter Nineteen

Hazel Renko wondered whether or not to put the newspapers on the breakfast table. Vidal was not working and when he was not working it was his custom to breakfast at leisure and to peruse all the national dailies, and whatever foreign newspapers his chauffeur had been able to get. The headlines

that Valentina, the screen goddess who had given up fame
and stardom for marriage, had given birth to a son in Athens
was in each and every one of those newspapers and Hazel
had no idea how her employer would react to the news.

He had changed drastically since the day that his protégée
had so inexplicably left Hollywood with her young husband
and had later announced her intention of never returning.
His rows with Theodore Gambetta had been monumental as
he strenuously denied every statement Theodore issued regarding Valentina.

The lines that ran from nose to mouth in the olive-toned
face had deepened. Almost overnight a flash of silver had
appeared in the night-black hair that tumbled perpetually low
over his forehead. At thirty-two he was still one of the youn-
gest directors in Hollywood and by far the most daring and
innovative.

Hazel walked out onto the terrace to the breakfast table.
Pretending that the chauffeur had been unable to obtain any
newspapers would be useless. He would know that she was
lying and would immediately be suspicious as to why. He had
to see them sometime and his reaction might not be as bad as
she feared.

She set them down beside his place setting, noticing the
cold duck, the iced beer, the *pâté de foie gras du Périgord*
and salami, the black pumpernickel bread.

Vidal had changed in more ways than one. When she
had first come to Villada to care for Kariana, Vidal had
breakfasted in typical American fashion. Melon sometimes;
hot buttered rolls, lashings of strong black coffee. Now he no
longer seemed to care whether he fitted into the society
around him or not. Even his accent had become more pro-
nounced, the stress falling heavily on the first syllable of
every word. He had become a man that people avoided.
Stern-faced and short-tempered, he rarely smiled and when
he did, his eyes remained hard and bleak. Hazel could not
remember the last time that she had heard him laugh.

"Good morning, Hazel." Kariana drifted across the terrace toward the table in a negligee of floating powder-blue
chiffon.

"Good morning, Kariana." It was a long time since she
had been on anything but first-name terms with both Kariana

and Vidal. The intimacy in which the three of them lived precluded rigid formality.

Kariana sat down and the maid hurried out, pouring her a hot chocolate. Kariana sipped at it, ignoring the newspapers, gazing out over the valley and toward the Pacific with vague, untroubled eyes.

Hazel regarded her and wondered again if the change they had all initially thought to be for the better, might not, in the long run, prove to be for the worse.

Kariana's turbulent changes of mood had stabilized. There had been no unfortunate incident since the last one, shortly before Valentina had left Hollywood. It was an incident that Hazel would never forget. Partly because of the fear she had felt on Kariana's behalf, and partly because it was the only time that she had seen the heroine of *The Warrior Queen* in the flesh. There had been something both vulnerable and defiant about Valentina when she had insisted on speaking to Vidal and then, briefly, before she had hurried from the room in search of Kariana, she had seen bewilderment on that lovely face and had felt pity for her. Why? It was a question she had often asked herself. Kariana was the one who deserved the pity. Yet it was Valentina whom her heart had gone out to.

She looked down at the front-page photograph of a smiling Valentina cradling her newborn son. Her pity had been misplaced. Even as they were all frantically searching for the missing Kariana, Valentina had been happily in love with her handsome Greek. The baby was described tactfully as premature. Hazel smiled. It had been only seven months since the wedding.

"I think I shall go shopping today," Kariana said dreamily, tilting her head back, her long, pale golden hair catching and holding the light of the morning sun. "We'll go down to Wilshire Boulevard and I'll buy some dresses, maybe a fur."

Hazel nodded in agreement, but her doubts returned. The expensive shopping trips had become almost a daily occurrence. The dresses and furs purchased were seldom worn. Hazel doubted if Kariana even remembered what it was that she had bought. She forgot things continually. She forgot what she was saying midsentence. She forgot which room she was heading for. There were even times when she forgot where she was and mistook her Hollywood home for her father's New England home.

Vidal had been too relieved that the moody highs and lows had ceased for Hazel to point out that the vagueness and dreaminess that had replaced them might be equally dangerous. To Vidal anything was preferable to the mania that turned his wife into a stranger and that came on like a devil of possession. He had even been able to invite people to Villada for dinner, and life had begun to take on a semblance of normality. But Hazel's inner instincts told her it was a normality built on dangerously shifting sands.

He strode out to join them, still wearing his breeches and riding boots from his morning ride.

"Good morning, Kariana. Did you sleep well?"

His wife turned her head in his direction, a slow smile curving her lips, and then she turned her head away without answering, contemplating the view that absorbed her for hour after hour.

"Good morning, Hazel. Do you have any plans for today?" Vidal asked as he poured himself an iced beer. He hated to be waited on at the breakfast table. The maid appeared only to attend to pouring endless cups of chocolate for Kariana and occasionally to serve her with slices of thin, dry toast.

"Kariana would like to go shopping."

If Vidal flinched at the prospect of another unnecessary onslaught on his bank account, he showed no sign of it. Shopping seemed to have become a palliative to Kariana. It had become her only interest and she seemed able to indulge in it with complete safety. The spiraling swings from deepest depression to dangerous exhilaration no longer occurred.

"Fine," he said, eating his cold duck and mentally going over the arguments he was going to need in order to persuade Mayer to finance the filming of Balzac's *Eugénie Grandet*.

Louis B. Mayer would refuse. He would say the subject was not commercial enough; that audience interest would be limited. He, Vidal, had to convince him otherwise. The whole project revolved around having the right star for the lead part. He pushed his plate of duck to one side. *She* would have been perfect. As Eugénie Grandet, Valentina would have had every studio in town rifling through the classics in a vain frenzy of imitation. Everything inside him was cold. It was as if losing her, ice had entered his heart, frozen it, and never thawed. He wondered if it ever would.

He reached out for the first of the papers and Hazel Renko steadfastly kept her eyes focused on Kariana.

A SON FOR THE STAR WHO GAVE UP ALL FOR LOVE the headline ran, and beneath it was a photograph of a smiling Valentina, in a hospital bed with a baby in her arms and Paulos Khairetis standing with his arm around her shoulders surveying his wife and son with pride.

For a second there was complete silence. There was no rustle of newspaper, no clink of cutlery. Hazel Renko drew in a deep breath and turned her head toward Vidal. He looked like a man who had been turned to stone. The night-black eyes, slanting above the high cheekbones, glittered with an expression that was unreadable. Scraping his chair back from the table, he moved swiftly onto his feet before she had even the chance to blink, striding away and into the house with a pent-up rage that could not be disguised.

Kariana did not even turn her head. She seemed oblivious of his sudden departure.

"I think," she said dreamily, "that if I were to be reincarnated, I would like to be a cloud. I would drift along against a blue sky and sometimes, sometimes, when there were storms . . ." Her voice trailed away, but Hazel noticed that though her face was perfectly calm, beneath the table her fingers were pulling fretfully at the lace edging of her negligee, pulling so that the delicate material was fraying beneath her carefully manicured nails.

Vidal strode through the house and out to the stables. He could not see Mayer today. He could see no one. He felt a jealousy and a fury burn through him, so devastating that he felt as if he were going to disintegrate. Paulos Khairetis had given her that which he never could have given her. A child. A child born in wedlock.

His heels dug into the horse's flanks. He rode hard, unmercifully. For the first time he realized the unspoken hope he had woken with each day. The hope that she would return. That she would leave Khairetis. The hope that would never now be fulfilled.

The sweat poured down his body and down his horse's flanks as he rode higher and higher into the hills, never slackening his pace. He was confounded with desire for her.

Convulsed with it. He was thirty-two. How could he live the rest of his life without her? How could he exist? He wheeled his horse to a standstill and flung himself to the ground, burrowing his head in his hands in an agony of despair. When he rose to his feet, it was dusk. He had spent the whole day in his private Gethsemane. He rode homeward, his face cold and hard. If he could not have the woman he loved, he would have other women. Scores of them. Hundreds of them. Thousands of them if need be. Eventually, he must be able to expiate his pain in the arms of one of them. There had to be more for him in life than the shallow playacting that awaited him at Villada.

Hollywood was stunned. Rakoczi took and discarded the most beautiful women in town with as little regard for their reputation as for his own. He became known as "The Hungarian Devil" and rumors of his sexual exploits were discussed at every Hollywood cocktail party, at every dinner table. It was said that he made love to three, to four, different women every night. That Paramount's leading female star had attempted suicide when he had abandoned her. That there wasn't an actress on the 20th Century lot that hadn't graced his bed. That Errol Flynn's romantic exploits were those of an inept schoolboy in comparison.

Hazel Renko read the gossip columns, answered the never-ending telephone calls to the house, and wondered if she was destined to go through life feeling pity for the people she most cared about. Whatever Vidal's exploits outside Villada, inside life continued as it always had.

Vidal was punctiliously polite to Kariana and everything and anything she expressed a desire for, she was given. Hazel was careful to see that no reporters were put through to Kariana on the telephone. That no newspapers were left lying around the house. Alone, in all of Hollywood, Kariana Rakoczi was unaware of her husband's sexual exploits. She had withdrawn into a world that nothing could penetrate. The shopping expeditions had ended. She was content to sit, the same piece of embroidery in her hands for days, her eyes fixed on the far horizon as if therein lay the answer to her problem.

Perhaps, Hazel thought as she tried to urge Kariana indoors long after the sun had set, it would be better if she *were* in a home or a hospital. Better if Vidal remarried. But none of the stars and starlets that his name was associated with brought a softening to the granite-hard face. Sometimes it seemed to Hazel that Vidal Rakoczi would never smile again.

Valentina had been able to hold the baby briefly, alone, before Paulos had been ushered into the room. He had weighed almost ten pounds and there was no way that his weight could be issued to the press. For the sake of Paulos's mother, the pretense that the baby was premature had to be continued.

She could see nothing of herself in his face; he was all Vidal. His hair was a wild, shaggy mop of jet-black. His eyes at first had been screwed up as he had yelled lustily. Then, when the nurse had placed him in her arms, his cries had ceased, and his eyes had opened. Mother and son regarded each other for the first time. Small, clenched fists fought their way free of the blanket the nurse had cocooned him in with a fury at the restraint that was worthy of his father. His eyes, though the nurse would later state categorically that *all* newborn babies' eyes were blue, were gypsy-dark and thick-lashed. Valentina touched the petal-soft face with wonder and with love, tracing the unformed features with her forefinger, knowing very well how strong the lines of nose and jaw would be. How high the cheekbones. How winged the brows. He was a son Vidal would have been so proud of. A son she and Paulos would love.

Paulos entered the room, the relief on his face still not quite disguising the lines of anguish he had suffered during the hours he had been barred from Valentina's side.

He crossed quickly to her, kissing her gently. His concern, as always, was first of all for her.

"Are you all right, my love? Was it very bad? They wouldn't let me near you, but I heard you cry out and . . ."

Valentina smiled, her love for him nearly as maternal as it was for her child.

"Darling Paulos, it was an easy birth. Truly."

He sat down beside her, his gaze traveling from her radiant face to the warmly wrapped bundle cradled in her arms. His first emotions were of wonder and astonishment. He had never seen a newborn baby before. He reached out tentatively to touch it and immediately his forefinger was seized in a sturdy grasp.

"She's marvelous, darling. Absolutely incredible."

"She's a he," Valentina said in amusement.

The bright black eyes screwed up again tightly, the face turning an angry red as the little mouth opened, emitting a deafening squall.

"I think he's hungry," Valentina said as the nurse hurried into the room.

"I daresay he is," the English nurse said scoldingly. "You've been holding him for far too long. Boiled sugar water is what he needs right now. You can put him to the breast tomorrow."

The baby was unceremoniously whipped from Valentina's arms and whisked from the room.

"They're very authoritative, aren't they?" Paulos said with a grin.

"Very," Valentina agreed. She could still feel the weight of the tiny body in her arms, the warmth of him against her flesh. "I don't want to stay here a day longer than necessary, Paulos. I want to be at home with you and the baby."

"What are we going to call him?"

"I don't know," she said helplessly. "I don't think an American name would suit him. He doesn't look American, does he?"

"With that mop of black hair, he looks very Greek," Paulos said, a gleam of amusement in his eyes. "Shall we call him Alexander?"

"Alexander would be a perfect name," she agreed, and raised her face for his kiss.

For several months they ventured no farther from the villa than the nearby village. They were forging a whole new life together as a family and Paulos spurned the offers that arrived for him to perform on concert platforms in London and Paris.

"This is where I want to be," he said when Valentina gently protested, fearing that he was neglecting his music for her sake. "My career can wait."

To Valentina, it was a golden, fairy-tale existence. Alexander thrived, gurgling on a blanket in the shade of a plane tree, sleeping to the strains of Bach and Liszt. She would sit at Alexander's side, sewing, overcome with love for him, the emotional barrenness of her childhood more than compensated for. She had Paulos; she had Alexander; and if sometimes her sewing lay neglected on her lap and her eyes grew pensive at the thought of the other person she loved and who no longer had any part in her life, no one knew but herself.

When Alexander was a year old, Paulos made a return to the concert platform circuit, taking his wife and child with him. *The Times, Le Monde,* and *Le Figaro* frequently displayed photographs of the Khairetis family arriving in London, Paris, or Rome prior to a Khairetis recital. They traveled lightly and with none of her usual entourage. Valentina would carry Alexander herself, smilingly but emphatically refusing any attempt to interview her.

In the winter they would ski at Gstaad and Alexander's first, faltering steps were taken in the snow. In the summer they returned to Crete. They entertained family and friends Paulos had known since childhood. In the evening they drank with the villagers in the local taverna and walked home along the moonlit shoreline, arms around each other's waists. Perfectly happy. Perfectly content. Sufficient entirely unto themselves.

Public interest in her didn't fade as her year of seclusion stretched into two years and then three. Hollywood producers tried ceaselessly to lure her back to the studio. And all failed. She was not returning to the screen, she told them, and she was not returning to Hollywood.

Alexander was no longer carried in her arms when they arrived and departed amid a host of reporters and photographers at train stations and airports. He scampered along at their side, accepting as natural the attention his parents attracted, dark curls tumbling low over his brow, referring to himself constantly as "Skander" and demanding that he, too, have a camera that he could make flash.

Paulos began to devote more and more time to composing, aware that however easily they now traveled together, the day would come when it would be a burden for them. He derived intense pleasure from this new departure in his career, especially when he was no longer referred to in the press as "Paulos Khairetis, concert pianist" but as "Paulos Khairetis, composer and concert pianist." His professional stature grew and Valentina was overcome with pride.

Alexander spoke English, Greek, a smattering of French, and a Cretan dialect that even Paulos had difficulty understanding and that he had picked up from their gardener.

"We'll have to think about schools, my love," Paulos said to her repeatedly, but Valentina would shake her head and say that it was much too soon even to think about them. Paulos laughed, knowing full well that no power on earth would separate Valentina from her beloved "Skander." When he reached school age they would have to settle in London or Geneva, where he could attend a suitable day school.

They spent the summer of 1938 in Crete. Europe was no longer such a comfortable place in which to travel and composing was definitely taking precedence over performing for Paulos.

The latest papers from England had arrived and Paulos read them with a deepening frown. The news was not good. Mussolini was looking increasingly aggressive, and Hitler was already causing havoc in Eastern Europe. Crete was no longer a safe place for his wife and child.

Through the window he could see them playing: Valentina throwing a bright red ball for Alexander, who ran laughingly to retrieve it. Alexander was sturdy and strong with a shock of black hair and sparkling dark eyes. If he had been his own son, Paulos knew that he could not have loved him more.

Reluctantly he rose to his feet, the wild flowers massed in the vase on the piano trembling at his movement. He touched their petals. Pink, lance-shaped anemones; stark white clusters of neragoula; tall purple and rose skilaki; tulip-shaped fritillarias. Valentina gathered them fresh every morning, walking with a chattering Alexander at her side, far up into the foothills of the White Mountains.

There would be no skilaki and fritillarias in New York and he knew that she would be appalled at the prospect of being separated from him. Heavyhearted, he left the room, walking down through the garden to the beach.

Alexander was gleefully chasing the waves as they creamed toward him. Valentina was watching him, her arms hugging her legs, her dark eyes alight with pleasure, her shining black hair held away from her face by two heavy tortoiseshell combs.

Never, in all the years of their marriage, had he become accustomed to her beauty.

"We should have named him Poseidon. He's more at home in the water than he is on the land," Paulos said, sinking down onto the sand beside her, wrapping his arm around her shoulders.

She turned her head to look at him, at the unhidden love in his eyes, the adoration that had not faded with time, the kindness and the compassion that were such an integral part of him, and smiled.

She had grown to love him more deeply than she had ever imagined possible. His goodness and gentleness she had been aware of from the moment she had first met him. Later, she had become aware of other things. Of his talent. Of the way other women looked at him and the knowledge that she was envied. Not simply because she was Valentina, but because she was the wife of Paulos Khairetis, the pianist and composer who looked as if he had been the original model for a hundred Greek statues. Tall, fine-boned, lean and graceful, his charm was not a social veneer that could be exerted or cast aside at will, but stemmed from a genuine interest in everyone he met. A deep concern for others that those around him instinctively sensed.

His face was unusually serious, and she felt a flicker of alarm. "The news from Athens is not good, Valentina. I think it best if we leave Crete."

Her alarm deepened. "But why? Surely whatever is happening in Europe will not touch Crete?"

"But it has already touched Crete, my love. John Pendlebury, the archaeologist who has been working on Crete for many years, was stopped by a local policeman and accused of being a spy."

"But that's ridiculous!"

"I know. Apparently, Pendlebury was so indignant that he suggested the policeman ring up the king, or the British consul, to check on his identity." He grinned. "The policeman sensibly remarked that to telephone would cost twenty-five drachmas and that it was cheaper to let him go."

"Then no harm was done," Valentina said, relieved.

"Not on that occasion, no. But it shows the way things are going. There are currency restrictions, and it is impossible to send money out of the country. Mussolini is baying for blood, and as for Hitler . . ." He shrugged his shoulders expressively.

"But if we left Crete, where would we go? If England goes to war with Germany, there will be no safety for Alexander there. If Italy invades Greece, then we cannot return to Athens."

His gray eyes were somber. "There is only America, Valentina."

"No!" America was in her past, and she did not want the past rising up and disturbing her newfound happiness.

He took her hand. "If the situation in Europe deteriorates any further, we shall have no choice, Valentina. You and Alexander will have to travel to America while it is still safe to do so."

Alexander ran over to her, depositing a tiny struggling crab onto her lap.

"See, Maman, pretty, pretty."

For once she ignored him, staring at her husband. "Only me and Alexander?" she asked unbelievingly.

Paulos removed the stranded crab from her lap. "Here, Alexander, put it back into the water. It doesn't like the dry land."

Alexander stared at them both, sturdy legs set wide apart. He had brought them something pretty and they had ignored it. His chin wobbled dangerously and then he picked up the crab and walked back to the sea to do as his father had asked him, the set of his shoulders unmistakably Vidal's.

"If Italy invades Greece, then I must fight, Valentina. Greece is my country. I have no intention of hiding behind my profession and fleeing to America."

Her eyes flashed. "I'm your wife, Paulos. My place is with you."

"Not if there is a war," Paulos said firmly. "As a wife, my love, you will do as you are told."

Valentina felt a surge of despair. "I don't want to leave Crete, Paulos. I've been happy here."

"So have I, my love."

He kissed the corner of her mouth and gently cupped her chin, turning her face to his. "We are two very lucky people, Valentina." His lips touched hers, butterfly light and then warm and demanding.

"I think," she said huskily when at last he raised his head from hers, "that it is time for Alexander to have a sleep."

They smiled at each other, the smile of two people with no need for words.

"I love you," he said as she rose to her feet. "I love you with all my heart, and all my body and all my soul."

She wound her arm around his waist, resting her head contentedly on his shoulder, calling her son to her side, walking back to the villa in order to put him to bed and to make love to her husband—the husband who had given her so much—before the sun had reached its midday heat.

That evening they dined on their little vine-shaded patio. As the maid cleared the table and bid them good night, Paulos looked out over the still, dark sea and said, "I think I'll go out in the caïque for an hour or so. Fresh fish for breakfast would be nice."

Valentina cradled a glass of mandarini in her hands. "I'll wait up for you."

Their eyes met. She would sit up for him and when he returned they would make love again. He blew her a kiss and ran lightly down the steps leading from the patio to the beach.

When the storm came, it erupted out of nowhere. One moment the sea was calm, the next it was a mass of seething foam. Alone on the patio, as the wind whipped savagely through the pines and jacaranda trees, Valentina waited in increasing anxiety. Lightning seared the sky and she ran indoors for a jacket, hurrying once more out into the gardens and down to the beach. The little jetty where Paulos moored the caïque was empty, the sea no longer calm and gentle but thundering up the beach in huge, tumultuous waves. The rain lashed her face, the wind tugging viciously at her hair as she ran back to the villa, trying to raise help on the telephone from the harbormaster at Chania.

Her Greek was not good enough for her to deal with the situation. The harbormaster was sorry; the storm was severe. The sea was too rough for any boats to leave the harbor.

Pulling her jacket high against the onslaught of the screaming wind and driving rain, she stumbled once again down to the beach, straining her eyes for the sight of the caïque. The blackness was impenetrable. Her eyes ached as time and time again she imagined a black speck, denser than the waves, heading for the shore. Always it was in vain. She began to run along the shoreline, calling his name, the roar of the elements drowning her voice.

He had to come back! He *had* to! "Dear God, let him be safe," she sobbed as the lightning forked again and all that could be seen were huge walls of surf crashing down in relentless fury.

Her jacket was no protection against the torrential rain. Her silk dress was saturated, clinging limply to her legs as she staggered toward the jagged outcrop of rocks that formed one arm of the bay. Perhaps there he had found shelter. Perhaps he was too injured to move. Alive, but too injured to make his way to the villa.

"Oh, Paulos! Paulos! *Please* be alive! Please don't leave me!" she shouted against the elements and then, as the outcrop was reached and she found nothing but a vortex of surging foam, she sank to her knees on the spray-drenched rocks and sobbed vainly, "I love you, Paulos! I *love* you!"

They found his body the next morning, washed up in a cove a mere two miles from the one that fronted the villa. Of the caïque only a few pieces of smashed wood were washed ashore. It was his mother's wish that he be buried in Athens. The Khairetis yacht was dispatched to Chania to take its tragic cargo home.

Valentina sat stiffly at the side of the coffin, Alexander's small hand held tightly in hers. She had closed up the villa and would not be returning to it. Without Paulos it was no longer a home. Beneath her black veil her face was ashen. She had known that she had loved him, but not until it was too late had she realized how much.

"Hush, darling," she said to Alexander as he began to cry again. "It's all right. Everything is going to be all right."

"Not all right," Alexander said with irrefutable logic. "Daddy's gone. Want Daddy."

She had made one fresh start in life; now she would have to make another. And with only a four-year-old child as comfort and solace.

"It *is* going to be all right," she said fiercely to Alexander. "Daddy would want it to be. He would want us to be brave," and she turned her head away so that Alexander should not see the tears that were coursing down her cheeks.

Chapter Twenty

Paulos's mother had wanted her to stay in Athens.

"I cannot, Mama. The last thing Paulos asked of me was that I take Alexander to safety in America."

Evangelina Khairetis sighed and nodded. Europe was no longer a healthy place in which to rear a child. She had lost her son and now she was to lose her grandson.

"Paulos was right," she said, the heavy drapes in her apartment barring the bright light of morning. "You must do as Paulos wished you to do."

Valentina kissed her cheek. "We will write to you, Mama, and as soon as it's safe to do so we will return."

Evangelina Khairetis nodded and patted Valentina's hand. Later would be too late. Maria was now married to the son of family friends. Aristea was betrothed to a banker of good family. She had lived long enough and death would reunite her with those that she had loved the most—her husband and her son.

Strange, she thought, that Paulos's child had never touched her heart in the way she had expected. He was a handsome little boy. Sturdy and vital. Yet she did not feel the fierce love for him that she had felt for her own children, and for the granddaughter whom Maria had presented her with a year ago.

She laid her hand on Valentina's head. "You brought my son great happiness, my child. Go with my love and with my blessing."

Valentina left. She went first to Lisbon and then to London. It was March 1939 and the weather was crisp and cold, the newspapers full of the dismal news that Hitler had annexed Bohemia and Moravia and proclaimed them a German protectorate.

Paulos had been right in his desire for her to leave Europe. The London she was now visiting was not the London she had known so briefly and so happily on her honeymoon.

As the black taxicab hurtled her and Alexander through the narrow streets, she saw that all four of her films were being shown simultaneously in the West End. Her image confronted them from a dozen billboards: "Valentina as Margaret of Anjou in *The Warrior Queen*"; "Valentina in *A Woman in Scarlet*"; "Valentina in *The Gethsemane Gate*"; "Valentina in *The Heiress Helena*"; and everywhere, below her name, Vidal's name was written in huge black letters.

Alexander had stared at them in wonder, not understanding why all the ladies on the giant posters looked so much like his mother. Valentina had looked away. The sight of them brought back too many painful memories. Memories she was not yet ready to face. She needed a breathing space. A time to think.

She found it in her suite at the Savoy. The large windows overlooked the windblown Thames. There were riverside gardens in which Alexander could run and play . . . and there was privacy. No one knew of her presence in London. There were no reporters to contend with. No phalanx of photographers whenever she took Alexander for his daily walk.

Three days before she was due to leave for Southampton and the *Queen Mary*, the telephone in her suite rang. She answered it absentmindedly, assuming it to be room service, her thoughts elsewhere.

When the thickly accented voice asked if it was Valentina to whom he was speaking, she sat down suddenly on the bed, feeling as if a fist had just been pressed hard into her belly.

"Welcome to London," Alexander Korda said jovially. "You have managed to keep your visit very discreet. Not a word in the press. I congratulate you."

It wasn't Vidal. Vidal's accent had never been so thick. Yet for a brief, unguarded moment . . .

"Who is it?" she asked, her breath once more coming evenly, her hands steadying.

"Alexander Korda. I heard only today that you were in London, and only then because I was lunching at the Savoy. I am still here. Will you have dinner with me?"

"No. Thank you for asking, but . . ."

"Is all right," Alexander Korda said expansively. "I know that you are recently a widow and I offer you my sincere condolences. My *very* sincere condolences. We *will* have dinner. We will talk of your movies, of your plans for the future. It will be extremely pleasant."

It was two months since Paulos had died. Two months since she had taken her leave of Evangelina. Since then she had spoken only to maids, waiters, bellhops, and a four-year-old boy. "We will dine early," Alexander Korda was saying. "I will meet you in the American Bar at seven o'clock."

Korda was a director of formidable repute. He would be an interesting and stimulating host. She had to emerge from her self-imposed seclusion eventually.

"Thank you, Mr. Korda. I will look forward to it."

She rang for a maid to sit with Alexander in case he woke and was frightened by her absence. Korda was Hungarian. Before she could stop herself, she wondered if there would be any similarity between him and Vidal. For the first time since Paulos had died, a wry smile touched her lips. No one could be like Vidal. He was unique.

She glanced across at the far twin bed and the small body buried beneath the blankets. No one, that was, unless it was his son.

Her face grew somber. When she returned to America, she would have to stay far from Hollywood, for if Vidal ever glimpsed Alexander, he would know the truth.

Alexander Korda was not remotely like Vidal. His hair was gray, his figure was stout, and he wore thick, shell-rimmed glasses.

"I am enchanted to meet you," he said, raising her hand and kissing it with genuine reverence. "You have brought a magic to the screen that is inimitable."

"I haven't made a film for more than four years, Mr. Korda."

"Alex, please," Korda said, realizing at once why his compatriot, Vidal Rakoczi, had dispensed with all other leading ladies and had worked with her and her alone until her departure from Hollywood.

Her beauty had a strangely haunting quality that captivated him immediately. He noted the simplicity of her black cocktail dress and remembered that she had been widowed for only a couple of months. The dress was long-sleeved and high at the throat, the waist minuscule, her only jewelry a wedding ring. Yet as they walked from the American Bar into the chandelier-hung decor of the River Restaurant, every head turned in their direction and a murmur of admiration and speculation followed in their wake.

"I'm afraid that by inviting you to dinner, I have put an end to your privacy," Alex said as the headwaiter deferentially seated them at the best table in the room. "Tomorrow, news that you are in London will be in all the gossip columns."

Valentina smiled, and Alexander Korda felt the blood leap along his veins. There was more to her than mere beauty. She had warmth and empathy and he knew instinctively that here was a woman who could listen as well as talk. Give as well as receive. A woman who was interested in other people more than she was in herself.

"It doesn't matter," she said as the waiter handed her the leather-bound menu. "Someone was bound to discover sooner or later that I was here."

"And you will be staying?"

"No. I am leaving in three days for America."

Alex cast his menu aside and leaned toward her, his hands clasped.

"No, no, and no!" he said with an intensity that was reminiscent of Vidal. "That is why I had to talk to you. I am preparing to make a film. The most expensive and daring film of my career, *The Thief of Baghdad*. Unfortunately, there is no leading female role in it, but I want to plan *now* for a film that we *can* make together!"

She shook her head. Alex frowned at her over the top of his glasses. "You have not decided to retire permanently, have you?"

"No. Now that Paulos is dead, I want to work. I *need* to work. Without work there is too much time for thinking and remembering."

Alex nodded understandingly. "Then you must work here. In England."

"No. There is going to be a war, Alex. I cannot remain in England."

"There will still be films to be made," Alex said vehemently. "Films that will lift the country's spirits; films that will fill the nation with hope and certainty of victory."

She shook her head again. "I'm sorry, Alex. I would have loved to have had the opportunity to work with you, but I have my child to consider. There is no way that I can remain in England."

Alex leaned back in his chair. He had forgotten about the child. "Perhaps," he said, reaching for the menu again, "if there is no war, you will return."

"If you want me to, then I will."

Alex visibly cheered. "We will make great films together, Valentina. Films to rival even the masterpieces that you made with Rakoczi."

"Yes," she said, her voice steady as she changed the subject. "I think I would like to start with the caviar glacé, Alex, please. And then perhaps the crepe Versailles."

Alex ordered, a splendidly majestic figure in his silvergray double-breasted suit, his Sulka shirt, his Knize tie, and his Lobb shoes. It was perhaps better the way it was. Merle Oberon, his bride-to-be, would certainly not have been pleased if he had made plans for a film starring Valentina and not herself. Time was on his side. He had met Valentina in the flesh. She was willing to be directed by him. The story would have to be exactly right. He would use Technicolor and in England at the moment, Technicolor was an expensive and difficult process. No, it was better as it was. For a little while.

The waiter served the hors d'oeuvres and Alex grinned. "I'll never tell Vivien, but you're the only other actress who would have been a serious contender for the part of Scarlett in *Gone With the Wind*. As Scarlett, you would have been *terrific!*"

"I imagine Miss Leigh will be pretty terrific," Valentina said, sipping her wine.

"Oh, she will be," Alexander said confidently. "Vivien is *my* protégée as you were Rakoczi's. When I first saw her, she had only played bit parts and was doing a play, *The Mask of Virtue*. I signed her up then and there, and now she has the plum part of all time." He beamed, as if he himself were responsible for David O. Selznick casting Vivien Leigh as Scarlett O'Hara.

Valentina suppressed a smile. She imagined that the avuncular Alexander Korda had made a substantial profit by loaning Vivien out to Selznick.

"Still, it would have been a hard choice," Alex continued, spearing a mushroom. "You or Vivien for Scarlett." He paused, wondering yet again why Valentina had turned her back on Hollywood when she had married. It had perplexed Hollywood. It had perplexed him. It still perplexed him.

Paulos Khairetis must have been a most remarkable young man to have lured a woman like Valentina away from her natural environment. Away from the soundstages and klieg lights. Away from the heady intoxication of moviemaking.

"We must make a *great* movie together," he said, leaning once more toward her. "Greater even than the movie Selznick is making now with Vivien. Greater than anything that has been made before. Where should it be set? Ancient Rome? Egypt? Or should it be a classic? A *Jane Eyre*? A *Madame Bovary*?"

The years of self-imposed indifference to the world of moviemaking fell away as if they had never existed. She was once again caught up in the fevered fascination of suitable parts, suitable films. This was how she had talked with Vidal. Suggesting projects, rejecting projects, discussing until the long hours of the night had pearled into dawn.

Alexander Korda's eyes twinkled behind his shell-rimmed glasses. Though the world would never know it, and Valentina herself would be unaware of it, he, Alexander Korda, had reawakened in her the lust to appear before the cameras again. It had been a good day. A satisfying day. A day he would not soon forget.

When they parted, it was on the understanding that Valentina would star as Queen Guinevere in a vast Arthurian epic to be made by Alex sometime in the unspecified future.

Alex left the Savoy humming to himself, and Valentina returned to her suite and her sleeping son. For a second, as the gilded elevator bore her upward, she imagined she could feel the heat of klieg lights against her face. She laughed at her fancy and stepped from the elevator. Soon, very soon, she would do so. It was what Paulos would have wanted, and it was what she now wanted for herself.

*   *   *

The crossing on the *Queen Mary* from Southampton to New York was rough and unpleasant. Given the choice, Valentina would have spent her time sitting in one of the splendid lounges with a book borrowed from the ship's vast library. The pleasure was denied her. To Alexander, the crossing of the Atlantic was the greatest adventure of his life and he raced the decks, tweed-coated by Harrods, an English muffler around his neck, his eyes sparkling, his cheeks glowing.

With the collar of her mink coat pulled high, Valentina followed him, terrified that he would fall and hurt himself. Even more terrified that in his enthusiasm he would do what the steward assured her was impossible and fall overboard.

The joy she found in seeing the return of his usual high spirits, spirits that had been utterly quenched when Paulos died, compensated her for the biting discomfort of the driving wind and the piercing cold.

She did not dine in any of the restaurants but ate privately with Alexander in her cabin. The ship was full of celebrities, some whom she knew personally, some she knew only by reputation. All seemed intent on making her acquaintance and only the complicity of her helpful steward prevented her from being besieged by unwelcome visitors.

The steward's protection ceased the minute the ship docked. A throng of reporters and photographers awaited her, pressing in on her on either side.

"Have you returned to make a movie with Vidal Rakoczi?"

"Are rumors of your reconciliation with Worldwide true?"

"What are your plans, Valentina?"

"I'm sorry, I don't know myself yet," she answered, smiling professionally, aware of Alexander's small hand tightening in hers. What *were* her plans, for God's sake? She didn't even know where they were going to stay the night.

"Why are those men shouting at you, Maman?" Alexander asked as she tried to force a way through the mass of bodies and hopefully find a cab.

"They're just asking questions, darling."

Flashbulbs popped on either side of them and she realized with despair that her efforts to keep Alexander out of the public eye could not possibly succeed. She only hoped that his heavy coat and muffler would make his likeness to Vidal impossible to detect.

"Could you find me a cab, please?" she asked a porter, cutting across the barrage of questions.

"Valentina! Valentina!" a familiar voice cried, and with a rush of relief she saw Leila's tiny figure swathed in fur, waving furiously.

"Am I glad to see you!" Valentina said fervently, hugging her close as Leila led the way to a chauffeur-driven Rolls. "I expected some reaction from the press when I returned, but nothing like this."

The porter stowed her bags in the Rolls' capacious trunk. The chauffeur opened the rear doors.

"Idiot," Leila said affectionately as the car, leaving the docks, moved into the wide, straight thoroughfare of West Fourteenth Street. "*The Warrior Queen* has grossed more than any movie in history. It's still playing to packed houses all over the country. *The Gethsemane Gate* picked up more awards than any other movie of its year. If it hadn't been for the hoopla over the way you left the country, you would have had an Oscar. *The Heiress Helena* had its premiere audience on their feet and clapping—and its premiere audience was Hollywood's crème de la crème. You're still a big, big star. What everyone wants to know, is what you intend doing now that you have returned."

"One thing I am *not* doing is returning to Hollywood. I shall stay in New York."

"And work?"

"If I can."

Leila threw back her head, her laughter pealing as delightfully as it had in the far-off days when they had worked together on the set of *The Warrior Queen*.

"Darling, I promise you that by tonight you will be inundated with offers from every producer in the country. Denton has already asked that he dine with us."

"Denton?" Valentina asked curiously as Alexander squirmed between them, trying to get a better view of the breathtakingly tall buildings and the incredible stream of vehicles speeding by on either side.

"Denton Brook-Taylor. He's a Broadway producer and" —Leila's eyes sparked mischievously—"my lover. You didn't think this Rolls was mine, did you?"

"What's a lover, Maman?" Alexander asked, returning his attention to the conversation going on between his mother and the lady who had hugged and kissed him so effusively when he had first scrambled into the rear of the nice-smelling car.

"A lover," Valentina said, "is someone you are very, very fond of."

"Is Grandma Khairetis my lover, then? And you and Auntie Aristea and Auntie Maria?"

"No, darling. A lover is someone special. Someone that you love even though they are not family."

"Like a friend?"

"Yes, Alexander. A very special and very close friend."

"I can see that I am going to have to watch what I say," Leila said over the top of Alexander's head as his interest returned to the chrome and glass buildings soaring skyward.

"And *I* am going to have to find somewhere to stay. Perhaps you could ask the chauffeur to drop my luggage off at the Plaza."

"Yes, but luggage only. You're both coming home with me and we're going to talk and talk and talk."

Liveried bellboys at the Plaza removed Valentina and Alexander's white calfskin luggage, and as she glided up the steps and into the foyer she was aware of at last stepping irrevocably from one world to another. There would be no more sunlit days laughing and talking with Paulos and Alexander in their flower-drenched sparkling white villa: no more stillness. No more quiet.

New York held bustle and noise and a completely new way of life. She secured a suite for herself and Alexander with ease, and then returned, Alexander's hand still in hers, to the waiting Rolls. For the first time it occurred to her that she would have to find a nanny for Alexander. He was too small to follow in her wake around New York. Even now he was rubbing his eyes, tired by the excitement of the morning. She would also have to find somewhere to live. The Plaza could not remain their New York home. Its sumptuous opulence was not the best environment for a healthy child accustomed to making as much noise as he liked, and running free on beaches and mountain slopes.

They passed Central Park and she gazed at it with relief. At least there was somewhere nearby where she could take Alexander and he could release his natural high spirits.

Leila's apartment was large, roomy and untidy and in total contrast to the sleek Rolls-Royce Silver Shadow that had deposited them on the curb.

"I don't live with Denton. He's far too proper for such an arrangement," Leila said unnecessarily, flinging her fur coat over a chair. She disappeared into the kitchen, returning with an orange juice for Alexander and a bottle of Mumm's Extra Dry for herself and Valentina, which she promptly opened.

Alexander, copying Leila, nonchalantly flung his coat on the nearest chair, crossing to the bookshelves to see if he could find a book with pictures in it. He was, Valentina thought as she watched him, every inch Vidal's son.

"Tell me about Denton," she said as the champagne frothed into her glass and Leila kicked off her shoes and curled on a comfortable-looking chair.

"He's a millionaire. He's at least sixty though *very* handsome. Well . . ." She paused and giggled. "He's very distinguished-looking and I guess if you're a millionaire, that amounts to the same thing. He's really a banker, but the theater fascinates him and he's begun backing shows."

"And putting you in them?" Valentina asked with a grin, aware that Alexander had found a book to his satisfaction.

"Of course. Only small parts so far. I'm still having voice lessons. Broadway, New York, is a hell of a lot different from Worldwide Pictures, Hollywood!"

They laughed and then fell silent. "I guess it was a success," Leila asked after a little while. "Between you and Paulos?"

"Yes." Valentina put down her champagne glass. "It was very successful, Leila."

Vidal's name hung, unspoken, between them. Alexander continued to turn the pages of a large book and Leila, noting the angle that he held his head as he perused the pictures with concentration, the tumble of childish curls falling low over his forehead, the already stubborn lines of jaw and chin, knew at last why Valentina had married Paulos and left Hollywood. And why she was determined never to return.

The doorbell rang and Leila sprang to her feet. "That will be Denton," she said, rushing across to a mirror to check her makeup. "Goodness, you'd think he would have given us a *little* longer together, wouldn't you?"

He entered the room and she clung to his arm, puppy-dog fashion. He barely glanced at her. He strode across the room and took Valentina's hand, grasping it firmly.

"I'm very, *very* glad to meet you at long last," he said.

Everything about Denton Brook-Taylor was gray. Not a dull, drab gray but a silver as glittering as that of his Rolls. He was tall and thin and carried himself with the air of an aristocrat. His hair was silver, slicked close to his head. His moustache was neat, carefully concealing a narrow upper lip. His suit was dove-gray, double-breasted, and he wore a white carnation in his buttonhole. His eyes were gray and his tie was gray, slashed diagonally with silver stripes. Despite Leila's assertion, he could never have been called a handsome man. But he was a man with presence. No one could possibly doubt that he had wealth and power and that he relished the possession of both.

"Did you have a pleasant voyage?"

"Yes, though it was rough. March isn't the best month to cross the Atlantic."

"You should have crossed on the *Normandie*. It rolls far less in heavy seas."

"I'll remember in future," Valentina said, aware that she was under close scrutiny.

"Do you mind if I smoke?"

"No."

It was almost as if Leila were not in the room. He removed a cigar from behind the silk handkerchief in his breast pocket and a few minutes later the aroma of good-quality Havana tobacco filled the room.

"Leila has told you that I am a producer?"

"Yes." Alexander had returned to her side and was regarding Denton Brook-Taylor with open hostility. Denton Brook-Taylor ignored him as he did Leila. Valentina thought that Denton Brook-Taylor would ignore with ease anyone or anything that was not engaging his immediate attention.

"I intend to put Ibsen's *Hedda Gabler* on Broadway. Will you accept the part of Hedda?"

Valentina stared at him as if he were mad. "I couldn't possibly accept. I've only acted before the camera, never on the stage."

"No, but as Hedda, burning with suppressed sexuality, you're going to be a sensation."

"Leila, explain to him. The idea is preposterous."

"No, it isn't," Leila said, perching on the arm of Denton's chair. "As soon as we heard that you were aboard the *Queen Mary* on your way to New York, Denton said he must have you for the part. I'm to play Thea Elvsted. It's the most marvelously challenging part that I've ever been given. Oh, you *must* say yes, Valentina. You must!"

Valentina stared at them. Only a stage actress could portray Ibsen's tortured heroine as she deserved to be played.

"Would you like to do it?" His eyes impaled her.

If she succeeded, she would have proved to herself beyond all doubt that her talent was not something that depended solely upon a camera and lighting. But if she failed . . . She shrugged her shoulders. She would not fail.

"I'd love to do it," she said to a delighted Denton Brook-Taylor. "When do we start rehearsals?"

It meant a nanny for Alexander. It meant voice lessons. It meant coaching every hour of the day and most hours of the night. It meant a return to life as a public figure. Interviews. Photographs. Ridiculous rumors printed in the gossip columns as truth. It meant the learning of a new craft. Stagecraft. It meant hard, unrelenting work, and it meant exhilaration as she slipped with pain and ecstasy into the multifaceted character of Hedda Gabler.

Stan Kennaway was the director. His string of credits included *The Cherry Orchard, Romeo and Juliet,* and Chekhov's *The Three Sisters*. He had been appalled when Denton had told him who was to play the part of Hedda.

"This play needs an actress, Denton! Not a lightweight glamour queen."

"Have you seen her movies? She *is* an actress."

"F'Christ's sake, Denton! Every scene she appeared in was probably shot a hundred times! Out there, onstage, she only has *one* chance."

"She only *needs* one chance," Denton said tersely. "Trust me, Stan. We're going to have the biggest Broadway success of the year on our hands."

Stan had considered stepping down as director and then had decided that nothing would be lost by at least seeing how the star of *The Warrior Queen* performed onstage.

She had arrived at rehearsals with none of the artifacts of

the Hollywood star. There had been no coterie of hangers-on, no pretensions. She had worn trousers and a cashmere sweater. Her hair was held back from her face by a headband, falling free to her shoulders. Her skin was devoid of makeup. She had listened to him with unnerving intensity and from the moment that she did her first read-through, he knew that Denton Brook-Taylor's judgment had been sound.

"You're going to be just fine," he said to her when they broke for coffee. "This is just the sort of play Rakoczi would have loved to direct. When he hears the news he's going to be wild that he didn't get to you first."

He grinned. It felt good to be one up on the brilliant Hungarian.

Valentina's smile was stiff and forced. Though the April sunshine streaming through the windows was pleasurably warm, the rehearsal hall felt suddenly cold. Denton Brook-Taylor was speaking to her, but she didn't hear him. She wasn't even aware of his presence. Her thoughts were elsewhere. On Vidal, and what his reaction might be when he learned of her return to America.

ChapterTwenty-one

The rehearsals were strenuous, and there was Alexander to take care of as well. The nanny she had hired was young, cheerful, and loving and Alexander quickly adjusted to his new way of life. Every morning, after a walk through Central Park, his nanny would take him to sit at the back of the drafty rehearsal hall and he would watch as his mother and Leila polished and repolished their lines. He never fidgeted or chattered. He would sit with his sturdy legs dangling from the seat of his chair, watching the various scenes being acted, and reenacted, with rapt attention.

Lunchtimes were always a special time of the day, for then he had his mother all to himself. It was the first rule that

Valentina had made. She would not socialize at lunch; she would not give interviews. She would not join in the heated discussions regarding the progress of the play with her fellow actors. Lunches were for Alexander, and were sacred.

Sometimes they would go for hamburgers; sometimes they would picnic in Central Park. But whatever they did, or wherever they went, it was fun. They would walk along, their clasped hands swinging, chattering, laughing, reciting poetry, relishing each other's company. The relationship between them was special: they knew it and so did everyone who saw them together.

"Why the hell don't I have that kind of relationship with my kid?" Stan Kennaway asked Leila one day as Valentina and Alexander left the rehearsal hall laughing at a private joke.

"Perhaps you don't love him enough," Leila answered dryly.

"Hell, that kid of mine gets everything he asks for," Stan said indignantly. "He goes to the best school in town. The tuition leaves me permanently broke."

"There's more to it than that," Leila said, pouring herself a coffee. "When was the last time you spent time together? Took him out on his own? Played ball with him?"

"I have a living to make," Stan protested. "Besides, he's only six years old. How can you have a conversation with a six-year-old?"

"Alexander is almost five and no one has a problem having a conversation with *him*."

"Maybe it's because the kid is advanced for his age."

"Maybe it's because his mother treats him like a friend and talks *to* him, and not just at him."

Stan shrugged and walked away. He didn't know what the hell it was. He only knew he wished he had the same kind of relationship with *his* son.

As a producer, Denton Brook-Taylor rarely graced his rehearsal halls. *Hedda Gabler* was an exception. At ten every morning the faint aroma of a Havana cigar would pervade the hall, and the cast and director would be aware that they were under close scrutiny. No one relished his presence. Stan preferred to work without the financier of the production breathing down his neck. His lack of praise or comment unnerved the cast, and even Leila's spirits dropped to zero whenever he appeared.

"I wish to goodness he'd go away," she whispered to Valentina. "I'm nervous enough as it is. Stan says I'm still not projecting my voice sufficiently."

Only Valentina was uncaring of Denton Brook-Taylor's presence. Her whole future career depended on her performance as Hedda Gabler. The news that she was to appear in a play, and not return to Hollywood, had, as she had expected, hit the headlines. The general consensus of press opinion was that Hedda Gabler was too ambitious a project for an actress who had never acted before on the stage, and who had not acted at all for five years.

As one leading New York critic wrote sagely, "Success on the screen does not necessarily mean success on the stage. The two arts are entirely different and very few stars have been able to achieve greatness in both media."

The *New York Times* predicted that her performance as the neurotic, sexually suppressed Hedda Gabler would be a disaster. The *Herald Tribune* commented that her return to America should have been crowned by her return to Hollywood and by the making of a movie to rival the much-talked-about *Gone With the Wind*.

Each day after rehearsals ended, she visited the celebrated English actress Dame May Whitty for further coaching in her part. The aging Dame May alternately bullied and coaxed her, drawing from her a performance she knew would stun the critics and have the premiere audience on its feet, roaring with admiration. But she kept the knowledge to herself. There was nothing more detrimental to an artist's performance than overconfidence.

"Take it from the beginning of Act Two," she said relentlessly. "Your movements on stage have to be more definite, more purposeful, than the movements you make for the camera. Your gestures must be subtle, but telling. Vocal intonation is everything."

Valentina began again and Dame May leaned back in her chair, watching her with shrewd eyes. Here was a natural, instinctive, intuitive actress whom it was a joy to coach. Her physical magnetism would spellbind theater audiences just as it had screen audiences. Together they researched the role of Hedda. Probed her tortured character; studied the reasons behind everything that she did and everything she said. And late at the end of every day, Valentina would return, bone-weary, to her luxurious suite at the Plaza, and kiss the fore-head of her sleeping child. Alexander had asked to be there on the night that the play opened. She hoped and prayed for his sake that her performance would be a success.

"Could we have lunch together?" Denton Brook-Taylor asked on the morning of the dress rehearsal.

Valentina looked up at him as the morning costume she wore in Act I was repinned. "I'm sorry. I always lunch with my son."

"Dinner, then?"

She nodded. Obviously her producer had something to say to her that he wanted no one else to overhear. It could only be about the play. Was he thinking of replacing her? Even at this late stage?

"What on earth can he want to see me about?" she asked Leila that evening as she slipped her feet into shoes of glacé kid, a worried frown puckering her brow. "I thought every-thing was going well."

"It is," Leila assured her, bending down and setting Alexander's train back on the rails of track that covered the entire floor of the hotel suite. "Maybe he wants to talk publicity. Whatever it is, it at least gives me a night of freedom."

"What do you intend doing with it?" Valentina asked, looping a row of pearls around her throat so that they fell lushly against the soft drapery of her dress.

"What I always do." Leila's eyes shone wickedly. "I'll slip downtown and see my boyfriend Rory."

"You can't two-time a man like Brook-Taylor for long without his finding out," Valentina scolded, picking up a small leather purse the exact shade of her dress. "When he does, it will be good-bye to your use of his Rolls; good-bye to any more furs . . ."

". . . And good-bye to any further parts," Leila finished for her. "I don't care, Valentina. I'm really in love this time. I just want *one* Broadway success. Just *one* play that I'll always be able to look back on with pride. When I have achieved that, I shall be quite happy to turn my back on it all, and live in happy poverty with Rory."

"Rory is very talented," Valentina said, spraying perfume on her throat. "He's hardly penniless."

Leila giggled. "He is compared to Denton."

"*Everyone* is, compared to Denton," Valentina said, smiling despite herself.

The telephone rang and Leila threw a pair of kid gloves across to Valentina. "That will be to say that he's waiting for you. Have a nice time, and if he mentions that he might call on me after he leaves you, *please* tell him not to. Tell him I'm having an early night. Tell him I'm having a nervous breakdown. Tell him anything, but make sure he doesn't find out that I'm not sitting chastely in my apartment, pining away with loneliness for him."

Valentina kissed Alexander good-bye, waved to Leila, and stepped out into the thickly carpeted corridor, wondering yet again why Denton Brook-Taylor should have asked to speak to her in private.

They dined at a French restaurant, so discreet and exclusive that not even one photographer captured the event for any of the gossip columns. The decor was formal with pale primrose walls in the style of Louis XVI, chairs and banquettes upholstered in gold velvet, and crystal chandeliers that would have done honor to Versailles.

Denton discussed the menu with the maître d' in perfect French and when he had ordered, leaned back in his chair, the elegant surroundings perfectly complementing his distinguished looks. She waited for him to speak, to enlighten her as to the reason for his dinner invitation. Instead he said, "You look very beautiful."

Her fingers tightened around the stem of her aperitif glass. She had seen that look in men's eyes before. Many, many times. Mr. Denton Brook-Taylor had not invited her out to dinner to discuss the play or anything to do with the play.

"Thank you," she said, her voice cold.

He smiled. "You don't like me, do you, Valentina?"

"Leila is my best friend. I thought you wished to see me tonight to discuss the play. If I had known otherwise, I would not have accepted your invitation."

"How very prim and proper." His gaze on her face never wavered. Her incredible eyes held him mesmerized. They were tip-tilted at the corners. Did those eyes give her face its uniqueness? Or was it the clean, sculptured lines of cheek and jaw? He was a connoisseur of beautiful objects. He collected them. Hoarded them.

His eyes narrowed as he surveyed her. The magnetism that set her apart from other women had nothing to do with her beauty, he decided. It came from inside. There was something unreachable about her. Unattainable. Denton Brook-Taylor smiled. Nothing was unattainable to a man of his wealth.

His rooms were hung with Rembrandts and Van Goghs; his library was full of leather-bound first editions. His collection of eighteenth-century porcelain figures was the largest in private ownership. He signed his checks at a Louis Philippe walnut bureau mounted with Sevres panels and ormolu mounts, and he sat on a seventeenth-century Venetian Baroque giltwood chair to do so. Whatever he wanted, he got, and he wanted the dream of a million men. He wanted Valentina.

"Don't concern yourself about Leila. No doubt she will now be in the arms of the man she loves. A bohemian Irish painter by the name of Rory O'Connor."

Valentina looked up at him sharply. He knew. Leila's days of chauffeurs and furs were numbered. It made no difference. She was not romantically interested in this man.

"I don't date, Mr. Brook-Taylor," she said icily. "I haven't dated since my husband died."

"I know." He knew everything about her. What she ate for breakfast, where she took her child at lunchtime. What size dresses she wore; what size shoe she took. That she preferred pearls to diamonds; simply draped chiffons and silks to extravaganzas encrusted with sequins and beads. That she read widely, enjoyed English and Russian authors as well as American. That she drank very little apart from wine and that she didn't smoke.

He smiled. He had no intention of rushing her; of deepening her hostility. "You've misunderstood my intentions, Valentina. They are perfectly honorable. Have some caviar. It's the best in New York."

She could hardly excuse herself and say she would rather be in her hotel suite with her sleeping child. The evening would just have to be endured.

"Why do you think such a strong character as Hedda Gabler lacked the courage of the milk-and-water Thea Elvsted?"

he asked as the wine waiter poured a 1929 Chateau d'Yquem into his glass.

Despite herself, her attention was caught. "I don't know. That is what makes the play so fascinating."

They discussed the complexities of Hedda Gabler's longings and frustrations. They discussed the dilemma facing England as Hitler grew more and more aggressive. They argued as to whether the isolationist statements made by Joseph Kennedy and Charles Lindbergh were wise or unwise. They praised Homer's *Iliad* and agreed James Joyce's *Ulysses* was unreadable.

When the evening came to an end, Valentina was surprised to find that she had enjoyed herself. He did not attempt to seduce her and did not even kiss her good night.

As the Plaza's gilded elevator bore her upward toward her suite, she decided that Denton Brook-Taylor was a far more interesting companion than Leila had ever intimated. And she also decided that it would be wise to inform Leila that Denton Brook-Taylor was well aware of her extracurricular activities downtown.

Leila was on the telephone the next morning, even before the maid had delivered her breakfast.

"How did it go? What did he want?"

"I'm not a hundred percent sure," Valentina replied cheerily. "We discussed Hedda Gabler, and Hitler, and Greek literature, and then he dropped me off at the Plaza and wished me good night."

"No hand squeeze or a kiss?" Leila asked mischievously, without the least jealousy.

"None at all, but he knew very well where *you* were last night. Be warned."

"Oh, God," Leila said feelingly. "I knew it couldn't go on for much longer. Never mind. At least I'll be free of pretending to be intelligent. Hitler and Greek literature would have sent me up the wall. I'll see you at rehearsals."

"With vine leaves in your hair?" Valentina asked, laughing, taking a recurring line from the play.

"Hell, no, with a hip flask in my pocket! Bye."

There was only a week to opening night. Rehearsals were now being held in the theater and Valentina was existing on little more than nervous energy. She ignored her breakfast when it was brought to her room and dressed hurriedly, drinking cup after cup of black coffee. The *New York Times* lay crisply on her breakfast tray, and she shook it open, wanting to see if the Broadway critic, Brooks Atkinson, was still predicting disaster for the play and an untimely end to her stage career.

For once her own name was not headlined. It was Vidal's name that sprang from the page. "Rakoczi's *Eugénie Grandet*, the most daring, innovative movie to have emerged from Hollywood . . ." The critics eulogized the film.

Valentina tried to tear her eyes away from the accompanying photograph of Vidal, his brows pulled together, the lines of his mouth harsh, and read the accompanying newsprint.

"In *Eugénie Grandet* there is a depth and subtlety rarely, if ever, encountered on the screen. Sutton Hyde as the miser Grandet is a masterly performance and Rakoczi's new protégée, Helen Kratzman, brings disturbing nuances and an underlying eroticism to the main part."

Valentina did not read on. Her eyes were drawn again to the photograph. So he had found a new protégée. She wondered if they were lovers; if he was happy.

"Maman, Ruby is taking me to the zoo today," Alexander cried, entering the room in a rush, his eyes bright.

He never referred to his nanny by anything but her Christian name. An eight-year-old English boy at the Savoy had told him that to have a nanny was to be a baby. Alexander had no intention of being thought a baby. Ruby cared for him because his mother worked long hours at the theater. But in Alexander's mind, she was *not* his nanny. She was just someone whom he liked, who looked after him and took him to nice places.

Valentina caught hold of him as he rushed toward her, hugging him tight. "Aren't you the lucky one? Seeing lions and tigers while I have to declare yet again that Ejlert Lövborg will return—with vine leaves in his hair!"

"Why is it so important to Mr. Kennaway that you say that line properly, Maman?"

"Because it means far more than it seems to mean, and the audience has to know that by the way I say the words. They have to know all I'm feeling, but not expressing. What is going on in my head and in my heart."

Alexander nodded. He didn't really understand, but he

was determined that he would someday. He liked watching
his mother and Leila rehearse. He liked listening to Mr.
Kennaway and the way he could change things simply by
asking people to move differently and to speak differently.
He would have liked to spend the day at the theater, but the
lure of lions and tigers had been too strong. Tomorrow he
would make up for it. He would persuade Ruby to forgo their
daily walk in Central Park, and to spend every single minute
of the day at the theater. Valentina kissed him.

"Enjoy yourself, darling. I must go now. Give my love to
the bears."

"Silly," Alexander said, giggling. "They wouldn't understand."

As she stepped from the Plaza's foyer there was the usual
phalanx of reporters and photographers. She smiled, wished
them all good day, answered none of their questions, and
stepped into the rear of the chauffeur-driven car she had
quickly realized was a necessity in New York.

"I think they must camp on the sidewalk," Ted, her
chauffeur, said as the limousine drew away from the curb and
entered the mainstream of traffic.

"It will be worse after opening night," she said dryly,
hoping that Ruby and Alexander would be able to leave by
their usual side door unmolested.

Ted grinned. Opening night was going to be magnificent, and so was the fuss and clamor that would follow it.
Already the reporters were treating him as if *he* were a
celebrity. Asking questions. Offering money. He never took
any. It was enough for him simply to have the honor of
working for her. He began to whistle cheerfully to himself as
he drove toward the theater.

"Hi," Stan said, kissing her affectionately on the cheeks.
"I see Rakoczi has been hitting the headlines again. Only he
could have taken a subject as apparently uncommercial as
Balzac and made a hit of it."

"Vidal could make a masterpiece of the telephone direc-
tory," Valentina said, sitting beside him, passing an appraising eye over the set.

Everyone knew of her previous close working relationship with Vidal. It had been one of the first major obstacles
she had had to overcome. The ability to say his name lightly

and carelessly, talk about him with the same ease as she might Theodore Gambetta or Wally Barren.

There came the sound of a firm footfall behind them. Both turned their heads. "Good morning," Denton Brook-Taylor said. "What is it today? A straight run-through of all four acts?"

Stan nodded. "When Leila arrives."

"She's here now," Denton said, smiling pleasantly. "It's my fault she's late. We had a little matter to discuss."

Valentina looked away from him and surveyed the stage once more, certain that his discussion with Leila had centered around her relationship with Rory O'Connor.

Denton left them, mounting the stage and examining the set with close scrutiny. "He'll want to direct soon," Stan said, his eyes narrowing as Denton Brook-Taylor fingered the heavy velvet cloth covering the oval table center stage.

"He'd probably do quite a good job."

Stan looked at her sharply.

He had thought her immune to Denton's chill charm.

Leila arrived as merry-faced as ever. "Sorry I'm late, Stan. What is it? A straight run-through? I'll be ready in five minutes."

As she and Valentina changed she shrugged her shoulders philosophically. "It's all over. Denton was quite pleasant about it. He said if I loved someone else, it would be better if our relationship ended." She fastened the wrist buttons of her dark calling costume. "He didn't react at all as I had expected. No vindictiveness. No ice-cold fury. He said that I could keep all the presents he had given me, and that until the play ended I could still have the use of the Rolls."

Valentina was aware of a feeling of relief. She had expected Denton's reaction to the knowledge that he had been cuckolded to be less than gracious.

"So what is it now? Wedding bells?"

"I think so. I'm never going to be a great movie star. I'm never going to be a formidable actress. But Rory *is* going to be a great painter. If I marry him, I can live in reflected glory. Come on. Once more into the breach."

Valentina smoothed down the heavy silk of her morning dress, grateful for the miracle that would take place when she stepped on the stage. Her pain at the loss of Paulos would be forgotten as she took on the pain of being Hedda Gabler.

Vidal's face would no longer burn in the forefront of her mind. Instead, as Hedda Gabler, Ejlert Lövborg's face would torment her. She heard her cue and stepped forward, no longer Valentina but Hedda Gabler. Her eyes lost their warmth. They were cold, clear, and calm. She was a woman married to a man she found physically repugnant. A woman of sexual passion who didn't have the courage to flout convention in her pursuit of it. A woman whose burning jealousy would drive her to destroy Ejlert Lövborg. A woman who found herself so trapped by her actions that her only release was through suicide.

"Good morning, my dear Miss Tesman," she said, uttering her first line. "What an early visit! It *was* kind of you."

Stan Kennaway sat crouched in the front of the auditorium, not moving, not speaking. Act I flowed into Act II, into Act III and Act IV. No one, he observed, as Leila's blue eyes filled with genuine tears when news of Eljert Lövborg's suicide was brought to her, would be able to say that Leila Crane could not act, and no one who saw Valentina's performance as Hedda Gabler would ever forget it.

The dummy-pistol shot rang out and Hedda's husband shrieked, "Shot herself! Shot herself in the temple!" and the prestigious English actor who played the part of Judge Brack, the man who had compromised Hedda into her actions, half collapsed into an easy chair. "But merciful God! One doesn't *do* that kind of thing!"

It was the last line of the play. For a long moment there was silence, and then Stan stood up and moved forward. Six weeks ago he had seriously considered stepping down as director. Now he knew that this play would be the pinnacle of his career.

"Ladies and gentleman," he said respectfully, "I congratulate you, and now let's get back to work. The beginning of Act II again, please. Hedda and Judge Brack."

Valentina had not prayed since the day she had left the convent. On opening night, alone in her flower-decked dressing room, she clasped her hands tightly in her lap and said, "Oh, God, *please* let me be a success. For Paulos and for Alexander." She paused and then added softly, "And for Vidal as well."

She had specifically requested she be left alone before

curtain time, declining even Leila's company. The night was
going to be the most testing night of her career. The theater
was packed. Every critic in town was out front, just waiting to
see a one-dimensional, frivolous performance. For an agonizing second she doubted her own ability. Stan Kennaway was
a brilliant director, but he was not Vidal. In the past it had
been Vidal who had drawn from her the performances that
had made her famous. Now she was trying something completely new to her. And because of her name, if she failed,
she could not do so quietly. The whole world would know.

The bell rang to indicate that the first act had begun.
She rose to her feet steadily. She could rely on no one else's
strength but her own. Paulos was dead, and Vidal was lost to
her. Neither of the men she had loved and needed would be
in the auditorium giving her their wholehearted silent support, but Alexander would be there with Ruby.

There was a tap on her door and she was given last call.
She tilted her chin defiantly upward. She was Valentina. She
could become anyone she wanted to be and tonight she was
going to be Hedda Gabler, General Gabler's daughter. She
swept from her dressing room, her head high, and a few
seconds later she heard her voice loud and clear as she spoke
her opening lines.

"Good morning, my dear Miss Tesman. What an early
visit! It *was* kind of you."

The fevered frustrations, the jealousy, the bitterness that
consumed Hedda Gabler, consumed her.

Stan Kennaway was aware of the army of hostile critics
listening in amazement. Of exchanged looks. Raised brows.
And then compelling attention to the stage and the central
figure of Valentina. She burned with suppressed sexuality. As
if she were a magnet, every eye in the house was drawn
toward her. She held the audience in the palm of her hand
and her performance was so powerful, so subtle, that even
Stan wondered from what depths she drew.

When the pistol shot reverberated through the theater,
when Tesman shrieked in horror and Judge Brack collapsed
into a chair and uttered the last line, there was a moment's
silence. To the cast it seemed to last for a lifetime, and then
the applause erupted. It soared and swelled, surrounding
them, deafening them. Hands clasped, they faced a house
that had risen to its feet, stamping and cheering. The critics

were running for the doors and their typewriters. The fans were throwing their boutonnieres, their corsages of orchids, down onto the stage.

The curtain fell, was raised, and fell again. The roar of applause grew louder, more intense. Only after curtain call after curtain call did the cast manage to leave the stage, and still the cheers rang in their ears.

"We made it! My God, we made it!" Stan was hugging her. Everyone was hugging her. Leila was crying. Champagne corks were exploding. A horde of people were trying to use their influence to get backstage. In seconds Valentina's dressing room was filled with a seething mass of admirers.

"Ruby's bringing Alexander backstage," Valentina gasped to Stan. "He'll get crushed in this mob. Can you get them out, Stan? Just for five minutes?"

It seemed to take forever before the room was empty. She gazed at herself in the mirror. Not Hedda Gabler anymore, but Valentina.

She had no need to wait for the morning editions of the papers to know she had been a success. She moved Denton's massive bouquet of white roses to one side, and reached for a glass of Perrier. Paulos would have been deeply proud of her. And Vidal? She pushed the thought away. She had lived without him for almost five years, and during those years she had not allowed her thoughts to dwell on him. Her loyalty had been to Paulos. She had been both physically and mentally faithful to him. Now, in New York, it was much harder.

She picked up a newspaper and saw his face. From a taxicab she saw billboards announcing his latest movie. In Stan's conversation his name occurred regularly. Yet nothing had changed. She had left him of her own accord. She had married, had been widowed. Their lives were separate and would continue to be so.

The desolation she had felt at the knowledge was reminiscent of the grief she had felt when Paulos died. The adrenaline that had surged through her veins when she stood before the wildly cheering audience evaporated. There would be no sleep for her. The whole cast would be partying at Denton's expense until the first of the papers hit the street.

There was a sharp rap on her door and she wheeled around, her eyes once more shining, her smile exultant.

"Come in, darling," she called, opening her arms to greet her son.

When Vidal strode instead into the dressing room, she froze into immobility.

"I apologize for not being the person you were so obviously expecting," he said, his voice tight and hard and barely under control. "I came to congratulate you. Your performance was masterful."

She couldn't speak. Her heart was slamming so hard against her chest that the sound seemed to fill the whole room. He had changed. There was a streak of silver in his hair. The harsh lines running from nose to mouth had deepened, yet there were no laugh lines around his eyes. He moved, commanding the room and the situation as he had always done. He picked up the card that had accompanied the roses, read it, and tossed it back into the array of white blossoms. Any moment Alexander would come bounding into the room; Alexander with his tumbling thatch of curls that fell across his forehead just as Vidal's did. Alexander with his flashing dark eyes and, beneath the childish contours of his face, the unmistakable budding of high Slavic cheekbones; of a strong nose and powerful jaw.

"Thank you," she said, praying for strength. Praying that Alexander would be delayed. "Now if you will excuse me, I am expecting someone."

"So I gathered!" His eyes flashed to Denton's card. "Are you intending to marry again with the same indecent haste as last time?"

Her face was as bloodless as the roses. She dug her nails into her palms and turned her back to him, saying stiffly, "My personal affairs are no concern of yours."

He seized hold of her wrist cruelly, swinging her around to face him, his eyes blazing. "Your personal affairs are everything to do with me! Why did you leave? In God's name, Valentina, *why*?" The pain in his voice ripped wide the years and sent them scattering. She tried to draw away from him but the pressure of his fingers increased. Their bodies were touching and it was too late for feigned indifference. Too late for rage. Lust, love, and longing surged through them, meeting and fusing.

"Because . . ." She tried to remember her reasons, the lies she told him so long ago, and could remember nothing.

She could feel his heat. She wanted to sink her teeth into his flesh. "Because . . ." and then the door opened and Alexander ran into the room.

"Maman! Maman!" he began, and then halted as he saw that she was held in the tight grip of a stranger. For a long moment they were a tableau. Every vestige of blood had left Valentina's face as her son and his father stared at each other for the first time.

"Holy Mother of God," Vidal whispered, slowly releasing her wrists, staring at Alexander and then Valentina and then back to Alexander again. "So *that* was why you left!"

"Alexander, please leave the room for a moment," Valentina said, her voice so high and brittle it was scarcely recognizable.

"Don't want to," Alexander said stubbornly, setting his feet apart, frowning steadfastly back at Vidal's devouring gaze.

"Do as I tell you, Alexander."

Alexander looked once more from the man who resembled the demon king in his fairy-tale book, to his mother. She had never spoken to him in that tone of voice before.

"All right," he said, his voice trembling dangerously as mystified tears welled up inside him. "I'll go to Ruby. Ruby wants me."

He stalked from the room on sturdy legs, the picture of outraged dignity. The door closed behind him and Vidal turned once more toward her.

"You not only left me," he said, his voice incredulous. "You took my son with you! Why did you do it, Valentina? Why?"

The years fell away as if they had never existed. She knew why. She remembered in agonizing detail.

"Because if you had known you would have left Kariana and acknowledged Alexander. Because your career would have been finished. Because our future would have been built on Kariana's misery. Because I love you."

"And so you married your Greek. Did he know that the child you carried was not his?"

She held his eyes steadily. "Yes, he knew."

"Did you love him?"

The question was uttered like the pistol shot that had ended the play. "Yes," she said. Now was not the time to explain that her love for Paulos had been different from her love for him.

He sucked in his breath, his eyes darkening. "So, for you there was happiness, while for me there was . . ." He made a sharp savage movement full of revulsion. "*Nem fontos*. What a fool I was. If I had only known."

They stared across the years at each other.

"You know now," she said simply.

"Yes."

Their eyes held fast. His rage and jealousy faded. Yes, he knew now, and he would not make the same mistake again. Fate was offering them a second chance.

"I love you," he said, reaching out for her and drawing her into the circle of his arms. "I love you and I will never let you escape me again. Not you, or my son."

"He was Paulos's son for four years," she said, raising her face to his. "You cannot claim him as your own so swiftly, Vidal. He will not understand."

"No." He traced the pure outline of her cheekbone and jaw with his forefinger. "But I can claim you, Valentina. Now. This moment." And he reached behind him and shot the bolt of the door home.

Chapter Twenty-two

At first the crush at Sardi's was so great that no one was immediately aware that the star of the play and Vidal Rakoczi were constantly in undue proximity to one another. Stan Kennaway was exultant at receiving Vidal's congratulations. There wasn't a Rakoczi movie that he had not seen. He had watched and watched again, constantly learning. Vidal Rakoczi did not work within the Hollywood system. He worked outside it and still he succeeded. To Stan the man was a living legend.

"Vidal Rakoczi says that no one who was at tonight's

performance will ever forget it," he said exuberantly to one of Broadway's leading critics. The critic could only raise his champagne glass high and agree with him. Even now he could feel reverberations down his spine at the memory of Valentina's outward tight control, and the naked eroticism so palpable beneath the surface.

The whole room was awash with congratulations, flowers, and the very best French champagne. Leila was drunk with success and happiness.

"Oh, pinch me, please, I think I'm dreaming," she said to another member of the cast who was rapidly becoming literally drunk. "Isn't that Larry Olivier over there with Valentina and Vidal?"

"He came right on over immediately after his performance in Behrman's *No Time for Comedy*."

"Oh, God! And is that Katharine Cornell with him? *And* Guthrie McClintic?"

"The whole cast is here and you'd better put on your best smile, darling. Elliott Arnold from the *New York Telegraph* is heading in your direction."

"What the hell is *he* doing here?" Leila asked, frantically seizing another glass of champagne with which to fortify herself. "He should be writing his review of *Hedda*."

"If he's here, it means he's already done it, darling. And don't worry about its content. I've a feeling that overnight we've all achieved fame and adulation."

"Thanks to Valentina," Leila said as Elliott Arnold approached. "No one could have failed as long as they were in her orbit."

Valentina. Valentina. The name was heard everywhere. She had stunned them. Dazed them. Inflamed them. The only person to stand aloof in the room was the host—Denton Brook-Taylor.

The others were too high on nervous hysteria to notice that Valentina had entered not only with Vidal at her side, but with her hand tightly clasped in his. Even if they had noticed, they would have thought nothing of it. There were hugs and kisses all around. Vidal had been Valentina's Svengali all through her moviemaking days in Hollywood. There was nothing more natural than that he should be sharing her evening of glory in New York. But Denton knew instantly that with Vidal Rakoczi's arrival, all his own careful plans were about to be disrupted.

That fervent handhold was not one of friendship. When their eyes met, they looked as if they were eating each other alive. A knot of cold fury tightened and hardened deep in his gut. *No one* cheated him of anything that he had set his heart on. His gray eyes were glacial. He would outbid, outmaneuver anyone who stood in his way in auctions for his exquisite objects. He would do so now. Whatever part Vidal Rakoczi had played in Valentina's past, he would be damned before he would allow him to step once more into her life. Rakoczi would have to go. But how and when?

Stan Kennaway threw an arm around his shoulders. "You were right, Denton! Boy, oh, boy, were you right!"

Denton gave him a thin smile, but his eyes remained on Valentina and Vidal. There would be a way. There always was.

Leila, who had been mesmerized by Larry Olivier as the wild-eyed, arousingly sexual Heathcliff in *Wuthering Heights*, which had just been released, was overwhelmed at being in her idol's presence. When he left her and made his way toward Denton, she pushed through the crowd surrounding Valentina and said, "My God! All this and Heathcliff too! I can't believe it!"

"Have you changed your mind about forsaking all for love?" Valentina asked wickedly.

"It's very tempting, but no. In fact, I'm leaving now. I've just *got* to tell Rory about tonight."

"You mean he wasn't in the audience?" Valentina asked, aghast.

Leila grinned sheepishly. "No. I was crippled with stage fright as it was. If I'd known Rory was out there, I would have been in a state of total collapse." She looked from Valentina's radiant face to Vidal's. The harshness had gone. His eyes were gleaming, his white teeth flashing as he smiled first at one of Valentina's host of congratulating admirers and then at another. Her eyes dropped to their tightly clasped hands and she grinned.

"Here, Valentina. This is my key. I'm going down to Rory's tonight. Bye."

"But why—" Valentina began. It was too late. Leila had been swallowed up in the crowd of well-wishers. She looked down at the key and a smile curved her lips. Leila knew. Leila had always known. She couldn't return to her suite with Vidal. Not with Alexander snugly occupying the twin bed in her room. And she had no desire to return to a strange hotel room with Vidal. Their lovemaking deserved less impersonal surroundings. Leile's untidy, comfortable, familiar apartment would be perfect.

"What is that?" Vidal asked, glancing down at the key in her hand.

"The key to Leila's apartment." She paused, her eyes sparkling. "Leila will not be occupying it. At least, not tonight."

The heat in his eyes made her bones melt. "Then let's go," he said, his voice thickening. "There's no need to wait for the first editions. The reviews are going to be raves. Come on." He began to force his way toward the door, Valentina in his wake.

"Just a minute," she said urgently, pulling him back. "We can't go straight there, Vidal. There's Alexander. I have to return to the Plaza and say good night to him."

"But won't he be asleep?"

"I doubt it after the excitement of this evening, but even if he is, he'll want to know where I am when he wakes in the morning."

"But surely his nanny will be there?"

Valentina smiled at him indulgently. "Yes, she will, but he'll want *me*."

Vidal stared down at her. She was right. It had never occurred to him before that being a parent could be highly inconvenient. He thought of his curly-haired, exuberant son and grinned. Like hell they were inconvenient. They were a privilege he had long been denied. "We'll *both* go to the Plaza," he said, managing at last to reach the cream and gold doors. "I've a lot to catch up on where Alexander is concerned."

They fled down the corridor and out onto the sidewalk, terrified that their escape would be seen. Their fears were groundless. Only Denton Brook-Taylor saw them slip from the room and he remained where he was, the center of a circle of congratulatory sycophants. Rakoczi. How many times had he heard the name and never given it a thought—other than that the man might prove useful one day as a director of extraordinary talent. Now Rakoczi stood between him and what he wanted most in the world. His knuckles whitened as they tightened around the stem of his champagne glass. He had ruined greater men than the upstart Hungarian. All it needed was a little thought. And a lot of patience.

"Is he asleep, Ruby?" Valentina whispered as they entered her hotel suite.

"No, ma'am. I've never seen a child so overexcited. He keeps talking about the people and the lights and the applause." There was a slight tone of disapproval in Ruby's voice. She couldn't understand why Valentina had allowed Alexander to witness her apparent death on stage. Surely it would be disturbing for him? Valentina had assured her that it would not be; that Alexander understood perfectly that she was only acting. Playing make-believe just as he did. Ruby was not so sure. She had a practical mind and had never indulged in make-believe.

"Don't worry, Ruby. I'll go in to him now and he'll be asleep in a few minutes."

"Yes, ma'am." Ruby eyed the tall, dark stranger standing a little behind Valentina and felt suddenly shy. No one but Miss Crane was ever invited into Valentina's suite. She wondered if he was a famous movie star. His face was very familiar. She knew that she had seen it in the newspapers and movie magazines. His nonchalant stance was reminiscent of Clark Gable's, and for a moment she wondered if the King of Hollywood himself was standing only feet away from her. Then he moved forward and she saw that he was clean-shaven, and taller, more powerfully built than her idol. Her disappointment was fleeting. He had a face that she could not tear her eyes from and his negligent sexuality was so overpowering that she abandoned worship of Clark Gable and transferred it instantly to the being before her.

As Valentina entered the bedroom he followed her, remaining in the doorway, watching her speak softly to Alexander and kiss him good night with an expression in his eyes that she could only describe as hunger.

Alexander, satisfied now that his mother had come and kissed him good night, snuggled down under the bedclothes and closed his eyes. For a long moment Valentina and the man stood silently watching him, and the atmosphere was so intense that for some reason it aroused in Ruby the same feelings of awe that she sometimes experienced when in church.

"I shan't be back until late in the morning, Ruby. I've already explained to Alexander. Good night."

"Good night, ma'am," Ruby said, aware that her thoughts were traveling along improper lines, and aware too that she felt no censure at her employer's behavior. Only envy.

They had driven from Sardi's to the Plaza in Vidal's Pierce-Arrow. Now, with Vidal again at the wheel, they sped through the deserted streets to Leila's apartment on East Sixty-first Street. She leaned close against him, her head on his shoulder. His hands on the wheel were strong and dexterous. She remembered the first time she had driven with him, knowing that she was quite willfully walking away from a world of safety and shelter and into a world where no path was charted. It was strange to think that if she had not left Lilli Rainer's party with Vidal years ago, she would be living quietly with Bob. Going to the movies occasionally, to the tennis club—that her life would have held nothing more exciting than an occasional barbecue or meal downtown.

Vidal took the corner of Park Avenue and East Sixty-first at a speed that would have brought him before the courts if it had been seen. She had not opted for a quiet, safe life with Bob. She had opted for the life she now led and she had never regretted it. It had brought her fame and adulation . . . and great pain. Her fingers dug deep through Vidal's tuxedo into the flesh of his arm. The pain was over now. They were together again. Nothing else mattered.

"Here it is," she said, the breath tight in her chest.

Vidal swerved to a halt. She didn't wait for him to open her door. She was out of the car and he strode around to her, seizing her hand, and then they were laughing, running up the flight of stairs to Leila's apartment, slamming the door shut behind them, discarding their clothes in a fever of impatience.

Their lovemaking in her dressing room had been savage and urgent, a physical explosion of the pent-up emotions of almost five years of hungry longings. Even now it was not sated. Neither of them could wait. There were no preliminaries. No soft words or caresses.

"Oh, please! *Please!* PLEASE!" she begged as her nails scored the lean, tanned contours of his body and his weight pinned her down, a willing captive, on Leila's bed. He did not take her body, he plundered it. Ravening it like a starving man. He entered her like an arrow entering the gold and she sank her teeth into his flesh, arching her body to his in an ecstasy of total submission. Past, present, future merged into one and in all the world there was only Vidal and Vidal and Vidal.

Afterward he made love to her again. This time with care and with skill and with a love so intense that he thought he would die of it. There was no time or place. No world outside. They were together again. Their bodies fused, their beings once again one. Her orgasm left her almost senseless. As it ebbed and she clung to him, she licked a rivulet of sweat away from his neck and wondered how she had ever imagined that she could live without him.

"I shall leave New York in the morning," he said as he rolled away from her.

For a moment she thought that she had not heard right, and then her blood chilled and it seemed as if her heart had ceased to beat.

"Why?"

He was leaning back against the head of the bed, drawing her against the heat and strength and familiar nakedness of his chest.

"To tell Kariana that it is the end. That I wish to marry elsewhere." His voice was deep, smoke-dark, and at the certainty of its tone her fear ebbed.

"Is she still . . . ill?" she asked as his fingers caressed her hair, the nape of her neck.

"Kariana will always be ill," he said gently. "But these last years have not been like the earlier ones. She is quieter now. Hazel is still with her. My divorcing her will not change the way she lives. I doubt if she will even notice the difference."

His voice held inestimable sadness, but there was no pain. That had long since been spent. Kariana would continue to live as she did now. He could afford to see that she was adequately protected against the encroaching world. But he could no longer sacrifice his life for her.

He touched her face tenderly. "Will you tell me now," he asked, ". . . about Paulos?"

She nodded. She had spoken about Paulos often to Leila, but she had never spoken about the dreadful night of his

death. Not even to Evangelina. Now she told Vidal everything. She told him of how good he had been to her. Of his
kindness and gentleness. She told him of their travels to
London and to Paris and to Vienna and of how they had
always been happiest in their little whitewashed villa on the
shores of Crete. She told him of the night he had died. Of
how, when it was too late, she had realized the depth of her
love for him. Of how she had wanted to tell him that he *had*
come first. That he hadn't been, as he always believed,
second best.

Vidal was silent. He had a lot to thank the dead Paulos
Khairetis for. The knowledge expunged all jealousy. He had
noticed that in her hotel suite a photograph of Paulos stood
on a low table in a silver frame. Wherever they went and
wherever they lived, he determined that the photograph
would remain in view. Though he had never known Paulos
Khairetis, he knew he would always remember him as a
friend.

Clasped in each other's arms, they slept, and when they
woke it was to a peace that both had thought lost to them
forever.

It was eleven o'clock before either of them thought of
breakfast or newspapers.

"Oh, God," Valentina said, sitting suddenly upright, her
naked breasts and shoulders flushed from lovemaking. "The
reviews! What if they're awful? What if last night was a fluke
and the critics weren't the ones applauding and they really
thought the play was dreadful!"

Vidal laughed at the agony in her voice. "You make the
coffee," he said, "I'll go out and buy every paper in town."

The reviews were ecstatic. Acclaim for Valentina's performance was lavish and unanimous. She rifled through them,
not fully convinced until she had read the very last one.

"Satisfied?" Vidal asked, quirking an eyebrow in amusement as he poured her yet another black coffee.

"Yes, thank God," she said devoutly.

"You realize that no one, apart from Leila, knows where
you are? Stan Kennaway is probably heading for a coronary."

"I must phone him. And I must get back to the Plaza and
Alexander. Ruby is probably under siege by reporters demanding my presence."

"And I must return to Hollywood," he said, his face suddenly grave. "I shall tell Kariana immediately. This time there is going to be no subterfuge. No lies. I don't care if the whole damned world knows that we are lovers."

Thirty minutes later they stood on the sidewalk. Vidal was driving directly to the airport; Valentina was returning to the Plaza by cab.

"When will you be back?" she asked, raising her face for his last kiss.

"Almost immediately. I'll speak to my lawyer later today. Don't worry, my love. Nothing will go wrong this time. I promise."

They kissed long and lingeringly, oblivious of the curious stares of passersby.

"I love you," she whispered as he stepped away from her. "I love you. I always have loved you and I always will love you."

"Then be patient," he said, his dark face brilliant with an expression of such fierce love that it was transfigured, "just for a little while longer. Then we will be together forever."

She stepped into her cab, looking through the rear window until the Pierce-Arrow had disappeared in traffic.

"The Plaza Hotel, please," she said to the driver, and wondered why, when she had at last all that she had yearned for, she was filled with a nameless fear.

The hotel *was* besieged by reporters and photographers and fans and Stan *was* pacing the room, clutching his heart.

"Where the hell have you been?" he yelled as she finally entered her suite after a near hour-long battle with the crowd hemming her in on all sides.

"Leila's."

"F'Christ's sake, Leila was here *hours* ago!"

Valentina tried to look contrite, and failed. "Sorry, Stan, but that's where I was."

Alexander pushed past Stan and hurtled into her arms. "Have you seen the flowers, Maman? There's hundreds and hundreds of them. Millions of them. *Trillions!*"

Valentina had indeed seen the flowers. They erupted from the suite and all the way down the Plaza's lushly carpeted corridors.

"Do stop pacing the room, Stan. I'm back. The show is a

success. For goodness' sake, stop looking as if you're on the verge of a breakdown and have a drink."

She poured him a Scotch and he took it gratefully.

"You don't understand," he said, sitting down at last. "I thought the excitement of last night had been too much for you. That you were suffering from amnesia. That you wouldn't be back in time for the performance tonight."

"Well, I *am* back," Valentina said spiritedly. "And I am most definitely not suffering from amnesia. . . ."

There was a loud knock at the door. "I *told* reception that no one was to be allowed up," Ruby said apologetically, "but people keep getting in. One gentleman said he used the fire escape and another that he used the service elevator!"

The sharp, authoritative knock came again and before Valentina could reach the door, it opened and a smiling Denton Brook-Taylor entered.

"Valentina, my dear! You were magnificent! Superb!" He was beaming in a way Stan had never seen before. "Now that we have scored one major success, I want to set about planning another triumph."

Stan stared at him. He couldn't possibly be planning another Broadway play. *Hedda Gabler* was all set for a long run.

"Would you like a drink, Denton?" Valentina asked, pouring herself a white wine.

"Bourbon, please," Denton said expansively.

Stan's eyes sharpened. He had known Denton a long time, but he had never seen him in this jovial, hail-fellow-well-met mood before, and he didn't find it at all reassuring.

"What is it you have in mind, Denton?" Valentina asked, her interest polite but not caught.

"Movies," Denton Brook-Taylor said, gratified at the sudden turn of Stan Kennaway's head in his direction. "I want to make you into a limited company, Valentina. That way *you* will reap the benefits from any further movies you make. The profits won't all go into the pockets of the movie moguls."

"And who is going to finance these yet unmade movies?" Stan asked dryly.

"I am, of course."

Stan smiled. "Then all you will be doing is putting *yourself* in the position of the movie mogul."

Denton's gray eyes were frigid. "I shall ignore that remark. I'm sure you are aware that it was ill-timed and in bad taste. I'm interested in putting my money behind movies in which Valentina stars and in seeing to it that she reaps the full benefits from such a deal."

Stan eyed him cynically. There was a lot more that he could say, but to do so would be unwise.

"From now on, Valentina, I want to take care of all your business affairs with my staff of handpicked experts. Agreed?"

Valentina laughed. "No. You're rushing me, Denton. I'm not convinced I *need* a team of handpicked experts to handle my financial affairs. I've managed fine on my own so far."

"But you haven't." Denton met her gaze steadily. "In Hollywood, your salary may have seemed enormous to you, but the profits Theodore Gambetta made from your movies was staggering. I don't want to see you ever go back to Hollywood and the studio system."

"After my court battles with Theodore, I have no desire to return to the studio system myself," Valentina said dryly.

"Then let us make you Valentina Productions!" Denton said triumphantly. "We can choose the stories. You'll have complete authority over what parts you play. Over who co-stars with you. Over everything. All I have to do is set up a proper company for you once and for all."

Valentina took a sip of her wine. Denton Brook-Taylor was a banker of sound reputation. When it came to finance, he undoubtedly knew far more than she did. More to the point, what he said was true. She had no desire to return to Hollywood under the old studio system. Yet she *did* want to make more movies. There was an awful lot of sense in what he was saying and she would be a fool to dismiss it out of hand.

"I'll need to think about it, Denton, and I'll need to talk about it to Vidal."

Stan's head swung in her direction. For a fleeting instant he wondered if Valentina and Denton had already got together and decided to make a movie with Vidal Rakoczi as director. The doubt immediately faded. Denton might wheel and deal behind his back, but Valentina never would. If she needed to speak to Vidal Rakoczi about a major decision in her life, it was because he was her oldest friend.

At the mention of Vidal's name Denton's eyes flickered momentarily and the telltale sign was immediately and ruthlessly suppressed.

"Of course," he said. "Vidal Rakoczi is just the kind of man whose advice would be invaluable."

Stan was tempted to say that the news came as a great surprise to him, as the last time Denton had mentioned Rakoczi's name it was to refer to him as a Hungarian bastard. He kept his mouth shut. So far he couldn't see that anything Denton was proposing could harm Valentina's life or career. If and when it did so, he would have a word with her. Till then it was easier to remain silent.

Before he boarded his plane for the West Coast, Vidal telephoned his New York lawyer, telling him tersely that he wanted a file for a divorce immediately and that he would speak to him at length when he returned to New York after informing Kariana of his decision.

He had no doubts or qualms. It had been years since he had been intimate with Kariana. He was a haven and a refuge to her, but he was not a real husband to her, certainly not a lover. The charade had gone on long enough.

When his plane landed at Los Angeles, he was tired but too impatient to telephone his Beverly Hills home and request that his chauffeur pick him up. Instead, he got a cab and as Hazel Renko saw it enter the gates of Villada, she was immediately filled with foreboding. Never, in all her years in his employment, had she known him to arrive home without a phone call announcing that he was on his way.

"Is Kariana in bed?" he asked as his coat was taken away by the butler and Hazel poured him a vodka and blue curaçao and soda.

"Yes, but I don't think she's asleep." She hesitated. Kariana's sleeping pattern had become very erratic. Her moodiness had returned. There were temper tantrums over the least thing followed by frightening displays of violence. The period of comparative calm and normality was coming to an end. Hazel knew that Kariana was heading once more into the snake pit of her illness. She was aware of an unusual tenseness about Vidal and decided that the news could wait till the morning.

Vidal drained his glass. Hazel Renko had been part of his

household for many years. When he divorced Kariana, she would need Hazel's calm presence more than ever. It was only fair that Hazel should know what his intentions were.

"I'm going to speak to Kariana tonight," he said, "and before I do so, I had better tell you what it is I am going to say to her."

Hazel felt her legs weaken. If Vidal had chosen this moment in time to tell Kariana that he wanted a divorce, it would send her over the edge completely. The next days and weeks would be a living nightmare. She sat down and waited, white-faced.

"I intend to divorce Kariana," Vidal said, his face somber. "I want to marry again, and I want to marry again quickly."

"Don't tell her now," Hazel pleaded. "There's been a complete turnaround in her condition." She wished she had poured herself a drink when she had poured Vidal's. "She's been moody and silent for long periods and then, for no reason, she has become hysterical. Wait till her mood swing changes, until she's calmer."

"I don't have time," he said, his jaw tightening. "There's a child. *My* child."

"I see." Hazel's voice was barely audible. He would want to marry before the baby was born. She wondered how Kariana would react to the shock of Vidal divorcing her, and a knot of dread grew deep within Hazel, tightening and twisting. It would be enough to plunge Kariana into a state of complete mania.

"When is the baby due?"

Vidal raised a dark eyebrow and said wryly, "The baby is almost five years old."

Hazel stared at him. "I'm sorry, Vidal, I don't understand."

For the first time since he had entered the room, a smile tugged at the corners of his mouth. "I don't blame you, Hazel. When Valentina left Hollywood, she was carrying my child. Now she is back and I am going to marry her."

Hazel exhaled slowly. Valentina. Nothing had ever been said, but she had always known. She had sensed it the first time she had set eyes on her. When Valentina had married and left Hollywood, she had thought for a while that she had been mistaken, but Vidal's behavior had shown that even if

Valentina's heart was elsewhere, his was not. For Vidal, it had always been Valentina. It always would be.

"Then you had better tell her," she said simply.

He nodded, put down his empty glass and began to walk toward Kariana's bedroom.

The drapes were pulled back as they were night and day. The moon was riding high over Cahuenga Valley, the stars low in the night sky. She was pacing the room restlessly, her lace-edged negligee whipping about her ankles as she reached the vast windows and spun on her heel, retracing her steps for the hundredth time toward the door. As he entered her head shot up, the pupils of her eyes mere pinpricks.

"You're back!" It was an accusation, not a statement. The lines of Vidal's mouth tightened. Hazel had been correct when she said that Kariana's condition had once more deteriorated. It never ceased to amaze him that Kariana's sweetness could change in an instant into vitriolic abuse. The tone of her voice was no longer soft and low. It was harsh and shrill. He gazed at her despairingly, remembering how exquisite he had thought her when they had first met. How refined. How delicate. Now, victim of her inner demons, her beauty was transformed into macabre ugliness.

"I need to talk to you, Kariana," he said, a pulse throbbing at his temple.

"Talk!" She whirled on her heel again, pacing back toward the window.

He had waited many years. He had protected her, pitied her, and now he could wait no longer. "I want a divorce, Kariana," he said, his voice as gentle as possible.

She spun round to face him, her brows high with surprise, and then she began to laugh.

"Don't be ridiculous, Vidal. You can never have a divorce. I'm a Dansart. Dansarts don't divorce."

"It will make barely any difference in our relationship. I will still see that you have the best care when you are ill. I'll make a large financial settlement. You can have the house and everything in it."

She flew across the room toward him, clawing at his face. "Ill? Is that what you think I am? Ill? There's nothing wrong with me, Vidal Rakoczi, except I married beneath me! Fuck you and your financial settlements! You're not going to discard me, you Hungarian bastard!"

Vidal passed a hand across his eyes. When she was well, Kariana never even uttered the word *damn*. He wondered where that other Kariana went to at moments like this. How it was possible to sleep and wake and have no recall of the ugly things that she had said. He had been a fool to try and talk to her when Hazel had warned him of her mood.

"Go to bed, Kariana," he said wearily. "We'll talk tomorrow."

He turned on his heel and left the room, ignoring her shouted obscenities. In the morning he would talk to Grossman. He was not going to be able to return to Valentina as soon as he had hoped. He needed Grossman with him. He could no longer handle Kariana alone.

"Bastard!" Kariana shouted as his steps receded down the corridor and her high-pitched laughter turned to tears. "I'll teach you to threaten to leave me!"

She rushed across the room to her bedside table and her cigarettes and lighter. It was Hazel he wanted to marry. She had always known it. That was why he had brought Hazel into the house and they thought her a fool who had not known what they were planning and scheming. Her fingers shook as she sparked the lighter into flame. He'd leave her the house, would he? She began to laugh again. When she had finished, there would be no house for him to leave to her. She would show him that he could not leave her. That she would kill both of them if he tried.

She bent down by the drapes and held the lighter to the edge of the velvet. It smoldered but did not burst into flame. Impatiently she ran across to the bed and lit a corner of the delicate draperies. They ignited immediately.

"Now see what I've done," she shouted triumphantly. "See if you ever *dare* to ask to divorce me again!"

Chapter Twenty-three

"The fire seems to have started in Mrs. Rakoczi's bedroom," the sweating fireman said to his chief as hoses sprayed gallons of water onto the roaring flames.

"Who got her out?" the chief of the Los Angeles Fire Department yelled, stepping back another foot as a fresh bellow of heat blasted him full in the face.

"Her husband. They've been rushed down to Los Angeles General. The wife is in pretty bad shape."

"Any other casualties?"

The fireman nodded in the direction of a blanketed body. "A member of the household staff. A woman. Probably the housekeeper or Mr. Rakoczi's secretary."

The fire chief nodded and began to walk back to his car. He had been at a highly prestigious dinner when he had received news that the Rakoczi place was burning like a torch. His immediate fear had been that he had a disaster of huge proportions on his hands. If the fire had started while Vidal Rakoczi had been hosting a Hollywood party, the casualty list could have consisted of half the movie community. As it was, there had been only the Rakoczis and the household staff in when the fire had occurred. He didn't have Gloria Swanson's or Clark Gable's body on his hands. Only the body of a woman employee.

"Keep at it," he said tersely, slipping behind the wheel of his car and revving the engine impatiently. If he hurried, there would still be time to return to his dinner party.

"Must . . . cable," Vidal gasped, fighting for consciousness as white-uniformed doctors and nurses rushed his stretcher along the corridors of the hospital. "Must . . . send a cable."

It was eight hours before he was able to do so. It was to

Valentina and it said only: SAFE STOP DON'T WORRY STOP BE WITH YOU SOON STOP PLANS UNCHANGED STOP VIDAL.

The second evening's performance had been as great a triumph as the first night. Denton had sent an army of servants into a vast, luxuriously furnished house at Oyster Bay, Long Island, and ordered them to prepare it for Valentina and her nanny and her son. He was now at the Plaza to inform her that she needn't worry any longer about being besieged by the press and by clamoring fans.

Leila was there, sorting through a pile of congratulatory cables as Valentina showered.

"She'll like it," she said crisply when Denton told her what he had done. "Living here is impossible. It's not fair to Alexander. I did suggest my place, but it's far too small and Valentina hasn't the time to find a suitable house herself."

"There's a pool and tennis courts, and I've told them to erect swings for the child and to put a pony in the paddock."

Leila pursed her lips. "You're really serious this time, Denton, aren't you?"

He brushed an imaginary speck of dust from his immaculately cut lapel. "I'm going to marry her," he said calmly.

Leila smiled. "No, you're not, Denton. This time you're going to find that your money won't buy you everything you want in the toyshop window. Valentina is going to marry Vidal."

Denton Brook-Taylor's eyes narrowed. "Rakoczi is already married."

"Yes, and his marriage has been on the rocks for years. He flew home yesterday to tell his wife he was divorcing her and that he intends to marry Valentina at the earliest opportunity." The telephone rang shrilly. "Damn, I've told them time and time again not to put any calls through." She answered it bad-temperedly.

"Would you please ensure that no more calls are put through? It's very disturbing and—"

The blood drained from her face. "Oh, my God," she said, swaying slightly. "When did it happen? How bad is he?"

When she replaced the receiver, her hand was trembling. "It's Vidal. There's been a fire. He's in Los Angeles General."

"Will he live?"

Leila's eyes flashed with venom. "Yes," she spat at her

former lover. "God damn you for your hopes, Denton, but he'll live!"

Through the adjoining door came the sound of Valentina singing to herself. Leila looked at Denton in horror.

"Who is going to tell her? *What* can we tell her? We don't know any details. We don't—"

"Who called?" Denton asked curtly.

"Stan. The *Los Angeles Times* called him with the news and wanted a comment."

"Telephone Los Angeles General and find out the truth of Rakoczi's condition. Not from here," he snapped as Leila reached toward the telephone. "She could walk in on the call."

"Yes." Leila's head was spinning. "I'll go down to reception. Oh, God, I can't bear to think of it. What if he dies?" She began to cry.

"Make that telephone call immediately," Denton said, grabbing her arm and leading her to the door. "When we do speak to her, let's have some facts to give her. He may be suffering from nothing more than shock."

Leila stumbled out into the corridor. Denton was right. Vidal might not be burned. After a fire they always took people to the hospital. Vidal couldn't be burned. Disfigured. It wasn't possible. It was unthinkable.

"I want to be connected to Los Angeles General Hospital, please," she said to the desk clerk. "Is there anywhere I can telephone from that is private?"

The desk clerk took one look at her ashen face and led her into the reception office.

"I'll get the number for you immediately," he said. "Use the phone on the desk."

Getting the call through seemed to take forever. When at last she had the hospital on the line, she found that her voice was trembling.

"Could you please give me some information regarding the condition of Mr. Vidal Rakoczi, who I believe has been admitted after a fire at his home."

"I'm sorry, madam, we are giving no information to the press at this stage," an arch voice replied.

"I'm not press." The breath hurt in her chest. "I'm a friend, Leila Crane. I'm calling on behalf of Valentina."

There was a slight pause. "Just one moment."

Leila could hear a hurried discussion and Valentina's name repeated, and then, "Mr. Rakoczi's condition is serious but stable."

"You mean he'll live?"

"Yes." The crisp voice left no room for doubt. "However, he is in no condition to receive any visitors."

She didn't know what else to ask. "Thank you," she said, and only when it was too late and she had replaced the receiver did she realize that she had not asked about the condition of Kariana Rakoczi. As she left the office she saw curiosity in the eyes of the staff. The newspapers were spread out on the reception desk, the headlines glaring.

WORLD-FAMOUS DIRECTOR RISKS HIS LIFE TO SAVE HIS WIFE FROM HOUSE INFERNO.

UNNAMED WOMAN DEAD IN RAKOCZI HOUSE FIRE.

VIDAL RAKOCZI SAVES WIFE.

She couldn't bear to pick up the papers and read the details. Feeling as if she had aged ten years, she made her way slowly back to Valentina's suite.

The telephone had begun to ring incessantly the minute she had left the room, and Denton had answered, saying sharply that no calls were being received. When the knock came at the door, he wondered if it was Stan. A bellboy stood there with a cable. Denton took it wordlessly, closed the door, and weighed it speculatively in his hand. Hundreds of congratulatory cables had flooded into the suite, yet some primeval instinct told him that this one was different. That this one concerned Rakoczi.

From behind the far door, the sound of the shower had ceased. Valentina was likely to emerge at any moment. With a decisive flick of his thumbnail he opened the cable. It was from Vidal. When he had read it, he paused for a moment and then a slight smile touched his mouth. Crushing the cable into a small ball and burying it in his pocket, he crossed to the telephone and asked to be connected with his Los Angeles home.

"Burton, is that you?" he asked sharply as his butler answered.

"Yes, sir."

"I want you to send a cable to Valentina, the Plaza Hotel, New York. Have you got a pen and paper?"

"Yes, sir."

"The cable is to read, "Am safe stop Kariana badly hurt in fire stop our previous plans cannot go forward stop please do not write or call stop all over stop sorry stop Vidal." Have you got that, Burton?"

"Yes, sir," Burton said dutifully.

"Good. Send it immediately."

Valentina emerged from the bathroom and he put the receiver down.

"Who was that?"

"Someone wishing to speak to you. They didn't leave a name."

Valentina sat at the dressing table and began to brush her hair. "People have been amazing. Did Leila tell you that Theodore Gambetta actually rang this morning and suggested we meet? He said it was time we forgot the past and began to look to the future." She smiled at Denton's reflection in the mirror. "Can you believe it? He actually thinks that I'd be willing to work for him again." At the somberness of Denton's expression, she laughed. "There's no need to look like that, Denton. I only told you because I thought it was amusing."

He stepped toward her. "Valentina, Stan rang a few minutes ago. He had some bad news."

At the expression in his eyes her hand froze in midair, still holding the brush. "What did he say? What's happened?" She swung round on her dressing table stool to face him and as she did so, Leila entered the room.

"He's safe," Leila said, her face haggard. "He's going to live. There's no need to worry. He's going to live."

"*Who's* going to live?" Valentina demanded, springing to her feet. The nameless fear that had haunted her ever since Vidal had left was now crystalizing, taking shape.

"Vidal. There was a fire at his house. One of the household staff died. But Vidal is all right, Valentina. I've just gotten through on the telephone to the hospital. He isn't in any danger."

Valentina's skin was like alabaster. "Which hospital?" she demanded, her hands already on the telephone.

"The Los Angeles General."

As Valentina waited to be connected, Denton Brook-Taylor held his breath. It had been a gamble and if it *was* true that Vidal Rakoczi was not seriously hurt, and if he was allowed to receive calls, then it was a gamble that would have failed.

Leila could dimly hear the same arch voice. The same answers to the very questions that she had asked. Valentina put the receiver down abruptly.

"I must go to him. Now. Immediately."

"You can't," Leila said, her eyes filling with tears at the sight of Valentina's anguished face. "There's the play. For the stand-in to go on tonight would be disastrous. Besides"— she paused uncertainly—"there's Kariana. I think she may be more badly injured than Vidal. There are newspapers downstairs . . ."

Valentina pressed her hand against her throbbing head. Kariana. For a brief moment she had forgotten all about Kariana. She felt as if a huge weight were pressing in on her, suffocating her.

"Have the newspapers sent up," she said through parched lips.

"You can't stay here." It was Denton speaking, quietly and authoritatively. "I've rented a house for you out at Oyster Bay. There's plenty of room for Alexander to play. There's a full complement of staff just waiting for your arrival. I think you should go there now. From now on, the pressure from the press is going to be unbearable." He put an arm around her shoulders. "Right now you need to be taken care of, Valentina. I'll make sure that we get news from the hospital on an hourly basis. And I'll make sure that you fly out to be at his side just as soon as he is able to receive visitors, play or no play."

She looked up at him gratefully. "Thank you, Denton. I'll tell Ruby to begin packing Alexander's things as soon as she returns from their walk."

When the newspapers were delivered, she read them in silence. Hazel Renko, who had cared for Kariana so diligently for so many years, was dead. The newspapers described her merely as the housekeeper. The rest of the household staff had escaped unscathed. The fire had begun in Kariana's bedroom and there were varying accounts of how Vidal had risked his life to save her. She pushed the newspapers away. None of them gave any clear indication of the severity of the burns he had sustained. The Los Angeles *Examiner* said that Kariana Rakoczi was near death. The *Los Angeles*

Times quoted firemen as saying that Vidal's rescue of her had been an act of almost suicidal courage.

The telephone rang again, and Valentina leapt toward it in agitation. It was a reporter wanting to know her comments regarding the Rakoczi house blaze. She put the receiver down without speaking, her hand trembling violently.

"Get dressed," Denton said to her. "At Oyster Bay I will be able to ensure that the only calls you receive are those that you want to receive."

Valentina turned to Leila. "Will you come with me, Leila?"

"Of course. I'll start packing. By the time Ruby returns from the park with Alexander, we'll be ready to leave."

As the dressing room door clicked shut behind her, Leila began emptying drawers. As she did so she glanced several times at Denton. His expression was grave. His manner all that it should be under the circumstances. Yet Leila could not help thinking that deep below the surface he was feeling triumphant.

She frowned. Vidal was not dead and was not near to death. Nothing had happened to change his relationship with Valentina. He would still divorce Kariana, still marry Valentina. Denton would still have lost the one thing he had openly declared he wanted above all others. There was no reason in the world for him to be feeling so self-satisfied, yet Leila knew that he was. They had been lovers. He could hide his true feelings under a mask from other people, but she knew him too well. His shoulders were set in the same way they were whenever he concluded a successful business deal or heard that a painting or sculpture he had been bidding for by proxy was now his.

She shrugged and continued with her task. Perhaps that was all it was. Perhaps he'd just acquired another Rembrandt or Van Gogh. She had more important things to think about. Valentina, and how she would survive the next few hours waiting for news from the hospital. How she would cope when she had to set foot on stage and put all thoughts of Vidal out of her mind.

Valentina dressed hurriedly. Denton was right. To continue living at the Plaza was impossible. At Oyster Bay she would at least have some privacy. The sooner she arrived there, the sooner she could establish an hourly link with the

hospital and make arrangements to fly out and be at Vidal's
side if he was badly burned. Her hand shook as she tried to
fasten a button. If he was badly burned, then she would stay
there. She didn't care about the play. She didn't care about
anything. Only Vidal.

"Will our new house be like our house in Crete, Maman?"
Alexander asked, snuggling up against her in the rear of
Denton's Rolls.

"No, darling. It will be much bigger and there will be
swings and a pony."

Alexander sighed ecstatically. He hadn't liked the hotel.
It had been full of furniture with long, thin legs and things
that fell over easily when he ran by.

Valentina glanced at her watch. It had been over forty
minutes since she had telephoned the hospital. A lot could
happen in forty minutes. People could die in forty minutes.

"I must go to him," she said urgently to Denton. "I can't
just stay here waiting for telephone calls, behaving as if
nothing has happened."

Denton patted her hand reassuringly. "We'll make one
more telephone call when we reach the house, then I'll see to
it that you're flown straight to Los Angeles. Jeanette Leeman
can go on in your place tonight."

The gratitude she felt toward him deepened.

"Thank you," she said with heartfelt relief. "I don't know
what time the flights are . . ."

"There's no need to worry about flights or seats. I have a
private airplane. It is completely at your disposal."

She managed a flicker of a smile. "You're a very useful
person to have as a friend, Denton."

"I'm very privileged to be one," Denton said, his white
hair silvered by the sun as they sped over the Queensboro
Bridge.

At Oyster Bay, Ruby discreetly absented herself with
Alexander, taking him out into the grounds, showing him the
pool, the tennis courts, and the pony. An army of household
staff ferried their luggage upstairs. The rooms were full of
exotic flowers. The satin sheets on Valentina's bed bore her
name in exquisite gold embroidery, as did the bath towels.
Leila eyed them cynically. Denton's suggestion that Valentina
retreat from the onslaught of the press at the Plaza had not
been made on the spur of the moment. The whole house had

been very carefully prepared for its visitor. Too carefully prepared for Denton to be satisfied with Valentina's staying there only briefly. Yet he was already on the telephone ordering that his private airplane be made ready for a flight to the West Coast. She didn't understand it. Denton was not behaving remotely like the unbending, autocratic figure she was accustomed to. Either he had undergone a complete metamorphosis or there was something funny going on. Something she couldn't work out at all.

"What *are* second-degree burns, for goodness' sake?" Valentina was asking frantically. "It could mean anything. Why the hell can't they speak in a language that people can understand."

"Second-degree burns are severe but won't kill him," Stan Kennaway said, crushing out one cigarette and immediately lighting another. He hoped to God he was right. If Rakoczi died, it was obvious that Valentina would go to pieces completely. The play would be a two-night wonder.

Denton heard the purr of a limousine and put the telephone down. It was the aide-de-camp he had left at the Plaza with strict instructions to drive out fast with any Los Angeles cables.

"The plane is ready, it's a short drive to the airport and then we'll be aboard," he said comfortingly, a small smile hovering at the corners of his mouth as he saw his employee run from the car and toward the house.

"Oh, God!" Valentina said, pacing the floor, a mink coat flung around her shoulders, her hands grinding together in a paroxysm of anxiety. "The flight will take hours and hours and hours. We'll have to land at places that probably won't have a telephone. I'll be out of touch with his condition for *ages*! I *knew* something dreadful was going to happen to him when he left me yesterday. I just *knew*."

"There's a cable for you," Denton said, dismissing its bearer and crossing the room to her. "It's from Los Angeles."

Stan Kennaway put down his glass. Denton looked grave. Leila said unsteadily, "It's probably from Theodore."

None of them moved as she took the cable and slit it open. She stared at the message for a long time, her dark hair falling forward and hiding the expression on her face. At last, when Leila thought she could bear it no longer, she raised her head and said in a voice that was oddly expressionless,

"The plane will not be necessary, Denton. Kariana is badly hurt and Vidal will be staying with her. It doesn't sound as though he is badly injured. Do you mind if I go upstairs and rest now? I need to sleep before tonight's performance."

She folded the cable carefully and slipped it into the silk-lined pocket of her coat and then she walked from the room. Stan and Leila stared after her.

"Why the hell is she so calm all of a sudden?" Stan asked, bewildered. "I've never heard her speak like that before. It was . . . toneless."

"I think I'd better go to her," Leila said uneasily. "She didn't look as if it were good news she received. Why did she look so waxen if all it said was that Vidal was not badly hurt? Surely she should have been relieved?"

"Perhaps she's distressed that Kariana Rakoczi's condition is so serious," Stan suggested.

"That wasn't distress on her face," Leila said slowly. "It was the way she would have looked if the cable had told her Vidal had died."

She hurried up the curving staircase that led to the upper floor and ran breathlessly along the corridor to the door of Valentina's bedroom. Then her footsteps faltered and she halted. From beyond the door she could hear Valentina weeping. Weeping as if her heart had broken and her world had come to an end.

She raised her hand to knock and then let it fall to her side. Whatever the cause of Valentina's grief, it was too deep to be eased by a few kindly words. Feeling inadequate, she turned on her heel and returned slowly to the sitting room.

Valentina did not emerge from her bedroom until it was time for her to leave for the theater. When she did so, she was perfectly composed, utterly in control. Leila steeled herself to ask about the cable, but her courage deserted her. Valentina had changed. It was as if a sheet of ice encased her, isolating her from those around her. She didn't respond to any of Leila's falsely cheerful chatter. When she spoke, it was in monosyllables and her gaze rarely met Leila's. When they did so, Leila felt as if she were looking into the eyes of a stranger. They were dark and full of shadow, disclosing nothing of what she was thinking and feeling.

At the door of her dressing room, Leila said impulsively,

"Valentina, whatever it is, let me help you. Share it with me, please."

Valentina turned to her, her eyes bruised with grief. "I shall never be able to talk about it, Leila. Not ever," she said unsteadily, and quietly and firmly closed the dressing room door behind her, leaving Leila alone in the corridor.

From the moment Valentina read the cable and isolated herself in her bedroom, Denton had taken charge. He had ordered that no cables were to be delivered to her. No telephone calls were to be put through. No visitors admitted.

"I don't want her distressed any further," he had said to Stan. "What Valentina needs now is a little calm and order in her life."

Stan had kept his thoughts to himself. Valentina would certainly have calm if she remained at Oyster Bay. Denton and his army of aides-de-camp and bodyguards were rapidly turning the place into a luxurious prison. He had wondered if Valentina and Alexander wouldn't have been better off remaining at the Plaza amid the healthy clamor of voracious newsmen. The isolated house and its silence and respectful maids was like a tomb in comparison, and he doubted if Denton would tolerate Leila's presence there for long. He wanted Valentina to himself and it seemed to Stan as if that was just what he was going to get.

His fears about her performance that evening were groundless. She was spellbinding. The very air throbbed with Hedda Gabler's sexual jealousy and need for vengeance. It was so intense, so all-consuming, that Stan felt as if he were looking into the very soul of the woman onstage.

He did not get the chance to speak to her afterward. Denton Brook-Taylor had her spirited away, with the greasepaint still on her face.

"You need a drink," he said to her when she entered the vast sitting room, after kissing a sleeping Alexander good night.

She didn't reply. She was beyond speech; beyond feeling any need for food or drink. There was, she thought, staring at the unlit logs in the marble-framed hearth, a threshold of pain that no human being should ever have to cross. A wilderness of the spirit, a world of desolation, that was beyond imagining.

Denton smoothed the pencil-thin line of his moustache thoughtfully with his forefinger and poured a large Scotch.

"Here," he said, pressing it into her hand. "Drink this."

She obeyed him, shuddering at the unfamiliar taste. Denton refilled the glass. "I have a proposition to make to you, Valentina."

She shook her head in protest. "No, Denton. Not now." She didn't care if she never made another movie. She didn't care about the plans for turning her into Valentina Productions. She didn't care about anything any longer. Vidal was not returning to her. She had lost him not once but twice. Kariana's hold over him was greater than hers. He didn't want to hear from her or to see her. Beyond this terrible truth nothing else mattered.

"I want you to marry me, Valentina."

Her head jerked upward, her eyes widening in shock and disbelief.

Denton swirled the bourbon around in his glass, saying smoothly, "You need protection, Valentina. It takes more than wealth to ensure peace and privacy. It takes power. I have that power." He smiled, superbly sure, utterly confident. "I would like us to marry as soon and as quickly as possible."

She stared at him dazedly. Whenever there had been a crisis, he had been there. Quietly and efficiently he had smoothed out any problems that had arisen. He had found a house that was suitable not only for her but also for Alexander. His plans for her future career were sound. He cared for her and she regarded him with the fond affection and respect that she might have held for an uncle. But she could never marry him. Not in a million years.

"No," she said gently. "I'm sorry, Denton."

His lips tightened. He knew instinctively that to pursue the subject at the present moment would be fatal. He had committed a rare error. He had miscalculated. He had thought that grief over Rakoczi had made her vulnerable. He smiled and shrugged.

"Nothing ventured, nothing gained," he said, kissing her paternally on the forehead as she rose to her feet. "You need a good night's rest. I'll see that you are not disturbed by the press in the morning."

"Thank you, Denton. Good night."

As she walked from the room his smile faded and his eyes narrowed calculatingly. He crossed to the telephone. When he was connected to his secretary, he said crisply, "No telephone calls will be received here for at least forty-eight hours. After that, if and when Mr. Vidal Rakoczi telephones asking to speak to Valentina, will you please inform him that she has given instructions that his calls are not to be accepted?"

"Yes, sir. Good night, sir."

He put the telephone receiver down with a smile of satisfaction. He would speak to the press, indicating that a marriage between himself and Valentina was imminent. The news would reach the source he wanted it to reach. Vidal Rakoczi, trapped in his Los Angeles hospital bed. If Valentina was distressed by the headlines, he would simply say that the press was fabricating their own stories and rumors. His chill eyes gleamed as he poured himself another bourbon. He had lost the battle, but not the war. Valentina was at Oyster Bay, and as long as she remained, he had a satisfying measure of control over her. Control he would not easily relinquish.

Chapter Twenty-four

Vidal woke disoriented and gazed around. Where was he, for God's sake? The white walls of the hospital room closed in on him and he blinked hard, struggling to maintain consciousness. His hands hurt like hell, pain searing up through his arms. He moved, struggling into a sitting position, and the effort made him gasp. His hands and head were swathed in heavy bandages and an intravenous needle was in his arm. Memory flooded back. Horrific and total.

He had been downstairs, pacing the room, trying to think of a way to make Kariana understand that their marriage was at an end. He had been too deep in his thoughts to be aware of the smoke. It was Hazel who had rushed in from the kitchen where she had been making herself a late-night cocoa.

"Vidal! Something is burning!"

He had turned to her quickly. "In the kitchen?"

"No. I thought it was in here. That you had gone to bed and left a cigarette smoldering."

As she spoke a trail of smoke curled into the room and the whole house had suddenly been filled with the pungent smell of burning wood. Instantly, they ran to the door. As Vidal opened it they fell back momentarily, engulfed in choking fumes.

"Wake the servants!" Vidal shouted to her, crushing his handkerchief against his nose and mouth. "Get them out and stay out!"

"But Kariana . . ."

Vidal was already racing across the hall. "*I'll get Kariana! Now get the hell out of here!*"

He couldn't see flames, but he could hear them. Gasping for air, he took the stairs two at a time. Chai and the maids all had quarters on the ground floor. Hazel would have them out by now. She would have called the fire department. There was only Kariana. The smoke was thicker, almost impenetrable. He began to run along the landing to Kariana's room, his lungs bursting. If Kariana had been asleep, she would have been overcome immediately by the smoke. Sweat broke out on his forehead. Dear God in heaven, how long did asphyxiation take? How long, behind closed doors, had the fire been raging?

The door of her bedroom was charring and splitting, the heat of the doorknob scorching as he flung the door open. She was in the far corner of the room, a small, huddled figure at the foot of the bed. The whole room seemed to be in flames. Great tongues of fire soared up the velvet drapes, raced hungrily along the lace-covered canopy of the bed. Blistering plaster fell from the ceiling, raining down on his head and shoulders. The heat blasted him, robbing him of air. The flames were licking at her feet. Even as he struggled across the room he saw the satin of her nightdress erupt into flame. There were sparks in her hair. The waxen doll in her hand melted and disintegrated before his eyes as he seized her, beating at the flames with his hands. A blazing beam fell down behind him and he turned, scooping her up in his arms, facing a wall of fire that seemed to stretch before him endlessly.

He remembered nothing else. When he had regained consciousness, he was on the grass outside Villada, the night sky seared a fevered orange by the flames.

"Kariana . . ." he had managed to say weakly as he was gently transferred to a stretcher and wheeled into an ambulance. "Kariana . . ."

"Your wife is alive and on her way to the hospital," the attendant had said reassuringly. Vidal was aware of blessed relief and a pain that was agonizing. "I must send a cable," he had said, fighting against the darkness that threatened to envelop him. "I must send a cable to New York."

"There'll be plenty of time for that later, sir," the attendant had said solicitously. "You just take it easy till we get you to the hospital."

He had tried to speak again, and failed. The roof of his mouth, his throat, his lungs, felt as if they had been scorched raw. Valentina. News of the fire would be in the papers the next day. He would have to send her word that he was safe, that there was no need for her to worry, that nothing had changed, that between them, nothing would ever change.

"Valentina," he had whispered, and then succumbed to the black rushing winds sucking him down to a place of darkness and ease.

As he struggled up against the pillows, the doctor entered the room.

"How is my wife?" Vidal asked fearfully.

"Your wife is in a very serious condition, Mr. Rakoczi. "Sixty-five percent of her skin area has been burned. Forty-six percent has suffered third-degree burns."

"*Remes!*" Vidal whispered, his face ashen. "Will she live?"

The doctor sat down by the side of his bed, his face grave. "It is impossible for me to say at this stage, Mr. Rakoczi. Generally speaking, when third-degree burns to fifty percent of the skin area have been sustained, then death is the inevitable result. Your wife has suffered forty-six percent of third-degree burns, therefore death is a possibility, but there is still hope."

"I want to see her," Vidal said, trying to swing his legs to the floor. The doctor restrained him.

"Your wife is not conscious, Mr. Rakoczi. I would ask that you remain where you are for the present moment. If there is the slightest change in your wife's condition, I will let you know."

The effort of moving had caused fresh waves of pain to surge up his arms. He looked down at his bandaged hands. The doctor followed his gaze.

"You are an extremely fortunate man, Mr. Rakoczi. The cuffs of your jacket protected your arms."

"And my hands?" Vidal asked, his voice tense.

"Your hands have been very badly burned. You will need skin grafts, and I can give you no reassurance that you will ever regain full use of them. I am sorry." Vidal's mouth tightened. "There is no need to worry about the face," the doctor was saying. "It will be marked only a little. Here," he said, gesturing to Vidal's hairline, "and perhaps some scarring here. The hair will cover it when it grows again."

Vidal received the news in silence and then said quietly, "I would like to speak to Miss Renko. There are people that I have to contact."

"I am afraid that it is not possible, Mr. Rakoczi," the doctor said in a low, serious tone. "Miss Renko died in the fire."

Vidal stared at him disbelievingly. "She couldn't have! She left the house! I *told* her to leave the house!"

The doctor's eyes were compassionate. "Once the rest of the household staff were safely outside, she returned. The Filipino houseboy tried to restrain her, but she ran back into the house. She was overcome by smoke and the firemen found her body at the foot of the stairs."

"Sweet Christ!" Vidal whispered, closing his eyes, fighting for control. Hazel had returned to try and save Kariana. Right up to the last moments of her life she had been loyal and steadfast. Utterly devoted to a woman rarely aware of her existence. He turned his head away, overcome with grief. Hazel dead. Hazel with her calm common sense. Her unfailing good nature. A new fear seized him. He swung his head back to the doctor.

"You did say the rest of the household staff escaped? There were no more casualties?"

"No. Only Miss Renko."

Only. To the doctor she had been a secretary. Perhaps a

housekeeper. To him she had been the best friend that he had ever had. Without Hazel, the last few years would have been impossible. She had cared for Kariana; protected her in his absences; shielded her from the press; been companion, confidante, nurse. Now she was dead and Kariana would never again have anyone to care for her as selflessly as Hazel had.

"I would like to see my houseboy," he said, his voice toneless. Hazel had no family. The funeral would be small. He would make the arrangements himself, and he would be in attendance if he had to crawl from the damned hospital in order to do so.

The doctor nodded and rose to leave. He had not expected Mr. Rakoczi to have been so overcome by the news of Miss Renko's death. Perhaps there had been more to the relationship than that of employer and employee. If there had been, it did not detract from the courage of the man. If Kariana Rakoczi lived, it would be due solely to the fact that her husband had braved an inferno in order to save her.

White-faced and still trembling from shock, Chai made a note of all the people Vidal wished to contact and then spent a long half hour on the hospital telephone. At the end of the half hour he had arranged that Vidal's secretary would occupy a room adjoining Vidal's; that Theodore Gambetta would visit Vidal but that no one else would be allowed to do so; that Hazel Renko was to be buried at Forest Lawn and that the gossip-hungry press would be kept away at all costs.

As soon as his secretary entered the room Vidal asked that she telephone Valentina at the Plaza. After a few minutes she replaced the receiver.

"I'm sorry, Mr. Rakoczi. Miss Valentina is not in her hotel suite."

Vidal's eyes darkened. He had to get in touch with her before the news broke in the press. "Send a cable," he ordered tersely. "And keep trying to contact her by telephone."

His carefully worded cable was sent. Arrangements for Hazel's funeral were made. He was periodically disturbed by the nursing staff and subjected to their ministrations. He asked on the hour and every hour for news of Kariana. And still he was unable to contact Valentina by telephone.

"Put me through to the hotel manager," he said at last in exasperation.

The hotel manager was courteous and apologetic. Mr. Rakoczi should have been informed earlier: Miss Valentina had checked out of the hotel.

As his secretary replaced the receiver for him, Vidal was filled with a mixture of elation and panic. She was going to jeopardize the play by walking out of it to fly to his side. Calculating the length of time it would take her to reach Los Angeles, he spent the night in a fever of impatience.

The morning newspapers mystified him. She had appeared onstage the previous night. There was no hint that an understudy was to take over.

"Where the hell is she?" he roared to Theodore when he visited him late the next day. "It's two days since I cabled her and I haven't heard a thing!"

"If she flew to your bedside, it would cause a lot of very unpleasant speculation, especially with Kariana so critically ill," Theodore said practically.

"Devil take it!" Vidal thundered. "She can telephone, can't she?"

"She will," Theodore said reassuringly. "Just be patient."

"Patience be damned," Vidal snapped. "Where is she? That's what I want to know! Where the devil is she?"

"Try telephoning Kennaway. He'll know."

Neither man spoke as Vidal's secretary waited to be connected to Stan Kennaway's New York number. Beneath his outward calm, Theodore was deeply disturbed. It made no sense for Valentina not to have cabled or telephoned. He would have staked his life on her rushing to Vidal's side the instant she had heard the news. He knew by bitter experience that when it came to personal relationships and her career, Valentina put personal relationships first. And Vidal had told him that they were going to marry. That not even the fire and Kariana's injuries were going to make any difference to their future plans. They would have to wait, of course, because Kariana's recovery would be slow. But he was going to divorce her and marry Valentina as he should have done years ago. Nothing and no one was going to stand in his way.

Theodore had remained silent. Their friendship had suffered badly in the acrimonious aftermath of Valentina's departure from Hollywood. Only in the last year had it been renewed, and he had no desire to place it in jeopardy again by reminding Vidal that Valentina had left him once before with no word of warning.

After what seemed an eternity, Stan's voice could be heard clearly. "Vidal! Thank God you're all right! We've been out of our minds with worry. The papers said—"

"Where is Valentina?" Vidal snapped, cutting Stan short abruptly.

There was a moment's awkward silence and then Stan said, "At Oyster Bay. Denton thought she would have more privacy there."

"I don't understand you. *Where* at Oyster Bay?"

"At Denton's place. He has a big house there."

Vidal's brows flew together and his face whitened. "What the hell is happening, Stan? She hasn't telephoned. Hasn't cabled."

"I guess she tried and couldn't get through," Stan said helplessly.

"A cable would hardly have gone astray and I've given orders that every call from New York is to be put through to me immediately."

"Well, I don't understand it, Vidal. She isn't talking to anyone and—"

"Give me her Oyster Bay number," Vidal said tersely. He got the number and then waited as his secretary tried to connect him, his eyes dark with a pain that had nothing to do with his savagely burned hands.

"I'm sorry, Mr. Rakoczi. The operator says that the telephone has been disconnected."

"That damned son of a bitch!" Vidal flared, swinging his legs from the bed to the floor. "Brook-Taylor would expire without a telephone at his fingertips! If that line has been disconnected, it's been disconnected on purpose! Get me some pants and a shirt, Theo, I'm flying out there right now."

"No, you're not," Dr. Jenson said as he entered the room.

The look Vidal gave him would have annihilated a lesser man. "I'm going to New York," he said curtly. "Today."

Dr. Jenson regarded him coldly from the foot of the bed. "Mr. Rakoczi, you are going nowhere. The wounds on your hands are still losing fluid. That fluid is blood plasma and you are just about to receive a further plasma transfusion to replace it." As he spoke he moved toward Vidal, forcefully restraining him. As a nurse inserted a tube into his arm, Vidal began to swear. Dr. Jenson ignored him.

"Get this bloody tube out of me! You can give me all the transfusions you want when I get back. Twenty-four hours is all I need. Just twenty-four hours!"

"If you leave this room now, the tendons in your hands will never heal. Your hands will be useless and the damage will have been self-inflicted."

"For God's sake, listen to him, Vidal," Theodore said imploringly. "Send another cable. Telephone the theater. I'm sure there's a reasonable explanation for Valentina's silence. Just wait a few more days. You *can't* fly east. Not like this.." He indicated the tubes entering Vidal's arm. The saline drip. The darkly flowing blood. The helplessly inert gauze-swathed hands.

Their eyes met and held and then, at last, Vidal fell back against his pillows. Theodore was right. He was trapped in this sterile white room, Oyster Bay as far away from him as the moon.

The secretary breathed an imperceptible sigh of relief. Theodore's massive shoulders relaxed and Dr. Jenson retreated triumphant.

During the next few days cable after cable was sent. Telephone call after telephone call was made. Valentina could not be contacted at Oyster Bay. Could not even be contacted at the theater. They were the longest, loneliest days of Vidal's life.

At last he could stand it no longer. "I'm going tomorrow," he said as Theodore entered his room. "Hire me a doctor and two nurses and tell Chai I want him to accompany me as well."

Theodore sat down heavily by the side of Vidal's bed. "Before you make any further arrangements, I think you should read this." He spread the *Los Angeles Times* open on the bed.

Vidal took one look at Theodore's face and his blood froze. Then slowly, fearfully, he dropped his eyes to the stark black headlines. The photograph showed Denton Brook-Taylor holding Valentina's fur-clad arm protectively as she walked from his Rolls to the theater. The newsprint proclaimed, VALENTINA AND PRODUCER TO WED!

"I don't believe it," he said, his face ashen. "Theo, help me with the phone."

For once Theo did not argue with him. Vidal gave him Valentina's number and he dialed, holding the receiver to Vidal's ear as his bandaged hands lay impotently on the white sheets.

For the first time ever there was a reply. Vidal sucked in his breath and then said tersely,

"Valentina, please. Vidal Rakoczi speaking."

"I'm sorry, Mr. Rakoczi," said a disinterested female voice in clipped tones. "No calls are being accepted from you."

"What the hell?"

Theo flinched at the rage in his voice.

"This is Vidal Rakoczi speaking! I *demand* to be connected to Valentina immediately!"

"I'm sorry, Mr. Rakoczi," the bland voice repeated. "Instructions have been given that your calls are not to be received."

"Whose instructions?" Vidal thundered, a pulse at his temple pounding, his eyes blazing.

"Valentina's," the voice said, and severed the connection.

"Nem," he said, his breathing harsh. *"Nem. Nem!* NEM!"

The days after were a miasma of pain. It was as if, until then, he had been unaware of his injuries. Now he was all too aware of them. There was surgery to undergo. There was the dreadful wait to see if the nerves in his hands had been destroyed. If he would ever regain full use of his fingers. There was the eternal screaming question. Why? For God's sake, *why?*

Had she been afraid that the fire had disfigured him so terribly that she would no longer be able to stand the sight of him? If so, her fears had been unwarranted. Only his hands were scarred. He looked down at them. They were not a pretty sight, but he would have thought it would have needed far more to send her racing into the arms of the nearest man. Had the woman he had believed himself in love with all these years been nothing but a creature of his own imagination? Was she really as shallow, as uncaring, as her actions declared her to be? He spoke to no one. Not even to Theo. The bitterness of the past was nothing to the bitterness he felt now. He wondered how it was possible to both love and hate one woman so intensely. He wanted to kill her. To destroy her. And then he thought of Alexander and his raging hate grew cold and murderous. She had taken his son away from him. A son he could never claim without destroying all their lives.

Kariana continued to improve. She would never regain full physical health, Dr. Jenson told Vidal. A wheelchair and round-the-clock care would be necessary for many months. Vidal didn't bother to inform the doctor that round-the-clock nursing had been necessary for the past five years. Since the fire Kariana had been calm. Despite her suffering, no one at the hospital had been given any cause to question her mental health and Vidal had remained silent. Even if they knew, they could do nothing. The disease that afflicted Kariana's mind would continue as it always had. There would be a constant spiraling between the depths of depression and wild, uncontrollable mania; occasionally, as now, there would be respite, periods of apparent normality.

Villada was no longer habitable and when he was discharged from the hospital, Vidal moved into a new house in Bel Air on Moraga Drive. It was built all on one floor and would be easy for Kariana to negotiate in her wheelchair. The ceilings were beamed in rich oak, the floors were of polished cedar wood, and he furnished it with deep, comfortable sofas and set about replacing his library.

Every book he purchased reminded him of Valentina. Jane Austen's *Emma*; Emily Brontë's *Wuthering Heights*; Tolstoy's *War and Peace*; Flaubert's *Madame Bovary*. He remembered the soft pink of the carpet in the Beverly Hills Hotel bungalow, the honey-gold of the sunlight as it streamed into her room and he sat cross-legged on the floor, reading, opening up a whole new world for her.

Over dinner one night Theodore suggested, in a moment of unaccustomed interest in the classics, that the tortured love story of Abelard and Heloise would make a surefire winner at the box office. He'd been stunned at Vidal's vehement rejection of the suggestion. Their meal had come to an abrupt halt; Vidal had thrown his napkin on the table and stalked from the restaurant. The subject had never been raised again. For Vidal, Abelard and Heloise were inextricably combined with his first early memories of Valentina. With the innocent happiness of the days before they had become lovers.

The day that Kariana came home from the hospital, Vidal braced himself for a return of the burden that could no longer be shared by Hazel. He had engaged two nurses, Irish girls, brisk and cheerful, but he had not had the emotional strength to explain to them that his wife suffered from a mental as well as a physical disability. The time would come soon enough. Until it did, he had no desire to think about it.

Kariana was not confined to her wheelchair and when she entered the house she leaned heavily on his arm as he showed her through it.

"It's a lovely house, Vidal," she said in the soft whispery voice of her normalcy. "And we'll be alone together here, won't we? There won't be anyone else. There won't be Hazel?"

"No," Vidal said gently. "There won't be Hazel." He had told her of Hazel's death himself. She had taken it silently, lying small and pitiful in her hospital bed. It had been one of the hardest things he had ever had to do.

He led her out onto the balcony and she sat down, leaning with her elbows on the railing, her face in her hands. "I'm glad," she said, and she began to smile.

At first he thought he had not heard her correctly, and then she turned to him, her smile deepening. "She thought she was so clever, Vidal, but you see, *I* was the clever one. I knew what it was that she wanted. Why she always prevented me from seeing you, telling you whenever you telephoned that there was no need for you to come home, that *she* was with me. *I* knew, and I knew that she would never win. I knew that I would die before I would let her win." She held out her arms toward him. "And I did, didn't I? Nearly die. For you."

Her eyes were dreamlike, only the tiniest pinprick of a pupil discernible. He didn't move. The moment seemed to spin out forever. He didn't want to speak; didn't want to ask the question that he must ask. The police and the fire department had been united in their view that the fire had started in Kariana's bedroom. He had been unable to offer them an explanation. Kariana did not smoke in bed. The fire had not been caused by an electrical fault. The cause of the fire was a mystery and had remained a mystery. Cold, so intense that it caught at his breath, seeped through him as he stood in the blazing sunshine, facing his wife.

"Did you know that Hazel would die?" he asked, the words so forcedly casual that he thought they would choke in his throat.

"I knew that it would frighten her. That it would teach her a lesson." Her eyes clouded over, their coloring unclear. "I only wanted a little fire. I didn't expect . . . didn't expect . . ." She shuddered and wrapped her hands around her arms.

"Why?" he asked, and knew that it was the last question that he would ever ask her, that after she had answered he would walk from the house and never willingly set eyes on her again.

Again there was the smile, feline and knowing. "Because you were going to marry her. You were going to leave *me*, a Dansart, and marry *her*. Now you can't, Vidal. You know now that you can never marry anyone else. You are married to me. You always will be married to me." She leaned back, her face toward the sun, her eyes closed.

"I was never going to marry Hazel." His voice was totally without expression. He could not, dare not, give vent to the horror and revulsion consuming him. "I was going to marry Valentina. Hazel Renko loved you. She died trying to save you. And you murdered her."

Kariana drew a lace-edged handkerchief lightly from one hand and into the other. "Ask the maid to serve me with some iced tea, Vidal. It is so hot. So very hot."

Her eyes were still closed, a small smile still on her lips. He wondered if she had heard him and knew that he would never know. For a long, long moment he looked at her and then turned on his heel and walked back into the room.

"An iced tea for Mrs. Rakoczi," he said to Chai, and then went into his study and picked up the telephone.

Ever since his honeymoon he had lived with the knowledge of her illness. He had pitied her and cared for her and he could do so no longer. She was a danger not only to herself but also to those who cared for her. He dialed Dr. Grossman's number and prayed to God that the doctor was in New York and not in Switzerland.

"Just one moment, Mr. Rakoczi, and I will put you

through to the doctor," said the familiar voice of the receptionist.

"What is it, Vidal?" Dr. Grossman asked. "Has Kariana had another serious relapse?"

"Yes," he said tersely. "There's no longer any question of caring for her at home. I want her to come to you, immediately."

"But why? I thought you said that after the fire she seemed calmer. As I have said before, some cases such as Kariana's can cure themselves spontaneously and—"

"Kariana started the fire deliberately. She knows that Hazel Renko died in it and she's showing not the slightest sign of remorse. She is beyond my control and I cannot assume the responsibility for the safety of the household staff caring for her."

"Do the police know?"

"No. There is no reason for them to know. It would only mean a public declaration of Kariana's insanity. Nothing can alter what has already happened."

"I agree. You have done everything for her that you can, my friend. You can do nothing more. I do not think it wise that you should escort her here yourself. You are too emotionally involved. I will have trained psychiatric nurses and a doctor accompany her here. I'll try to arrange for her move immediately . . . today, in fact."

"Thank you," Vidal said, replacing the receiver. He could not have escorted Kariana anywhere. He could no longer stay beneath the same roof. The last, lingering shred of affection had been destroyed. He would never be able to look at her and not see Hazel's image. He went upstairs and packed the new clothes that had been awaiting her on her arrival. The telephone rang and he answered it swiftly, terrified that it was Dr. Grossman calling to inform him that there would be a delay in the arrival of the doctor and the nurses. It was Theo.

"Have you heard the news? Hitler has invaded Poland and England has declared war! Two of my leading men are Britons and the bastards say they're returning home to fight. It's going to cost me thousands to replace them. Vidal, are you there? Are you listening to me?"

"Yes, Theo," Vidal said, holding the telephone receiver in one hand and closing Kariana's suitcase with the other.

"What am I going to do, for Christ's sake? How can I finish *Dark Quintet* without a leading man?"

"Or without a director," Vidal said, swinging Kariana's case from the bed to the floor.

"What do you mean, without a director? *You're* the goddamn director!"

"Yes, and I am also a European. If there is a war in Europe then it is *my* war as well, Theo. I am sure the British will find a use for me."

"*Vidal!*" Theodore thundered, but it was too late. Vidal had already replaced the telephone receiver, and by the time Theo stormed around to the house in his car, it was to find Kariana Rakoczi inexplicably absent and Vidal packing his bags.

"Where the hell do you think you're going?" he yelled, panting for breath after his rush through the house.

"London," Vidal replied, carefully placing his passport in his breast pocket. "After these last few months, the battle-fields of Europe should be a picnic for me."

Chapter Twenty-five

Valentina received the news that Vidal had left for Europe in silence. She could not talk about what had happened, not even to Leila. The hurt was too deep. A raw wound that nothing, not work or time, could heal. Denton's proposal of marriage was repeated, and repeated again. At her third refusal his attitude toward her changed. He became more autocratic. He no longer made requests of her. He demanded. She tried to be patient. To convince herself that he only had her welfare at heart, but when she discovered that he was contacting boarding schools and intended to urge her to send Alexander away to be educated, her temper broke.

"It's a ridiculous suggestion, Denton! Alexander is so young! He needs me."

Denton's mouth tightened. All her love, all her affection, was centered on her child. It was no longer Rakoczi who stood between him and his goal. It was Alexander.

"All mothers feel the same," he said smoothly. "What I am suggesting is for the best, Valentina. Alexander needs the benefit of the best education possible. I've vetted the schools very carefully and—"

"*No!*" Her eyes flashed. "My son's education has nothing whatever to do with you, Denton! He is my responsibility and my responsibility alone!"

"Nothing is your responsibility alone, Valentina. I thought I made that clear to you long ago when I took over your financial affairs."

"My financial affairs are not my personal affairs, Denton. Leila tells me she can't get calls through to me. Stan says you told him I would not be interested in another Broadway play when *Hedda* closes. How *dare* you tell him such a thing? We've never even discussed it, and for your information, I would be *very* interested in doing another play with Stan."

"Broadway is prestigious, but it is movies that make the money," Denton said coldly. "As soon as the play closes we have to go ahead with the plans we made long ago. That is one of the reasons why it is imperative that Alexander be settled at school. His constant presence is distracting."

"Not to me, it isn't!" she flared. "You're talking about my *son*, Denton!" There was not even a glimmer of understanding in the chill gray eyes. Her rage ebbed. She felt oddly deflated. Oyster Bay's walls were stifling her. Denton wanted more from her than she could possibly give. He wanted to possess her as absolutely as he did his antiques and his works of art. She pushed her hair away from her face. "I've been here too long, Denton. I'm going to move in with Leila until the play closes."

"In a two-bit apartment not fit for a maid?" Denton asked derisively. "You're a star. What will your public think if you move into an apartment any one of them could rent?"

"I don't know and I don't care. Alexander adores Leila. The apartment is home to him. That is all that matters."

"Don't be ridiculous." There were white lines etching his mouth and his voice was sharp. "You're overtired. If it disturbs you so much, we'll forget about sending Alexander away to school. Alternative arrangements can be made."

"And I will make them," she said quietly. "You don't like Alexander, Denton. No matter how hard you try and disguise it, it shows. He will be happier and more settled at Leila's." He began to protest and she said steadily, "And so will I."

The parting had not been amicable. It had always been Denton's intention to marry her. Without marriage, he saw little future status in merely handling her financial affairs. He had been rejected and he did not take kindly to rejection. His comments about her to the press were scathingly derogatory. Valentina remained firmly silent.

"For goodness' sake, Valentina," Stan said in exasperation. "You'll have to make a statement in retaliation. He's saying that in abandoning his own business affairs to conduct yours, he lost hundreds of thousands of dollars."

"It isn't true."

"I *know* it isn't true! But what about the gullible public? Are they going to believe that? Denton can be most convincing when he chooses."

"I know," Valentina said with a wry smile. "But I'm not going to descend to the level of hurling insults in public. Denton wrongly believes that his dignity has been offended. He needs to get the bitterness out of his system. If this is his way of doing it, good luck to him."

Stan shook his head in mock despair and grinned. Denton's statements made headlines but carried no weight: in the eyes of the great American public, Valentina could do no wrong. She was admired and emulated by women from coast to coast. She was a star. Bigger and brighter than any other star of stage and screen. She was Valentina and Stan adored her.

In the summer, Europe had plunged deeper and deeper into chaos and her letters to Evangelina had received no reply.

"If only I knew if she was safe," she had said despairingly to Stan.

He had patted her hand. "All you can do is to keep writing," he'd said compassionately. "Things must get better. They can't possibly get worse."

But they had. On September 1, Germany had invaded Poland.

"I doubt if you'll hear anything now until the war is over," Stan said as they sat drinking coffee. "I had a letter from David Niven the other day. He thinks America is bound

to pitch in soon and that, once we do, it will quickly put an
end to the war."

"David left Hollywood and enlisted almost immediately,
didn't he?"

"Yes. He went without any hesitation."

"And Vidal is Hungarian, and he went too," she said, her
voice thick with suppressed emotion. Stan looked at her
sharply. Vidal's name was rarely mentioned.

"Yes," he said, keeping his voice casual. "It was a strange
thing to do. Leaving Hollywood the day the British declared
war on Germany."

"Vidal would hate the Nazis and all they stand for,"
Valentina said, her hair swinging down softly on either side of
her face. "He wouldn't sit on the sidelines. Dear God, why
can't this country see what is happening? I'm so sick of
Charles Lindbergh and Joseph Kennedy and their pompous
isolationist statements. People are dying and we're just sitting
here, waiting for Hitler to defeat Britain. What sort of Europe will it be if he does?"

"God knows," Stan said wearily, thinking of his own
cousins in bomb-blitzed London. "But you can't do any more
than you are doing. You've organized more benefits for British War Relief than anyone else I know."

"It isn't enough!" Valentina said passionately, her fists
clenched. "Not for people like Evangelina and Maria and
Aristea. It isn't enough, Stan."

"What are you two looking so gloomy about?" Leila
asked as she joined them.

"War," Stan said briefly.

Leila shrugged her shoulders dismissively. "Can't you
two ever talk of anything else? Sex, for instance. Glorious,
glorious sex."

Stan and Valentina laughed. If it wasn't that she was still
performing nightly as Thea Elvsted, both doubted if Leila
would ever surface from Rory O'Connor's bed.

"Korda is going to make a romance-adventure based on
the life of Lord Nelson, one of England's foremost naval
heroes, and Lady Hamilton," Leila said, lighting a cigarette.
"Rumor has it that he wants Laurence Olivier and Vivien
Leigh in the lead parts."

"There's a film originated by the war spirit if I ever heard
of one," Stan said, rising to his feet. "More coffee, anyone?"

* * *

When the Japanese attacked Pearl Harbor and brought
America into the war, Valentina felt only relief. She threw
herself totally into the organization and support of cocktail
parties, concerts, bazaars, all in aid of the American Red
Cross, the French *poilus*, the British War Relief. James Stewart
enlisted in the United States Air Force, and was stationed in
Britain; Clark Gable followed suit. Valentina corresponded
with both, asking casually after the welfare of David Niven, of
Vidal, of the many other Hollywood personalities stationed in
Great Britain. But it was Vidal whose name she fearfully
searched for every time a letter arrived in return. Vidal, who
was never far from her thoughts every time she read a
newspaper or saw newsreel pictures of the fighting.

Sutton Hyde and his wife were staying in New York.

"You look tired. You really must take a rest," he said
to her one evening as they sat nursing after-dinner coffees.
"You'll have a breakdown if you continue at your present pace."

"I'm fine, Sutton. Please don't worry about me."

Sutton noticed the faint blue shadows beneath her eyes.
She was lying and he knew it.

"What costume drama is Theodore planning to star you in
now?" she asked, changing the subject. She enjoyed Sutton's
company. Being with him reminded her of the making of *The
Warrior Queen;* of her marriage to Paulos. She had not one
unhappy memory connected with him and she was grateful that
his age made it pointless for him to return to Britain and
that he had so much time for her here in New York.

"*Captain Black,*" Sutton replied, raising his eyes to
heaven. "I am to be an English earl captured for ransom. It
will be a debacle, of course. Theodore has no historical bent.
He's lost without Vidal."

The name fell between them like a shadow and both of them
them fell silent. Vidal. Her heart ached. Was he safe? Was he
happy?

"I'm cold," she said, though the evening heat was stifling. She drew a cardigan around her shoulders and asked
the maid to set fire to the logs in the hearth of the living room.
Their warmth did not ease her. The cold she suffered from
was too deep. It was a cold that she was never free of. It had
pierced her heart on the day she had received Vidal's cable
and it had never left her. It never would leave her.

"What happened between you and Vidal?" Sutton asked gently. "I saw the photographs taken at the premiere party of *Hedda Gabler*. When I saw you together I thought . . ." He raised his shoulders expressively. "I thought there would be a happy outcome for you both."

The maid brought in a tray with wafer-thin china cups and a pot of Sutton's favorite Earl Grey tea. Valentina waited until she had set the tray down and departed and then she said, speaking of it for the first time, "So did I, Sutton. That night was the happiest night of my life."

The firelight shone on her hair, accentuating the purity of her cheekbone and jaw. His breath caught in his throat. She was the loveliest woman he had ever seen. And the saddest.

"When Vidal left for home the next day, it was to tell Kariana that he was divorcing her. We were going to be married, Sutton. We *would* have been married if . . ." Her eyes darkened and her fists clenched. "If it hadn't been for that damned fire!"

The naked anguish in her voice seared him. "I can understand the fire meaning a change in your plans. Kariana was badly injured, but surely, in time . . ."

"He didn't wait for time," she said, and the anguish had gone. Her voice was bitter and hard. "He cabled me from his hospital bed the next day. There was to be no divorce. He would not be seeing me again. He was staying with Kariana. He had a choice to make and he made it." Her expression was bleak. "He chose Kariana."

When *Hedda Gabler* came to the end of its long run, she did not embark on any of the movies that had been offered. Instead, she went to the United States Organization and offered to help in any way that she could.

The officer interviewing her was overawed but cautious. "We need entertainers for the troops. Singers, dancers, that sort of thing."

Valentina's eyes gleamed. "Lieutenant, I *am* an entertainer. I can make those men forget for a short time the horrors that they are living through."

The lieutenant grinned. "One sight of you, ma'am, and they'll certainly do that!"

*　　*　　*

Sutton presented her with a pearl-handled .44-caliber revolver that he had carried with him throughout World War I. "I hope you never have cause to use it, my dear, but if you do, don't hesitate. It's hesitation that loses the day." He had kissed her good-bye affectionately, his eyes suspiciously bright.

When Rogan Tennant heard of her plans, he asked if he could accompany her. They could put some sketches together. He could sing. He was tired of playing war heroes behind the safety of studio lights while his compatriots were dying on real battlefields. It was too late for him to enlist, but he could at least do this. It would be something. It would ensure that he retained a measure of self-respect.

Valentina had taken Rogan to the USO headquarters at One Park Avenue. The military had been delighted at the offer of his services, and he had been delighted with the honorary rank of colonel he was given in case of capture by the enemy.

In a battered C-54 they flew via the Azores to Casablanca and then on to Algiers and Italy. The past was never mentioned between them. It was as if they had never been romantically involved but had always been friends.

"Don't you miss Alexander?" he asked her one day as they drove through the blackout to the theater in which they were to perform.

"Yes, but he understands why I am doing this. He's staying with Leila while I am away."

She looked out of the car window at the night-black city streets of Naples. In the future, wherever she was, wherever she worked, Alexander would be with her.

The tour was arduous. They traveled in great discomfort and often in great danger, but the tumultuous welcome she received everywhere she went more than made up for it. Onstage she wore the most daring, breathtaking gowns of her career.

"Those men haven't been close to a woman in months," she said when a colonel timidly suggested she dress a little more modestly and avoid a riot. "I'm here to remind them of what one looks like."

"You sure do that, ma'am," the colonel said, loosening his collar.

She had been dubious of her singing voice before the

tour began, but her choice of songs, sexually explicit, full of double entendres, had the troops cheering until they were hoarse. She had gone to the front lines to provide battle-weary men with glamour, and she gave it to them in abundance. By day, her sequins and rhinestones were abandoned. She wore GI uniform: Eisenhower jacket, regulation trousers, boots, and a helmet when necessary. She still looked so stunning that they were often delayed for hours as admiring soldiers surrounded the jeep she was traveling in, slowing it to walking speed.

In London she took a few days off and Rogan drove her down to David Niven's cottage near Windsor. It was a relaxing weekend. She played in the garden with the Niven children, listened in amusement as Rogan recounted their exploits, and caught up with the news, both professional and personal.

"And Rakoczi?" Rogan asked David, when they had brought each other up-to-date on their mutual friends from Hollywood who were serving in Europe. "Does anyone know where he is?"

Valentina's hand tightened on the arms of her cane garden chair. She could no longer hear the children laughing or the birds singing in the branches of the nearby trees.

"He's in the Peloponnesus acting as a British liaison officer between our chaps and the EDES, the Greek guerrillas under Zervas," David said. He grinned suddenly. "God knows how he got a pip like that. I thought he was a Hungarian, not a Greek."

"If it got him into hand-to-hand combat, he would have convinced the powers that be that he was Ghenghis Khan," Rogan said, laughing.

A precious bottle of Scotch that they had brought with them from the American PX was passed around and the conversation turned to other things.

Valentina did not join in. Her fingers tightened around her glass. Vidal was in Greece. What if he died there, as Paulos had? She closed her eyes and fought back a wave of nausea. He *couldn't* die. He may have abandoned her for Kariana. He may have turned his back on her and not given her another thought, but he couldn't die. She wouldn't be able to bear it.

"We'll have to be going," Rogan was saying to her. "You're dining with the top brass tonight."

She smiled and rose to her feet. Though she could not say so, she was dining with Britain's prime minister, Winston Churchill. She wondered if he would give her any up-to-date information on a Hungarian serving as a British liaison officer in the Peloponnesus, and doubted it. As they drove back to London she stared out over the darkened fields. How long would it be before she ceased to care? Before he ceased filling her thoughts, waking and sleeping? The answer came back like the roar of surf. Never. As long as she had breath in her body, he would be a part of her.

"Rome next week and then Aachen," Rogan said buoyantly. "How do you feel about the prospect of setting foot on German soil? Doesn't it scare you to death?"

"No," she said, smiling at his boyish enthusiasm. She had only ever been afraid of one thing in life. Losing Vidal. Now that she had lost him, there was nothing left to fear. She was seeing a special operations officer in the morning to map out the rest of her route. He would be able to tell her what the present situation in Greece was. But he would not be able to tell her if Evangelina was still alive . . . or Maria . . . or Aristea . . . or Vidal.

Chapter Twenty-six

If Britain's prime minister was working a twenty-hour day, and fighting for the future freedom of untold millions, he showed little sign of it at dinner. His interest in Hollywood was unlimited. Over champagne he disclosed to Valentina that he knew Alexander Korda well and that Korda's film *Lady Hamilton*, starring Laurence Olivier and Vivien Leigh, had been his own idea.

"In 1940 a great mass of public opinion in America was against any involvement in the war," he said, his full, heavy lips pursing. "I recommended the subject of Nelson to Korda. I wanted him to produce a movie that would create a more sympathetic attitude towards England and ultimately create a demand in America for the United States to help us."

"And the Japanese did it for you," Valentina said impishly.

Churchill chuckled. He was enjoying the company of his dinner guest. "They did, but never tell Korda. He believes he orchestrated the whole event himself."

As brandy was poured for the prime minister and Valentina lightly covered the top of her glass with her hand, she asked, "Would it have been easy for a Hungarian to have become a British liaison officer?"

"It would have been damned odd," Churchill replied, regretting that the dinner would soon have to come to an end.

"A friend of mine did so. Vidal Rakoczi, the film director. I believe he's in the Peloponnesus. I've had no news of him for a long time. . . ."

Churchill patted her hand reassuringly. "When there is news, I will see to it that you receive it. Now, I'm afraid that you must excuse me," and he returned to his desk and his maps and his staff officers.

The special operations officer the next morning was no more helpful. For a man serving in Vidal's capacity, no news could be expected. Valentina sought solace in writing a long letter to Alexander and wondering if it would be delivered. God, how she hated the war. Its effects had scarcely been noticed in New York. Here in Europe they were all around her. Bombed-out cities and derelict houses; long lines for the necessities of life. Refugees. Hideously wounded soldiers.

The tour went on. In France they were lost in fog, their fuel running dangerously low before their straining eyes saw a break and their pilot made an emergency landing.

In the Netherlands a bomb fell so close to them one evening that the power failed and Valentina sang, the headlamps of a jeep her only spotlights.

"We're a damned sight too near the front lines," Rogan said one evening when Valentina had specifically requested they visit an area that was not on their schedule. "There's no need for it, Valentina. If we're captured, we'll be executed. I want to be a *live* conquering hero, not a dead one."

Valentina smiled tolerantly at him and took not the slightest notice. They were entertaining fighting men who were at war. They couldn't expect to do so in comfort and safety.

They were in Belgium when the real danger came. Rogan had been edgy ever since they had crossed the border. North Africa and Italy he could handle. Belgium was too near to Germany for his liking. "I'll be glad to get the hell out of here," he said to her as GIs, jubilant at her presence, were noisily erecting a rough wooden platform on which he and Valentina could perform. "That road was so heavily mined I could hear my knees knocking."

"They're fighting what could be the last and most important battle of the war," Valentina said soberly. "We might not be fighting ourselves in the Battle of the Bulge, Rogan, but at least by being here we're revitalizing the men who are."

Rogan didn't think he was doing much to revitalize them, but he knew damned well that Valentina was. She pulled out all the stops where glamour was concerned. Her sequined gowns were slit to the thigh, revealing a length of leg that had the men whistling, clapping, and shouting themselves hoarse. She was woman personified and there were times when Rogan feared for her safety, certain that, like a pack of wolves in heat, the men were going to rush the stage and literally devour her.

That evening the lieutenant colonel came to see them, his expression grave. "I have to tell you that the military position is changing by the minute. We are now virtually surrounded. The Germans have cut us off north, south, and east, and there is fierce fighting to the west."

The blood drained from Rogan's face. "But there'll be reinforcements? More troops?"

The lieutenant colonel nodded, but his face was still grim. "The point is, this area is going to very shortly be a battlefield. The only way of getting you out is to fly you out. I'm sorry, Mr. Tennant, I'm doing my best, I assure you."

When he had gone, Rogan turned to her, his lips bloodless. "What do we do now?" he asked, fumbling for a cigarette.

Valentina shrugged a slender shoulder. "We do what we came out here to do. We entertain the troops and we keep calm."

"Shit, Valentina, don't you *ever* get scared?"

A sad smile tugged at the corners of her mouth. "Yes," she said quietly, "but not of the Germans."

It seemed to her that the applause they received that night was the most intense they had ever received. In the

distance bombs dropped; the rickety stage vibrated dangerously; there were no jeeps to give light and the men focused
flashlights on her as she sang of love and peace and home.

For the thousandth time she wondered where Vidal was.
If he, too, was under bombardment, wishing with all her
heart that he was one of the men in the darkness only yards
away from her. When she sang, it was to Vidal, and tears
glittered on her eyelashes. Somehow, by being in danger,
she felt closer to him.

"*Down!*" a voice suddenly cried, and mayhem broke
out. An explosion ripped the air, robbing her of breath,
throwing her forward. She could hear feet stampeding, voices
shouting, and could feel a warm trickle of blood as it seeped
down her face from her temple. Debris rained down on her
and then strong hands were holding her.

"Are you all right, ma'am?" a young officer was asking
urgently.

She nodded, trying to see where the stage had been,
trying to locate Rogan.

"Mr. Tennant . . ." she gasped as she was swept high
against a uniformed chest. "Where is he? Is he hurt?"

There were flames shooting up into the night sky, men
running, the hideous stench of burning cordite.

"He'll be all right, ma'am," the officer shouted. "Just
keep your head down!" Even as he ran with her to shelter,
they were strafed, bullets ricocheting around them. Valentina
felt sick with fear. Not for herself but for Rogan, who had
never wanted to venture so near the front lines. "Please!" she
panted, "I must find him!" Another bomb exploded and wood
and metal flew through the air. It was impossible to speak
anymore, impossible to be heard. The officer threw her down
behind an upturned jeep, shielding her with his body.

She longed desperately for her revolver, but it was in
her dressing room and there was no way that she could
return to it. For the first time she ceased to regard it as a
memento. It was a lethal weapon, and at any moment she
might have desperate need of it.

A medical officer was running low toward them. She
shouted to him that she was all right and then there came
another blast and the jeep rocked and she was being sucked
down and down as if she were in the eye of a hurricane.

When it was over, it was discovered that her scalp had

been cut open but that her face was unmarked. Rogan's arm had been severely cut by flying metal, but he seemed more proud than disconcerted. He had been bloodied in battle, and it gave him pride and assurance. Valentina knew that, if they survived, it was a story he would dine out on for years.

"Do you think they'll get a plane in for us before the Germans attack again?" he asked her, nursing his arm.

It was a cold day and Valentina shivered, her army jacket pulled up around her ears. "I don't know. They're going to do their best."

They stared upward at the empty sky, their faces grim. The alternative was to be killed or captured, and neither alternative appealed to them.

"Listen, can you hear something?" Rogan said at last. "An engine?"

Valentina held her breath and then relief shot through her. It was a plane and she could both hear and see it.

"Lucky devils," the lieutenant colonel shouted, herding them at a run toward the makeshift airstrip. "Give my regards to the folks at home."

"We will when we get there," Valentina said, flashing him a dazzling smile, "but it won't be for several months. We have a lot more places to visit yet."

Rogan groaned, scrambling into the barren interior of the plane, shouting his good-byes and thanks over the roar of the engines.

When at last they took off, he stretched his legs out on the cold, vibrating metal and said, "There used to be a time when planes had seats."

Valentina grinned. "There used to be a time when dressing rooms had showers, not just buckets of cold water." They laughed and then she said quietly, "You don't mind if we continue with the tour, do you, Rogan?"

"No," he said, surprised to know that it was the truth. "For as long as you want me to be shot at, Valentina, I'll be shot at. Where do we go next?"

"Wherever the top brass will allow us to go," she said, but as their plane droned to safety she wasn't thinking of Western Europe but of Greece and the EDES and of a danger that she could never share.

*   *   *

Three months later they were back in New York. The USO had recalled them and though she did not want to return, she was under orders, just as the soldiers she had been entertaining were under orders.

After a joyous reunion with Alexander, she boarded the Santa Fe Chief and headed back to the town she had left so many years ago.

Hollywood welcomed her back rapturously. On her first evening she attended a concert at the Hollywood Bowl and as she entered, the star-studded audience turned in her direction and whispers began to cascade from tier to tier. Then, quite simultaneously, before the performance even began, they rose to their feet and began to applaud. Valentina smiled and waved and felt the tears sting the back of her eyes. She had never thrown herself into the heady social life of the Hollywood set, yet she was being received back among them with an unprecedented show of love and affection and a complete lack of professional jealousy. She was home, where she belonged. Where she had always belonged ever since she had first walked onto the set of *The Black Knights* at Worldwide.

It took Theo a bare twenty-four hours to call on her. It was the first time they had met since she had walked from his office nearly ten years previously. He eyed her appreciatively. Only a few of the stars who had been famous when Valentina was the queen of Worldwide had managed to retain their success and their beauty. Drink, drugs, disastrous love affairs had taken their toll on all but a precious few. Yet, at thirty, Valentina was more beautiful than she had ever been. He reflected yet again that her beauty was not a surface thing. There was an indefinable quality about her that he had never encountered in all the thousands who sought to imitate her. There was an air of elusiveness about her. A fey quality. A mystery that was bone-deep and utterly natural. Not for the first time, he wondered where she had come from. What her history had been before she had caught Vidal's eye. No one knew. He doubted if even Vidal knew.

The long, shoulder-length fall of hair, partially obscuring the face and so beloved by his current leading ladies, was not affected by Valentina. Her shining black hair was held away from her face by two heavy tortoise shell combs. Adulation had given her no tiresome pretensions. Her dignity was innate.

Her world-famous success was worn with the casual ease of the mink he had once draped around her shoulders. Yet she had changed. The quick laughter that had always been in her eyes during the years she had worked with Vidal, was no longer there. Instead, there was a far more disturbing quality. A haunting sadness that not even her smile could disguise.

"Good morning, Mr. Gambetta," she said, walking forward to greet him with gentle hip-swinging grace.

"What's with the 'Mr. Gambetta'?" Theo said expansively. "The name is Theo."

"It was Mr. Gambetta the last time we met," Valentina said, with a spark of mischief.

Theo had the grace to flush. "A lot of water has flowed under the bridge since then."

"And a lot of bucks," Valentina added demurely.

Theo, remembering the huge settlement she had paid for the privilege of leaving his employ, threw back his head and guffawed. She had always been bright. Always been more than a match for him in their verbal battles. There were not many women he had liked as much, and yet . . . His laughter faded. This was the woman who had deserted Vidal when he lay in a hospital bed with appalling burns. The woman who had never telephoned to ask about the condition of the man she had been going to marry. Who had never even had the common decency to write, and who had allowed Vidal to learn of her engagement to another man through the dispassionate columns of the *Los Angeles Times*.

He thrust the memory from him. He was here on business and personal feelings had no place where business was concerned.

"Sit down, Theo. Tell me why you are here."

"As if you didn't know," he said, his dark thoughts banished, his grin once more relaxed. He looked around the room. It was light and airy with floor-to-ceiling windows looking out over the canyon below. Outside was a patio with a glass-topped dining table surrounded by birds and flowers, and in the distance he could see the shimmer of a pool and white blossoms floating on the surface. She had always had a talent for making any house she moved into instantly a home.

He sat down on a pleasingly comfortable, deep-armed sofa and said, "I want you back at Worldwide."

A smile tugged at the corners of her mouth. "I can work

for any studio in town, Theo. Why, after all that has happened between us, should I ever again work for you?"

Her dress was of ivory silk, molded gently at the waist and over her hips and falling into a delicious swirl around her knees. Her only jewelry, a rope of pearls.

"Because we understand each other, Valentina. Because we've made great pictures in the past and can make even greater ones in the future."

She shook her head. "No, Theo. I'm never going to be bound to a studio again. I shall do the movies that *I* want to do, and I shall never again allow myself to be put under contract for years at a time."

"There's no need for you to be," Theo said, leaning toward her, his hands clasped. "We'll do it your way. One movie at a time."

"And what if we disagree about the subject matter?"

"We won't. You'll have the final say in everything."

There was an unmistakable gleam of amusement in her eyes. "Theo, you're impossible. What you are suggesting is unheard-of and you know it. No writer, no star, no director, has a final say. The most important directors in town are often replaced in mid-picture. Even worse, they often have their finished work taken out of their hands and completely recut and reshaped by the front office."

"I know," Theo agreed equably. "And the front office does so on my orders. I have a responsibility to the banks, to stockholders. Picturemaking is a business. A picture that does poorly at the box office, no matter how creatively made, is a poor picture. If the public doesn't turn up in droves to see it, it's a failure no matter what I may personally think, or what the critics may think. Box-office returns are the name of the game. You know that as well as I do."

"Yes, and I want no part of it," she said emphatically. "I want to make *good* pictures. Creative pictures. Pictures with artistic depth and pictures that make people think and feel."

"You will," Theo said with maddening complacency. "With me. The war has changed people, Valentina. There's a new spirit in this country. The public is becoming more discerning. They want more than the froth we've been giving them. I'm willing to take a chance, but I'm only willing to take it with you. I'm prepared to be as daring and as innovative as you like. Now, what do you say?"

It was ridiculous. She had vowed never to set foot on a Worldwide set again. Yet it was Worldwide that was her spiritual home, and Theo was offering her everything that she most desired.

Her smile deepened, effortlessly, unknowingly sensual. Theo felt a rise of pleasure in his loins. He had thought it impossible to forgive her for the agony she had caused Vidal, and yet already the memory was dimming. It was unthinkable that woman before him should have behaved in such a callous fashion. Perhaps Vidal had been in delirium. Perhaps she never had agreed to marry him. Perhaps the whole, awful horror of those days of waiting had been nothing but the fevered longings of Vidal's own imagination.

He said carefully, "The war has brought a lot of talent to Hollywood. Refugees from Hitler are here in droves. Thomas Mann, Bertolt Brecht. We've got some of the best writers ever assembled in one place at the same time. But we don't have the best director."

Her smile faded. Her face went suddenly still.

"All your former movies for me were directed by Vidal. Until he returns from Europe you will have to work with other directors."

Her long, beautifully shaped hands tightened imperceptibly in her lap. "It is impossible for me to work with Vidal again," she said, and he was shocked at the sudden flash of suffering in her eyes.

He rose to his feet, shaken, and mixed himself a drink. A strong one. Whatever had happened between Valentina and Vidal had brought neither one of them happiness.

"I have some scripts I'd like you to look through," he said, turning once more toward her. "And there's a Maugham short story that has distinct possibilities."

The Maugham short story was discarded. They settled on a Christopher Isherwood script and Theo promised that he would pull out all the stops and have the filming under way as soon as possible.

Leila, married to a prospering Rory, moved into a ranch-style house just off the intersection of Mulholland and Coldwater Canyon. Valentina began to entertain; to give parties as well as to go to them. She had her work. She had her friends. She had her son, and when the war ended she had the joy of hearing from Evangelina and learning that, although they had undergone dreadful privations, the Khairetis family was safe.

"These last few months have been quite something, haven't they?" Leila said to her, sprawling over one of Valentina's white-upholstered sofas, a Bloody Mary in her hand with a tiny rose petal floating on its surface. "David Niven's back. Clark Gable's back. Jimmie Stewart's back."

"Vidal isn't back," Valentina said, her voice tight, as it always was whenever Vidal's name was mentioned.

"That's just where you're wrong," Leila said, wondering how Valentina would take the news. "He arrived home late last week. He's been keeping a low profile so it only became public knowledge today. The gossip is that he's going to direct Rogan in *The Last Tsar* for MGM."

Valentina's relief was total. She began to shake, overcome with the ridiculous desire to laugh and cry at the same time.

"Forgo the wine and have a Bloody Mary," Leila suggested, seeing the effect that her news had had. She swung her legs off the arms of the sofa and rose to her feet. "Stay where you are. I'll mix it."

Valentina clenched her fists hard, struggling for control. It was over. He was safe. God damn him. Her fears had been unfounded. He wasn't lying dead on some remote Greek mountainside. He was alive and he was back in Hollywood.

"Do the gossips say whether Kariana has returned as well?" she asked, trying to keep her voice steady.

"No. No one seems to have had any news of her since Vidal left for Europe and she returned east. I expect that now he is home she will be coming out and joining him."

"Yes," Valentina said, her voice suddenly hard, "I expect she will."

Leila regarded her with concern. It was hard to say whether Valentina still loved Vidal or whether she hated him. Whatever her emotion, it was one that consumed her and the meeting between them would be traumatic. It would also be unavoidable. In the close-knit society of Hollywood, everyone met everyone else eventually.

For two miraculous weeks, by dint of obtaining the guest lists prior to any party or event that Valentina was invited to, Leila, with the aid of Valentina's secretary, managed to avoid the inevitable confrontation. When it finally took place, it took place, ironically, at a party given by Theodore Gambetta.

"No Vidal Rakoczi?" Leila had asked Valentina's secretary when the invitation had arrived.

"No, he must be out of town."

"Good," Leila said fervently. "Let's hope he stays out of town!"

Theodore's parties were always on the grand scale. Anyone of any consequence at all had been invited and Leila and Rory accompanied Valentina in her chauffeur-driven limousine.

"Am I seeing a mirage?" Leila asked as they descended from the car into the balmy night air. "Or is the band walking on water?"

"Not even Theo can accomplish *that* for dramatic effect," Valentina said dryly. "They're on an island in the middle of the swimming pool."

"Thank God. I was beginning to think that Theo's power was ultimate."

Laughing, they strolled up the vast, porticoed steps and as they entered the house heads turned and conversation faltered. Alone, in a room where sequins, crystals, and gold lamé glittered, Valentina wore a dress of stark black. High at the throat, it plunged waist-deep at the back, needing no other decoration but her flawless skin and hip-swaying grace.

"No one can move in a backless dress like Valentina," Sutton Hyde said reverently as she crossed the room to Theo, demonstrating the truth of his statement superbly.

Theo kissed her warmly, disguised his surprise at her acceptance of the invitation when it was obvious that Vidal would be present, and introduced her to a young man of indecent Latin good looks who had come out from New York to help him convince the United States Department of Internal Revenue that their assessment of Worldwide's profits was vastly excessive.

"Oh, dear, there's Clark Gable with another Carole Lombard look-alike," Leila whispered to Rory. "When *will* he get over her death, poor lamb? And La Swanson eyeing Valentina as if she were poison. . . ."

Rory regarded the stars around him with indifference. There were very few people in the room whom he knew, or cared to know. Catching sight of Sutton Hyde, he crossed the room toward him, grateful that there was one person at least he could have an intelligent conversation with.

"There are a hundred people waiting to say hello to you," Theo said, extricating Valentina from his new protégé's overeager attentions. "Errol Flynn says he's going to abduct you unless you come quietly. I wonder if he feels a heel about not going to fight when so many of my guests had such a hell of a bad time in Europe?"

If he did, he showed no sign of it. He was as ebullient as ever. "Look, sport," he said when he had kissed her and she had carefully removed his hand from a place it had no right to be, "don't you think this chastity lark has gone on long enough? You're an insult to my reputation."

It was familiar repartee. Errol had long since given up any hope of adding her to his list of conquests. In a bizarre way he preferred it the way it was. He wasn't a man who made friends with women. They were for using and discarding, not for befriending. Valentina was a rare exception. She kissed him indulgently and moved away from him toward Rory and Sutton.

"Have one of Theo's atrocious new cocktails," Sutton said, handing her a glass as Rogan Tennant joined them. "God alone knows what the alcoholic content must be. Even Flynn's looking glassy-eyed!"

She took the proffered drink, looking up and beyond him. As she did so her smile froze and the blood left her face.

He was at the doorway, his stance negligent, his hands in his pockets. It had been six years since she had last seen him. Six long, lonely years in which there had not been one day when he had not occupied her thoughts. The war had changed but not ravaged him. He was leaner, his body harder, if that were possible, than it had been before. He had the air of a man it was impossible to take by surprise. A man it would be wisest not to tangle with. He raised his eyes, looking carelessly across the room, and she felt faint; her hurt as raw and as fresh as the day when she had first known he would not be returning for her.

"Oh, Lord," Leila whispered unnecessarily. "It's Vidal."

"With my ex-wife," Rogan added bitterly.

For the first time, Valentina became aware of the immaculately red-lacquered nails clinging to Vidal's arm, the slender crystal-and beaded figure at his side.

He began to stroll through the throng and her throat tightened. He moved with the deceptive ease and suppleness of a man who was always wary. A man who would be swift to turn on an attacker. A man capable of killing unhesitatingly if the need arose. The years with the EDES had left their mark.

In another moment, another second, he would see her. There would be no more delaying the moment she had both dreaded and craved for so long.

His hair was as dark and as lustrous as ever, curling thickly into the nape of his neck like a ram's fleece. There was no hint of gray, only the startling flash of silver falling low across the black bars of his brows. The incisive lines running from nose to mouth had deepened and there was a disturbing, almost merciless quality about the set of his mouth. Alone, in all the room, he was spared the effusive kisses, the hearty backslappings that were the obligatory Hollywood greetings. Only a brave man or a fool would have proffered undue familiarity to Vidal Rakoczi.

Romana had seen Rogan and was blowing him a kiss provocatively in his direction, pointing out their tiny group to Vidal. Valentina tried to move, to avert her gaze, and failed. He had seen her. She saw him suck in his breath; saw the skin tighten like parchment across his cheekbones, and then, in stunned incredulity, saw the bitter, burning hate.

She swayed and Sutton grasped her elbow. She could no longer hear the noise in the room, the laughter and the chatter. Even Leila and Rogan seemed blurred and indistinct as Vidal began to move toward them. There was no escape. Nowhere to run. Nowhere to hide. He was so near that she could smell the clean starched linen of his evening shirt; the familiar aroma of his cologne. She drew in a deep, steadying breath and lifted her head high.

"It's nice to see you back, Vidal," Leila said stiffly as Sutton and Rory maintained an uneasy silence and Rogan glared at Romana.

His mouth quirked in a humorless smile. "You surprise me, Leila. I would hardly have thought my absence would have given you cause for concern."

At the mockery in his voice Leila flushed and then, slowly, his gaze slid away from her and rested on Valentina. The moment seemed to stretch into infinity, and then, with careless insolence, he said, "I'm told that you discarded Mr. Denton Brook-Taylor with practiced ease. Have you another would-be husband hovering on the horizon?"

Leila gasped and Rory's eyes widened. Valentina raised her head a fraction higher, the long, lovely line of her throat flawless. This was the man who had promised always to love her. The man who had promised to marry her and be a father to their child. Who had abandoned her and had abandoned Alexander to stay with his badly injured wife. A man who, on his return to Hollywood, had chosen to forget his wife's existence and had escorted Romana de Santa to one of the most public events on the Hollywood calendar.

"If I had," she said, each syllable dripping ice, "you would be the very last person to know, Mr. Rakoczi."

For a horrified moment Leila thought that he was going to strike her, and then he shrugged his shoulders and said with careless indifference, "And to care," and he turned on his heel, striding quickly from the room, Romana hurrying in his wake.

"What devil is riding him?" Rory O'Connor asked in bewilderment.

"A devil that will eventually destroy him," Sutton said, his aristocratic face pale. "Commandeer some more drinks, dear boy, will you? Brandy, I think, would be most suitable. Extremely large ones."

Chapter Twenty-seven

Valentina remembered very little of the remainder of the party. She left early, stiff and unspeaking, locked into an inner world that not even Leila could penetrate. The promise he had made to her six years ago on the sunlit streets of New York was as vivid as if it had been made only yesterday. His breaking of it had almost destroyed her, but she had understood. His duty had been to Kariana. Knowing that, she had managed to endure the intervening years. If there had been no fire, he would have been with her. It had been comfort of a kind. His arrival at Theo's with Romana on his arm meant that there could be comfort no longer. He had not married her; not because of Kariana, but because he had not chosen to.

Her hands clenched on her lap, the knuckles showing white. He had hurt her for the last time. From now on, life for Valentina, the enigmatic star of Hollywood, was going to be very different. She smiled grimly to herself in the dim interior of the limousine. Louella Parsons and Hedda Hopper would have so much to write about in the coming weeks, their pens would run dry.

"Would you like me to come in with you?" Leila asked tentatively as they glided to a halt outside the burnished oak doors of Valentina's hilltop home.

"No, I'm fine, Leila. Good night."

Her chauffeur opened the rear door and she stepped out onto smoothly raked gravel, not even turning to wave as the chauffeur returned to the driver's seat and the limousine slid away in the direction of Leila and Rory's Mulholland Drive home.

Her maid brought her a nightcap of cocoa and wished her a respectful good night. Valentina slipped off her evening pumps and kicked them carelessly across the room. Then she picked up the mug of milky cocoa, walked barefooted into the kitchen and poured it down the sink. Back in the living room she surveyed the well-stocked bar and removed a bottle at random. It was bourbon. She grimaced at the taste and swallowed. In a little while she no longer grimaced.

"Vidal! Wait. Please wait!" Romana cried, teetering after him in her suicidally high heels, her speed hampered by her figure-molding gown.

"*Vidal!*" she wailed as he yanked open the door of his limousine, then revved the engine savagely. By the time she had reached the bottom of the porticoed steps, the limousine was speeding down the drive, its taillights flashing as it swept around the corner of the drive, disappearing from view.

He took the coast road. The road he had taken so many years ago when he and Valentina had left Lilli Rainer's party together. He had known that she would be there. Theo had warned him. Yet even after all this time he had not been prepared for the physical impact she would have on him. Looking at her across the crowded room, it had been as if a fist had been thrust hard into his belly. Nothing about her had changed. She didn't merely glitter, she shone. Her smoke-dark hair had been coiled softly into the nape of her neck and knotted with stunning simplicity. Her pale ivory skin had gleamed and he had felt the irresistible urge to reach out and touch her.

He looked down at his maimed hands on the wheel and his mouth crooked in a mirthless smile. It was to avoid such obscenities that she had severed all contact with him. Had she imagined that his face, too, would have been similarly scarred? If so, her fears had been groundless. Only his hands bore the marks of the fire and he had long ago come to terms with their disfigurement. He had regained full use of them. They still functioned, still moved, still felt. And somewhat to his astonishment, he had yet to find a woman who was repelled by them. He swerved to a halt and stared out over the dunes and the silk-black motion of the sea. He had yet to find a woman that he could love. Why, in God's name, was he still tied to her by invisible bonds that he could not break? He swore softly to himself as a bank of clouds scurried across the face of the moon. He had made love to so many women that he had lost count, and yet he still hadn't met a woman who could drive her from his heart. The abrasive lines of his face hardened. He would find that woman. He would be damned to hell and all eternity before he would continue loving a woman who had betrayed him not once, but twice.

"Darling, why so many different escorts all of a sudden?" Leila asked, reclining on a chaise by Valentina's pool.

Valentina dipped a toe experimentally into the azure depths and shrugged. "Why not?" she asked, and executed a perfect dive into the sun-dappled water.

Leila watched her surface and swim with clean movements to the far side of the Olympic-size pool. The Valentina she had known no longer seemed to exist. Whenever the conversation grew too personal, she retreated behind a dismissive smile and a careless shrug of her shoulders. What she thought, what she felt, no one knew. It was as if the actress in her had taken over completely. The only time the facade slipped and her eyes warmed with genuine emotion was when she was with Alexander.

He was almost twelve now, tall and loose-limbed, and with the unmistakable look of his father.

"My God," Leila had said, horrified, when Valentina had first brought him to Hollywood, "you can't educate him here, Valentina. You have only to look at him to see that he's Vidal's son."

A dangerous spark had flashed deep in Valentina's eyes. She no longer wished to be reminded that Vidal had fathered Alexander. She wanted him to grow up like Paulos. Sensitive and gentle. The harsh methods that Vidal employed in order to obtain Oscar-rating performances from his actors had become legendary; as had his womanizing. Valentina had no desire to see either trait in her son.

"We've been separated for too long," she said to Leila obstinately. "I'm not going to be separated from him any longer."

"Then send him to school in San Diego. You can see him on weekends and holidays. If he remains here, you're going to have problems."

Valentina had tensed her jaw, knowing that what Leila said was true, but not wanting to accept it.

"Does Alexander know that Vidal is his father?" Leila asked, and flinched as Valentina rounded on her in a moment of rare rage.

"*No!* Why should he? What has Vidal ever done for him? He *knows* that he is Alexander's father! I told him in New York!" She paced the room, resisting the urge to sweep her collection of rare glass figurines crashing to the floor. "He could have divorced Kariana and married me. He could have been a father to Alexander, but no. It wasn't convenient. There was Kariana to care for." She whirled around, her dark eyes blazing in the pale oval of her face. "But he *did* divorce Kariana during the war, didn't he? Perhaps he did it for Romana? For another of his girl friends? But he didn't do it for me! And he didn't do it for Alexander."

She stormed from the room and a few seconds later Leila saw her through the window, striding across the lawn, her hands dug deep in the pockets of her skirt, her jaw clenched, her rage and pain so great they apparently could find no outlets.

Alexander had gone to school in San Diego. Valentina had taken a permanent suite at the nearby Hotel del Coronado, and if she was happy, it was a happiness reserved for the precious hours when she was far away from Hollywood and in the company of her son.

"No, Theo," Valentina said, sparks flashing in her eyes. "No power on earth will persuade me to make a movie with Rakoczi!"

Theo strove for patience. "Valentina, *I* want to make this movie. *Vidal* wants to make this movie. And the only star who can make the title part worthwhile is you."

"Get Joan Crawford. She would be sensational."

"Mayer won't loan her out," Theo said tersely, "and it's not Crawford I want. It's you."

"No. Never. Good-bye, Theo." She swept from his office in a swirl of white fox, the door reverberating on its hinges behind her.

Theo sighed. He *had* to have her for the part. The movie had all the ingredients of *The Warrior Queen* and only Vidal and Valentina together could give it class as well as splendor.

"What did she say?" Vidal asked when Theo walked into the projection room later that day.

"She said 'No. Never.' That no power on earth would persuade her to make another movie with you."

"Then we don't make it," Vidal said, returning his attention to the screen. "It would be nothing more than a costume epic with any other actress in the lead."

"There's always Romana."

Vidal looked at him pityingly. "Romana only plays Romana."

"There's Hepburn," Theo said, desperation in his voice.

"True, but she doesn't have Valentina's translucent beauty. No Valentina, no movie."

"Oh, Christ!" Theo thundered. "What is it with you two? Other people have affairs that end and they still work together! Other people marry and divorce and still work together! All I want to do is make a movie. I don't care if you don't even *speak* to each other off the set. I'm going to make *The Empress Matilda*, you're going to direct it, and, so help me, Valentina is going to star in it!"

* * *

"It's a good script," Leila said, passing a hand reflectively over her burgeoning stomach. "It almost makes me wish I were under contract again, and not about to become the great earth mother figure of all time."

Valentina remained stonily silent.

"You haven't had an Oscar nomination for several years. Your best work was done with Vidal. Why let personal feelings come between you and your acceptance speech?"

There was still no response. Leila sighed and pressed a hand into the center of her aching back.

"If you want to give Vidal satisfaction, you're sure going about it the right way. He knows the part is tailor-made for you. If you turn it down, he's going to think it's because you're still in love with him."

"Like hell I am!" Valentina flared.

"So take the part," Leila urged, sipping at a glass of milk, then grimacing. "Show him that you are as indifferent to him as he is to you."

The costumes and setting were so similar to those of *The Warrior Queen* that Valentina was filled with an almost overwhelming feeling of *déjà vu*. She shook it from her determinedly. She was the Empress Matilda, not Margaret of Anjou. The young woman who had played the part of Margaret was transformed.

The first morning she walked onto the set, the atmosphere was charged with tension. "Okay," Vidal said tersely. "Let's start. I want to go over this morning's scene with everyone who's in it."

The script girl drew her canvas chair toward Vidal's. Valentina's co-star did the same. The second assistant nervously picked up the black velvet-covered chair that bore Valentina's name in letters of gold, and placed it alongside. Valentina glared at him and marched toward the tight-knit circle, her nails digging deep into her palms.

They began to read the scene and professionalism calmed the tumult of emotions in Valentina that Vidal's nearness aroused. He made subtle changes in the dialogue. The scene was repeated.

"I want one work light on the set," Vidal said at last. "Then we'll go through the scene and see how it feels."

He rose to his feet, pushing his chair away from the circle impatiently with a leather-gloved hand.

"Move around, see where it seems natural to stand."

Her co-star was nervous of her reputation and Valentina sensed it and gave him a reassuring smile, enslaving him immediately.

Vidal strode toward them, his brows pulled together as he studied the set. "More to the left," he said to her dispassionately.

She obeyed, her pulse pounding. He was the father of her child and he was speaking to her as if they had never met before. When he dismissed them and called Harris over to discuss the camera setups, she returned to the chair and her script, so unapproachable that not even crew members who had known her for years dared to say how pleased they were to be working with her again. She closed her eyes, overcome by a feeling of unreality.

The long, lonely day finally drew to a close. Her secretary deflected the reporters who were anxious to speak to her after her first day back on the set. Her chauffeur sped her swiftly through the small crowd of fans at the studio gates. They looked after her enviously, seeing only the beautiful face, the exquisite clothes, the symbol of a life-style they could never hope to emulate. She smiled sadly to herself. They had nothing to be envious of. They would doubtless return home to family and friends and she would return home to no one. Alexander was in San Diego. Leila had a family life of her own to lead. And the man she loved was uncaring of her existence.

"Will I be needed again this evening, ma'am?" her chauffeur asked, concern in his voice as he noted the sadness in her eyes, the weary droop of her lovely shoulders.

"No, thank you," she said with a smile so sweet it caught at his heart strings. "Good night, Ben."

Her housekeeper had prepared a light meal for her. Her maid had run a deep, foam-filled bath and laid out a sequined cocktail dress and evening pumps on her bed. She paused, staring at them with a slight frown and then remembered. She was due at a film premiere with one of her innumerable and tedious escorts later on in the evening.

She kicked off her shoes and picked up the telephone.

She had been mad to have agreed to it. She never partied when she had to be on the set early the next morning.

"But, Valentina, darling . . ." the male voice said in hurt tones.

"I'm sorry," she said gently, and put the receiver back on its cradle. Ever since the traumatic night at Theo's party she had dated constantly. With almost feverish zest she had plunged herself into a round of gaiety in an effort to drive away her pain. The gaiety had been false and brittle and the pain had remained.

She walked quietly through the white-carpeted rooms, dismissing her maid and housekeeper and telling them that she had no further need of them that evening. Then she poured herself an ice-cold glass of white wine and stood at the giant window that looked out over the darkening Hollywood Hills. The sense of déjà vu that she had experienced in the studio returned in full measure. It was as if, despite all her struggles, she had come full circle. The lonely little girl who had stood staring out through the high wrought-iron gates of the convent at Capistrano was still lonely. Still without the love that she craved.

She drew the drapes, shutting out the sight of the twinkling lights of nighttime Hollywood. A Hollywood she no longer had the heart to be a part of. Her mother had abandoned her and slowly, over the years, she had come to terms with that abandonment. Vidal, too, had abandoned her and she knew with despair that it was an abandonment she would never accustom herself to as long as she lived. She walked slowly back into the bedroom. She was the most feted woman in Hollywood and she was going to go to bed alone. Tonight and for all the nights of the future, as far ahead as she could see. With a heavy heart she undressed and turned off the light. She had her son; she had her work; and those two loves would have to sustain her.

"The newspapers advertised your absence from last night's premiere more lavishly than they did other people's presence," Leila said to her over the telephone the following evening. "What was the matter? Were you sick?"

"No," she said, knowing that she was lying. She had been sick. Sick of an old passion. "I never burn the candle at both ends when I'm working."

"Then come to lunch on Sunday. The English contingent will be here, including Sutton. It should be fun."

"Thanks, Leila, but I'm going down to San Diego to see Alexander."

"Then stop by on your way home."

Valentina paused. She had no desire to socialize. She felt like a wounded animal who needed to be alone to heal its wounds.

"Thanks again, Leila, but I'd rather not. The script is going to keep me busy."

"Okay," Leila said easily, disguising her concern. "But if you change your mind, you know where to come."

It took the newspapers and fan magazines only a week before they were publicly proclaiming her a recluse. If Vidal saw the headlines, he gave no sign of it. Not one unnecessary word passed between them. It was as if he could no longer bear the sight of her. The lines of her jaw were continually tense with the effort she made to remain calm and composed in his presence. Occasionally, when he would demand that a scene be replayed yet again, she would give him a withering look, but it was lost on him. Whenever she did so, he merely shrugged and waited for her to do as he asked.

Just as she had retreated within herself when she was a child and the hurt became too much to bear, she retreated now. Her inner self became her citadel. When the day's work was finished, she went home and ate alone, reading her script and going to bed early. On the weekends she visited Alexander and took long walks on the beach, her identity disguised by a silk headscarf and dark glasses, her couture clothes exchanged for white slacks and a simple cotton shirt.

There were times when she wished that she had never agreed to work with Vidal again. It was all so different from before. A travesty of the closeness of purpose that had bound them when making *The Warrior Queen*. On *The Empress Matilda* there was no closeness. No discussion. Her views on the part went unspoken. He wanted her to do as she was told and that was all. She did so, sublimating her unhappiness in the blessed routine of filmmaking.

Her studio car came for her at six every morning. Once there, she went straight into makeup, then hairdressing and wardrobe. On the set there were her lines to concentrate on. Rehearsals; changes. The daily phrases repeated time and time again. "Hit those marks. Watch those lights. Quiet, please! Hold it down! Roll 'em! Take six! Speed! Go." It was a world that gave little time for personal misery.

After the first few weeks, the crew and cast accepted as normal the palpable tension between their director and his star. Gossip columnists revealed to their readers that Valentina was being kept a virtual prisoner by Vidal Rakoczi until filming on *The Empress Matilda* had ended. Others stated that when her last scene had been shot, Valentina would stun the world by announcing her decision to become a nun. Valentina shrugged the rumors aside. It seemed impossible for the columnists to grasp that she was alone because she was unhappy. It was too simple a reason for them. They wanted something more exotic, more bizarre.

"I hope this nun thing is a joke, my dear," Sutton said to her one evening when he had invited her to spend the weekend on his yacht and had been gently refused.

"It is," she said, managing a rare smile.

"Well, hurry up and get whatever is troubling you out of your system," Sutton said gruffly. "We miss seeing you."

"I miss you," she said truthfully. "Shooting comes to an end this next week. I'll see you then, Sutton. I promise."

She put down the telephone receiver, not wanting to think about what she would do when shooting was over. At least for the last eleven weeks she had been able to see him; to hear his voice. She closed her mind to it. It would be survived as everything else had been survived.

Vidal's voice was terse as he called, "Cut, print," and the last scene was shot, the movie finally completed.

She drew in a deep, steadying breath and walked off the set toward the privacy of her bungalow. As she did so, his shadow fell across her and he barred her way.

"Just a moment," he said, his voice snaking across her nerve ends, scorching them raw. "I want to speak to you."

"Then do so," she said tightly.

Fury flared in his eyes and was immediately suppressed. "Not here. In my office."

"I'm sorry. No—" she began, and was cut abruptly short as his leather-gloved hand shot out, imprisoning her wrist so tightly that she thought he would crush the bones.

"*Yes!*" he said, the menace in his voice naked.

She tried to wrench herself away from his grasp. "Let me go or I'll cause a scene here, in front of everyone."

"Do that and every grip and electrician will hear me ask after the welfare of *my* son!"

She sucked in her breath, her eyes widening with horror. "Even you wouldn't do that!"

"Try me," he said, and at the savagery in his features, she physically flinched.

"It's true what they say about you," she said, her voice low and harsh. "You *are* a devil!"

"Then let's talk about the devil's spawn," he said grimly as he marched her off the soundstage, out into the sunlight and up the wooden steps leading to his office.

Not until he had closed the door behind him did he release his hold on her.

"What is it you want to know?" she asked, her rage white-hot.

"I want to know where he is."

"Why? You've shown not the slightest interest in him since the one and only time you set eyes on him."

"Within days of that meeting you were planning to marry Brook-Taylor," Vidal snapped, his eyes narrowing dangerously. "You were going to provide him with a stepfather and I thought it highly unlikely that you would have told him his real father was a man you had no intention of having anything further to do with."

"I never married Denton."

"No. No doubt you had other diversions," he said cruelly. "And I went to war. I want to see my son."

"No."

"*Yes!*"

They faced each other like two warring animals, eyes blazing, every muscle in their bodies taut.

"I will *not* let you destroy Alexander's happiness!"

"And I will not let you keep me away from my son any longer!"

His determination was ferocious. Looking at him, she knew it was a battle she could not win. If he wanted to find out where Alexander was, he would do so easily enough. He was a man who always got what he wanted. Her rage ebbed on a tide of despair.

"If Alexander must know the truth, he must know it from me," she said at last.

"And will you tell him?"

"Yes," she said, knowing that when she did, the close bond between her and Alexander would never be the same again.

Her fear of what Alexander would think of her when he learned the truth showed on her face. At the sight of her inner pain, Vidal turned away abruptly.

"Then I promise that until you have done so, I shall make no attempt to see him."

"Thank you," she said quietly, and a moment later the door closed behind her and he sank down into the chair behind his desk, clenching his gloved hands against the pounding pain above his eyes.

"I'm going to New Orleans for a short vacation and would like to take Alexander with me," she said to Mr. Leavis, the headmaster of Alexander's school.

Mr. Leavis felt his neck flush as Valentina's almond-shaped eyes regarded him coaxingly. In all the time that Alexander Khairetis had been a pupil at his school, he had never been able to accustom himself to the fact that his mother was the legendary Valentina.

"Yes," he said, overcome that an action of his could bring her pleasure. "Of course that can be arranged."

"Could I see him now, please?"

Mr. Leavis summoned his secretary. "Please tell Alexander Khairetis that his mother is in my office and would like to see him," he said, and continued to gaze happily at Valentina. "New Orleans should prove interesting for Alexander," he said, wishing there was some way he could prolong her visit.

"Yes." Her eyes were on the door, eager for the moment when Alexander would enter the room.

"No doubt it will change him."

"I beg your pardon?" She turned toward him, startled.

"I said, no doubt New Orleans will change him. I believe the city has that effect on people. They're never the same when they return." He smiled beatifically.

She sat very still. For a moment he wondered if she had heard him. Then, despite the heat of his study, she shivered, pulling the high collar of the mink coat closer around her throat. Things would be said in New Orleans that would have an irreversible effect on Alexander, and she didn't want them to be said. She didn't want him to change.

There was a knock at the door and she wheeled around, chasing the shadows from her eyes as he entered the room.

"Hello, Mother," Alexander said with a broad grin.

Valentina sprang to her feet and they met in the middle of the book-lined room, hugging tightly. It was not behavior that Mr. Leavis would normally have approved, but Valentina was Valentina, and young Khairetis was half-Greek by birth, and the Greeks, as everyone knew, were an emotional race.

Chapter Twenty-eight

The days they spent in New Orleans were to be etched in Valentina's memory with searing brightness. Her son had become a companion. An exuberant, intelligent, fun-loving friend who teased her, showered her with affection, and instigated adventurous forays into the bayous and swamplands that surrounded the city.

"But, Alexander, there are *alligators* out there," she had protested when he insisted that they take a trip by pirogue into the dim green world of overhanging mosses and whiskered trees.

"And American bald eagles and brown pelicans and Catahoula hog dogs," Alexander had said with relish.

The eagles and hog dogs had failed to appear, but they had glimpsed a pelican and Valentina had shuddered as their guide lured an alligator to the surface of the sluggish bayou with a lump of meat pierced through the end of a pole.

"Now it's *my* turn to choose where we will sightsee," Valentina said determinedly the next day. "We'll go on another boat trip, but an *elegant* boat trip. We'll take a trip on one of the old paddle steamers."

"I think I would have enjoyed being a riverboat gambler," Alexander said, leaning against the rails of the *Natchez* with all the unconscious panache of his father. "I would have lived in the Vieux Carré, drunk mint juleps, and sported a gold sateen waistcoat."

"I should never have taken you to see *Gone With the Wind*," Valentina said in amusement. "You've been modeling yourself on Clark Gable ever since."

"No, not Gable," Alexander said reflectively as he gazed down into the churning water. "If I were to model myself on anyone, it would be Vidal Rakoczi."

Valentina froze. She had still not told him about Vidal. A score of times she had framed the words, but her courage had always failed her.

"Why?" she asked faintly.

"I like him. I like the movies he directs. I like the way he works outside the system and not in it. He does what *he* wants to do. He sees things in a way other people don't and it shows in his movies. That's the sort of director I want to be."

Now the moment had arrived. Her fingers tightened over the arms of her cane chair. "I never knew that you wanted to be a movie director," she said, wondering how he would react when he knew the truth.

He turned to face her, leaning back on the rail with his elbows, his grin wide. "It's all I've ever wanted to be. Ever since Ruby used to bring me to the theater when you were rehearsing *Hedda Gabler*."

"Alexander, there's something that I have to tell you." Her heart was racing. "I should have told you before, but. . ." Her words were drowned as the band picked up their instruments and the sound of jazz filled the air.

"Aren't they just *great*?" Alexander said ecstatically, his tousled hair shining blue-black in the sun as he moved away from the rails. "I'm going down to hear them better. Just *listen* to that saxophone."

Valentina closed her eyes. The moment was past and gone. It would come again and when it did, she would be better prepared. She would not let her courage fail her again.

"This is the deep South," Alexander said as they picnicked in the grounds of an antebellum mansion. "We should be eating jambalaya or bananas Foster or crabmeat salad, not tucking into pâté and Brie."

"Rubbish," Valentina said good-naturedly, reaching into the picnic basket for French bread and caviar.

Alexander began to laugh. "You're hopeless, Maman. *No one* picnics on Beluga caviar." The old childhood name. He still used it and she still liked to hear it.

"*I* do," Valentina said firmly. "And champagne!" Triumphantly she withdrew a bucket of crushed ice and a bottle of Lanson.

"This is *some* picnic," Alexander said, his eyes sparkling as he lounged on the grass by her side.

"The champagne, young man," Valentina said in mock chastisement, "is not for you." She withdrew another bottle from the hamper and Alexander groaned. "*This* is yours."

"I *loathe* soda," he protested as she plunged it into the ice bucket with the champagne. "I'm eleven now. Surely I'm old enough for champagne?"

"When *I* was your age I . . ." she began, laughing, and then halted in midsentence. At Alexander's age she had been living in the convent. She had not known that there were such things as champagne and caviar. Or that it was possible to love and to be loved.

"What's the matter, Maman?" Alexander asked, the sparkle dying in his eyes as he reached a hand out to her in concern. Their fingers interlocked. "Nothing," she said, chasing the years away. "Just a silly memory."

"If it makes you sad, don't think about it. Just think about how *fantastic* New Orleans is. How happy we are and how much I love you."

"I do," she said, the smile back in her eyes. "And for that gallant speech you deserve something a little more daring than soda. Open the champagne, Alexander. Let's enjoy ourselves!"

"Do I *have* to go back to school next week?" Alexander asked a few days later as they strolled through the market in the French quarter.

"I'm afraid so. I told Mr. Leavis we would only be away for two weeks."

Alexander regarded the riot of fresh fruit and vegetables gloomily.

"I much prefer it here with you," he said, pausing to buy some Louisiana oranges.

"I prefer having you here with me," Valentina said, averting her gaze from the sight of live crabs writhing on a tray in a fish stall. "But you would get terribly bored on your own all day and if I keep you away from school any longer, Mr. Leavis might not take you back."

"That'll be no loss," Alexander said. "I'm never going to learn how to direct at school. I'd learn far more returning with you to Hollywood. I might even be able to watch Rakoczi direct. I never got the chance while you were filming *The Empress Matilda*."

A shadow darkened Valentina's eyes. Her ivory skin suddenly seemed a shade paler. "I want to talk to you about Vidal Rakoczi, Alexander. I was seventeen when we first met. I had just arrived in Hollywood."

"Where from, Maman?" he asked, throwing an orange in the air and catching it.

"From a convent on the outskirts of a small California town."

"A *convent*?" Alexander's eyes widened. "You weren't thinking of becoming a nun or something, were you?"

A smile hovered at the corners of her mouth. "No, Alexander. I was there because that was where my mother left me."

Alexander digested this information in silence. His mother had never spoken to him of her childhood and he had never asked. He knew that her parents were not alive, but it had never occurred to him to wonder *when* they had died. People just died, that was all. Like his father. After a little while he said, "Do you mean that she didn't die? That she simply left you?"

"Yes," Valentina replied, her dark hair swinging against her neck as she walked. "She simply drove up to the convent, deposited me in the arms of a nun, and disappeared from my life. I didn't leave there until I was seventeen."

They had somehow veered away from the subject of Vidal. She tried to steer it back. "The Reverend Mother had arranged that I should go as a maid to a lady living in San Diego. Instead, I hitched a lift north. If the truck that stopped for me had been going to San Francisco, my whole life would have been different. As it was, it was going to Hollywood. To Worldwide Pictures."

"That's fate, Maman," Alexander said, his olive-toned face intense.

"Yes, Alexander," she said, briefly reaching out and touching his hair. "I think it was."

Faint strains of music came from the direction of Jackson Square, immediately catching his attention.

"Let's go and listen," he pleaded. "School is going to be so *quiet* after New Orleans."

"You go," she said. "We'll have dinner in the Vieux Carré tonight, and then talk some more."

"Okay." He flashed her a dazzling grin and then sauntered through the crowds toward the source of the music. She stood in the sunlight, watching him. A tall, loose-limbed boy, his hair a black tangle of curls, his walk confident. He was her son. Her beloved son, and she hoped fervently that the truth about his parentage would not diminish her in his eyes. He disappeared in the crowd and she turned, walking back with unaccustomed tiredness to their hotel.

Later, relaxing in the fragrant heat of a deep bath, she thought how strange it was that, of all men, it should be his unknown but natural father that Alexander had singled out to admire and to emulate. Whether it would make the fact that Vidal was his father easier or harder for him to accept, she had no way of knowing. When the water began to cool, she stepped out of the bath and toweled herself dry, slipping into a silk robe. She had been in the bath for over an hour, and there was still no sign of Alexander. She frowned and rang his room. There was no reply. The magic of the music had obviously made him oblivious of the time. She opened the doors of her closet and ran her fingers speculatively over her evening gowns. At last she selected a gown of deep raspberry chiffon with long, full sleeves and a tiny waist that exploded into a skirt so full and fragile that, when worn, it billowed softly around her. Alexander called it her antebellum dress and had said that the color reminded him of his favorite ice cream.

She laid it on the bed, realizing with a pang that in another few days this precious time of privacy would be over. She would once again be Valentina: star. Not just a fantastically beautiful woman sightseeing with her son. There would be maids, hairdressers, chauffeurs. An endless succession of newspaper reporters and photographers. A complete lack of personal privacy.

There was a knock at the door. She opened it and smiled at the hotel manager in his sober pinstripe suit.

"Madam . . . I am awfully sorry . . . I do not know how to tell you . . ."

Her smile faded. His face was ravaged. For the first time she saw the policeman at his side; the huddle of maids at the far end of the corridor.

"What is it? What has happened?"

"Madam, please sit down." They were ushering her back into the room. Someone was pressing a drink into her hand. She thrust it away, choked by fear. *"What is it? What has happened?"*

"It was a new building, madam. The accident could not have been avoided. The beam of wood fell and—"

"My son! Where is he? Where IS he?"

"In the hospital, madam. He is unconscious and—"

Valentina pushed him aside. He was alive. He was hurt, but he was not dead. He was alive and these fools were keeping her from him.

"Out of my room while I dress! Is there a car?"

"Yes, mada—"

She didn't wait for them all to exit. She tore off her robe and scrambled into her discarded street clothes. "Please, God, let him be safe," she prayed aloud as she ran down the corridor, still doing up the buttons on her blouse. "Please, God, let him be all right. Please. *Please!"*

A small group of photographers were already at the door of the hospital as she hurtled from the car and up the stone steps.

"It was a glancing blow, madam. Another fraction and he would have been killed outright," the doctor who hurried to greet her said.

"Let me see him! Just let me see him!"

There was another doctor at her elbow and yet another hurrying ahead to open door after door.

"Please, God. Please. *Please!"* The words reverberated through her head. The last door was open and she halted. It was a very small room, and the tall, handsome son she had said good-bye to only hours ago looked very small and very young. His head was heavily bandaged. His eyes were closed.

His face was still. For one horrendous moment she thought that he was dead and then she heard the doctor saying, "He should recover consciousness at any time. If you would like to sit with him?"

"Yes." Slowly she crossed to the chair at the side of Alexander's bed and sat down. Her hand reached out and held his. He was alive. Everything was going to be all right. She raised her head, her eyes huge in the pale ivory of her face.

"How did it happen?"

The doctor sat a few feet away with her, tiny lines of tension around his mouth.

"He was walking along the street and a beam of wood fell as it was being hoisted to the first floor of a new building. It did not fall from a great height and it did not fall on your son with its full impact. If it had . . ." He spread his hands expressively. "Nevertheless, it gave him a glancing blow and the cut on the scalp is severe."

"And he'll be all right?" Her eyes were pleading.

"Don't worry. It is a common injury. He will regain consciousness soon."

She remained for the rest of the afternoon at Alexander's bedside and only the warmth of his hand in hers assured her that he was alive. The long eyelashes on the suddenly child-like cheeks never flickered.

"I am sorry, but it is late," the doctor said at last. "By the time you return tomorrow . . ."

"I'm not leaving," The steel beneath the femininity that so many others had encountered was focused on the doctor.

"But, dear lady, we have tests to conduct because he should have regained consciousness by now."

"And I will stay. There must be a room for me somewhere, even if it is only a linen closet. If there is not, I shall sleep on the chair in the corner. I am not leaving until my son regains consciousness." Her eyes flashed dangerously and the doctor accepted defeat. She was as superb in real life as she was on the screen. Stunning. Spectacular. A tigress fighting for her cub.

"There is a small storage room a few yards farther down the corridor. It has no window, but I will see that a bed is made up for you in there."

"Thank you."

The doctor returned his attention to Alexander, the lines of tension around his mouth deepening. The longer the boy remained comatose, the less chance there was that recovery would be uncomplicated. He lifted first one of Alexander's eyelids and then the other, flashing a thin pencil of light onto each pupil. Neither pupil dilated.

"I want reflex tests taken every half hour during the night," he said in a low voice to the head nurse, "and if there is any change, for good or for bad, I want you to call me."

Not until the hospital was quiet and only the night-lights burned, could the nurse at Alexander's side persuade Valentina to rest. She did so reluctantly. She wanted to be there when he regained consciousness. She wanted to see his look of recognition; the familiar smile. She lay on the narrow bed in the darkened storeroom, listening as the head nurse entered Alexander's room every half hour to carry out the tests the doctor had asked for. Waiting to be roused and told that the crisis had passed. That Alexander was conscious and asking for her. When she awoke in the morning, no one had summoned her.

She had slept in her slip. She dressed hastily and hurried into Alexander's room. A nurse was at his side. Her son was as still, as deathly pale, as before.

"Oh, God," she said shakily, and sat down once more at his side. It was a long, lonely vigil. The doctor entered the room with a colleague and both of them examined Alexander and then stood quietly conferring together, their expressions grave.

"What is it? What is happening?" she asked, the beautifully etched face pale, the dark eyes shadowed with fear and weariness.

"We think that perhaps the blow has caused a hematoma," the doctor said gently. "We are going to prepare Alexander for surgery and operate to release the pressure."

She sat outside in the corridor on a tiny chair. She had no one in New Orleans to offer her the comfort of friendship. Leila was far away in Los Angeles and Sutton was in London. There was no one. She was as alone and lonely as she had been as a child.

The doors opened and two hospital porters wheeled the stretcher carrying Alexander out of the room and into the corridor. She rose instinctively to reach out and touch him, but a nurse gently restrained her. The stretcher and its attendants disappeared through swinging doors on their way to the operating room. She sat down slowly and began the long wait.

It was three hours before the stretcher and its small cargo returned. She was not allowed into the room with him. As the doctor steered her away, she caught a glimpse of something black and shiny protruding from Alexander's mouth.

"Why does he have that tube in his mouth?" she asked fearfully.

"The tube is to keep the trachea open. It will not be necessary for long."

"And the operation was a success?"

"The operation went exactly as planned. The pressure on the brain has now been relieved and when the effects of the anesthetic wears off, we can expect to see an improvement in his condition. There is nothing we can do now but wait."

Never before in her life had Valentina appreciated the agony that could accompany the simple act of waiting. She remained on the uncomfortable chair in the corridor, her eyes on the clock opposite her. At last the head nurse emerged from Alexander's room and said quietly, "You may go in and see him now, but only for a moment. There probably will be no change in his condition until morning. It would be best if you tried to get some rest."

She stood by the edge of the bed. The ugly monstrosity had been taken from his mouth. He was lying on his side and a nurse was sitting in the chair that she herself had occupied earlier. She could never remember seeing him so still and so silent. Even in sleep, Alexander had always been vital, his cheeks bronzed by the sun, his dark curls tousled. There was no sign of his hair now. She presumed that they had shaved it off. His head was swathed in white bandages and a frightening-looking tube snaked from beneath the sheets and into a bottle on the floor. She touched his hand lightly and then turned and left him to the nurses. There was nothing she could do for him; she could only continue to wait.

The next day she was allowed to sit beside him and to hold his hand. She no longer asked questions as a succession of doctors came in to examine him. At midday on the fourth day after the accident, the nurse checking Alexander's pulse stiffened and then whirled from the room. Within seconds there were doctors at the bedside and Valentina was hurried away.

"What's the matter? What's happened?" she cried imploringly, but the doors closed on her and she was left to sink with a strangled sob onto the all-too-familiar chair in the linoleum-lined corridor.

It was the surgeon who had operated on Alexander who was the first to speak to her.

"I'm awfully sorry, Mrs. Khairetis, but your son's condition has deteriorated. I think it would be best if his father were informed."

Valentina stared at him blankly. The surgeon was accustomed to the effects of shock. "Your husband," he said gently. "I think he should be contacted."

She shook her head dazedly. "My husband is dead."

The surgeon remembered. Her husband had been the pianist Paulos Khairetis who had drowned. She had already been struck by tragedy and was about to be struck again.

"Then I think it would be best if you could be joined by a member of your family," he said compassionately.

Valentina's eyes were huge and dark as she looked up at him. "Are you telling me that my son is going to die?"

The surgeon shook his head. "No. There is always hope. But if he has other close kin, they should be informed that his condition is grave."

"No," Valentina said, seeming visibly to shrink inside the crumpled linen of the pale blue suit that she had arrived in. "There is no one."

"I see." The surgeon held out his hand and helped her to her feet. "You may go in now and sit with him."

He opened the door for her and she paused for a moment on the threshold, gazing across to the small, still figure in the bed.

"Mr. Vidal Rakoczi," she said unsteadily. "Would you please contact Mr. Vidal Rakoczi," and then she crossed to the bed, took Alexander's hand in hers and began to weep.

All through the night she refused to leave his side, willing him to open his eyes, to smile, to speak to her. As the first faint rays of dawn seeped through the blinds she began to talk to him as if he were conscious, reminding him of the happy days on Crete; of how they had walked in the mountainous foothills picking wild flowers. Of the music Paulos had played; of the sun and the sand.

She pressed her hand against her cheek, recalling London and how they had walked by the banks of the Thames and he had worn an English muffler to protect him from the cold.

No one deterred her. The act of talking to her child seemed to comfort her. A faint smile tinged her lips as she reminded him of their trip across the Atlantic on the *Queen Mary*. Of how he had raced the decks; of their time at the Plaza Hotel and of how Ruby had taken him daily to Central Park and then to the theater to watch the rehearsals of *Hedda Gabler*. She spoke of everything they had done together. Of all the people they had loved: Paulos and Leila and Sutton. Of how, but for the simple act of turning north on the highway, and not south, she would have become a maid in San Diego. Of New Orleans. Of their boat trip by pirogue into the sinister swamplands; of the elegant paddle steamer and of how he had declared he would have liked to be a riverboat gambler. Of their picnic; of the champagne, of the music that permeated the city, the Creole food that he had loved.

"You can stay, darling," she whispered, a sob in her throat. "I won't send you back to school. Just open your eyes and smile at me, please. *Please.*"

There had been no response. The door opened quietly and Vidal's shadow fell across the bed. She raised her eyes to his.

"Help me not to let him die," she said desperately. "Help me, Vidal!"

For a long moment he stood gazing down at the still, pale features of his son. The son he had never known. With bitter anguish he thought of the time that had been wasted. Time that could never be recaptured. The harsh planes of his face hardened. There would be no more wasted time. No more separation. He put his hand on her shoulder and as he did so the long, lonely years went whistling down the wind as though they had never been.

"He will not die," he said gently, his smoke-dark voice full of utter certainty. "Trust me, my love."

She covered her hand with his, her eyes shining with tears. He was never wrong. It was impossible that he should be wrong now.

"Vidal is here," she said to the small, comatose figure. "He wants to talk to you about movies, darling. About riverboats and gamblers." The long, lustrous eyelashes never stirred. All through the long night they sat in silent vigil by the side of his bed, disturbed only by the nurse as she checked Alexander's respiration and reflexes, and by the doctor as he entered the room every hour to repeat the examination.

The night sky dulled, presaging dawn.

"I never told him about you, Vidal," she said, breaking the silence, her voice thick with suppressed tears. "I kept going to and going to. We went on a paddle steamer and he said that he would have liked to have been a riverboat gambler. I teased him and said it was because he wanted to be like Clark Gable in *Gone With the Wind*, but he said that it wasn't Gable he wanted to be like. It was you." Her voice trembled and a tear ran down her cheek. "He wanted to be a director like you."

"He will be a director, Valentina. He will be everything that he dreams of being."

His voice held no room for doubt. His eyes held hers, his strength filling her. She felt suddenly calm. She was not going to lose Alexander. Vidal would not allow her to.

The doctor walked quietly to the bed and carried out his examination of Alexander's reflexes. When he had finished, he turned to her and said gently, "There is no sign of any change, Mrs. Khairetis. You must go back to your hotel and rest."

She shook her head and the doctor sighed. Coma cases could live for weeks, for months. There would have to come a moment when she finally accepted defeat. He raised his eyebrows slightly in Vidal's direction.

"Could I have a word with you, Mr. Rakoczi?"

Reluctantly, Vidal left his son's bedside and walked with the doctor toward the door.

Valentina took hold of Alexander's limp hand and pressed it against her cheek.

"*Please*, Alexander. Please come back to me, darling," she whispered pleadingly.

The sky was streaked with pearl. In the far distance the bell of a riverboat rang mournfully. Almost imperceptibly the hand held in hers stirred.

Her heart began to race and the blood slammed in her ears.

"Alexander!" she said urgently, leaning toward him. "Alexander, can you hear me?"

The moment seemed to stretch out into infinity and then his hand moved again.

"Maman, is that you? I'm thirsty, Maman."

"*Alexander!*" Her voice broke on a sob. The dark, girlish eyelashes trembled and opened and he was looking at her as if heavily drugged, his expression dazed and uncomprehending.

"Alexander! Oh, thank God!" Tears coursed down her cheeks. She was laughing and crying, kissing his hand. She heard the doctor call for a nurse, was aware of Vidal's swift footsteps to her side and then the doctor was saying, "Excuse me, Mrs. Khairetis," as he leaned over Alexander, flashing a thin pencil of light into the pupils of his eyes. When he raised his head, he was smiling. There would have to be extensive tests, but the worst was over.

"Perhaps now," he said to a radiant-faced Valentina, "you will return to your hotel and rest?"

"Who is that, Maman?" Alexander asked as Vidal's hands tightened on her shoulders.

She knelt down by the side of his bed, kissing his cheek. "It's Vidal Rakoczi, Alexander. He wants you to hurry up and get better. He wants to talk about movies with you."

"Gosh," Alexander said feebly, but in awe, and then to Vidal, "It's very nice to meet you, Mr. Rakoczi."

Vidal's eyes were unnaturally bright. "It's very nice to meet you, too, Alexander," he said, and then the doctor was ushering them away so that he could examine Alexander thoroughly and Alexander was saying plaintively, "I'm not just thirsty. I'm hungry, too."

Vidal smiled down at her. "He's going to be all right, my love. Let me take you back to your hotel. You need to rest."

"Yes." She leaned against him, her heart at peace. As they stepped out into the pale sunlight of early morning, a trumpet could be heard, the sweet sound of jazz mixing inextricably with the sound of birdsong. She paused at the foot of the hospital steps, listening to it with a smile on her lips, and then with Vidal's arm around her waist, she stepped light-footedly toward the waiting limousine.

Chapter Twenty-nine

When she awoke, she was wearing only a lace-trimmed slip and the room was dark, the drapes drawn against the searing light of the afternoon sun. She pushed herself up against the pillows, crying out in fear. Alexander was ill; he was in a coma at the hospital and he needed her.

"It's all right, Valentina." Vidal crossed the room quickly to her side.

"Alexander! He's unconscious! I must go to him!"

She swung her legs from the bed and Vidal caught her hands restrainingly.

"Alexander is conscious and eating and drinking and there is nothing to fear, little one."

Little one. How many years had it been since she had heard his deep, rich voice utter that endearment? They had parted in hostile silence and then Alexander had been hurt and she had sent for him. He had left Hollywood and the studio and the movie he had been making, and Alexander had opened his eyes and smiled, and the doctor had said that there was no further cause for fear. Memory brought with it a relief so intense that she half fell against him.

"Has the hospital telephoned while I've been asleep?" she asked urgently as his arms slid around her, steadying her.

"Yes. Alexander's condition is stable. Everything indicates that there will be no detrimental aftereffects, though I imagine he will have quite a headache for a while. They want to keep him under observation for at least another week." He tilted her face up to his. "You've been asleep for nearly ten hours."

She turned her head to the bed. She had been asleep there alone. "And you?" she asked, her heart beginning to pound against her chest.

He smiled down at her. "I've been waiting," he said, and

352

he lowered his head, his mouth covering hers. For a second she was absolutely still and then she warmed against him, her lips opening softly like the petals of a flower. His kiss was long and slow, banishing the past and all its pain.

When at last he raised his head from hers, she said simply, "I love you. I have always loved you."

"And I you."

He kissed her again. This time with a passion that made her tremble. No one else had been able to arouse her deepest emotions. Only Vidal. His lips brushed her temple, her eyelids, her hair.

She looked up at him, her eyes eloquent. "Why did you hate me when you returned from Greece? Why were you so cold? So cruel?"

He held her very close. "Because I was jealous," he said, and at the intensity in his voice she shivered. "I was jealous of Brook-Taylor. Of all the other men you had loved."

"There were no others," she said, her face pale. "And I never loved Denton."

Their eyes held. The moment a pulsebeat in the stretch of time. An eternity in the course of their lives.

"After the fire you didn't come to me," he said quietly. "You didn't write. You didn't telephone."

His eyes were black pits full of remembered pain. She tried to speak, but at first the words would not come. It was like being on the edge of a precipice. She was terrified of what she might hear. Terrified and full of desperate hope.

"Your cable asked me not to," she said unsteadily.

As the expression in his eyes changed to one of slow bewilderment, she felt the blood pound along her veins and her doubts became a certainty. "Your cable said that Kariana had been badly hurt in the fire. That our plans could not go forward. That I wasn't to write or to call you. That everything between us was over."

His bewilderment had changed to an expression of sheer incredulity. "Like hell it did! I dictated that cable to Chai within an hour of reaching the hospital. It read, 'Safe. Don't worry. Be with you soon. Plans unchanged.' "

She began to cry, joy and pain so inextricably combined that she didn't know where one began and the other left off. "Oh, God," she whispered softly. "Let me show you, Vidal. Let me show you."

She stepped away from him, drawing back the drapes, rifling feverishly through the contents of her handbag. At last, as Vidal towered at her side, every nerve and muscle in his body taut and tense, she withdrew a monogrammed leather wallet.

"It's in the inside pocket," she said faintly. "I tried to destroy it, but I couldn't."

The ink on the page was as black as if it had been sent only yesterday. The silence spun out between them till she could scarcely bear it. Slowly he refolded the piece of paper that had changed the direction of their lives.

"I never sent it," he said quietly.

"I know," she said unsteadily, slipping her arms around his neck. "I've known ever since you kissed me."

It had been Denton. Denton with his ice-cold single-mindedness. She shivered in revulsion, thrusting the memory away from her. "Let's go to the hospital," she said huskily. "Alexander is waiting to see us."

Vidal drove the wine-colored Cadillac limousine himself, his hands gloved in soft black kid. She remembered the first time she had watched him drive, the power and fascination he had exerted over her and from which she had never been able to free herself. As they drove past the sycamores and oaks of Audubon Park he said, "How will Alexander take the news that we are to be married?"

She gasped, her eyes widening. A smile tugged at the corners of his mouth. "I've waited a long time, Valentina. I'm not going to wait any longer."

"You can't propose to me driving at fifty miles an hour," she protested, her heart slamming against her breastbone as though it would burst.

"Then I'll do so stationary," he said equably, skidding to a halt, plunging the traffic around him into horn-blaring chaos.

He cupped her chin in his hand, gazing down into her eyes, his dark face brilliant with an expression of such fierce love that it was transfigured.

"I love you, Valentina. I want you to be my wife. Will you marry me?"

The shadows of the sycamore dappled the leather interior of the limousine. "Oh, yes!" she breathed, touching his face lovingly with the tips of her fingers. "Oh, yes, Vidal. I

want to marry you more than anything else in the world."
The love she felt for him flooded through her with such an
intensity that she could hardly bear it. Desire, so long suppressed and denied, scorched her blood.

"*Szeretlek*," he said hoarsely, taking her into his arms
with the gentleness of absolute love. "I love you, Valentina,"
and he lowered his head to hers, kissing her with all the
hungry passion of the long, dividing years.

When at last he raised his head, unshed tears of joy
trembled on her eyelashes. He brushed them away tenderly.
"There is one more thing."

She looked up at him questioningly, and very slowly he
began to take the gloves from his fingers. She had not known.
He could tell by the first, fleeting expression of horror that
darkened her eyes. She had held his hand in the trauma of
the hospital and in the darkness of the hotel room and had
not guessed that the flesh beneath her touch was maimed and
dead. Slowly he let the gloves drop to the floor.

"Your hands," she said, her voice breaking. "Oh, Vidal!
Your poor, poor hands!"

"I'm surprised that you didn't know. That you hadn't
been told."

"No." She shook her head, the tears spilling down her
cheeks. It was the fire, of course. He had saved Kariana from
the flames and this had been the cost.

"Do you mind?" His tone was casual, but she caught the
inflection of fear behind it.

"No," she said, taking hold of his hands with their strange
white skin, and pressing them against her cheek. "Of course I
don't mind, Vidal. How could you think it? How could you
ask?"

"I don't," he said. "Not anymore."

The doctor refused to let them stay with Alexander for
long, saying that a speedy recovery depended on his being
kept calm and rested.

"But Mr. Rakoczi will have to return to Hollywood soon,"
Alexander had protested, terrified that his idol should disap-
pear before he had the chance to talk to him about moviemaking.

"I don't have to return anywhere," Vidal said easily,
wondering if Theo's blood pressure would survive the news.
"I thought we might all vacation together. There's splendid
fishing in the south."

Alexander's eyes glowed. "I used to fish in Crete with my father, when I was little."

"And I used to fish in Hungary with mine," Vidal said. His father: Alexander's grandfather.

"Did you fish in rivers or lakes?" Alexander asked with immense interest.

"I used to live in a castle, and in front of the castle was a large lake filled with carp. The very first thing that I remember is fishing for carp in the castle lake."

"Who else lived in the castle?" Alexander asked, fascinated.

"My grandmother, whom everyone called 'the Old Excellency' with her *dame de compagnie* and her maid; my father and mother; my mother's maid; Ferencz, who had been my father's footman since he was in his teens; and my two sisters and our governess and a nursemaid or two."

"That's an awful lot of people," said Alexander, who, apart from school, could barely remember living with anyone except his mother.

"There were more people at the castle when it was summer and the time for the harvest. The men who came for the harvesting brought their wives and children with them. The women worked in the fields following the reapers and we children played in the woods and fields."

"I've never been in a real castle," Alexander said reflectively. "Don't you miss yours awfully?"

"Not now. My sister and her husband live there. I enjoyed the fields and the harvesting, but I enjoy other things more."

"Like making movies?"

Vidal grinned. "Yes, Alexander. Like making movies."

Valentina sat back, regarding them with a curious expression in her eyes. No one seeing them could doubt that they were father and son. They had the same winged brows, the same night-black eyes: Alexander's jaw was as firm as Vidal's; his mouth as finely chiseled.

Her eyes lingered on the dark hair curling low on the nape of Vidal's neck. It seemed to her that she had known him all her life. There had been only the convent. And Vidal. Yet never before had she heard him speak about his childhood. She listened as raptly as Alexander as he described the acacias that drowned his family home in heavy, fragrant blossom. Of the ice-cold lakes that he and his sisters had swum in. Of village festivals celebrating saints' days; of his grand-mother, the Old Excellency, and of how she had always worn heavy ornate dresses of black silk.

"Is that your family crest on your ring?" Alexander asked.

"Yes." Vidal stretched out his hand.

For the barest fraction of a second Valentina held her breath and then Alexander took Vidal's hand, uncaring of the scarred flesh, and said, "The engraving is so fine that I can't read it. What does it say?"

"*Tempora, non mutamur.* It means, times may be changed, not we."

"I like that," Alexander said, leaning back against his pillows, suddenly tired. "If I had a family motto, I'd like it to be a sensible one."

The nurse coughed and raised her eyebrow at them. Vidal rose to his feet. "We have to go so that you can rest, Alexander. Would you like me to bring some strawberries in for you tomorrow?"

"Please," Alexander said, his eyes brightening. "And can you tell me what movie you are going to direct next?"

"I don't think it's going to be a movie," Vidal said lightly. "I think it's going to be a play."

Valentina kissed Alexander good-bye and when they were outside the room she said, "I didn't know you were going to direct a play, Vidal. Who is it by? Is it cast yet?"

He grinned, his arm around her shoulders as they walked down the corridor. "The play is Turgenev's *A Month in the Country*, only the part of Natalya has been cast."

Valentina felt a pang of jealousy. She wondered who Vidal's choice had been. Vivien Leigh would be superb as the dazzling, romantic Natalya, and so would Olivia de Havilland.

"Who has the part?" she asked, unable to suppress a longing ache for the excitement of performing before a live audience. For the nerve-racking wait for reviews. The heady intoxication of applause.

He turned her around in his arms. "You have," he said, silencing her gasp of disbelief with a long, deep kiss.

As they drove back to her hotel she asked hesitantly, "How is Kariana, Vidal? Is she still sick?"

His hands tightened momentarily on the wheel. "Yes," he replied briefly, swinging out onto River Road.

Valentina was oblivious of the Mississippi rolling in splendor down to the Gulf. She had no desire to talk about Kariana, but she had to. Kariana's ghost had to be laid to rest before they could marry.

"Is she in New York?" she persisted.

"No, she's in La Jolla."

Valentina's eyes widened in surprise.

He took one hand from the wheel, running it through his hair. "I'm sorry for being so brusque, my love. I find it nearly impossible to talk about Kariana."

His eyes had darkened with remembered suffering and she was instantly remorseful.

"Then don't," she said, laying a hand lovingly on his arm. "I'm sorry, Vidal. I shouldn't have asked."

"No." His voice was firm. "You had to ask and you have to know." He allowed a car to overtake them and said, his voice oddly flat, "The fire wasn't an accident, Valentina. I didn't discover the truth till the day Kariana was discharged from the hospital." His eyes never flickered from the road ahead of him. "It was Kariana who set fire to Villada. She told me so herself. I had asked her for a divorce and she thought it was because I wanted to marry Hazel Renko. God knows why. There was never anything between Hazel and me except mutual liking and respect."

Valentina knew that the blood had drained from her face. She wanted him to stop. To tell him that she didn't want to hear any more.

"It was then that I knew I couldn't accept the responsibility for her any longer. The only other person who knows the truth about the fire is Dr. Grossman. I telephoned him immediately and he made arrangements for her to enter his New York clinic." His voice was tinged with weariness. "Grossman still had hopes that her condition would stabilize, but it hasn't. When he opened his new clinic in La Jolla six months ago, he brought Kariana with him. If she were to make any signs of progress, I think that he would marry her. As it is . . ." He shrugged helplessly. "Her illness follows the pattern it has always done. Outwardly she is sane for weeks, sometimes months on end. Then, for no discernible reason, she plunges into mania."

His eyes were filled with pain. "It is a nightmare she is

never going to be free of, but at least with Grossman caring for her, it is a nightmare that will harm no one but herself."

"Do you still see her?" she asked gently.

"When I knew that she had caused Hazel's death and that she felt no remorse for what she had done, I never wanted to see her again. Later, after the divorce and the years in Europe, the revulsion died. She wasn't to be blamed; she was to be pitied. I began to visit her regularly while she was in the New York clinic, but Grossman asked me to stop. He said that my visits disturbed her and that she was happier not seeing me."

"Poor Kariana," Valentina said quietly.

He slewed to a halt under the hotel's porte cochere. "Grossman cares for her very deeply. Perhaps, with his help, her condition will eventually improve. She's happier in La Jolla than she was in Hollywood. She has no awareness of being a patient. She knows that Grossman is in love with her and she enjoys the attention he gives her. She is as content as she can be."

They walked silently into the hotel, and in the shadowed lobby he turned to her, taking her hands in his.

"No more talk of Kariana," he said, and at the expression on his face the blood surged through her veins. "We're together again, and alone. I've waited too many years to make love to you to wait another minute." His eyes gleamed devilishly, and ignoring the startled gasps of the desk clerks, he swung her up into his arms and strode with her toward the stairs.

The sensuous joy of their reunion was a memory she knew would live with her always. The warmth of his touch on her inner thigh; the smell of his skin and the feel of his body pinioning hers. The glorious giving without restraint. The expression in his eyes as he looked down at her. The fusing together of their bodies and their souls. The words whispered in the darkness. The knowledge that she was safe in the world of his love. That the satiety and rapture was not transient but would be hers through all the long years ahead of them.

As the sun-gold afternoon melted into dusk she lay beside him, lightly caressing the strong muscles of his arms and chest.

"Let's marry tomorrow," he said, pulling her head down

to his, kissing her long and lingeringly. When at last he released her, her eyes were clouded.

"We can't marry tomorrow," she said, sitting upright and hugging her knees. "We can't marry until Alexander is well enough to be told the truth."

A slight frown furrowed Vidal's brow. "That could be a long time, *liba*."

"Then we will have to wait," she said quietly. "We have waited a long time already, Vidal. Now we must wait a little longer."

Alexander, discharged from the hospital, and ecstatic at the news that he would not be returning immediately to school, watched Vidal direct his mother in Turgenev's *A Month in the Country*.

Valentina looked at him as he stood at Vidal's side during rehearsals. The last test results had arrived and he was fit and well. There was no cause for any further delay.

"It's going to be good," Sutton Hyde, who was playing the part of her husband, said to her. He was sitting by her side, a paper cup of coffee in his hand. "I've always liked opening a play in San Francisco. It bodes well. San Francisco, Chicago, Boston, and then—New York, here we come!"

He beamed at her beatifically and she squeezed his hand. The weeks they had been together in San Francisco had been the happiest of her life. Alexander had spent each day at rehearsal with her. His relationship with Vidal had blossomed and deepened. And now the time had come to tell him the truth and she felt a frisson of fear.

"Would you mind if Vidal didn't dine with us tonight, Alexander," she said as Vidal summoned Sutton forward. "I want to talk to you."

"Sure," he said easily, engrossed in a sheaf of photographs that had been taken during rehearsals. He paused at one of Vidal and himself, his lips pursing, his eyes suddenly troubled.

His hotel room was next to hers and Valentina had arranged that dinner would be sent up to them and that they would eat it on the small patio that led from her room. They usually ate in a threesome with Vidal and Alexander passionately discussing her part and everybody else's part. It seemed suddenly quiet with only the two of them on their own. She picked listlessly at her chicken salad and then moved her plate away. "I want to talk to you, Alexander. About Vidal."

He looked up at her, his eyes oddly bright. She took hold of his hand. "We're going to get married," she said gently.

"That's *fantastic!*" His voice held no doubt or hesitation.

"I'm glad that you're pleased," she said, wanting to hug him tight. "I wanted to marry him very much once before, Alexander. Shortly before I married Paulos."

He was very still. "Why didn't you?"

She said carefully, "Vidal was already married and I thought it best that I leave him, and Hollywood."

"Because you were having a baby?" he said, his gaze holding hers steadily.

Her heart began to slam violently against her chest. "Yes," she said. "Because I was having a baby, Alexander."

He removed his hand from hers and stood up unsteadily, his face pale. "I was the baby, wasn't I? Old Jemmy who sells newspapers outside the theater always refers to Vidal as my pa. I didn't pay it any attention at first. But then, this afternoon, when I was looking through the photographs, I suddenly knew." He looked very bewildered and near to tears.

She pushed her chair away from the table and walked around to him, vividly remembering the child who had flung herself against the convent's iron gates and sobbed and sobbed for the mother who had left her.

"Vidal never knew about you, Alexander. He didn't know until Paulos was dead and we returned to America and he saw you for the first time. He wanted me to tell you. That was why I took you with me to New Orleans. I intended telling you there, but then you had your accident and afterward the doctors said that you shouldn't be upset."

"I don't understand!" he said, turning around to her passionately. "Why did you marry Papa? Did he know? Did you tell him?"

"Papa knew that I was having a baby. He loved me and he wanted to protect me. He loved you too, Alexander. He loved you just as much as if you had been his own son and he always thought of you as his son. Paulos was very special, Alexander. I loved him very much."

The color had begun to return to his face. "You should

have told me when I came out of the hospital. I would have understood."

"I *wanted* to tell you, Alexander, but the doctors said that you were to be kept quiet until all the tests had been proved negative."

He said, a trifle defiantly, "I've always been proud that Paulos Khairetis was my father and I will always be proud that my surname is Khairetis. I won't change it."

"No one wants you to, darling," she said, her hand tightening on his.

He looked at her, his face oddly mature. "I don't mind, Maman. Not now that I know." He grinned suddenly. "At least I understand now why I'm not musical!"

She began to laugh, hugging him tight. It was going to be all right. He knew and he didn't think any less of her. She was not diminished in his sight. He was her son and he still loved her, would always love her. As she would love him.

Vidal had remained in the theater. She stepped into the quiet auditorium and walked down to the stage where he was studying the set for Act II.

"I've told him," she said quietly.

He spun round to face her, his expression one of overpowering relief. She slid her arms around his waist and rested her head on his chest. "He had already guessed, Vidal. He was bewildered and he was angry. At first."

"*Ertem!*" Vidal said, his eyes darkening in dismay. "Should I go to him? Talk to him?"

She shook her head. "There will be plenty of time for you to talk to him later. For the moment I think that he needs to be on his own a little while."

His arms tightened around her. "Did you tell him that we were going to be married?"

"Yes." She smiled up at him. "He was pleased, Vidal."

His voice was rough with tenderness. "And you don't want to wait any longer?"

"Not another day."

His teeth flashed in a sudden down-slanting smile that rendered her breathless. "Then we will get married as soon as possible. A week from today."

"A week from today is opening night."

"A week from tomorrow then," he said easily.

Her eyes were full of tears of joy. "A week from tomorrow is Saint Joseph's Day."

"And is Saint Joseph's Day special?" he asked, outlining the curve of her cheek and jaw with a fingertip.

"Very special. When I was a little girl, Saint Joseph Day was a day filled with hope. It was the day when I knew that anything was possible. It was the day the swallows returned to San Juan Capistrano."

"Is that where you lived?" he asked curiously.

She nodded, remembering with unexpected clarity the white, imprisoning walls of the convent; the lingering odor of carbolic soap; the heavy swish of the nuns' habits on the tiled floors. The overpowering longing to be free. As free as the swallows that swooped and dived with a grace so beautiful, it had made her want to cry.

"Tell me," he said gently.

She leaned against him and in the stillness of the empty theater she told him all about her childhood. Of the mother who had left her. Of the nuns who had cared for her. And of the swallows who, year after year, had filled her heart with hope.

"I wish that you had told me before, little one," he said when she had finished, his heart aching as he thought of her loneliness, her lovelessness.

"There was no need, Vidal," she said softly. "It was all a long, long time ago," and she pressed her mouth against his, closing the door on the past, happy in the certainty of the future.

A few days later Vidal gave Valentina a prewedding present from Van Cleef & Arpels. It was a gold swallow on a fine chain, so delicate that it looked as if it were in midflight.

"It's beautiful," she whispered as he fastened it around her neck. "The most beautiful thing that I've ever been given."

She didn't take it off, not even for dress rehearsals. She slipped it beneath the high neck of the flowered chiffon morning gown that she wore as Natalya Petrovna.

The part fascinated her. The romantic, capricious Natalya was, in her way, as strong and compelling as the part of Hedda had been. The story centered on a house party on a country estate some miles from Moscow. It is a summer at the turn of the century and the heat is palpable. Natalya Petrovna is a woman in the full bloom of her beauty, a twenty-nine-year-old woman married to a much older husband. When she becomes irrevocably infatuated with Belyaev, her son's tutor, she spreads devastation throughout her household. It scatters them "like partridges," as her bewildered husband puts it, and some of the partridges are fatally wounded. She becomes a primitive force out of control, and the ruthless course of her love has disastrous consequences.

It was a part that demanded a virtuoso performance, the whole dramatic impetus of the play concentrating on the one character. Valentina played the part with glowing self-awareness, so Russian in her animation that Vidal would say as she finished a scene, "You were wonderful, *teccik!*" and then add teasingly, "but on second thought, *ketlem*, you were very bad!"

They worked together in utter harmony and with total commitment.

"It's magnificent," Leila said when she had seen the first rehearsal. "Even more compelling than Hedda."

"I must have been mad agreeing to get married the day after opening night," Valentina said as her dresser unhooked her gown. "I *still* haven't found a dress that is suitable. They're either too virginal or they don't feel like a wedding dress at all."

"Wear your antebellum gown," Alexander said to her, perching on the corner of her dressing table. "All raspberry flounces and exotic ruffles. It will be like no other wedding gown ever!"

She had laughed at him, but after another two days of fruitless, frantic shopping she had contemplated the antebellum gown with a new eye. The vivid raspberry was a perfect foil for her pale skin and dark hair and it was Alexander's favorite dress. She would carry a bouquet of white freesia and stephanotis. It would look sensational.

As she sat in her dressing room on opening night she didn't know whether her nervousness was because of the performance ahead of her or her wedding the next day. Theo was driving up from Los Angeles to give her away. Leila was going to be her bridesmaid. Alexander was jubilant at the prospect of being his father's best man. Her fingers closed over the golden swallow on its delicate chain. She had waited so long and now the waiting was almost over. Only another few hours and she would be Vidal's wife.

"The streets outside the theater are knee-deep with clamoring fans," Leila said as she helped Valentina's dresser shovel an armload of congratulatory telegrams to one side.

The first call came over the loudspeaker. "Half hour, please, half hour."

Her hand trembled as she put the finishing touches to her makeup. She had worked at the part of Natalya night and day. She had been calm when they had begun to hang the set ready for the technical rehearsals. She had stood patiently while the lights were adjusted for every scene, for every move, from stage left to right, downstage to up. Only now did she experience pure terror. If she failed tonight, it would be not only her career that would suffer, but Vidal's, too. Her triumph as Hedda would be regarded as a fluke. Vidal would be scorned as a director who should have stuck to movies.

Her chin tilted defiantly as she stared at herself in the mirror. She would not fail. She would go out there tonight and show the world what a magnificent director Vidal Rakoczi was. Tonight, as Natalya Petrovna she was going to give the performance of her life. For herself; for Vidal; for Alexander.

Vidal stepped into the dressing room, a gleam of amusement in his eyes. "It's like a Broadway first night out there. Brooks Atkinson from the *New York Times* is leading the East Coast contingent. There's a London theater critic trying to look as if it's the most natural thing in the world to have Louella Parsons on one side of him and Hedda Hopper on the other."

"Is Theo out there?"

"The whole of Hollywood is out there," Vidal said dryly, kissing the nape of her neck. "I doubt if San Francisco has ever seen anything like it before."

"Fifteen minutes," the stage manager's voice said over the loudspeaker. "Fifteen minutes, please."

Valentina's dresser fastened the last button on her dress.

"Do you want a drink, sweetie?" Leila asked, her hand trembling violently as she tried to carry her own glass of vodka from the dressing table to her lips.

"No," Valentina said calmly. "I'm fine."

"Five minutes . . . Five minutes," the voice said relentlessly.

Vidal's arms surrounded her. He could feel the beat of her heart fast and light against his chest.

He kissed her forehead. "Let's go," he said softly, and led the way toward the wings.

Valentina squeezed his hand, took a deep, steadying breath, and forced her whole being into the thoughts and feelings and mannerisms of Natalya Petrovna.

"Places, please . . . Places, please," the stage manager said quietly. She stepped onto the stage and moved soundlessly toward the chaise longue, reclining on it gracefully. There was utter silence, the tension of the audience palpable, and then the strains of a Chopin mazurka filled the theater and the curtain rose.

A bead of sweat broke out on Vidal's brow and then she said her first line and he let his breath out slowly. She was in total command. No longer Valentina, but Natalya. He could feel the ripple of excitement that ran through the auditorium, the vibrations that her voice sent down a hundred spines. She was compelling, mesmerizing, magical.

"Excuse me, Mr. Rakoczi," a stagehand whispered nervously. "There's a lady to see you."

"*Nem fontos.* Not now!" Vidal hissed furiously.

"Sorry, sir, but she insists." The stagehand's face was troubled. "She says she's your wife, sir."

Chapter Thirty

Vidal spun around. "She said *what*?" he rasped out.

"That she was your wife, sir."

Vidal pushed past him, ignoring the startled looks of the others in the wings, racing down the narrow stairs to where Kariana waited for him.

Her blond hair dipped and curled fluffily around her

heart-shaped face. She was wearing a pretty evening dress of rose silk and a gardenia was pinned to the pastel-mink coat that hung around her shoulders.

She smiled at him. "Hello, Vidal."

He breathed a sigh of relief. She was calm. Her voice, low and whispery.

"Hello, Kariana," he said, taking her hands in his. "Is Dr. Grossman with you?"

"I'm not sure." Her eyes were vague and uncomprehending.

"Who brought you to the theater?" Vidal asked, his relief brief.

"I don't know. No one. The *New York Times* said that Valentina was opening in *A Month in the Country* in San Francisco and so I knew that you would be directing . . ." Her voice faded away. She looked like a small child who was lost and did not understand why.

He took her arm and she smiled uncertainly. "I just thought that I would come and see you. It's been such a long time, Vidal."

He took her arm, wondering if Valentina's dressing room would be the best place to take her.

The confusion in her eyes cleared at his touch. "*That's* why I had to see you. I need your advice, Vidal. Dr. Grossman is in love with me. He wants to marry me."

Vidal began to lead her along the corridor toward Valentina's dressing room. "I have to go back to the performance, Kariana. We'll talk about it later."

She pulled away from him, her eyes clouding over, the sweetness disappearing. "We have to talk about it *now!*" she insisted, her voice rising hysterically. "It's important."

Vidal flinched. An octave higher and her voice would reach the stage. "Wait in Valentina's dressing room until intermission," he said soothingly. "We'll talk then."

"No! I won't wait!" She lashed out at him, a nail scoring his cheek, drawing blood. "I want to talk to you now!"

An electrician eyed them curiously. "Anything wrong, Mr. Rakoczi?"

"No," Vidal said abruptly. "Nothing." He had to get her out of the theater and out quickly. She was beginning to sob, to descend into the pits of despair that presaged mania.

Hurriedly he propelled her toward the stage door, his jaw clenched. It was obvious that she was sick and it was beyond his imagination why Grossman had allowed her to make the visit alone.

"Where are we going?" she asked as they stepped out onto the sidewalk.

"Somewhere quiet where we can talk," he said tersely, opening the door of his car. When she was seated, he marched around to the other door, opened it and slid behind the wheel. He had to calm her down; find somewhere safe to leave her. Valentina was onstage until the end of Act I. There was nearly an hour before she would be aware of his absence.

"Now, Kariana," he said, his patience on a very tight rein as he sped down Geary Street. "What is it that you want to ask me?"

"Why, whether I should marry him or not?" she answered, round-eyed, her flare of rage forgotten.

Vidal drew in a ragged breath. One wrong word and she would be a howling banshee again.

"Do you want to marry him?" he asked, forcing his voice to be easy and casual. Forcing his mind away from the time. Away from the theater.

"He's kind," she said simply. "But he doesn't know . . . He doesn't know about . . ." She began to tremble violently.

Vidal headed out of the city toward the house that Stan Kennaway had rented. He could think of nowhere else to take her.

"About what, Kariana?" he asked gently. Her eyes were on his hands. On the maimed, dead-looking flesh. He shot her a quick glance and understood. He swore inwardly, taking a corner at high speed. Damn Grossman. He could have spared him this. He could have told her that he knew the truth about what had happened the night of the fire.

"He knows, Kariana. I told him a long time ago."

She shook her head vehemently. "No! He can't know! He wouldn't want to marry me if he knew!"

"He *does* know." He couldn't bring himself to mention Hazel's name. "He knows that you were sick. That you didn't know what you were doing."

"You don't believe that, though, do you?" The hysteria was back in her voice. "You sent me away! You couldn't bear to look at me."

"I sent you away so that Dr. Grossman could take care of you."

She seized his arm, digging her nails through his tuxedo and into his flesh. "You sent me away so that you could marry Valentina! You lied about Hazel! It never happened. You made it up so that you could get rid of me!"

"Kariana, for God's sake . . ." The car veered into the right-hand lane and then back again. He tried to shake himself free and she scrambled to her knees on the seat, pummeling his head dementedly with her clenched fists.

"You wanted to marry Hazel and now you want to marry Valentina!"

"For Christ's sake!" He flung her away from him as the car swerved crazily across the highway. The lights of an oncoming car hurtled toward them and he swung the wheel savagely to the right, missing the car by a hairsbreadth. The pretty blonde in the rose-pink dress no longer existed. Her face was contorted with fury; her hands clawed as she tried to strike out at his face.

"I'll die, but I won't let you marry her! I won't! I won't!"

He tried to fend her off with one hand and keep control of the car with the other. He was aware of cars whizzing past in the opposite direction; of their horns blaring.

"You promised me that I would never have to face the dark alone!" she screamed, flinging herself bodily across him, pulling the wheel savagely to the left with both hands. *"You're going to keep your promise to me, Vidal! You're going to keep your promise!"*

The car careened across the darkened highway as he struggled to wrest the wheel from her grasp. The world swung in a sickening lurch and then time hung suspended. Kariana's eyes were wide with horror, her mouth a gaping hole as the car slammed into the solidity of concrete and the night split and wheeled.

He was plummeted into a world of spiraling blackness and then, as if from a great distance, he saw the first stabs of flame shoot high into the sky and heard the roar as they sucked in air and exploded upward. He tried to call Valentina's name, but no sound would come. He was aware of an insane desire to laugh. It had all been for nothing. Kariana and the consuming flames had been victorious after all.

"Where's Vidal?" Valentina asked as she came offstage at the end of Act I.

"He was called away," said Sutton, who was playing the role of her husband.

She frowned, perplexed. So much of their professional future hung on the outcome of the performance she was now giving. What could possibly have been so important that it had called him away?

All through the second and third acts her anxiety grew and then, as the final curtain fell, there was no room for anxiety: only the heady intoxication of triumph.

The applause was thunderous. The audience rose to its feet in a united act of unstinted acclaim.

"*Bravo Valentina!*" "*Bravo Rakoczi!*" "*Bravo Valentina! Val-en-tina! Val-en-tina!*"

The applause intensified, deafening her. The moment belonged to her and Vidal. She ran toward the wings to draw him onstage, her face radiant, her hands outstretched. "Vidal! Vidal."

The curtain rose and fell and rose again and the stage remained empty. Sutton grasped her hands, his eyes black pits in the whiteness of his face. The telephone call had been received only minutes earlier.

"He's dead," he said, his voice full of disbelief. "Valentina, Vidal is dead."

Chapter Thirty-one

The applause reverberated around them; feet were stamping and shouts of her name echoed and reechoed backstage. She didn't cry out. She simply stood and stared, a carved effigy with a bloodless face. All around her, people were crying. Sutton put his arm around her shoulders, tears streaming down his cheeks.

"Where is Alexander?" she said, her voice strange and disembodied.

"Out front. Leila has gone to get him away from the theater."

She stared at Sutton. "What did the police say?" she asked stiltedly.

"That Vidal's car had crashed on the highway. That they were on their way here to speak to you."

"Let me fix you a drink, darling," someone was saying. Someone else rushed to get her mink and placed it around her shoulders. She shook her head. She wanted no drink; no company; no empty words of sympathy. When she walked away, no one had the temerity to follow her.

"Oh, Jesus God," Sutton said, and wiped his eyes with his hands as the stage manager went on stage to quell the almost rioting audience.

She didn't go to her dressing room. Still in the emerald velvet gown she had worn in the last act of the play, she stepped out into the night air.

Why had he left the theater? Where had he been going? The crowds that would surge any second around the stage door were still mercifully absent. The night wind was cool on her face. There was no answer. For the rest of her life she would wonder, and she would never know.

"Is anything wrong, ma'am?" her chauffeur asked hesitantly.

She looked across at him, the tears glittering in her eyes. "He's dead," she said simply. "Vidal is dead and I will never see him again." And then she took the keys from his gloved hand and slid behind the wheel of the Rolls.

"Ma'am—" he protested as she started the engine. She ignored him. Vidal was dead and life no longer had any meaning.

She took the road south, her eyes blinded by tears. She could not remain in the theater, surrounded by helpless pity. She could not face the police and their clinical details that were of no interest to her. He was dead. She needed to know nothing more.

She left the city behind her. It was not their city. He had not lived to enjoy the knowledge that, together, they had triumphed. The Santa Cruz Mountains stood high and gaunt against the moonlit sky. He had not heard the applause. He had not been there when she had, for a brief second, thought that the world was at their feet.

She seldom drove and rarely drove fast. Now her eyes did not flicker to the speedometer as the needle wavered

from sixty to seventy. From seventy to eighty. Monterey Bay
gleamed silkily on her right, and then the Pacific was lost to
view and she was speeding south through Paso Robles, through
San Luis Obispo.

When she entered the massive sprawl of Los Angeles,
she did not take the route that would have led her to Hollywood, to Worldwide Pictures, to home. Instead, she kept her
foot hard on the accelerator and kept going south. An instinct
as old as man was driving her. Like the swallows, she was
succumbing to primitive nature and without thought or reason she was returning from whence she had come.

She didn't drive into Capistrano. She parked on the
outskirts and walked through the darkness, far off the road
and high up into the hills. The heels of her shoes dug deep in
the soft earth, the hem of her dress she had worn as Natalya
Petrovna trailing in the grass behind her. She hugged her
mink coat around her and halted, her hands deep in the
silk-lined pockets as she waited for the dawn.

It came slowly, the sky pearling from black to gray to the
first faint hints of gold. She could see the town and the
convent some distance from it. The high wrought-iron gates
that she had flung herself so passionately and so vainly against
as a child.

The sun rose, tinting the convent's coral-pink tiles with
soft light, sparkling on the fountain in the center of the small
courtyard. A black-robed figure hurried across to the chapel
and early morning prayers. The drone of childish voices
carried on the still morning air. She pulled the mink closer
around her throat, her hair blowing softly against her face.

It was Saint Joseph's Day. Her wedding day. Camera-
slung tourists were beginning to stroll the streets. Perhaps, in
the distant convent, a small child in a coarse linen dress and
heavy shoes was waiting eagerly for the first swallow to wing
magically in from the sea as she had waited so many years
ago.

"Take the road south," she whispered to the child of her
imagination. "Take the road south to San Diego and anonymity," and then her hand closed around the gold swallow at
her throat. She could never willfully have taken that road.
It had not been in San Diego that Vidal had been waiting
for her. And now he was waiting for her no longer. She

raised her face to the sun and let the tears fall and then she turned on her heel and began to walk blindly in the direction of her car.

When they had told him that she believed he was dead and that no one could find her, he had known where she had gone and he had followed her through the night, his broken ribs strapped tightly, his fractured arm in a sling. They had all tried to stop him. The doctor, the nurses, Sutton, Leila. He had ignored them all. It was their wedding day. He had to reach her. Had to find her.

He had taken the turning for San Juan Capistrano and had thanked God when he saw the parked Rolls. In a cloud of dust he had swerved to a halt behind it and then, agonizingly, had eased himself from behind the wheel and surveyed the hillside with anxious eyes.

She was standing on the crown of the hill, her face raised to the sun, her hands deep in the pockets of her coat. With a sob of relief he began to cross the road to the foot of the hill.

At first she did not recognize him. Through the mist of her tears all she was aware of was a dark figure climbing the hill and coming toward her. His coat hung awkwardly around his shoulders and she saw that it was because one arm was strapped close to his chest in a sling. Her heart began to slam and the blood began to beat in her ears. He looked like Vidal. He moved like Vidal.

She halted, not daring to breathe, poised on the hillside, the high collar of her fur brushing against her chin and jaw.

"Vidal," she whispered unbelievingly, and then, as he raised his head and she saw the unmistakable tumble of dark hair falling low across his brow: "Vidal! Oh, God, *Vidal!*"

She was running, stumbling, hurtling over the dew-wet grass. He was alive and he was waiting for her and the nightmare was over. As she fell against him and he caught her with his uninjured arm, his mouth crushed hers and the last shadow of doubt was banished.

"Oh, my love, my life," she whispered, raising her radiant, tear-streaked face to his. "They told me that you were dead!"

Tenderly he brushed away her tears. "Kariana is dead," he said gently. "I was thrown clear of the wreck before the

car exploded. When the police arrived at the theater to tell
you, you had gone."

"What happened?" she asked, touching his face with rev-
erent fingers.

"Quite a lot," he said with a grin. "Hospitals don't like
their patients walking out on them in the middle of the night.
Sutton told me that you hadn't been seen since he had
broken the news to you, and so I came here."

She stared up at him in bewilderment. "But why here?
How could you possibly have known?"

A swallow circled over their heads, swooping and soaring, its dark plumage glistening in the sunlight. He gazed up
at it, his arm tightening around her shoulders.

"How do the swallows know when and where to return?
I came here because I knew that this was where you would
be." He tilted her face up. "Because I am Rakoczi and
because I love you. Because you will never be lost to me.
Never." And as he bent his head to hers, the first swallow
was followed by another and another until the air was filled
with the soft churr of their cries and the sound of their
endlessly beating wings.

Rusty's Story

By Carol Gino
Author of NURSE'S STORY

When Carol Gino first met Barbara "Rusty" Russell, the young woman was working as a nurse's aide in a nursing home. Immediately, Carol was impressed by Rusty's compassion and understanding of her often difficult elderly patients, and the two women quickly became friends.

As their friendship deepened, Carol began to uncover the layers of Rusty's life. At the age of fifteen, Rusty suffered a seizure at a football game and the incident propelled her into a medical nightmare. Rusty was institutionalized, over-medicated, and misdiagnosed as everything from a paranoid schizophrenic to a dangerous psychotic. Struggling to maintain a normal life, Rusty fought back against the medical system and appeared to have won by the time Carol met her. But, her nightmare was just beginning . . .

Rusty's Story
The harrowing true tale of the friendship between two women who join forces for the fight of their lifetime.

BANTAM
SHOP-AT-HOME
C·A·T·A·L·O·G

Special Offer
Buy a Bantam Book
for only 50¢.

Now you can have an up-to-date listing of Bantam's hundreds of titles plus take advantage of our unique and exciting bonus book offer. A special offer which gives you the opportunity to purchase a Bantam book for only 50¢. Here's how!

By ordering any five books at the regular price per order, you can also choose any other single book listed (up to a $4.95 value) for just 50¢. Some restrictions do apply, but for further details why not send for Bantam's listing of titles today!

Just send us your name and address and we will send you a catalog!
